SPIKES
AND
EDGES

131 DAYS

BOOK 3

SPIKES AND EDGES

KEITH C. BLACKMORE

Podium

*TA special thanks to Mark E. Crouse, Sean Meadows,
and Miguel Tonnies.*

Published in 2024 by Podium Publishing
www.podiumaudio.com

SPIKES
AND
EDGES

1

The mug clattered off the countertop, loud enough to frighten the old man tending bar amid the raucous crowd filling the alehouse. *As right the servant should,* Strach concluded, tonguing the inside of his cheek and exploring the gaps left by missing teeth. He leaned over the worn wood, his tall frame stretching, and placed both elbows down while fixing the barkeep with a red-eyed look of murder. The white sleeves of his shirt slid back just a few fingers—enough to allow the old bastard a glimpse of black tattoos covering white flesh.

The barkeep's eyes bulged. He sputtered, momentarily paralyzed with recognition. Even the few lads standing on either side of Strach quieted and pulled away, as if he were touched by some deathly affliction.

A strand of graying hair fell across one of Strach's eyes, and he left it, knowing it made him appear even more sinister.

"Give us another one of those," Strach commanded in

a dangerous voice, indicating the tapped barrel of Sunjan Black and daring the man to deny him.

The old barkeep glanced around. A large man, thick necked and well muscled, appeared in Strach's side vision, but the white-bearded barkeep warded the guard off with a shake of his head.

Strach's smile widened unpleasantly as a curl of smoke drifted past his eyes. "Smart, you ancient shite rag. Now, give us that drink."

Strach didn't care how many alehouse guards the old man might employ. The serpentine markings on the Son of Cholla's wrist exuded an aura as menacing and dangerous as the Axemen surrounding King Juhn. The black-ink tattoos caused brave men to shiver, caused wenches to give him his way, and more often than not, allowed Strach to drink for free wherever he pleased. The Sons of Cholla disliked him venturing into taverns and alehouses for the single purpose of causing such stirs—disliked him showing off his markings. That bothered Strach. What good were the badges if he couldn't use them? He'd *bled* for his markings, and though he doubted he'd live to see his fiftieth year, he'd make certain he lived every moment between now and then. Not even the Sons—his own *brothers*—would deprive him of his pleasure.

That included imposing his will upon ordinary Sunjans.

The barkeep reached for his mug.

"Use a clean one." Strach flashed a warning smile

spotted with gold teeth, enunciating every syllable like the hellion he knew himself to be.

The barkeep produced a fresh mug from a well-stocked shelf behind him, worked the keg's spout, and poured the drink. Strach didn't take his eyes off the man.

"That serving wench your daughter?" Strach asked.

The momentary disruption in the flow of Sunjan Black confirmed that she was.

"She's a pretty one," Strach knew the barkeep hung on every word, despite the surrounding roar of good times threatening to bring down the roof. "Can't be more than twenty—if that."

The barkeep moistened his lips and struggled to stay composed. The mug almost overflowed, and he jolted into action.

Strach placed his drink directly between his hands. Others called for the barkeep, but the man wouldn't leave, remaining in sight of the Son. Strach drank, made a show of swallowing, and studied the contents of his mug before making a spectacle of licking out the rim. Once he'd finished, he sought out the barkeep's daughter, flashing a sinister leer in her father's direction.

"That honeypot's more than ripe, I'd imagine." Strach winked. "You're smart to have her working here. That figure would bring them in from as far as Vathia—I daresay—just to drink in her goods. Wouldn't you?"

Wicked Strach regarded the barkeep.

Clearly not wanting to, the tortured father gave the barest of nods.

"Come *on,* Willfar," someone bawled and jostled Strach's back with a gruff chuckle. "Apologies, lad—"

Strach whirled upon the drunken man, gripped him by the thick hair, and bounced his face off the hard countertop, leaving a dark blot of red. The offender crumpled to the floor. The hard *whump* of face on wood didn't disturb the ongoing merriment. The incident didn't bother Strach as he placed his elbow upon the dab of blood as if nothing had happened. He studied the barkeep, curious what the old punce would do.

A nervous Willfar again warded off his guards—three of them now. One powerful-looking lad resembled the barkeep.

That interested Strach. "Your son, old man?"

Again, Willfar nodded, obviously wishing that this nightmare would end.

"You want to fight me, lad?" Strach inquired of the younger man, a full head shorter than the towering Son of Cholla. Strach cocked his head like a prickly vulture and waited. He didn't have to look to know Willfar was shooing his son to stand back.

And like a good boy, he did just that.

But Strach didn't like the vengeful gleam in the young man's eyes, so he stepped in close and peered down the sun-scorched shard of his nose. "You want to fight me, lad, you follow me out these doors. I'll wait outside. I haven't killed anyone since dawn. You may as well be the night's entertainment, even as boring as I expect you to be. You come look for me like a good son protecting the family's business. You do that. You see, I understand *everything* about family. Outside. Just follow me out."

Strach lifted a hand to the pommel of a well-used shortsword, hanging off his hip in a battered scabbard. "And I'll use this. To cut you open. Just like a full wineskin."

The son of Willfar did not appreciate being spoken to in such a manner, and it showed on his conflicted face. The old man would later explain the nature of the tattoos on Strach's forearms. Strach knew he would. But whether Willfar's seething boy would dare follow the Son of Cholla out into the night was another question.

Smirking in the guard's face, Strach brazenly sauntered toward the open entrance. Some men got out of his way. Others, he pushed. Not one retaliated. The few who considered confronting the tall, rakish ghoul of a man struggled to find something else to occupy their thoughts.

And on his way out the door, Strach grabbed the firm bottom of Willfar's bent-over daughter, drawing a startled peal of shock and a glare. Strach very much approved.

Outside, he gasped at the night air and stopped just beyond the door. Strach placed his fists into the small of his back, popping his spine. He sighed with the stretch, fully intending to meet Willfar's son and at least smash that saucy look off his youthful face. Whether or not Strach would kill him was another matter, but he did smell blood on the night's air, and he had to admit he longed for a fight.

Blood.

Strach rolled his neck upon his high shoulders and stopped to stare. To his left, a one-legged man gripping crutches regarded him with a look of pure terror, as if he were a diseased hellion. Strach studied the lad with growing interest, tugged along by a feeling of familiarity he couldn't quite place—cropped hair, wide, unblinking eyes, and a haunted look that reeked of fear. The single leg was obvious but not entirely uncommon. Strach suspected he knew this punished frame of skin and bones. He took a step toward him.

The one-legged mystery gasped as if he'd forgotten something and tried to speed away. Strach watched the spectacle with amusement. Tonguing that gap of missing teeth, the Son snorted and forgot about the alehouse guard. This *runner* was much more interesting.

"Run, lad, run! That's right! Swing those nubs of yours." Strach strode after the fleeing cripple, harsh features splitting into a sly smile. He couldn't place the man's face, but in time… he would.

A few people in the street noticed the developing chase, but one evil glance from the tall poleaxe of a man, and they quickly looked elsewhere. And well they should. Throttling a few peasants wasn't beyond Strach's wicked whims. He believed *everyone* should bash a commoner's head or two in the morning. It set the day.

"You get by well on those sticks," Strach yelled and chuckled when the cripple worked frantically to outpace his pursuer. Wood tapped fitted stone. Strach followed, enjoying the hunt and a little mystified about who he shadowed. He grew more determined to discover this rabbit's identity.

The cripple disappeared down a dark alley. Strach's broad grin blazed at the turn of good fortune. He knew every street, back way, and crawlspace of Sunja like the crack of his own ass. He intimately knew the narrow alley his puzzling prey had taken.

The path ended in a wall.

Strach had cornered several street minions in that very dead end over the years. A loose iron grate covered a chute that emptied rainwater into the city's underground sewer system—a particularly deep hole, which made it quite impossible to extract the numerous bodies Strach had pushed and even stomped through its narrow opening over the years.

Taking a firm grip of his shortsword, Strach made certain no one would disturb him and pursued this rabbit down its hole. The alley housed deep, forbidding shadows and walls that towered over three stories. He eyed the stone and wood backs of merchant shops with the lowest windows entirely boarded up. Shutters loomed above, below a cloudless night, brilliant with stars, shining through a gauze of smoke.

Strach became a hunter, well aware that a cornered rat would fight to the death. The human kind were just as quick when faced with being killed. He placed his back to a wall and allowed his eyes to adjust to the dark. People walked past the mouth of the alley but paid him no mind. Strach moved deeper down the gullet of the passageway and paused at the first corner some ten paces away from the street.

"I think I know you." The unpleasant rasp of Strach's voice carried. "It's your leg. There are more than a few men in the city with missing limbs, a handful with missing legs. One lad doesn't have any ears, a fact that amuses me to no end. You might wonder how I know. Wait, wait, I'll tell you. It's because I cut the ears off that squealing asslicker. Now, I know of only one street maggot with a single leg, but you *can't* be him, can you? You can't be that wasted hellpup—the one I know would gratefully eat scraps off the ground."

He leaned around the corner, peering down another empty length, and judged it safe to proceed. Strach gripped the hilt of his shortsword and treaded deeper into the alley.

"Not to mention the smell coming off his hide. You *can't* be him. You're much too clean. It would take every bathhouse in Sunja to scrub that shite of a man clean again. And the rags he wore? Corpses are dressed with better care. Wretched, wretched pisser. I'll say this, however: those pitiful looks brought in his share of coin. Which reminds me, I haven't seen him in quite a while…"

Strach stopped in his tracks halfway to another turn. He regarded the heavens above.

"Perhaps that he-bitch kept a coin or two for himself." Anger undercoated that thought, and Strach's hand tightened on his blade's handle. "But you couldn't be him. Not even he would be so stupid as to hide coin from me.

The last street-crusted louse to steal coin from me lost his hand—amongst other pieces—before I shoved his carcass into the sewers. All of my beggars knew that man's fate. I made it known. I carried around his blackening paw for a week before tossing it to the rats. So it *couldn't* be you."

The sound of a quickening breath reached Strach's ears, belonging to a person realizing he was trapped. Strach smiled at the frightened noise and placed a shoulder to the final corner.

"You couldn't be that unfit," he whispered and eased into view.

There, at the end of the alley, shying away not three steps behind that very loose sewer grate, stood Strach's one-legged prey with his back against a stone wall.

Strach loosed his most disarming smile and extracted his shortsword. "There you are." He glanced at the night sky, fingers flexing on his blade's hilt. "Blessed night, this one. Now, let us see who you are."

His towering figure filled the narrow confines of the alley, and Strach crept forward with one hand extended, as if testing a very hot pot. "Just enough light to see. Just enough to see your gurry face. Seddon above…"

Strach stopped and peered at the cripple. "It *is* you."

Garl whimpered, bared terrible teeth, and tried merging with the wall at his back. In the brilliant starlight, his gray eyes appeared as cloudy as Vathian marble. He hopped to a corner, allowing one crutch to drop as his arms shot out for balance. He brandished the other crutch as a club.

"Haven't seen you in days," Strach hissed. His smile widened. "You've become quite prosperous at my expense, haven't you?"

Garl shivered. Whimpered. A bubble of snot exploded from one nostril. "Stay back."

"Have you forgotten my reputation?" Strach asked solemnly, just beyond the range of the crutch. "Have you forgotten the eyes I've dug out? The tongues I've ripped free? Evil deeds done just because a street maggot like yourself failed to greet his lord and master?"

Garl trembled as if facing unholy Saimon himself. "I remember."

Strach disagreed with a sad shake of his head. "No. I don't think you do. But you will." With a smile of spotty gold, the Son of Cholla waved his sword at Garl's face, flicking it one way and then the other.

The crippled man flinched and moaned.

Strach's eyes widened, savouring Garl's terror. "Yes, you certainly—*whuuu!*"

The sharp intake of air straightened Strach's back. He dropped his blade a split beat before his shirt bloomed darkly and elongated a foot from his abdomen, right before his bulging eyes. Strach gasped as a ruby-colored blade popped through his clothing and slid forth as if fashioned from starlight. All strength fled him, and he fell to his knees, clawing at a wall for support. Blood saturated his clothes and puddled around his knees. Strach's mouth hung open, and his eyes threatened to burst from his head.

"What's that?" Borchus asked through clenched teeth,

wrapping a powerful arm around the tall man's neck. He forced his blade deeper. "I didn't hear you."

The dying man *whuffed,* popping a gloomy bubble around his lips.

Borchus twisted the blade, and Strach shivered. The agent held on until the spasms stopped. When he pulled his blade free, the dead man crumpled.

"How are you doing?" the agent asked his spy.

"Damn near pissed my trousers," Garl squeaked and swallowed.

"Happens to the best of us."

"Damned near—but I didn't."

"Good for you, then."

"What *kept* you so long?"

"Shadowing a man takes time and patience, good Garl. You should know that."

Borchus's lips tightened as he wiped the blade, a cheap shortsword he'd purchased that evening, upon Strach's person. A weak moan escaped the fallen Strach, surprising the agent. The miserable sound didn't sit well on Borchus's nerves.

"Make it hurt," Garl whispered.

"Oh, it hurts," Borchus assured him.

"Well, make it hurt *more*, then."

That surprised the agent, and it showed as a question on his face.

"You don't know this dog blossom," Garl explained. "The man's tortured and killed street beggars for *years.* He's right and proper vicious, a sewer rat that'll feast on everything. Not a drop of mercy in him. Anything you do to the likes of him isn't enough for—"

Borchus screwed up his face and nodded emphatically, cutting the beggar short. "So you've said a few times now. Well then…"

He stabbed Strach again. The man writhed and gasped as if surfacing from very deep water. Then he settled back down.

"Done," Borchus declared.

Strach let out a wheezy peep and clawed at the stones. Borchus frowned at the not-quite-dead man and stabbed yet again, withdrew his blade, considered the corpse, and stuck Strach twice more.

The last thrust did the deed.

"Not done yet," Garl whispered with venom and smashed his crutch across the fallen man's head. The once-beggar staggered off-balance from the blow. He righted himself and brought the crutch down like an axe a second time across the dead man's skull.

Bone cracked.

Borchus retreated from the display, wary of the widening pool of blood and conscious of his good boots. The stones had been well dappled, and Borchus found himself stepping back a few more paces, minding where he placed his feet. He had no issue with Garl avenging painful memories upon the dead predator. Borchus would've done the very same thing. He looked up and took in the night, appreciating the starry heavens and trying hard to ignore the disturbing pummelling in front of him.

When the spy exhausted himself, he fell back against the wall, breathing heavily.

Borchus regarded the stones and sighed. There'd be no escaping that mess. "All done?"

Garl nodded.

"Care to stomp on those final pieces? Hm? Shatter them just a little more?"

"That's unfit."

"Well, you've gone halfway on the poor bastard. Why stop now?"

"I'm tired."

Borchus shrugged and glanced around. "Well, then. Suppose I should've expected to get dirty this night."

"You mean there's a clean way to do a stabbing?"

The agent leveled a look at his companion, not appreciating the sarcasm. "Where's this grate you talked about?"

Garl waved a hand. "Behind you."

The agent turned and spotted it. "Damnation. I should have stabbed him back here."

"Well, whose fault is that?"

"Nobody's fault. Just stating the obvious. The man's huge."

"The man's a punce."

"Yes, well, he's a dead punce now."

"You don't understand—"

"Yes, yes." Borchus cut him off, not wanting to hear it. Seddon above, Garl could prattle on once he got started.

"Why don't you go to the corner there and keep watch? Send any wanderers on their way."

Borchus struggled with a grip on the iron grate. Once he had his hands in place, he pulled the porous barrier free, exposing the dark hole.

"Will he fit?" Garl asked.

The agent sighed. "Not right now." He brandished his shortsword. "But give me a moment."

Drawing back from the sight, Garl collected himself and righted his crutches. He moved further away from the smaller man and stopped at the corner, peering down its deserted length. Fabric ripped wetly behind him. Limbs thumped, and gastric delights slipped from holes.

Garl lifted a hand to his nose.

"He smells worse dead."

"Yes, well," Borchus said in a strained whisper. "Be even worse in a few moments. He's isn't going to be buried in flowers, this one."

There was a meaty *whuk,* followed by a short period of silence.

"Well, dying Seddon," Borchus swore.

"What?" Garl turned and saw the man poised above a dark lump.

"The bastard's bones are thick too."

"You should've brought an axe."

"Or a saw."

"Or a saw."

"Oh." Borchus winced, the raw smell of offal offending his finer senses. "That's simply terrible."

"Are you all right?"

"Just keep watch. I'll finish this. Oh. Dying Seddon. Dying *Seddon*."

Steel filleted flesh. Fluids spattered stone. Sinews snapped, and bones splintered. Garl screwed up his face at the butchery at his back and kept his eyes focused on the alleyway.

Then everything stopped.

"Garl."

"Yes?"

"What's this?"

"Hm?" Garl turned around and saw the bloody torso in front of the glistening hole, the shirt ripped free of its back. The pallid flesh gleamed despite the gloom of the high walls, revealing the intricate drawings etched into the skin all the way down to the man's wrists.

Borchus stood above the carnage and glared.

"Oh." Garl swallowed.

"Who *is* this man?"

"He's a pisser—"

"These markings make him an *important* pisser!"

Garl fidgeted and nervously licked his lips. "There's been whispers. Rumors."

An impatient Borchus waved him to get on with it.

"We never knew exactly," Garl explained. "No one did. There was only Strach. But sometimes, there might have been two or three others with him."

Borchus sighed with dawning realization. "He's part of a gang."

Garl didn't say a word.

"We've killed a punce belonging to a gang," Borchus repeated, inspecting the bleeding body at his feet. He shook his head in disbelief. "Dying Seddon, take me now."

"You don't know…" Garl whispered.

"How many?"

Garl clearly didn't understand.

"How many are *in* this gang?"

"I don't know."

"All right," Borchus huffed. "Which gang? It's been a while, so refresh my memory."

Garl didn't immediately respond. Recognizing hesitation when he saw it, Borchus scrunched up his brow and dredged his memory for names. "The Twisted Pikes?"

"Long gone."

"The Fists? Zarbastus?"

"No. Neither."

"Cholla?"

Garl stiffened and held his tongue.

An incredulous Borchus arched his head back on his shoulders. "Cholla's pack still exists?"

"Cholla's long dead," Garl said. "But his sons have taken over the family trade."

"Cholla's sons?"

Garl shrugged. "They call themselves the Sons of Cholla now."

"Why not?" Borchus scratched his brow, feeling sick to his stomach.

"Most of the gangs and cutthroats were crushed by the

Sons years ago," Garl continued in a whisper. "They rule the undercurrents of Sunja without challenge. Well, until recently. A while ago, a pack of Sujins entered the black trades."

"Sujins?"

"Aye that. Right and proper evil animals. They bled just as many men as the Sons. Perhaps even more."

"How could Sujins be doing this?"

"I don't know." Garl groaned miserably. "I've only heard whispers. They don't rightly walk around in armour when they're breaking necks or digging out tongues."

Borchus supposed that made sense. "All right then. What about these Sons of Cholla?"

"As I've said, some whisper that they control most—if not all—of Sunja's undercurrents, that they've tortured, stabbed, and throat-slit all their adversaries or meddlers and disposed of them. At least to the point where any survivors fled the city."

A reflective Borchus regarded the body once more.

Garl nodded at his reaction. "The Sujins, however, they keep to the shadows, and there are rumors they have influence over the Street Watch. Some say the Sons have an agreement with the Sujins. Others say each pack is aware of the other and are already wrestling for control over certain areas of the city. But it's all either rumors or outright lies."

A wave of dizziness assailed Borchus, and he struggled to clear his head. The smell wasn't helping, so he started pushing Strach's cut-up carcass into the sewer. He kicked at shoulders and wrestled with flopping arms. The body sank deeper into the ground. Sections that didn't fit entirely required more effort, so Borchus cut off the troublesome parts, his breath becoming gasps and curses.

Garl watched the alley, ensuring no one approached while this gruesome work continued.

In short time, Borchus released the dead man's legs, and the body slipped from sight. A distant splash echoed far beneath the streets. He stood over the chute and marveled at its depth.

"I can see why Strach chose this place to rid himself of bodies," he said with a touch of disdain. "This hole must be directly over a drop in the sewers. It's quite deep."

"We should be going."

Borchus inspected himself. He stripped off his stained vest and the white tunic underneath, exposing a body not yet fattened by age. He bunched the clothing into a ball, swipe-cleaned his blade, and dropped the bloodied garments into the sewer.

Garl glanced back. "What are you doing?"

"Trying not to look so much like a butcher," Borchus said, naked from the waist up but much cleaner. He returned his shortsword to his scabbard and replaced the heavy grate over the sewer chute.

"You still have the trousers," Garl pointed out.

Borchus joined him at the corner. "And the boots. All of which you'll be replacing. Don't worry about the cost. My tastes aren't so grand. You can pay me out of your wages."

Garl kept his mouth shut.

"And, Garl?"

The spy regarded him.

"Don't ever do this to me again."

Borchus glowered at his henchman, waiting until the man reluctantly nodded. For a fleeting moment, the agent wasn't so sure if he should trust Garl. Suspicion could rot a man's mind, so he made the mental effort and pushed it aside. Having done that, he led his one-legged companion out of the alley of death.

It had been too long a day.

And a murderous night.

2

Under the same night sky, three wagons rattled through unmoving fields of tall grass, breaking the quiet with creaking wheels, squeaking wood, and half-hearted flicks of reins. A single horseman with a torch held high guided the wagons along the pockmarked road. The first wagon's driver glanced away from his team of four horses and cast his attention toward the starry horizon, where shadowy islands of forest sprouted from vast plains. A wheel dipped into a deep rut, and the driver shifted in his seat, turning his gaze to what lay ahead.

The passengers crammed into the rear of the vehicle huddled without conversation, their faces somber as they reflected on the past few days' events. Their dead filled the last wagon in the tiny procession.

Clavellus sniffed, swiped a trembling hand over his face, and glanced at Machlann sitting across from him. The trainer's eyes drooped with sleep. Koba sat beside him, a motionless lump of scarred muscle. Goll was across from the big trainer on Clavellus's right. None of them spoke. Words felt like lead, so no one bothered with them.

Tumber dead.

Kolo dead.

Sapo deserted.

Of the three, the desertion bothered Clavellus the most. Sapo's intimate knowledge of the Ten's house fighters would be a concern. It wasn't unheard of for a warrior to leave one house for another, but it was understandably rare. Gladiators remembered those breaking ties and took it personally, if not with vicious intentions. The brutal consequences of such perceived betrayals swayed most men from ever switching houses. Clavellus recalled one hellpup, who amazingly changed houses *twice* before being butchered upon the sands in exceptionally violent fashion.

Gladiators remembered. That alone kept most from ever changing houses.

But every now and again, one attempted to do that very thing.

The wagon's jostling stirred the taskmaster's thoughts. Clavellus knew Borchus would keep track of the big Sunjan's whereabouts. The House of Ten would meet Sapo another day, of that the old taskmaster had no doubts. It would not be a pleasant reunion.

Pushing Sapo from his mind, Clavellus returned to happier thoughts. The House of Ten had taken more victories than losses, and even with Junger sparing his opponent, a message had been sent. The house would give as good as it received. Clavellus's shaking hand hid his little smile. He couldn't wait to tell his wife the news. Nala would hate it.

Clavellus smoothed the white bush covering his jawline. Three victories—over Free Trained mongrels charged with killing the Ten's pit fighters. The other heads of houses wouldn't be too concerned with the Ten's fighters.

Not yet.

Another flicker of a smile spread across Clavellus's aged features.

It was a good start for his lads, a good showing, one to build upon, to build confidence and to remember before they fought the other house gladiators.

But first, the House of Ten would honor their fallen sword brothers. Seddon help him, Clavellus had already prepared for such a solemn occasion. No one came through a season without losing at least one life. Both he and Goll had previously agreed that their dead would not be cooked in the fire pits of the arena. Not one corpse would be dumped in those foul flames. Thus, the bodies of the Ten's deceased had been prepared for travel and loaded into the third wagon.

Machlann's eyes had finally closed. The trainer snorted and loosed a short and sleepy mumble. Clavellus felt the same way.

The day's fights had awakened him with a jolt and energized him, but unlike his dozing companion of many years, the taskmaster eagerly looked to the future. These men had potential. With Clavellus overseeing the training, he could perhaps make his name respectable once again in the blood sport he so loved. He reached out and parted the canvas flap just a crack, enough to peek over the driver's shoulder.

The fiery star of a torch burned, held high by the lone horseman.

The road ahead could not be seen.

*

The wagons stopped atop a low rise in the meadow, leaving tracks in tall grass. The lone rider plodded ahead while the others unloaded themselves with groans and stretches, forcing blood back into limbs that had fallen asleep. The weary travelers saw the rider lighting an arrangement of four torches. The flames burned high above a small clearing encircled by a sea of grass. Eight graves waited within the yellow light, some dug underneath a tree with wide, far-reaching limbs. Mounds of dirt separated the deep holes. Those pits silenced the returning gladiators, and they quietly unloaded their fallen from the third wagon. They laid the cloth-wrapped bodies of Kolo and Tumber into two of the holes. Once the dead were in place, Brozz and Junger shovelled dirt atop the corpses. For moments, the earthy tempo of their efforts filled the warm night air while flies with glowing bellies buzzed around the onlookers' heads.

The burial troubled Halm. The torchlight colored his brutalized face. Clavellus studied the devastation wrought upon the Zhiberian and mentally cursed in morbid wonder. The fat man was a gruesome mess: a broken nose for certain, while his left profile was distorted and swollen to the point where the taskmaster doubted the man would ever get a helmet over his head. The eye on that side was nothing more than a black slit, and it amazed the taskmaster Halm still managed to keep all those terrible fangs intact. And that was just the face. The body and arms beneath had been equally punished in the day's contest, adding more cuts and bruises to a devastating record of pain—a litany of punishment.

After the Zhiberian's fight, the sight of him had paled even Shan, the healer. That was never a good sign. Clavellus doubted if Halm had seen worse and wondered if his victory over the Free Trained Targus had come at a great cost. It might very well have been his last of the season. It certainly appeared so. Corpses seemed in better shape than the bulky warrior.

The Zhiberian met the taskmaster's gaze, the left eye cracking open against the fleshy sludge surrounding it. The chubby man offered a ghastly smile.

Tight-lipped, Clavellus smiled right back, admiring the man's raw push. Though his body looked broken, his spirit remained hard as iron. Clavellus liked that.

The last shovel of dirt tossed upon Tumber's grave invoked a period of silence while the lit torches flickered in the faintest midnight breeze. Some faces looked expectantly to Goll, but the Kree remained quietly focused on the ground.

Clavellus cleared his throat. The words flowed easier than expected. "Remember this," he said gently, regarding each gladiator in turn. "Tumber and Kolo rest with Seddon—or whatever gods they prayed to—this night. If they prayed at all. Remember them. Remember their strengths, their weakness, their manners, and even their voices when you have a moment. Do that, and they will never truly be gone. Do that, and if you were friend to them in this life, perhaps they'll help you on your own journey when the time comes. So remember every time you enter Sunja's Pit. Tumber and Kolo will most certainly not want you to perish there."

Clavellus paused and drew breath to continue.

Goll, however, found his own voice. "Sleep well this night. Tomorrow, once again you'll sweat and strain and bleed upon the training grounds. There's no time to waste."

The men waited for more, but Goll had none to give.

"That's it?" Torello blurted in shocked disbelief, his face partially hidden in the tree's long shadow. "That's all you have to say? Sleep well, and training continues? Truly?"

Goll faced the pit fighter.

"Don't die."

3

Snoring woke Pig Knot.

He scowled, for his sleep had been a pleasant one, filled with dreams of chasing young women through smoky taverns. He'd been happy and whole again, and wenches with beaming smiles had nuzzled his neck. All yanked away in a gurry snore. Pig Knot despised waking from his dreams to the nightmare of no legs, and he cursed the scant few bars of light penetrating his private quarters. Pig Knot lay on his cot, fingers laced together atop his head. His nose itched, so he rubbed it. Sounds of sleeping men came from beyond the curtain of his alcove, and for a moment, the immolating blend of self-loathing, pity, and volcanic anger lessened.

The lads had returned late and hadn't disturbed him at all. He mentally thanked them for that. Another snore ripped from beyond the alcove's curtain, an explosive, piggish snorting that widened Pig Knot's eyes and summoned anger.

He dearly wanted to plug that noisy hole.

The muscular snakes of his forearms flexed as Pig Knot pulled himself up, fighting the urge to open his mouth and move his broken jaw. The cuts in his left shoulder and arm stretched and strained dangerously. He didn't care. The ugly yellow and purple blooms covering his midsection—bruises sustained during his short fighting season—had faded. The stitches in his forehead itched while his nose ached and remained clogged. *Pain.* Every moment of his day ached, itched, choked, or outright crippled him. He fixed his eyes upon the space where his legs would've been. The bruised stumps vexed and horrified him, as they had every morning since returning to Clavellus's estate. He hated the knobs of sawed-off bone and meat covered in stitched flaps of skin.

Pig Knot sighed.

How could he have lost so much? The question flash-burned in his mind as he willed new flesh to burst forth from the old. Failing that, he reached out to a bundle of cloth bandages Shan had provided him and began to aggressively wrap his stumps to keep them somewhat clean, a new chore he had to do before moving about. A clay container filled with that evil concoction of ointment—no doubt squeezed from a cat's blossom—lay just to his left. That foul-smelling crack grease used to promote healing soured his stomach. Pig Knot couldn't be bothered applying the ointment and turned away from it. He finished wrapping his legs and, failing to control his frustration, lowered himself to the ground, ending in a slip, a painful raking across his naked back, and a solid pounding to his ass.

Pig Knot growled through his clenched jaw and forced the pain down. At least he hadn't squashed his balls. Fuming, the Sunjan gathered his wits and slowly, tenderly, shuffled his body through the curtain on hands, buttocks, and thighs. The movement was awkward, cringe-worthy, and ungainly, and any moment Pig Knot believed he'd start a fire down there, but he far preferred moving along on his own than being lugged about like a sack of maggot shite. If Shan saw him, he'd be annoyed. Right and proper annoyed. A part of Pig Knot wanted to make the healer right and proper pissed just because he possessed legs. No one, including Shan, could understand Pig Knot's plight.

Shan. The healer had specifically instructed him to apply that smelly, gurry stew to his stumps and cuts. Pig Knot had already left it behind. Perhaps tomorrow, he'd smear it over himself. He wouldn't waste the strength this morning.

Growling through the bandages fixing his jaw in place, Pig Knot scuffled toward the common room, careful to lift the meaty ends of his legs through the door and avoid slamming them into the frame as he'd done the night before. That one sudden lance of agony was something Pig Knot wouldn't soon forget. The basic movement itself was familiar—a short, energetic thrust of the hips—not unlike rutting. He simply had to be mindful of lifting his stumps when he moved.

Sweat beading on his flesh, he waddled past tables and

benches, determined to see the world beyond. Let the earth slap, scrape, and tickle his balls and buttocks for another day. The thought made him growl louder. Perhaps he should strap planks onto his bottom.

A straw mat waited for him, just to the right of the living quarters' entrance in the shade of the bathhouse's eaves. He greeted it with a relieved huff and maneuvered himself over its spread, taking his time to become properly situated before lowering his bulk. His plums felt fine, unharmed during the short journey, which pleased him. Pig Knot slumped. That little morning grunt and shuffle damn near exhausted him. Having one's limbs hacked off robbed one of his strength. He wondered if he'd ever be strong again. An evil chuckle bubbled from his throat at the thought, and he threw his head back in a lapse of sanity. As his fit of giggling receded, he settled in against the wall. His breath steadied.

He looked up and cursed Clavellus's mansion for blocking the majesty of the rising sun.

"You *would* build it there," Pig Knot muttered with venom. Damned if he was about to move.

The pleasant smell of bread baking reached his nose but did nothing to lift his foul mood. Above the main gates of the villa, two guards with spears stood together at one point of the ramparts, keeping watch of the lands beyond Clavellus's walls. One of them noticed Pig Knot.

The sentry wandered over and stooped to address him. "They got in late last night." The guard's voice carried in the morning calm.

"How did they fare?" Pig Knot asked through clenched teeth.

"What was that?"

"How… did they… fare?"

"Well…" The man leaned on his spear. Pig Knot recognized him. One of the newer guards Goll had hired, an old Sujin, but he couldn't remember the name. "I believe they won four of their matches and lost three. Two of them died."

"Died?" Pig Knot lurched, his wounds protesting. "Who?"

"Don't know."

"Not the Zhiberian?"

With a doubting look the guard indicated that he still didn't know.

"Seddon above," Pig Knot whispered. "You've put poison in my head now."

"Apologies." The guard straightened. "One moment."

He walked off to join the other man at the gate, leaving Pig Knot to squirm. The bandages covering his left stump had come undone, so he occupied himself reapplying the dusty streamer, knotting the ends with an annoyed huff. Halm had perished yesterday, and he'd slept straight through the news. Cold overtook him, shooting up from his backside and turning his guts to ice. Pig Knot suddenly *knew* that his friend had died in the blood games of the Pit. He slumped again and swore oaths of pure misery.

"Not the Zhiberian." The guard returned from the gate. "He sleeps inside. But the one called Kolo?"

Kolo? Pig Knot remembered the quiet man, but sympathy eluded him. He was too gladdened by the news of Halm's survival. Still, he recalled the Sunjan's face and his mild temperament.

"And Tumber."

The black-bearded Vathian. Pig Knot grunted in disappointment. Unfortunate. The fighter had trained hard under Machlann's guidance.

"Who deserted?" Pig Knot asked.

The guard held up a hand and looked at the other lad. "Who deserted again?"

"The big one called Sapo."

"Sapo," the guard relayed.

"*What?*"

"He deserted. Right there on the sands. In front of thousands. But the others won their fights."

The news stopped Pig Knot's flow of thought. He raised a hand in thanks, and the guard drifted away, leaving the legless pit fighter to sit and ruminate. News of Halm's survival had lifted his spirits, but the loss of Kolo and Tumber disappointed him. Sapo's desertion wasn't surprising in the least. Images of vengeful glares flooded Pig Knot's mind, and every one belonged to Sapo when Machlann or Koba ordered him to strike harder, move faster, or to repeat a drill. A man didn't need a nose to smell the hatred smoldering off the big lad. Sapo despised training. He'd probably only joined the house for the food and bed.

Like them all, perhaps.

The sand around his mat glowed in the morning heat. Pig Knot squinted at the empty training area and the wooden men bracing for the storm of practice strikes. He regarded his missing legs. Self-loathing and despair welled up inside, and Pig Knot sank deep into its depths. His legs. *Why did it have to be his legs?*

The sound of footsteps lifted his head, and *she* walked toward him.

Ananda, with her blond hair tied back, was enough to mesmerize any man fortunate enough to gaze upon her. Concern clouded her pretty face, but her presence dissipated Pig Knot's dreary gloom.

"Good morning, pretty one."

That ignited a smile.

"Good morning, Master Pig Knot," Ananda greeted him. "I'd thought you were perhaps ill."

"Ill? No more than what you see here." He waved at his crippled predicament. "Seeing you this morning is as good as any of that sauce Shan smears upon me—without the smell, I might add."

Ananda smiled again. It improved Pig Knot's mind and heart considerably.

"You're up quite early this morning," she said.

"I am. Right and proper."

"I'll bring you something to eat and drink."

"Just something to drink."

A frown of indecision shaded her lovely face, and Pig Knot drank it in. "Or just sit here and take in the morning with me." He patted the ground beside him.

"I'm afraid I've work to do."

"When you're finished, then. The offer will stand because you're you."

"I imagine the tavern ladies often hear the very same," she countered with a sly twinkle in her eye.

Not so naïve as Pig Knot thought, and he liked her more because of it. "They do, but that doesn't lessen the truth."

"The truth?"

Pig Knot's smile widened. He drew breath to deliver a well-used compliment, but he never got to utter a word. Shan stepped through the door of the living quarters, eyes closed as he finished a deep yawn that could have summoned cows from pasture. He scratched at his head of light-brown hair.

"You're up and moving around," Shan sleepily greeted the once-pit fighter. "Excellent. Ananda, would you be so kind as to bring us something to drink?"

With an energetic nod, she walked away. Pig Knot watched her go, his depressing mood returning. He regarded the healer with annoyance. "Why did you send her off?"

"Oh, she'll be back," Shan mumbled good-naturedly and combed his thinning sandy hair with a few fingers. "Let's see those bandages. You made it out here by yourself, I see. Impressive."

"My arms work fine."

"Yes, I can see that." Shan dropped to a knee and unraveled the bandage from one stump. His aging eyes narrowed in puzzlement. "What's this?"

"Hm?"

Shan blinked. "You didn't use the saywort."

"The what?"

"The saywort! That ointment you're supposed to rub on your legs to speed the healing. You must put it on every morning."

Pig Knot looked away and grunted his opinion.

Shan undid the other stump's bandage. "This one as well? Did you forget? You mustn't forget in the future. It's very important. Here. Where's your saywort?"

Lips puckered, a sour Pig Knot indicated the living quarters with his chin.

"I'll get it then." Shan stood. "But remember from now on. It requires no effort on your part."

A growl emanated from the pit fighter.

Shan went inside. No sooner had he disappeared when the unmistakable, towering form of Koba the trainer walked around the corner of the main house.

Just what Pig Knot needed. "You unfit kog lasher," he growled, not caring who heard. "My, but you strut about like a cock amongst hens."

Ananda emerged from the house with wooden cups and a water jug. She spied Koba and greeted him with a few words and a smile. The trainer responded with a few friendly words of his own, almost dispelling the image of the right and proper bastard Pig Knot knew him to be. The one-eared trainer—normally brooding at the best of times—exchanged pleasantries with the young lady. Not only did he speak with her, she seemed to *enjoy* it. That little nugget of mystery lodged in Pig Knot's craw. If he had his legs, there would be no contest for her attentions. None. He knew it.

Ananda broke away from Koba and crossed the training sands. The trainer with the gruesome scar snaking up the left side of his face stood and watched her all the way… until he spotted Pig Knot.

The friendly face vanished.

Pig Knot smiled, knowing full well it annoyed the trainer.

"Here you are." Shan emerged from the nearby doorway, causing Pig Knot's grin to frost over. The healer held a small container as well as clean strips of cloth. He knelt and placed everything on the ground.

"Ah, thank you." Shan took the water Ananda offered and served himself. Ananda handed Pig Knot a cup as well.

Not one to allow an opportunity to slip by, Pig Knot touched the back of her hand during the exchange. "You've soft skin."

"What's that?" Shan asked.

"*Not you,*" Pig Knot blurted.

"Well, then." Shan handed the empty cup back. "Thank you again. Now, let me take care of this."

The healer got to work upon his patient, unaware of the scene unfolding before him. Pig Knot's compliment had taken Ananda aback for a heartbeat, but then a little smile crept across her face. She waited for Pig Knot to finish his drink. He took his time, eyeing her over the brim of his cup.

She eyed him right back while Shan obliviously tended to his legs.

Pig Knot didn't return his cup. "For later. When you bring me a jug of beer. Or wine. Whichever's more plentiful."

"I'll look."

"My thanks."

"Master Pig Knot," she addressed him formally, smile still in place, and walked away. Pig Knot watched her go, taking evil pleasure from the stoic expression on Koba's face. The trainer slowly showed his back, moving in the direction of the stables.

"She's a treasure," Pig Knot commented, his eyes returning to Ananda's retreating curves. No doubt he'd dream of her later.

"What's that?" A gob of ointment coated Shan's fingers.

"I said, she's a treasure."

"Who?"

"The girl."

Shan glanced over his shoulder. "Oh."

"That all you can say about her?" Pig Knot cocked a brow. "How old are you, anyway?"

"Barely crossed into my fifties." The healer smiled.

"Then you should appreciate *that*." The gladiator stuck his chin out at the departing woman.

"I'll praise her name if it reminds you about the

saywort."

"Perhaps I'll ask her to butter me up when it's needed."

Shan chuckled, appreciating at the double meaning. "Well then, you'd best pay attention to how I'm applying it now."

Pig Knot ignored him.

"Is he making morning difficult for you?" Muluk hobbled from the barrack's doorway. The Kree appeared exceptionally brutalized this morning. His dark eyes stared out from darkened caves of flesh and bone. Water moistened and speckled his thick beard. Sleep had flattened one side of his wild bush of hair, while the rest appeared ravaged by a windstorm. The bandages covering his muscular shoulders, legs, head, and midsection needed changing. Seepage of some kind had dampened them during the night. His left hand curled, the stumps of the missing fingers doing their best to become a fist.

Legless he might be, but at least Pig Knot didn't look as though he'd just clawed his way out of a dead man's hole.

"No more than you." Shan studied the Kree with a critical eye. "And when I'm done with him, you'll sit and allow me to change those bandages."

A sleepy Muluk smirked. "More of that pissy salve?"

That struck a mortal blow, and it showed on Shan's tanned features. "I really wish you wouldn't call it that. That salve is the reason you're walking around right now. And you'll be mended even faster if you'd sit still long enough and allow it to do its work. Both of you. *All* of you."

Muluk dismissed the healer with a wave of his butchered hand. The Kree looked about and spotted the mat off to one side of the barracks. He bent over with a groan, exposing bandages under his short skirt and loincloth. He fetched the straw mat and swung it over next to Pig Knot before dropping it, stirring up the dust. A thunderous groan left him as he lowered himself, wincing when his buttocks hit the ground. He hissed when his back touched the barrack's wall.

"Unfit," the Kree said through a rack of yellow teeth that had seen better years. He watched Shan fuss over Pig Knot's wounds. "Lords above, that was unfit. I'll piss myself before I rise again."

That brought a scowl and a headshake from the healer.

"What?" Muluk asked.

"Men died yesterday," Pig Knot informed him.

A suddenly reflective Muluk raised his face to the sun. "I know."

"As do I." Shan regarded each of them before returning to his task.

"Where did you hear?" Muluk asked Pig Knot.

"From one of the guards here, just this morning."

"A bloody business all 'round." Shan slapped and lathered saywort onto Pig Knot's right stump. The smell of strong onions permeated the air, wrinkling the noses of the recovering former gladiators.

"That smells… horrible," Muluk muttered through puckered lips.

"Where did you hear?" Pig Knot asked the Kree.

"Heard them come in last night. They'd just finished burying the dead. Unfortunate. That Sapo lad left the house as well. Gone."

"I know why." Shan applied cloth to the stump. "One of the houses placed a bounty on the House of Ten. Three times the gold for any man who could kill a Ten's pit fighter. Sapo found out about the bounty and didn't care for it, said he was done with the house. He was very… vocal about it."

Pig Knot squinted at the rising sun. "Harsh."

"Very harsh," Muluk agreed.

"And to think, we'd be respectable by now," Pig Knot added with a cold smile. "What of the others?"

"Did they renounce the House of Ten, you mean?" Shan asked.

"Aye that."

"Surprisingly, they did not."

"That is a surprise," Muluk said. "They must like it here."

"Truly," Pig Knot added.

"Or nowhere else to go." Shan eyed each of the men.

"Or don't care," Pig Knot finished. "Being out of the hell of general quarters is reason enough to stay. A bounty. Pah. The Pit is life or death most days anyway. What's a price on one's head?"

"The House of Curge placed it," Shan informed them. That silenced them.

"Seddon above," Muluk breathed in dismay.

Pig Knot screwed up his lips in contempt. "Dog balls, why not Curge? If we're going to make enemies, why not the best? Why not, I say? As it is today, we'll all have to attend to Seddon's fleshy crack to escape Saimon's hell. What's another hellpup? Dying Seddon, Halm must have chuckled hard enough to make his bells ring upon hearing that news. Another reason for Curge to kill him—for being a part of an upstart house of Free Trained hellpups. Well then, my rosy bastards, I don't know your intentions, but I believe this bit of news is all the more reason to drink this day, and I mean to drink until my eyes cross and my kog becomes a fountain."

Shan drew back from the second stump and glowered. "Spirits hinder the healing."

"The healing can lick my crack," Pig Knot scoffed. "I'll not spend my waking hours simply *healing*."

The healer rolled his eyes before returning to work.

Machlann appeared with Koba. The old weapons topper engaged the taller brute in a quiet chat, turning his back to the recovering gladiators.

"They gather," Pig Knot observed darkly. "Training as usual, it seems."

"Aye that," agreed Muluk. "No rest for our bastards. And I can see the reasoning. With the season half done, our lads need every waking breath spent on the sands."

"And they're the bastards to see to it," Pig Knot said with contempt. The urge to shout and berate the trainers came upon him, but Goll stepped through the entrance of the living quarters, his limp much less noticeable.

"Ho, the master rises," Pig Knot remarked with a sneer.

The Kree squinted at the rising sun and regarded the trainers, ignoring the Sunjan's jab. Two manservants pushed a cart around the corner of Clavellus's main residence. They labored toward the barracks. Goll lowered his gaze to Shan.

"Good morning, Master Goll."

"Good morning, good Shan. Master Muluk. How are the wounds?"

"Sealed but still raw," Shan reported as he leaned back from Pig Knot's fresh bandage. "He'll be recovering for a time yet." The healer then took to fussing about Pig Knot's broken jaw.

"You lost a few lads yesterday," Pig Knot growled through teeth and probing fingers, glaring at the housemaster. "Two dead and one deserted, I hear. What happened, *Master* Goll? Sapo refused to lose?"

Instead of answering, Goll focused on Muluk. "What about you then? Feeling any better?"

The man shrugged halfheartedly.

"I asked if Sapo refused to lose," Pig Knot repeated, smiling at being snubbed. "Did he? I'll keep asking the same question until I get an answer."

"Ask if it amuses you," Goll said, uninterested. "But I'll save you the breath. Sapo left when he discovered a bounty had been placed upon his head, a large sum offered by the House of Curge. No loss to us. I'd wondered who was truly loyal to the House of Ten and who was pretending."

"I have a feeling… you know all about pretending."

Goll smiled coldly and faced the Sunjan. "You asked a question, and I gave you an answer. Anything else you wish to know?"

Pig Knot pushed away Shan's fingers. "Let me think about that, *Master* Goll. I'm finding I have plenty of time to think about things these days, all paid for in flesh and bone. If I think of anything, I'll be sure to call for you."

"I'm sure you will."

"Ah." Pig Knot's face brightened. "I just thought of something. The coin! All that coin won from wagers placed by our fighters. I suspect I'm entitled to a portion of it. A *sizeable* portion since I'm a master of this house. Isn't that right?"

Silent and sour-faced, Goll straightened and focused on the servants bringing breakfast into the gladiators' living quarters. "Get something in you. All of you."

To Pig Knot, he said, "Try not to choke while you're eating."

With that, Goll marched off toward the trainers.

"Bring us back something to drink, *Master* Goll," Pig Knot shouted. "Some of Clavellus's Sunjan Gold if he'll part with it. I'll pay for it myself. Out of my *large* share of yesterday's winnings. How much was there, by the way?"

If Goll heard, he did not answer.

*

Brozz selected one corner of the common room and walked toward it, his dark head and shoulders hunched over to clear the ceiling. The imposing Sarlander wore no shirt, displaying the lean and wiry muscle coating his tall frame. He didn't wear his intimidating necklace of crow heads this morning, but he'd chosen the farthest corner of the common room to sit and eat breakfast, implying that he wished to eat alone. In peace.

He sat down at a bench and table with a bowl of warm porridge and sliced apples. Breakfast. A *warm* breakfast. Not something Sunja's Pit would offer if he'd remained in general quarters. The fitful sleep he'd managed despite returning late was something he favored as well. Not that many bothered him while in the Pit, but he had to admit he appreciated the sense of security with the House of Ten. Thus far, the choice to join the young and brash house pleased him. Brozz regarded the nearby open window and saw the sky was clear. He regarded his food and wiped his forked mustache down. Then he started in with great bites.

Junger sat down across from him, causing the Sarlander to stop mid-chew. The shirtless Perician didn't seem to notice, however, as he fussed with his own bowl of hot oats sweetened with diced apple. He glowered at his food for a moment, then at Brozz's, and stood. He returned to the serving area where two men doled out food. Junger found the water barrel and poured himself a mug. Then another.

His hands full, he returned to Brozz's table and placed one cup before the big man. Junger sat once more with his own cup. He smiled faintly at the staring Sarlander and, without a word, inspected his food again.

Brozz's dark face pinched in puzzlement. He finished his mouthful and, scowling a question, watched Junger eat. Holding his spoon in an overhand grip, Junger shoveled food into his face. The man apparently enjoyed his morning meal. Brozz looked out the window once more, decided to carry on, and returned to his own food.

The two men ate in silence.

"Well," the Perician declared softly after he'd finished. "That isn't bad at all. You think they'd mind if I had another?"

Brozz stopped chewing and regarded the man.

"They have plenty." Junger glanced over his shoulder. "If we don't eat it, I daresay they'll only throw it away—or feed it to the pigs. I'd prefer to have one more bowl, in any case, in memory of the lads underneath the Pit. You know they aren't enjoying their morning."

With that, he stood and walked back to the serving area, leaving a puzzled Brozz to consume tentative bites.

In short time, the Perician returned.

"You fought well yesterday," Junger said. "Short. Clean strikes. No waste. To the point."

Brozz lowered his spoon.

"You're from Sarland." Junger took a drink. "I know a little about that place. You know about the elite guard? The Vanzani? Deadly warriors. Very much to the point. Like yourself."

Brozz straightened ever so slightly, his scowl deepening with curiosity. Torello entered the common room, distracting him. The Sunjan barely acknowledged anyone. He got his breakfast and retreated to a table on the far side of the common room. As he passed, the smell of sour sweat drifted past Brozz's nose. Torello wasn't an easy man to behold at any time, but this morning, he seemed particularly disheveled. His black hair and beard hung about his scarred features in matted clumps and greasy strands, rendering him almost frightening. He sat alone at his chosen table, lowered his face, and starting eating.

After Kolo's death, the man had quieted considerably. He'd barely made a sound on the journey back to Clavellus's villa.

"The Vanzani guards the Grand Vir," Brozz said quietly, out of respect for the mourning Sunjan.

Junger stopped eating. "They aren't the feared killers of the Sarlander army?"

"No."

"Oh."

"You are thinking about the Gorsha."

"The Gorsha." Junger brow twisted in thought. "That means… what?"

Brozz's grand moustache lifted at the corners. "There is no meaning. The Gorsha are… reavers. They kill upon a word. They're summoned when the regular army cannot complete a task."

"Ah." Junger prodded his food.

"There are those in the Gorsha who would even kill the speaker for saying their name in the same breath as the Vanzani."

"That so? Puzzling. Why?"

Brozz took his time in answering, studying the rustic interior of the common room for a moment. "The Vanzani only have a reputation. The Gorsha have history."

A look of surprise spread across Junger's face. "You know the difference?"

Brozz nodded in dramatic fashion, the ends of his moustache nearly reaching the base of his neck. "I do."

"Perhaps you know firsthand?"

Brozz said nothing.

"As if you might've been a part of that group…" Junger met his dark gaze. "Or at least *one* of them. I know something of the Gorsha. Fearless warriors. But you can't be one of them. Can't be. Please, correct me if I'm wrong. My knowledge of the Sarlander military is foggy. There's the Spears of Seddon, the regular army. The Vanzani. And the Gorsha. The Vanzani and the Gorsha are the harsh ones. From what I've heard, there's no leaving any of either one of those groups, not until you die or become old and feeble. Deserters are hunted down and killed, but that's common with any army. But if you desert the Vanzani or the Gorsha, they take particular offence. And also take extreme measures to *find* the deserters. At least that's my understanding. Again, please correct me if I'm mistaken."

The Sarlander waited a beat. "You're not."

Junger absorbed that. "I've seen a few of the Vanzani fight and the Gorsha, for that matter. You actually… remind me of them. Isn't that interesting? A young man like yourself, obviously well trained with a blade, fighting in such a faraway country like Sunja for the amusement of her citizens? But you can't be a soldier from Sarland. They wouldn't allow such a thing."

Brozz didn't answer. His posture remained rigid, and his eyes didn't leave Junger's face.

"It is a mystery," the Sarlander finally answered.

Junger's expression remained unconcerned. "It is."

"There are several mysteries surrounding these games."

"Are there?"

Brozz nodded. "I'm speaking with one this very morning."

That brought an expression of *really?* to Junger's face.

"I find myself wondering…" the Sarlander began, sucking on a tooth, "how is it that a warrior in these games—a very *skilled* warrior—sides with a house of unproven pit fighters? A house of Free Trained, for that matter. What kind of man excels at the day's exercises when the others are just learning? Struggling, even. And what manner of gladiator fights in the arena without any armor at all? It isn't often one will witness such… confidence. Some might even call it brazen foolhardiness. Then there's the matter of skill with his weapons. One seldom sees a warrior so skilled he leaves all who behold his mastery in a near-sorcerous daze."

Junger nodded. "Well, I can solve one of those mysteries."

Brozz waited.

"I remove the armor because it's hot. Nothing more."

"That's it?"

"What more could there be?"

Brozz turned to the nearby window. "So simple."

"Some mysteries aren't so difficult to unravel."

"I suppose not."

They stared at each other for a short time, sensing no ill will.

Junger resumed eating.

Brozz did the same.

*

Halm woke upon a single blanket laid over a cot stuffed with straw to make it comfortable. Movement beyond the curtain drawn across his sleeping area drew his attention. He lay there, hearing the remaining house fighters lumber along the floor into the common area, and realized it was morning. The lads were probably getting some food into their guts before the day's training.

Training.

Memories rushed through the Zhiberian, along with relief at having paid off Skulljigger and avoiding fighting the father of at least one son. At least Skulljigger *said* he would stay away from the remainder of the games, but who truly knew if he would honor his words? Halm could only hope. A pang of uncertainty twisted within his guts as thoughts of Targus entered his mind. Somehow, the man had witnessed Halm handing a sack of coin to Skulljigger and sought to profit from the knowledge. He'd died instead.

Targus had reminded him of Pig Knot, but the Sunjan was not his friend.

Were any of them? They were his companions. But friends? Could any of them be trusted?

Certainly not Goll. Halm realized he'd been blindly following the Kree, allowing the man to think for him. He'd been far too trustworthy, far too quick to leap into Goll's plans of establishing a house and challenging the upper houses for supremacy, to lift them up from the ranks of the Free Trained and fashion them into true fighters. It was a grand dream to tell around any table, but the Zhiberian had doubts. He doubted the men around him were his companions. He questioned Goll's motives. The man seemed more like a sly weasel than the young warrior who'd killed Baylus the Butcher. Halm's head ached when he attempted deeper thoughts about everything that had happened in the very season where he'd been performing at a personal best. Still breathing and undefeated. This string of victories was the most he'd ever amassed during the games. Any other year, he'd have been long finished by now and his purse half-empty.

But he'd be happier, or so he suspected, for it seemed the longer he'd remained in the games, the deeper he'd sunk into a mire of shite. He'd taken it all too lightly, too carefree, and only now did the weight of it all strike him.

Should he remain with the House of Ten? Would it be wiser to walk away and leave the headaches behind? The House of Curge would be livid, as the opportunity for blood matches ended with the season and weren't carried over to the next. If they wanted him next season, they would have to wait until the Madea paired them.

If Halm decided to return for another round, that was. *And go where?*

He knew a place. A woman's face came to mind. That memory made him smile.

A knock distracted him.

"Are you awake?" Shan stuck his head inside.

"I am, good Shan."

"Still alive, I see."

"Still."

"May I look at your wounds?"

Squinting one eye at the healer, Halm rolled onto his back and waved for him to enter. The appearance of Goll surprised the battered pit fighter.

"Master Goll," Halm said.

"Master Halm."

"You look well this morning."

"And you look ready to perish."

Halm smiled. He supposed that was truth. Shan placed a stool next to his cot, distributed fresh bandages upon a small table, and tugged at the dressings and poultices he had placed the day before, giving each one a solemn peek before moving on to the next. Each inspection seemed to darken the healer's face a little more.

"Well?" Halm asked, the hateful bruises upon his swollen face lending him an evil appearance.

"This one cut. Here along the ribs… is a nasty one," Shan reported. "I'm going to have to prepare a mixture in case of infection. Truth be known, I wouldn't send him back into the Pit."

That news melted Halm's ghastly smile. Nor did it please Goll.

"Oh, I'll fight again," Halm reassured the Kree. "Don't worry."

A frowning Shan directed his attention to the man's head and dabbed at the gruesome slash across Halm's scalp. The healer ran fingers along stitches.

"These are unbroken," Shan said. "Thankfully. A wonder they held when the rest of his face looks like a squashed plum. Are you able to see from that eye?"

"Aye that," Halm's smile returned, thinking himself clever, and he forced it open wider.

Neither effort impressed Shan.

"I'm sure you've seen worse," Halm said.

"No, I haven't. That's as wide as you can open that eye?"

"Ah, yes—I can see from it."

Shan exchanged a dire look with Goll before inspecting Halm's broken nose, a painful parting gift from the fearsome Iron Games fighter called Sibo. Shan picked daintily at the maroon crust about the nostrils, gently blowing away the resulting flakes. He stopped when the Zhiberian hissed in discomfort. Shan lifted Halm's left arm and checked on a bite-sized chunk of flesh missing from the forearm, the result of an unfed Iron Games pit fighter. Purple and sepia bruises had yet to fade from where they exploded across Halm's face and abdomen.

"Take a breath," Shan asked. "As deep as you can."

Halm did, only a shallow one before his broken ribs caused him to grimace.

The healer drew back and shook his head. "You shouldn't even be standing, let alone going back into the arena."

"You're saying he's finished?" Goll asked.

Shan took a deep contemplative breath and faced the housemaster. "Oh, yes. Exactly what I'm saying. He's been brutalized too often in too short a time. The stitches are holding, but those missing bits of flesh snacked from his person still need to be checked daily for infection. His lower ribs are perhaps the most telling. He can't draw a deep breath without feeling pain, correct?"

Not liking what he was hearing, Halm nodded.

"Time to heal?" Goll asked.

"Three weeks, under my care," Shan informed him. "No training, no fighting, and certainly no bloody surprises like the Iron Games. I'm surprised he isn't dead already."

That caused Halm to unleash a horrid chuckle. "And if I refuse?"

Shan frowned. "Well, *you* might refuse." He placed two fingers against the stitches in Halm's hair line. "But your body won't. Listen, lad. That eye alone makes me ill. The white is entirely red. You look like you fell off one wagon and got rolled over by the next half dozen. Your skin's a meadow of wildflowers in full bloom. Dezer hounds would sniff at your hide and leave you for dead.

Are you understanding me now? A dead man's hole is in finer shape than you, if you'll forgive my being crude. Those ribs? They'll burst with one deep breath. Might even snap apart with one good sneeze. It's a wonder you even competed yesterday, much less survived and *won*. Now, I can keep you walking… but I only have so many bandages to keep you together, and I certainly can't resurrect the dead."

The Zhiberian's smile faltered.

The healer's eyes twinkled. "So come now, good Halm. You're smarter than this."

A resigned Shan leaned back and regarded Goll.

"He's done."

4

The rasping of feet on stone roused Arrus from his sleep. He shifted his head, realized he faced a wall, and squinted toward the crossed bars of his cell door, hard iron he'd long given up pulling on. Voices sounded from beyond. Some asked for food and water. Others screamed, laughed, or complained the rats were eating them alive.

Rats.

Arrus reached down and scratched his instep where an unwanted visitor had bitten him only a fortnight ago. He shivered at the memory of his sleep disturbed by the sharp pinch of teeth. Up until then, the only bites he'd received had been from fleas or other unknown pests—little Sunjan bastards that waited until he was asleep before feasting on his blood. And those bites didn't wake him, but the wicked itching afterward did. He couldn't see his legs, as the Sunjans kept them all in perpetual dark, but he imagined his bare skin ravaged with welts and worse. He also suspected he'd lost weight. Whatever fat had clung to his bones had long since melted away. His hair and beard seemed to be the only things growing. And his toenails.

Darkness. Arrus now knew what it must be like to be buried alive, to exist without a sun. The dungeon was like that, an enforced night so deep, so brooding, that it had already driven some of the prisoners to madness. Or at least it *sounded* like madness. He didn't understand the Sunjan tongue or any but his own. Based on what he'd heard, he suspected the dungeon contained not only Nordish and Sunjans but a handful of prisoners from other countries as well.

Arrus sat up from the straw floor. The cell didn't allow him to stretch out when sleeping. If he stood, his head grazed the cool stone of the ceiling. *Cramped.* The Sunjans had entombed him in a box of rock, clothed in a filthy loincloth, with scarcely enough room to even piss. When the need did arise, he'd shuffle to the unclean latrine at a back corner. The foulness wafting from that opening had repelled Arrus at first, but Dogslaw told him to be thankful there was a latrine in the cell at all and that he didn't have to sleep in his own filth. Several nights, Arrus had awoken with a foot dangling over the hole, which no doubt attracted the toothy hellions. They were down there. Many times, when the dungeons' occupants were quiet, he could easily hear them. Rustling. Scratching. Even chattering, letting him know that they'd visit soon enough.

Rats. The vermin stalked the prisoners whenever they sensed it quiet in the perpetual dark. The only light came at mealtimes when the jailor and his assistants waded through, holding torches high whilst they fed the prisoners. The jailor's name was Balazz. He'd thumped his chest and introduced himself to the Nordish prisoner, stressing the word until it was understood as a name. Balazz, a powerful brute who would grab any hands reaching for him and cut them, towered over the dungeon cells. Or he would break them between the iron bars. Balazz and his men fed the prisoners twice a day, and Arrus couldn't tell which was breakfast or supper. During each visit, Arrus cringed and shied away from the torchlight, finding it unbearable in the rank blackness of the dungeon. He stole glimpses, however, recognizing Balazz's meaty frame.

Over the days and weeks spent in Sunja's dungeons, mealtimes became the high points in Arrus's life. Though he could not understand the words Balazz spoke, he and his men were proof that a world still existed beyond the iron bars and stone walls.

Arrus slapped at an arm, flattened a body, and flicked it in the direction of the latrine. He scratched at his hair and beard, feeling things crawling there. Fresh bites tormented him. Blood. Arrus had seen enough blood on a battlefield, but being imprisoned made him realize *having* blood was perhaps his sole remaining worth.

"Arrus."

The voice belonged to Dogslaw in the cell to his right.

"Yes?"

"Sleep well?" the voice asked, a whisper compared to

the wailing misery in the other parts of the dungeon.

"Not really. Something is truly devouring me a piece at a time."

"The rats in this place are ravenous."

"And the fleas. Or gnats. Or whatever lives here in the straw."

"Have you taken to eating them?"

"The fleas and gnats?"

"The rats," Dogslaw answered calmly.

That took Arrus off guard. "No."

"Lokan has."

Lokan. *Mad* Lokan lurked in the cell to the left. Others spoke of how Lokan had always been a touch insane. Arrus never fully understood just *how* mad until he'd been jailed next to him. Arrus didn't like speaking to Lokan. He was thankful to have a barrier between them. Since his imprisonment, the man had become increasingly disturbed. Many times, Arrus awoke to Lokan pounding on the stone walls or having extensive conversations with himself, heated whispering punctuated by curses and grunting and, of course, the unnerving fits of giggling.

"I hear him eating them. Feasting, at times," Dogslaw continued, much to Arrus's swelling horror. "He waits for them to crawl up through the latrine, up over his open hand. When they do, he grabs them, and that's it. One squeak. Maybe a crack. Then…"

"You're not joking?" Arrus whispered. "You heard all of that?"

Dogslaw didn't immediately answer. "And worse."

"I don't want to know."

"And I don't want to speak of it." Dogslaw chuckled softly. "Don't worry. There's a wall between your cell and his."

"Unless he worms through the latrine system."

"If he attempts it, then yes… worry."

Words failed Arrus. The sound of a fist striking rock caught his attention.

"Someone is busy." Arrus scratched at his crotch. Almighty Curlord, the fleas had infested him.

"Little to do." Weariness lay heavy upon Dogslaw's voice. "At least when sleep comes, one can escape in a dream. I bedded two tavern wenches last night."

That made Arrus smile. "Only two?"

"I'm not complaining."

"And then you woke?"

"And then I woke to things crawling around in my beard."

Arrus chuckled. He savored that for a moment before asking, "Do you think we'll ever be executed?"

They never spoke about freedom.

"Possibly," Dogslaw admitted. "But if you're truly interested in leaving these fine quarters, I'd suggest getting on the bad side of that jailor, Balazz. He seems quite willing to brutalize a person."

"He does."

A blood tick chomped into Arrus's thigh. He crushed the insect with a slap before rubbing it away into nothing.

Somewhere nearby, a door clattered open, and

unmistakable Sunjan curses echoed through the corridor. A terrible hush fell over the dungeon as the Sunjans approached. Most prisoners feared drawing the wrath of the jailor.

Orange light grew outside the iron bars. Arrus grimaced and withdrew deeper into his cell. Chains rattled along the stone. Metal scratched metal and resulted in a *clack* that stirred Arrus's curiosity. More shouting and a scuffling of feet, followed by a slap of flesh on flesh.

"What's happening?" Arrus asked, enduring the light.

"Can't see," Dogslaw answered.

"They'll kill us," Lokan hissed. "Butcher us. Our day's finally come at last. They'll kill us, but I'll take the life of that curnos hellion called Balazz. I'll thumb the eyes from his skull."

Arrus didn't doubt the Jackal would try.

The racket continued along the corridor. Men shouted. Heelslik yelled out in Nordish that they were at his cell door. An unseen force silenced his voice. Noll, always pleasantly pessimistic, was oddly quiet.

"Something is happening," Lokan said.

The light grew stronger. Men's long shadows flittered through the glow.

"Lokan! Can you see anything?" Dogslaw asked.

"They're at my door. They're at my door. So many of them. Damned Sunjans. Oh, how I hate—come in, come in, you ugly bastards. Come in, so Lokan can hook your eyes out!"

A rusty yawn of hinges and Lokan shrieked at his

invaders, startling Arrus. He peeked toward his own cell door as Sunjan voices yelled. A thick knot of men gathered there. Lokan continued shouting, followed by the sounds of a hard struggle. A dull clap silenced the crazed Jackal, and he said not a word more.

They continued hitting him, however, the punches hard and meaty.

He hoped Lokan had killed the jailor at least before they struck him down.

The light swung over to float outside his door, illuminating wicked faces. Mail shirts gleamed. Perhaps eight or more men, all very interested in Arrus, stood beyond the bars. The Nordish man pressed himself against the wall of his infested chamber, mindful of the latrine hole. Balazz barked, and a man fumbled with the lock. The door opened, and Balazz—at least the man was big enough to be Balazz—bent over and motioned Arrus to come forward.

He refused.

Balazz bared half a rack of bad teeth and gestured again, growling words that made no sense to Arrus. Light needled his eyes until he covered them with a hand.

Cursing, Balazz stepped into the cell and grabbed Arrus by his neck. He slapped the smaller Nordish man against the wall, holding his throat in an iron grip. Arrus pawed at forearms as thick as firewood.

A fist smashed into his face.

His world went lopsided, and he crumpled into hard hands. A powerful force yanked him along by his lifeless limbs, and Arrus became distantly aware of a bubbling buzzing in his head, as if he'd been submerged into deep water. Light flashed hotly before his face, causing him to moan. His feet and toes slapped against stone steps, and the sensation of rising touched his floating consciousness. He stole painful peeks at his surroundings, glimpsing Sunjan warriors on either side of him, their flesh shining in the light.

They're going to kill me. The thought lanced through his addled brain. *Finally.*

More Sunjan voices. Shouts. A hand grabbed his chin and whipped his face about. Another hand pulled him along before shoving him through a portal.

Into a world of agony.

Arrus landed on his hands and knees, scuffing them hard enough to draw blood. Daylight flooded his sight. He squeezed his eyelids shut in reflex, moaning. After existing for so long under the earth, the sun rejected him. Hated him. Its glare caused his naked skin to sizzle. He smelled his cooking flesh.

Callused hands lifted Arrus to his feet and dragged him toward another cell, one perched upon a wooden chassis. Five other men were crammed into the prison wagon. Arrus glimpsed faces before his knees painfully clacked against the wagon's lower lip, leaving behind blood and skin. They heaved him into the cell. Arrus sprawled into the tangle of bodies as the door slammed on his feet. Hands grabbed him while foreign curses flowered the air. Others crowded in, forcing Arrus to stand with his face shoved into a lattice of iron bars. He grabbed on for dear life and pressed his cheeks to the metal, taking deep breaths. *More* bodies crowded into his back, almost crushing him. Arrus gasped and squeezed his eyes shut. He stood with his face wedged between the bars and sucked in hot air.

A shout and the prison wagon lurched into motion. Arrus's knuckles whitened from tension. Hips squished into his lower back while hands held onto his shoulders for support. Warm fluid rushed around his bare feet. No one could fall, but every bump rippled through the caged men, causing them to shift one way or the other. Torsos mashed against his back.

The wagon rolled onward.

Sunlight, denied to him for so very long, glowed through his lids and needled his eyeballs, yet Arrus wanted to see life above ground.

People.

Sunjans and non-Sunjans went about their business, glimpsed over the helmets of armed guards walking beside the prison wagon. As much as Arrus wanted to look, he couldn't bear to open his eyes for anything longer than a painful blink.

Women fussing with merchants.

Children running.

A man studying a length of fabric while another babbled nonsense.

Washed clothes hanging above bustling side streets.

And the *smells*. Arrus gasped at the good smells—

roasting meat, stews, even baked bread, which stirred memories of his mother's brick oven. Whiffs of exotic spices, herbs, and mysterious pots left to simmer cut across his nose. After weeks of stale bread and beef slivers, the smell of real food tormented his hunger.

The wagon dipped. Bodies squashed Arrus against the metal until he thought his ribs would snap. The prisoners recovered and righted themselves, allowing him to breathe again.

He chanced another glance at his enemy's capital and glimpsed an architectural behemoth, squatting upon the land like a monstrous, unmovable weight.

The sun forced his eyes closed before he could better see the structure. Daylight glowed through his eyelids until all darkened. Arrus glimpsed red brick. The wagon had entered a wide tunnel and left the sun behind. He opened his eyes. Dusky murals appeared, adorning the walls in a scrolling history. He watched the striking visuals, painted by a master of the art, leaving no question as to meaning. Men fought one another in a constant stream. They killed with sword, spear, or mace and appeared as armored hellions or bare-chested monsters. Tiers of empty faces watched. Arrus glimpsed one figure, devoid of features yet held high above all, wearing a crown.

A king.

A faceless audience. An indifferent ruler. Fighters killing fighters on a canvas of brick.

The breath caught in Arrus's throat. His eyelids fluttered in discomfort, unaccustomed to seeing so much for such a length of time. The images he saw left little doubt as to where they were going or the fate awaiting them there. Even Nordun knew of Sunja's blood sports and the season when they took place.

Pit fighters. Gladiators.

Arrus struggled to remember the name the Sunjans had called their arena.

The Hole?

Arrus wasn't sure, but he understood why they'd been fed actual meat instead of rancid, why they'd received stale bread instead of moldy crusts, and why a punishing jailor like Balazz had left them largely unharmed.

For the games.

The prison wagon halted among a large host of armed guards Arrus believed were called Skarrs. Swords gleamed while a corridor of shields led to a grim entryway. Fear rippled through the prisoners. Four Skarrs walked past Arrus and stopped at the rear of the cage. One spoke curtly, his voice strained, perhaps from shouting.

Arrus could guess the meaning.

They were to fight in the Hole—probably to the death.

For the amusement of the Sunjan populace.

A sword tapped the cell bars. Another Skarr babbled a stream of unintelligible gibberish, but the Nordish man could guess that meaning too.

You're about to be released. Attempt to fight, and you'll die. Flee, and you'll die.

Arrus preferred to live.

The cell door opened, and men spilled onto the

ground. The weight slackened and eased off Arrus, and he took the opportunity to right himself. His features twisted into a near-permanent squint. He held a hand to his eyes and stepped down out of the cage. A line of wagons had stopped behind the one that had transported him. There were too many prisoners to see, all surrounded by Skarrs.

Guards herded him toward the waiting portal along with other prisoners. Arrus did not resist when the Skarrs grabbed his arms and walked him through the opening into another wide passageway. Torches burned at intervals. Arrus passed more watchful soldiers. There were enough Skarrs to deter even Lokan from escaping.

The prisoners descended steps as the Skarrs led them through a dismal maze of stone, past doorways reeking of excrement and sweat. Arrus sighed. His eyes welcomed the absence of the sun, but now his nose suffered. They marched through an arched door and down another staircase, deep into the ground, where the walls crumbled and the torches colored the corridor. More grim Skarrs appeared out of the dark, their armor gleaming. Arrus kept his eyes downcast while passing them, sensing their eagerness to hack away at Nordish flesh.

Another door materialized, and the stream of men flowed through its arched frame. A Skarr shouted. The guards directed Arrus to a waiting cell. They shoved him inside and slammed the door. Cranky tumblers turned over as other cages closed. Arrus went to the bars. Locked away like animals yet again. Outside the new cell, braziers burned, illuminating a wide corridor. Arrus gripped the iron bars, tugged them, and placed a cheek against the metal. Another prison, but this one was situated beneath a mighty arena.

On impulse, he called out to his companions. Harsh voices answered. Arrus rubbed his bearded face and scowled at the noise. No Nordish man answered. Either his companions had been shoved into a different cellblock or killed outright, perhaps for resisting or attempting to escape.

Arrus stared at the shadowy floor. He supposed the Skarrs would come for him soon enough.

And when they did, death would follow.

5

The constant clatter of wood on wood filled the training grounds of the House of Ten.

"*Eeee*, that's it," Machlann bellowed with heat, smoothing his bushy moustache. He marched back and forth, watching the three gladiators from behind as they smashed swords into the practice men. "Flow from one strike into the other. Twist the hips. Make those wooden frames tremble. That's it! That's it! Make them buckle with each and every strike. *Eeeee*."

"Why do you suppose he makes that noise?" Muluk asked the two companions sitting to his right.

Halm shrugged and immediately winced.

Pig Knot didn't seem to hear at all.

"*Eeee!*" Machlann stopped and held his hips, nodding. The gray tuft of hair atop his head bobbed and waved. "Only three this day. *Three*. Saimon's dewy sack, we're getting down to the core here. The almighty core! The *heart* of the slop. Two fallen, Seddon take their souls. And one deserted like a treacherous leech no longer wishing to suckle. That rots my guts. *Rots* my guts."

Machlann rolled his shoulders and walked past Junger going through the motions, performing the drill with effortless perfection. The tall and shadowy Brozz worked beside the Perician, not as crisp or smooth as his sword brother, but he rattled the target with solid blows all the same. At the end stood Torello who, upon Kolo's death, had quieted his complaining. The housemasters all noted Torello seemed a changed man. Upon finishing a solitary breakfast, he'd stood and walked onto the sands before anyone, reached for a wooden sword, and started swinging, practicing what he'd learned up to that point. Muluk had even thought that Machlann and Koba would drive the man back, away from his wooden target, but the trainers did not. The constant noise had even roused Clavellus from his roost.

The taskmaster sat on his balcony, leaning forward and effectively concealing his face behind a silver mug resting on the railing. One hand held the vessel while the other rubbed his bald scalp. At times, his forehead rested on the railing. He barely watched the morning's action.

Goll was nowhere in sight.

"How does Clavellus look to you?" Muluk asked.

"Like the wet hole of a dead man," Pig Knot grunted.

"He's swinging that stick hard," Halm commented, returning his companions' attention to Torello.

"Think you can do better?" Muluk smiled.

"I could if it wasn't for fear of bursting apart at the

seams."

"Unpleasant thought," the Kree muttered and scratched at the fresh bandages lashed to his person. Shan had tied them off rather tightly. The healer had checked on the long stitches and slapped on gobs of the smelly saywort. Shan had assured Muluk that his cuts were healing well—wounds the Kree had sustained while preventing thieves from stealing the future House of Ten's coin. Muluk felt somewhat sad this day and glanced at his right shoulder. A red mass of tissue had filled the depression of missing meat there. Shan warned him that his right shoulder might never be as strong as before, but the arm would still function. Shan could not do anything for Muluk's missing left ear, however, which was now a knot of ugly tissue surrounding a spider's hole, a battle scar concealed by the Kree's black bush of hair.

No, Muluk didn't want to think of anyone bursting apart at the seams. It would remind him too much of his own barely kept-together body.

"Stop!" Machlann bawled, breaking the Kree's thoughts.

Junger and Brozz did as told, but Torello delivered three final strikes to his target before relenting.

"Furious this morning, my missus?" Machlann asked when the man stepped back.

Shoulders heaving, sweat dripping, and glaring at the trainer, Torello didn't bother with a reply—not even so much as the dirty, petulant look he might've given a few days earlier.

"Well, that's good," Machlann said, realizing he'd be waiting a very long time for an answer. Koba stood near the dark-haired Torello and eyed him warily, as if no longer trusting the man. The lad had certainly changed since Kolo's death. Muluk could see it. Anyone with eyes could see it.

"That's good," Machlann repeated and regarded his gladiators. "Today, we practice more combinations. Combinations. A skilled gladiator knows *hundreds* of combinations that'll slice you open and let slip the red, purple, and pink, an unfit *deluge* of spikes and edges that will overpower most hellpups and rip the meat from their very bones. *Combinations.* Right and ready to unleash upon his opponent in an instant. When you fight, the basic strikes over and over will not assure victory over your opponent. You must be different every time, to confuse your foe, to keep him at guard long enough for your weapon to find its mark. You mustn't worry about being faster, although speed is helpful, but rather focus on *striking…* the exact moment the opportunity arises, to *steal* the initiative, and unleash your weapons before your foe can initiate his own combinations against you. *Eeeee!* Here, we devise and practice those sets of pain and punishment. We've started with simple breezes, you miserable hellpups. As of today, we'll begin raising blood-chilling *storms!* Ferocious bell-wringing *squalls* meant to ravage maggots and leave them thrashing in their own shite!"

The word hung in the air as Machlann marched away from the wooden practice men to a rack filled with wooden swords. He selected one and walked to the uncluttered sands in the middle of the training area. There, he turned and regarded his three gladiators.

"Now then, my missuses," Machlann growled. "I'll show you what I mean… Brozz. Stand over there."

The tall, swarthy Sarlander complied, the forks of his long mustache soaked in sweat. He stopped five paces away from the wiry old trainer. Machlann fixed him with a withering look, a gaze of sheer flesh-burning acid. It was harsh enough to make one wonder what Brozz had done to deserve such a hateful look.

"All right. Come at me," the trainer commanded. "And I mean *swing* for all you're worth. If I sense anything less, the pinch you feel will be my boot between your sun-scorched cheeks. Understood?"

Brozz nodded behind his upraised sword.

The imposing Sarlander lunged, his arm streaking for the older trainer's heart. But Machlann deflected it to the side and nimbly retreated a step. Brozz recovered quickly, sizing up his opponent while gripping his sword with purpose.

"That's it, my missus. *Eeeee*, whatever you can give."

The big man again stabbed for Machlann's heart, only to have the trainer deftly parry and twist, taking control of the other's weapon. The unexpected move almost put Brozz into the sand, but he lurched out of range and quickly retreated, placing distance between himself and Machlann.

"Good," the old trainer said. "He's trying to use his

combinations, but I stopped them. You see that? And he's kept enough sense to get out of reach before I could counter. Watch, now, watch."

Pig Knot, however, admired Ananda's slender form.

"You still eyeing that one." Halm nudged his companion.

"You have to ask?"

"The trainer's been eyeing her as well."

"Koba, you mean."

"Aye that. Koba."

"Man's a punce," Pig Knot grumbled.

At that moment, Machlann deflected yet another of Brozz's attacks before striking back in a flourish of stabs and slashes. The Sarlander parried one thrust and another, but then Machlann pressed forward, taking away the taller man's advantage of reach. Short cuts and ruthless thrusts erupted, a startling, probing series of expert attacks punctuated with grunts and yells. Silence fell over the onlookers.

Brozz gave up ground, no longer countering and entirely on the defensive.

Machlann's sword smoothly sliced the air, flowing from one attack to the other. A jab to the gut would flick up and transform into a slash for the jaw. A cut would revert into a spin and slanted chop. The onslaught backed Brozz up several strides, well out of reach of the whirling sword.

"*Eeeee*, you see that? You see that?" Machlann gasped, his chest heaving.

Junger and Torello nodded.

"Stand away, Brozz," the old trainer huffed, gesturing with his sword and struggling to compose himself. A sheen of sweat coated the older man.

"*Eeeee*, you see… how he retreated… when I started swinging? Hm? That's intelligence. *Intelligence*! I tell you now that only the experienced, the skilled, and the *thinking* will have the sense to get out of the way of a set of strikes. If a dog thinks he's up to the challenge, he might stop the first blow. Maybe even the second. May even get lucky and stop the third, but if he stays in front of you…you'll eventually get through. The stupid ones will bleed. The big ones will bleed. The overconfident ones will bleed."

Machlann waved his wooden blade at the attentive pit fighters. "They'll all bleed. Remember that. Sharpen your strikes, always be aware, and don't be afraid to get out of the way. Do anything less, and by Saimon's black hanging fruit, I'll pummel you so right and proper you won't feel a thing when I juice your bells."

From the safety of the barracks, Muluk swallowed. "That man frightens me at times."

"I think that's his intent." Halm glanced at Pig Knot. "Has that honeypot moved at all?"

Pig Knot didn't answer.

"Not so, ah, subtle about it, is he?" Muluk knew full well the pit fighter was taken with the woman.

"Like a starving dog." Halm grimaced in annoyance, displaying his horrid, overlapping teeth. "A good thing he doesn't have any legs. He'd be at her this very moment."

Muluk cringed. Halm's face slackened in shock as he realized what he'd said. "I spoke too quickly, good Pig Knot. No offence was intended. I've many things on my mind."

Pig Knot appeared not to have heard. "Not offended."

"Well, apologies again."

Halm squirmed and traded a worried look with Muluk. Machlann lectured in the background as Pig Knot sighed. "Said I'm not offended, Zhiberian. I'm not some old woman here. Don't concern yourself with me. As for the wench, you watch what you will, and I'll do the same."

But the downcast look on Halm's shameful face spoke volumes. "Shan has said my season's done," he abruptly reported.

That drew surprised looks from both men.

"Told me this morning." Halm sighed.

"Does Goll know?" Muluk asked.

"He was standing right there when the healer said it."

"You were doing so well."

"Undefeated this year," Halm said. "And yet done in by this old body of mine."

"What will you do?" Muluk asked. Pig Knot's drawn features spoke of deep thoughts.

The Zhiberian shrugged. "My season's done. I'm a master in this house, or so Goll informs me, so I'll have a say in matters, I suppose. I have coin now, food on my table, and a roof overhead—for a short time anyway. I have much more than when I started his season, much more than before I met any of you. I'll talk with Goll."

Pig Knot looked at his stumps before returning his gaze to the training men.

Muluk remained speechless, crestfallen. Of them all, Halm had managed to keep on winning, defeating those who should have beaten him, defying the odds. The man was inspiring, and learning that he would no longer be fighting saddened them. Muluk felt almost as if he'd just learned of the man's death instead. He shook that morbid thought loose and wished all four of them were in an alehouse somewhere, with women in their arms and pitchers filled to the brim.

"I'll talk with him," Halm repeated. "He'll suggest something."

"Don't trust him in the least," Pig Knot muttered, squinting against the daylight. "Not in the least."

"I won't argue it." Halm chose his words carefully. "But…despite everything he's done, he's brought us here. Here. He's provided us with shelter and food and even coin. He's given us direction—dare I say a future with this place? Would any of this have happened without him?"

"It's not ours," Pig Knot muttered. "He'll never let it be ours. In his mind, it's his. That man has plans of his own."

That made the others think.

"Aye that," Halm reluctantly agreed.

"Truth be known." Muluk shifted on his mat and scratched at his beard, not entirely certain where to take the conversation from there. Then it came to him, as plain as rain. "Time for something to drink." He waved until he caught Ananda's attention.

Smiles appeared on the bandaged faces.

All three men knew a bout of drinking would not help solve their problems.

But it certainly wouldn't hurt.

*

After a lengthy session in the latrine, Goll climbed the stairs of Clavellus's home, seeking to join the taskmaster on his balcony and watch the morning's training. Concerns for the future weighed heavily on his mind, plaguing his sleep. He'd twisted and turned the night before like a snake with a spike through its middle. Yesterday's victories had introduced the House of Ten to this season's games, but with a pair of deaths on his hands, Goll had to carefully consider how to proceed. Two deaths and a desertion. The desertion couldn't be helped, but it bothered him more than he cared to admit. Goll had no doubt that Sapo would be disgorging everything he knew about the Ten's warriors. That thought alone made Goll's blood boil. The Ten would deal with the Sunjan.

The deaths, however, would have to be avenged, and Goll questioned who would do the killing. Halm couldn't. Goll was no stranger to the horrific wounds and injuries sustained in a fight, but the Zhiberian's condition was appalling. He should never have participated in that unacceptable night of brawls called the Iron Games. The cuts and bruises from that mockery had finished him. The

Free Trained warrior called Targus had only made it official.

Goll had to choose another to avenge the house's fallen, to send warning to any who might attempt the same.

Blood matches. No doubt it would prove to be an interesting topic of discussion with the taskmaster.

The smell of wildflowers enveloped him as he reached the second floor. He walked along a short hall, musing that he'd stepped into a fragrant cloud.

"Good morning, Master Goll." Clavellus's wife, Nala, stepped out of a doorway and smiled. Long white robes covered her frame, while her silver hair, long and lustrous, hung tastefully over one shoulder. Her fingers fiddled with the ends.

"My lady." Goll noted her warm hazel eyes and how they sparkled. "I hope the morning has found you in good spirits and health."

"They most certainly have. Waiting for my husband to return last night wasn't a pleasant affair. I don't like him traveling to the city, even with a troop of trained gladiators."

Goll kept his thoughts unspoken. He knew of Dark Curge's warning to Clavellus, but he wasn't certain how much she knew. "We returned safely."

"Oh, I know. And with some measure of success on the sands, I hear."

"Some."

"I am very sorry to hear about the deaths of those two

men."

Goll nodded.

"I truly don't understand what any of you see in such blood sport. Master Goll…why do you do it?"

Why indeed? Goll had asked the question of himself once. He studied the art for several reasons, he discovered. He was drawn to the discipline of the sport, the dedication, the training, and the lifestyle. He enjoyed learning how to use weaponry, discovered he had a talent for it, just as much as a vase maker was drawn to pottery, or a carpenter to wood. He enjoyed the challenge of competing in perhaps the most dangerous event of the age—against others like-minded and similarly trained— and surviving.

And somewhere in there, he wanted to become a master at what he did. Whatever he did.

"I have my reasons," Goll stated with a rare smile, "as does every other gladiator. Wealth. Fame. Women. The danger. The… rush of competition."

"It's no better than war."

"Ah…" Goll dipped his head with respectful sympathy. "I believe it *is* better than war. There are many deaths in war. In an arena fight, perhaps only one. Think of the lives saved if only kings fought in an arena."

"You sound like my husband now."

That didn't surprise Goll at all.

Nala straightened. "Although my husband returned late last night, I must say, he was in the best spirits I've seen him in for a very long time."

"I suppose he drank his fill before retiring to bed."

"Retiring?" Nala questioned with a knowing look. "My good Master Goll, he never came to bed at all."

Her reply stunned Goll as effectively as a plank to the face.

"Don't be too upset with him, please. I'm not. As much as I despise the games, they've given me a comfortable life and my husband a purpose. When he was exiled from the games, a part of him perished, one I was powerless to replace or heal. Many a day I kept him in sight, you see, for fear of him taking a blade to his wrists or deciding to hang himself from a rafter. Foolish thoughts, I realize. He would never do such a thing, you understand, but when a person reaches the very bottom of despair, of misery, it changes one. He turned to drink just as much as he turned to me. Spirits kept him sane—dare I say it—while I kept him focused, or at least tried to, until he found his will to return to the world once again. That all happened a long time ago, a dark time in our lives. But since your arrival, he's slowly gone from existing, as he'd been doing for a very long time, to actually looking forward to the next morning. So thank you for that, Master Goll, and more. You may not see it, but your presence has lifted my husband's spirits in ways I never could. He's probably still drunk from last night…"

Goll looked to the balcony.

"Don't be upset with him," Nala pleaded. "He's quite happy, you see. Let him have this day, and he'll be much better for it. You'll see."

Goll saw that she waited for him to speak, but words failed him. Drinking since last night? Was the man even alive?

Somehow, he managed a semblance of a smile. It convinced Nala, who returned it with one of her own. Having spoken her mind, she pardoned herself and disappeared into the house. Goll watched her white robes glide along polished stone until she was out of sight.

Dread stole over him as he continued to the balcony. He took a steadying breath and went to his taskmaster, hearing Machlann's shouts from outside. Goll didn't want to see the state Clavellus had gotten himself into. Memories resurfaced of first arriving at the taskmaster's walls and subsequently being driven away. That verbal lashing alone could have turned stone to dust.

Things had certainly changed.

Goll smelled the man before he saw him: that sickly sweet aroma that seeped from a man's pores when he'd had far too much to drink far too often.

Clavellus leaned over a table, his head on folded arms. The taskmaster didn't stir, so the Kree studied the picture of inebriation before him. The old man's shirt and trousers were stained. A pitcher stood next to Clavellus's bald head while his right hand lay relaxed around his silver mug. Sweet, rancid sweat hung on the warm morning air and wrinkled Goll's nose. *Seddon above*, he thought, casting a look at the training grounds and seeing Halm, Pig Knot, and Muluk sitting at the sand's edge.

They hadn't noticed Goll standing behind the white

railing. Or if they had, they hadn't made a spectacle of it. Not yet.

Sensing he was under scrutiny, Clavellus snorted, shivered, and sat up as if being hoisted by hooks. He blinked at the sun in confusion. Half of his snowy beard was soaked with something. Goll hoped it was beer.

"Dog balls," Clavellus rasped. His glassy eyes bulged at the sound, and he immediately sought to smooth it out. He lifted his mug and downed a sloppy mouthful of whatever it contained. Two swallows later, he noticed the Kree, blinking in surprise.

"Well, then." He belched softly and squinted. "I thought you were Nala."

Goll scowled.

"We're both relieved." Clavellus smacked his lips. He inspected his drink and found it all gone. With a look of determined concentration, he reached with his shaky hand for the pitcher. He didn't offer any to the Kree.

Goll sat down on a chair on the opposing corner of the balcony.

"Say it then."

Goll gave him a look of, *say what?*

"Go on, you tightened ring of a dog's ass. You know you want to. And I know… I *know* you do." Another chest-expanding belch escaped him, one that almost felled the taskmaster from his chair. His eyes alternated between narrowing and widening. He righted himself and, while his left hand trembled, poured another drink.

"I don't care what you say—or think," Clavellus said

with exhausted venom. "We won yesterday. We lost three, but we won four. That calls for a celebration. Ordinarily, in season as we are, I wouldn't partake, wouldn't think of it. But this is different. This is a new beginning. So I'll drink, drink until my pisser lets loose with a flood."

Clavellus's words slurred. He gripped his chest as if in pain. "This is a new *beginning*, you crust of Kree shite. *New.* And it would be dishonest. No, dis… des*picable* to …"

The taskmaster lost his trail of thought, and it showed on his face.

"How much have you had?" Goll's scowl darkened.

"More than…" Clavellus screwed up his mouth, white beard going with it, and struggled to think. "More than the river Trysis. More than the Southern seas. I'll die of old age long before I finish pissing myself dry. Guaranteed, you righteous he-bitch. Guaranteed. And I fully intend to drink for most of this day, too. I don't care *who* you are."

Clavellus's red eyes blazed, but the Kree decided not to rise to the bait. Instead, Goll turned and studied the men under Machlann's and Koba's instruction. "Isn't it early for drinking?"

"*Pah.*" Clavellus spat and lifted his mug to his near-hidden lips. "It's only early if I stopped the night before. Which I didn't."

The sight of Muluk waving caught the taskmaster's attention. He leaned over the railing and bawled. "*Ananda*, go into the cellar and take out whatever spirits we have plenty of and bring them to those three punces sitting over there. I've already asked Clurik to have more delivered, so whatever we have left, let them have it. I've seen bastards happier dead. Send over as much as they wish, whenever they want it."

He flicked a warning glance at Goll, daring him to say otherwise. But Goll heard Nala's voice in his head, so he took a settling breath and got comfortable. For some unknown reason, he didn't want to disappoint her.

Below, Machlann bellowed instructions for his remaining students to devise and practice four- and five-strike combinations.

"We did win, you realize," Clavellus stated with effort. "You have… you have the coin to prove it."

And the bodies, but Goll didn't say that. "We have plans to make."

"Then let's make them."

"When you've finished drinking."

"That could be a long time. I just started."

"You can't drink the entire day away."

Clavellus felt his wet bread and appeared disgusted with himself. He fixed Goll with a drunken look of irritation. "You're a pinch in my pisshole. Can't drink—why *not*? You're here now. And I have plenty of kegs to crack."

"I'm surprised there's any wine or beer remaining in this place. I'd've guessed you would have downed it all last night."

"Ha. You don't know me, you unfit flicker. Of shite. And asses. A drinker…" He took a huge gasp of breath as if about to take a lengthy pledge. "A drinker *always* hides away a few kegs for mornings just like these." Clavellus finished with his lips puckered and listed to one side. He straightened himself by grabbing onto the railing, nearly upsetting the pitcher. He nodded and took a well-timed mouthful. "And we have cause to celebrate."

"With two dead?"

"I understand that. I do, you hateful bucket of soup scutters. I had wine. Wine in their memory. I'm… grieving."

Goll glanced away. At least Clavellus wasn't disrupting the training.

"Take comfort, Master Goll," the taskmaster said, his voice much smoother than before. "I see… I see your bruises are almost gone. That's good."

Clavellus swung his shaking hand at the gladiators below. "Watch the training… for any improper technique, any fault in their execution. Watch for… anything Machlann might miss. Or Koba. They'll both have them—have them practice striking all day. Up to five strikes now. All day *long*. By morning's end, their arms will be on fire. By day's end, that fire will have exhausted itself."

"What happens after five-strike combinations?"

Clavellus shrugged, his eyes red and glassy. "Six-strike combinations. Different patterns, of course."

Goll sighed. Different taskmasters. Different methods of training.

"I'm surprised at you, Master… Master Goll. I'd have thought you'd have done—have done all of this—with your renowned Weapon Masters of Kree."

"Ask me that again when you're not unfit from wine."

"Just wait a few moments." Clavellus winked. "The older one gets, the faster things flow. And I'd rather not think about you thinking about my frequent pissing. So just answer the gurry question."

Very well, Goll thought. "We never trained like this. It strikes me you're missing some important steps."

Clavellus palm-wiped his mouth and inspected his beard. He checked his loose-fitting shirt and frowned at the stains. "Nala made this for me. That woman's..." Clavellus took a shoulder-shrugging breath, and his tone softened considerably. "You're correct," the taskmaster explained in a firmer voice. "We discussed it early this morning before you rose, while I was still stumbling about in the cellar. Machlann and Koba and I. The season is half gone, and our lads—well, some of them—can't be expected to... absorb everything from a lifetime of learning. So. The best we can do is prepare them to survive."

Goll's scowl caused Clavellus to wince, remembering an earlier conversation. "And *win,* of course. I'm not being brazen. Too happy to be here. But in *winning*... in winning, they'll survive to fight. Next season. So we're teaching them to win *and* to survive. But I mean win. After the games, we can properly put them through their paces—all the paces—not simply *choosing* bits as we're doing now. Our opponents? And I mean those sunbaked, shite-trough *bastards* poising as house gladiators. All of them. They'll have prepared longer. Harder."

The clatter of wooden swords connecting with targets distracted Goll, and Clavellus interpreted the Kree's silence as a sign to continue.

"I've known trained pit fighters who knew hundreds of different combinations. Countless sets of strikes. Defensive movements. Not that a man has ever used so many, but… *seeing* a warrior move through a set—at full speed, mind you—against one foe or several, real or imaginary, well, it's a spectacle. One to admire. Respect."

Clavellus whispered that last word.

"Savor," he blurted dreamily. "*Admire*. Did I say that, already? I did? Well, it's true. Those who can perform such magic deserve to be called sword master or weapon master, for that matter."

"I'm glad you think so." Goll eyed the older man.

"Don't worry, Master Goll." Clavellus smiled behind the bulk of mug. "I've as much invested in our lads doing well as you. My thoughts of them, of their worth, has changed. Dramatically."

The word popped from the taskmaster. His brow knotted. "These plans you speak of. Are they concerning blood matches?"

Though the man was pickled, smelly, and near senseless, Goll couldn't help but smiling at him.

6

The Gladiatorial Chamber member called Soranthus hobbled through the dungeons underneath the Pit. He clutched a cloth to his mouth, despising the foul air and fearing that every breath blackened his innards. Of the nine appointed Chamber members, he was the youngest at fifty-eight. He trimmed his gray beard to a modest length to maintain a youthful appearance, and his ample belly, gifted to him from a fondness of beer, bulged under his gold-and-white Chamber robes. Unlike the others, Soranthus's wounds from a career of arena combat did not seriously cripple him, thus he was chosen to inspect the meat being transported to the Pit.

How fortunate for Soranthus. It almost made him wish he'd lost a toe or two.

A handful of Skarrs surrounded him as befitted a man of his considerable position. They stopped before an iron door that led to the lower levels. A soldier slid a pair of locking bolts free and pulled the door open with both hands. Hinges squealed. An expulsion of breath—a subtle yet ageless reek of spilled blood and excrement soaked into stone—yawned into the men's faces, and Soranthus squeezed his eyes shut, almost burying his face in his cloth.

Saimon only knew what existed in such a place, and Saimon only knew what Soranthus would find. None of the nine members relished descending into the history of Sunja's Pit, but Lord Schull, speaking for King Juhn himself, demanded it.

The forward Skarrs held their torches high, illuminating solid stonework that refused to break or crumble. Moisture lined the walls. As Soranthus descended steps with his armed escort, he recalled the arena's history, back to an age when criminals fought within the Pit. Thieves and cutthroats, hellions and the insane, all fought. They hacked and stabbed at each other for the amusement of the crowds. For those earliest pit fighters, victory meant living another day, a brutal existence and one fit for the condemned. An age not widely remembered.

And now, King Juhn had charged the Chamber—Soranthus in particular—to bring back those ancient blood spectacles, where untrained brutes butchered each other under a red sun. The arena was a much different place now, Soranthus knew, for the *quality* of the games had long since improved. Sunja's sport had evolved from those primitive shows of butchery to the battles of today, where the masses gathered once a year to witness an unrivalled level of skill at arms, where a mastery of weapons, mind, and body could ensure victory within the Pit.

Sunja's rulers had supported and funded the arena with coin from abundant treasuries. Honor and prestige had been heaped upon the event. The populace hailed skilled gladiators as heroes, and champions were arguably elevated to a status rivaling kings. Coin, women, and even property awaited the victors battling their way through the yearly games.

Men were no longer sentenced to the life of a gladiator but rather chose and embraced it.

Soranthus glanced over his shoulder at the Skarrs, secretly glad for their number. He'd even slipped his scabbard onto his belt and filled it with a thirty-year-old short sword, the very blade Soranthus had wielded when he became a champion of the games. He'd enjoyed the blissful afterlife and still enjoyed watching the sport, even though the antics of the Free Trained sometimes annoyed him. But at least the Free Trained weren't as low as criminals.

Soranthus gripped the hilt of his sword, drawing comfort from the weapon's serviceable weight.

Make the experience… dramatic if at all possible. Uplifting. Anything to take minds off what's happening on the front. Anything to instill pride in the watching populace. The king wishes to see sport and theater if you can manage it.

Words read from a delivered scroll and signed with Lord Schull's scrawl. The message had stirred the Chamber into an outraged, yet fearful, twitter: the wishes of the king, commanding them to foul the games with the condemned.

Dark times, Soranthus thought. Dark times indeed. The Chamber wondered how bad the Nordish war had become. One only needed to walk the streets and listen to know the people wondered the very same thing. It was a disturbing thought, disturbing enough for Soranthus to consider abandoning his city and country of birth. Perhaps the time was nigh.

At the bottom of the stairs, the former champion followed his Skarrs through an open archway. Glowing braziers spaced at regular intervals illuminated a wide corridor. Domes of red brick loomed in the ceiling. The walls appeared as grills of iron bars that eventually vanished into the smoky black. Faces and squinting eyes peered through the nearest cell. They tracked the Skarrs and Soranthus, perhaps curious about his robes.

Three jailors emerged from the warm gloom and approached. Their faces and arms were filthy with dungeon grime.

"Master Soranthus," the lead man greeted them with a dip of his chin.

Impatiently, Soranthus nodded back and lowered his hand cloth. He twirled a finger. "This isn't all of them," he said, aghast.

"Not all," assured the lead man, a beefy fellow with a mangy beard. An unclean leather vest covered his torso. Keys dangled from a belt. "This block contains two hundred cells. We couldn't possibly fit the rest of the prisoners in here, unless you wish us to place two in each cell."

Soranthus scowled at that notion, dismissing it.

"Not the wisest course, is it?" the jailor asked. "As it is, we now have almost half a prison here: two hundred strong out of four hundred and seventy-three. As the bastards are killed off, we can send for the remainder."

"What's your name?"

"Runson."

"Many years at this?"

Runson smiled, exposing half an upper shelf of teeth. "About twenty-two or so. I kept watch over these dogs with Balazz at King Juhn's dungeons."

"These same dogs?"

"Aye that, Master Soranthus."

"So you're well acquainted with them?"

"Most of them, sar," Runson said as Soranthus inspected one of the closer cages. "You have the worst of the lot, if I might say so. These are the right and proper bastards, whose crimes were so foul, not even the Sujins wanted them. That should tell you all you need to know right there. Murderers all. Of men, women, children, and animals. Anything that breathed in the light of day, well, they butchered it. Some of these unfit pissers even dabbled in rape before pulling steel. Balazz and the lads and I vowed to never allow any of them to ever see a dawn for what they've done. Not one. They're hellions wearing the skin of men, you see—bloody savages, and those are the ones still sane. I daresay Seddon above won't have anything to do with this pack of gurry, and Saimon, well, Seddon only knows what he'll do with them below. Unfit. Unfit, the lot. If I may, I think letting them slaughter each other in the Pit is a fine idea. Considering what some—"

"They're in fair health?" Soranthus cut in as he walked toward one of the cells, prompting the Skarrs to move with him. The prisoner leered at him like a starving rat.

"Ah, fair is fair to say." Concern marked Runson's face. "About a month ago, we were told to put them on a diet of meat. Usually, it's only bread and water, you understand, nothing but the best for our guests."

The jailor chuckled.

"Who?"

"Beg your pardon, Master Soranthus?"

"Who gave you that order?"

"Ah, a man working for a king's official. I have the document about somewhere. The official wouldn't set foot into the dungeon."

Soranthus scowled. King Juhn had been mulling his decision for some time then.

"And what did you feed them?" the Chamber member asked, confronting the prisoner. The man grinned, displaying rotten teeth worn down to needles.

"Ah, well, they're a pack of right and proper ass-lickers, Master Soranthus. As I've said, these are the ones the Sujins *didn't* want. And they'll press almost anyone into service. Cooked meat was a bit of a luxury for these maggots, so I confess, they might not have gotten exactly what was ordered. We heaved scraps their way, mind you.

And they were glad to have them."

A pungent, eye-watering stench of unwashed flesh emanated from the imprisoned man. He shuffled back into the depths of his cell, where the meager light didn't reach. All the while, his feral gaze and smile fixed upon the visitor. Darkness enveloped the criminal until only the gleam from his unblinking eyes remained.

"And how long have these men been in cages?"

Runson glanced at the other two jailors. "Difficult to say. Balazz was told to bring along all the bastard savages who could fight. Most of these unfit dog blossoms are perhaps eighteen, nineteen, all the way to forty or so. I don't think there are any alive over fifty-five years. Some who'd been passed over were missing limbs: arms, legs, that sort. A few had been blinded. Them with one eye we brought over if they had their limbs. And there's the ones who've been in a cage long enough to have their minds rot."

Soranthus realized he'd been choking his sword's hilt the whole time he'd inspected the ghoulish prisoner. He didn't release the weapon.

"Murderers," Soranthus said, distracted with sizing up the surrounding brickwork.

"Cutthroats," Runson emphasised. "Savages all. The worst of the lot. The unruliest and the unwanted."

And they'll grace the majesty of the Pit. The thought seeped through Soranthus's skull and made his mind ache and his heart heavy. Suddenly, the Free Trained were entirely tolerable.

But these men?

A nearby voice chortled, the sound unpleasant and taunting in the scant dungeon light. One of Runson's jailors excused himself and marched off to a cell, smashing a club across a set of iron bars.

Truly not wanting to be there, Soranthus sighed heavily and scratched the side of his face. "Runson. That's your name?"

"Aye that, Master Soranthus."

"I hear you even have Nordish prisoners. What of them?"

"They're not all here, but eight of them are."

"Eight? How many in total do you have?"

"Rare to have any Nordish as prisoner, but we managed to gather nineteen as permanent guests. The largest group, numbering a dozen or so, arrived about a month back."

"Infantry?"

"Ah…" Runson searched his thoughts. "I believe so. Jackals, I think."

Jackals. Soranthus scoffed. Among these prisoners, the name seemed to fit well enough indeed. "Move them all to the arena. Squeeze them into the same cell if you must. You understand these men are to fight and die upon the sands."

"Aye that, I do."

"Bear in mind that they *must* be able to fight, so continue feeding them scraps along with whatever else you've been throwing to them. Try not to starve them too badly. And no severe beatings. The audience will greatly enjoy seeing them killed in the Pit."

"Imagine so, Master Soranthus."

"Try not to maim or kill any before their time in the arena," Soranthus cautioned, knowing the Nordish warriors would be a high point in the games. "If they're being unreasonable, you have my permission to execute one to bring the rest to heel. And if you do that, replace them with the regular fare from the larders of the king's dungeons. Keep these cells full."

Runson nodded that he would do as instructed.

Soranthus thought for a moment. "I'll trust your judgment in such matters, but bear in mind, this fighting season has been lengthened, by order of the king, and we only have so many gladiators." He waved at the surrounding cells. "These will be the bloody prelude to the real games."

Runson's forehead crinkled in puzzlement. "Wasn't that the role of the Free Trained?"

"To a point, yes. But it appears their worth has just doubled—in comparison to this lot."

"The Skarrs will be present to march them to the surface?"

"All the way to the white tunnels and portcullis leading to the sands. Have no worries about that. Do you need more guards here?"

Runson shook his head and smiled. "I have twenty jailors with me here. We won't have any trouble. I've made a profession doing this."

"I don't doubt," Soranthus deadpanned. *The unfit to guard the unfit.* Soranthus saw no issue with allowing the jailor's chest swell a bit in self-worth. A man should have some pride in his profession. Even if it was caging a savage pack of hellpups.

"Ah, one last thing, Master Soranthus," Runson asked with a touch of concern.

"What is it?"

"When do they fight?"

Soranthus looked about the corridor. The scant glow of the braziers revealed spying faces and white-knuckled hands gripping iron bars. The thought of this rancid stew of human meat befouling the most prestigious of all the games filled him with loathing. His features twisted. Only Seddon above knew what was going to happen.

"Soon."

7

"This is your first match… with a quality opponent." Salwark peered into Blacktooth's eyes as if they'd been blinded by hot pokers. The son of Vavar Slavol, of the Stable of Slavol, possessed much finer teeth than Blacktooth, but his demeanor sickened the veteran fighter. Excitement shook the man's frame, and Blacktooth knew an unchecked stream of flattery would soon gush forth, intended to build his confidence, one last rush as ill timed and unnecessary as the forced enthusiasm in Salwark's voice.

Not that Blacktooth *didn't* need words of encouragement. He did, especially in the twilight of his career, but old Slavol had a much better way with words than his son. It was a shame that the years had taken away the strength in the owner's legs. The man spent all his hours in bed, surrendering his livelihood to the care of his only son.

Vavar Slavol's voice possessed a soothing note. He

could calm his gladiators with just a whisper. His measured words, spoken almost lyrically, channeled his pit fighters' energies to all the right places, readied them to crack open skulls and snap bones, charged them to perform at their very best. When he spoke, men listened, for they knew Vavar cared. They knew Vavar wanted them to fight their best fight. The owner of the Stable of Slavol conjured *magic* with the resonance of his voice. He inspired pit fighters, charmed monsters, dispelled thunderheads, and summoned the sun.

Vavar knew how to talk. Knew *when* to talk, as if life itself was an act within a dramatic Perician play. And his gladiators would fight to win because they knew Vavar watched, and they so very much wanted to please him.

Blacktooth missed the old man.

Salwark, however good his intentions, did not possess his father's gift of speech. And his breath smelled of fish and beer.

"You've had an easy run thus far," said the younger man. "You fought a handful of Free Trained and one unseasoned gladiator who probably let slip a cow kiss before he walked out onto the sands. Now, however, you have your work before you. Now, you have no room for sloppy strokes or slow defense. Brontus has had more days at this than you, and he's two years younger, which tells me he's faster of foot. If there's anyone who could end your undefeated run, it is *this* man, today. Don't think about how he's defeated you twice already in years gone by. And don't think about the two ass lickers he's already executed this season. I've placed a considerable amount of coin on your head, hoping you can defeat this sick topper from Ustda. A *considerable* amount. Keep that in your head. You can defeat this man. You can. It's your time. *Your* time. He's nothing more than a crust of scab fallen from Saimon's black hanging bells. You must win. You *must*. Remember the strategy. Remember what we talked about."

Blacktooth's expression remained unchanged, unmoved, but inside, he thought, *Sweet Seddon*, embarrassed at the flow of shite issuing from Salwark's toothy mouth. The man would do more good if he'd simply shut up and slap the pit fighter on the shoulder.

As if Salwark sensed a bout of physical contact would do wonders, he hesitantly lifted a hand, studied Blacktooth's armored form for the best place to make contact, and struck. *Hard.*

"Considerable coin," he squeaked, trying hard to keep a brave face, his pained hand clenching and unclenching by his side. "The remainder of your season rests on this match's outcome. Don't allow it to slip by. Do not!"

Blacktooth absorbed the uninspired, nerve-rattling rant. If only Salwark were ailing and bedridden. The man didn't know when to shut up or when to allow a moment of silence. Lords above, Blacktooth missed Vavar.

"Now *go!*" Salwark yelled.

Left cold by the mildly insulting outburst, Blacktooth glanced at the other fighters in the private viewing room. Aidas wore that blank expression whenever he attempted to hide his disdain. A faint smirk skewed Villari's features, brazenly showing what he thought about the older pit fighter's chances. Blacktooth wished he could smash the arrogant Marrnite bastard into the floor. A few others filled his side vision, but Blacktooth walked past them all, toward the open door and the mind-cleansing serenity of the white tunnel. Punder held out a spiked fist, and Blacktooth pressed his own armored knuckles against it. Punder wasn't as old as Blacktooth, but he traveled the same road.

Blacktooth, however, was going to enjoy it more.

"*Victory!*" Salwark shouted, the sound blasting past the departing gladiator as he turned a corner, escaping the brunt of the windstorm.

Blacktooth walked the white tunnel, taking his time, savoring the experience. The depths of the underpass muted the screaming crowds above. That would change the closer he got. At thirty-five years of age, his career as a gladiator was nearly over. He knew it, though there was the part of his mind that scoffed at the notion, telling him he was still young, that hard training would sharpen his mettle and keep him competitive. His body ruefully said otherwise. Wounds ached more these days and took longer to heal. The strength was still there, but somehow he'd gotten slower, or the younger lads had become faster. But the worst, the absolute *worst*, was seeing his flesh age, like fruit blackening in the sun. That disturbed him.

Still, he'd give what he could this day, even though the man he faced had defeated him twice over the years in the

Pit.

Skarrs stood with their backs to the walls, shields and swords at the ready, their visors worn but gleaming. Blacktooth nodded casually at one and marched on, relishing the moment. These days, he wrung every drop of enjoyment that could be had out of life, well aware that one of these walks to the arena would be his final, one way or the other. Every walk was potentially the last for any fighter. Now, however, in the sunset of his career, that haunting feeling of becoming too old had fused itself to his bones.

Blacktooth took his time, tasting the dust-tainted air and relishing it. His twin short swords swung at his side like faithful dogs. Lightning and Thunder, he'd secretly named the blades. He gripped Lightning in his left hand and Thunder, the splitter of skull pots, in his right. He remembered the weapons merchant, the haggling, and how they'd finally settled on ten gold apiece. No finer purchase had Blacktooth ever made. He lifted Lightning halfway, torchlight rippling along the fine lines of the steel. Nicks and scratches pitted the weapon, and he recalled how they got there.

A vest of ringmail covered Blacktooth's body, while bronze greaves protected his muscular legs. Bronze bracers appeared nailed to his formidable forearms. A cage screened his helmet. A single battered fin, iron and screaming respect, adorned the top of his helm to the nape of his neck. Most of the scars lashing Blacktooth's person were below the neckline.

Most of them. Except for one match. When he was twenty-two, he'd fought a Free Trained bastard, who'd bashed his head with two solid strikes. The first blow, from a sword, smashed the protective cage from his face. The second one, from a fist made from steel, struck him in the mouth and removed all of his upper teeth—except his right incisor.

His lucky tooth, Blacktooth snorted, remembering how his sword brothers had howled over his ruined mouth. He'd chuckled as well. His smile had never attracted any ladies before, but at least after losing his teeth, he'd received sympathy, if not outright curiosity. And on more than a few occasions, blatant horror. He pursued the women who pitied him and knew Seddon frowned on him for doing so.

Twin swords. Armor. Subdued and focused. The blood rose. Quickened. *Eager.*

Blacktooth turned a corner and walked toward the gatekeeper. He didn't worry about how many fights Seddon had remaining for him. Didn't care. The only one that mattered was the one ahead.

And he'd enjoy it as such.

*

Inside the private chamber assigned to the House of Ustda, Burco Ustda inspected the timbers holding up the ceiling and the mortar between the red brick.

"What do you think?" Brontus asked, the caged visor of his helmet hiding his features. As was his habit, he rolled his shoulders, feeling the weight of his spiked mace and shield pull on his thick arms.

"Fine work." Burco slapped a callused hand against the window arch. For a flicker of time, the opening framed the owner's upper body perfectly as he gazed upon the sands.

"How many others have looked out this very window? How many, I wonder? This is history, you know. We fight within history here, cut from rock. Stacked with brick. Dusted by the years. Marvelous."

Brontus had figured Burco would say something of the like. In his fourteen-year career, all spent within Ustda's walls, he couldn't remember Ustda's oldest son ever uttering a negative sentiment about anything. In this business, Brontus thought that spoke volumes about Burco's character. Old Ustda had raised his children well.

"You'd best remember that," Burco said, mischief twinkling in his eyes.

Brontus chuckled softly. Only a year after prime, and Burco was already nudging him toward another profession—one with less blood. Some of the older fighters took up employment with the Ustdas as guards around their private residences, training grounds, or warehouses. Perhaps Burco would offer him the same opportunity when the games were over or Brontus could no longer fight.

The Ustdas didn't have a long or rich history with the games. Unglo enjoyed the sport enough to establish a house of pit fighters, a stark contrast from his family's legacy with procuring and selling cloth. The Ustdas were wealthy, comfortably wealthy, and successful enough to believe they could manage a house of gladiators. They didn't have the same success in the Pit, however, despite hiring good trainers and taskmasters. The House of Ustda consistently placed somewhere within the third rank, along with the usual occupants of Razi, Vandu, and the Stable of Slavol. Coin wasn't an issue for the Ustdas, but good fortune within the Pit was. Unglo had never really attained an eye for sifting through ranks of potential fighters and developing them. Missed opportunities and bad fortune abounded. On the rare occasion they did find a warrior with the potential to advance all the way to a championship round, the other houses found someone better.

Burco was somewhat better than his father at overseeing the business of gladiators, but he was still, by and large, a man of cloth learning a very different trade.

None of the house gladiators disliked the owners. Even though they normally finished the season ranked low, their living and training conditions, as well as the opportunities after the Pit, were second to none. The Ustdas treated their fighters well.

Brontus wasn't the only one wishing he could claim a title in their name. But with the years pressing in, he didn't believe he possessed the time or the skills to do so, much to his quiet chagrin. This day, his path crossed with Blacktooth from the House of Slavol, an older dog of the games, perhaps three or four years Brontus's senior. He'd defeated the man twice already over the years. The first time they'd clashed, Brontus's speed gave him victory. The second time had been much closer, as Blacktooth remembered his opponent's speed and attacked his legs in an effort to take away that natural advantage. Even when Brontus had recognized the strategy and began countering it, Blacktooth had pressed, refusing defeat—even when the blood truly began to fly.

Burco and Master Torgul believed this fight would be just as close and perhaps even more dangerous. Blacktooth was nearly finished with the Pit. The gladiator would want to steal a victory from Brontus.

Brontus knew he would. And for the House of Ustda and all they'd provided for him, he would do everything he could to take a third fight from the man called Blacktooth. That included killing him.

"Fight hard," Master Torgul growled. "Fight smart."

Lines crossed the old taskmaster's face, deep enough to make one think he'd pulled an angry cat off it.

Brontus would do as told. He checked his vest of hardened leather and the bronzed greaves protecting his lower legs. Long spikes protruded from metal cups covering his knees.

"Bring us back something." Burco smiled, his meaning clear. "And we'll share a drink this evening."

Brontus grunted that he'd do that as well. Having their leave, the gladiator walked for the door. A handful of armored men showered wishes of good fortune, bolstering the fighter's determination. The door opened, and he marched into the white tunnel. He'd traveled the way so often he could do it in his sleep. In a short time, Brontus stopped beside the gatekeeper without realizing it. The gatekeeper was a younger sort this day and didn't so much as acknowledge the pit fighter. Brontus didn't care. All his thoughts focused on that bottom step, the first leading to the portcullis at the end of the stairs, the deep blue stamped with bars of iron.

Blacktooth.

Brontus inhaled deeply. The Orator bellowed far above, followed by the approving crash of thousands packed into the Pit. They were eager to witness a match fought by professionals. He'd give them one. Blacktooth would do the same. The people would see a spectacle. Brontus had no doubt.

The Orator started his introductions. The portcullis rattled open.

Sniffing hard, Brontus shrugged and climbed the stairs, focused on the blazing sky. Thousands greeted him with a cheering roar as he stepped into daylight. The stands teemed with people. Arms, open hands, and fists waved like a colorful, maddening mass of worms.

Brontus shook his shoulders, the day's heat already cooking unprotected flesh. Moisture fattened the air, heavy and ominous, and over the din of the spectators, he heard the Orator.

"...*Sunjan* born. He is an accomplished reaper, a collector of skulls, and a breaker of wills. Already this year, he's taken two lives in Saimon's name. His mace is a thing of nightmares, a black moon spiked with iron teeth, fashioned to smash bones and flesh alike. Children fear him, as do any and all within his freezing aura. You called upon Saimon's name, and you have summoned… *Brontus*! From the House of Ustda!"

The cheering spiked in volume, staggering in its power.

In the beginning of his career, the gladiator had gushed at the Orator's epic introductions. After the first two years, however, the colorful speech only brought a smile to Brontus's face. At times, he might've even shaken his head at the fearsome accolades. Now, understanding the theatre of the sport for what it was, Brontus knew better, and concentrated on the other side of the arena—and the figure emerging from an iron-and-wood maw.

Blacktooth.

"Men and women of the Pit," the Orator began, holding out his arms, "this gladiator turns my blood cold. This man is a hellion with his twin blades. Once he starts swinging, his foes drop in spouting chunks. He too is Sunjan born, but he won't hesitate to hack the head off a fellow countryman. He is not a man but a fiend freed from enchanted chains, released upon this existence, knowing only war, smelling out flesh to slaughter and blood to sup. You wished for a beast? I give you… *Blacktooth* from the Stable of Slavol!"

The portcullis dropped in Blacktooth's wake as he casually, confidently, walked toward his opponent. His shadow stretched across the ground as if attempting to free itself. Blacktooth took his time, and Brontus remembered that he did the very same in their previous battles.

"Both are undefeated this season." The Orator strained to be heard. "You wanted a *war*, men and women of the Pit? *I give you one!*"

That final, raw shout rose above the insanity of the audience, before being lost in the cheering of thousands.

Blacktooth sauntered on, bare swords swinging at his hips. Brontus went forth to meet him. As the gap closed, Brontus stopped five or six strides away and nodded a greeting.

"Brontus," the other replied cordially, tapping his head with a blade.

"Back for more?"

"Aye that. Looks that way."

"Well, maybe your luck will change this day."

Blacktooth didn't share his thoughts on the matter.

"Is this to the death?" Brontus asked.

"Should be asking you that. You've killed two men already."

"Free Trained, good Blacktooth. They don't count."

"Oh, but they do." Blacktooth smiled behind his face cage, revealing his infamous incisor. "It's been recorded, regardless of what you might think. History will remember the names and not the class. You decide if it's to the death or not."

Brontus sighed. That really wasn't an answer.

"Ready?" asked the battered gladiator with two swords.

Brontus raised his shield, turned his aging body to the side, and nodded.

Blacktooth's left blade stretched out as if measuring the

distance while his right blade rose to his shoulder.

Always the same, Brontus thought.

Hell came at him.

Blacktooth's whirling blades lashed out from over his shoulders, churning and cutting in a frightening, bloodletting weave like some diabolical machine. Sunlight flashed off steel.

Brontus instinctively got out of the way of such killing madness.

But Blacktooth lunged at the last instant, stomping his foot as he slashed, his right blade a flat arc of armor-splitting power. Brontus deflected it off his shield, but the blow staggered him. Blacktooth recovered first. He chased his opponent, tearing into the younger gladiator, swords scintillating in the sun, cutting for a leg, a head, a shoulder, a leg again, *stomach…*

Brontus ducked and parried, moving his shield with an uncanny speed as if dispelling bad magic. He feinted one way, failed to fool the older fighter, and nearly got his head half-lopped off for the effort. He backtracked at an angle, circling the pursuing Blacktooth, keeping his shield between them.

Blacktooth struck it twice, ringing the barrier as if demanding entry. Brontus got away a few steps, ignoring the ache in his shield arm. The crowds loved the action and let it be known.

"Seddon's rosy ass," Brontus commented over the rim of his shield. "Most hellpups slow *down* with age."

That made Blacktooth smile. Then he attacked.

The gladiator's swords lashed out in a dazzling series of strikes that rendered Brontus completely on the defensive.

Leg, arm, arm, head, head, shoulder, *leg*—

Blacktooth spun on a heel, arm powered by the torque of his hips. His left sword clanged off Brontus's forehead when he couldn't raise his shield fast enough. The Ustda man's head cracked back, the impact yanking a chorus of *OOOOOHs* from the audience. Brontus stumbled a retreat, holding a shield suddenly far too small for him.

Blacktooth didn't wait for a recovery. Smelling blood and opportunity, he charged in, left arm pulling back as if to strike but his right arm *stabbing*—

Brontus swatted the sword away and backpedaled, placing distance between them. His uneven gait smoothed out into a ready, if not playful, prance.

Half the crowds responded with cheers. The others were much harsher.

"Saimon's shite trough, old man," Brontus exclaimed. "You're throwing steel."

Blacktooth didn't pursue his dallying quarry. The Stable of Slavol fighter tracked his opponent's movements with one sword extended and the other ready to stab from the shoulder.

"You're slowing down," Blacktooth huffed.

Not caring for the comment in the least, Brontus sprang ahead, holding his shield like a battering ram. He twisted and swung for Blacktooth's head. The mace hissed over the fin-adorned helmet like a catapult shot, missing by a finger. Blacktooth answered by cutting for a left leg and striking a greave.

The men righted themselves and returned to circling.

"That's what I remembered," Blacktooth puffed.

"The difference a year makes."

"Everything."

Blacktooth snarled as he launched himself at his foe, swords hacking. Again, Brontus backpedaled, his shield turning away the storm of Blacktooth's lethal twins. Metal clattered. True to form, the Stable of Slavol fighter did not overextend himself, nor did he make a mistake. Blacktooth pressured, advancing while Brontus retreated. He slashed for limbs in daring flurries, lengthy sets of combinations that kept the younger man ducking and moving.

Then the storm broke, and Blacktooth retreated before Brontus could execute his own attack.

"Those last few strikes felt lighter." Brontus hunched over, stalking his foe.

"I'm an old man." Blacktooth sucked in air. "I should be… drinking by now."

"You make me laugh. Be a shame to kill you."

With that, Brontus attacked.

He crossed the space between them in a blink and smashed downward with his mace. The iron head crashed into one of Blacktooth's upraised swords, nearly tearing it from his grip. Brontus's shield whistled through the gap and exploded into Blacktooth's face cage, denting it. Sweat sprayed. The older pit fighter staggered backward amidst a blend of hearty approval and fearful shrieks.

Brontus pursued, readying his mace for another blow.

Blacktooth stopped and ducked, unleashing Lightning and Thunder in a silver *one-two* blur of cutting power.

Brontus stopped Lightning on his shield. He missed Thunder.

The blade cut him across the gut, and Brontus retreated, his attention suddenly divided between his midsection and Blacktooth, who did not come after him.

"Is it bad?" The older pit fighter asked, taking the time to adjust the squashed cage of his helmet.

"Give me a moment."

Blacktooth gestured that he would.

Brontus immediately probed himself with his a fist, a chill overcoming him. He pressed the leather armor sheathing his abdomen. A gill-like slit opened, revealing an untouched stomach underneath.

A hiss of relief left him.

"A near thing," he said. "Unfit."

"Your leather's too light." Blacktooth pointed with a sword, his shoulders heaving.

"My hide's too slow, truth be known."

"Truth be known."

"I'll change it if I get by you."

Blacktooth grunted with grim amusement.

They hunched over, seeking weakness like a pair of slick adders ready to spit venom. Slower now, the initial rushes of the battle behind them, they settled into counterstriking.

"I remember old Sawklaw," Blacktooth panted through his dented grill. "He bled to death from such a cut. Much deeper, of course. Straight through to the spine. A right and proper *mess*."

Brontus made a face. "Unfit way to perish."

"Unfit business."

"Aye that."

Brontus kept his shield moving, for fear of tempting his adversary. "So come on then, you piece of gurry. Enough with the dancing."

"This dance might end with your head."

Brontus snorted and swung at the warrior's helm. Blacktooth slapped it away in annoyance.

"What was that nonsense?"

"Just seeing, is all."

"That sort of—" Blacktooth's words died when Brontus swung for his hip, the mace cleaving space at a downward angle. Blacktooth jumped, avoiding the blow, but Brontus followed, closing the gap and swinging for pain. Blacktooth dodged right, then left, and ducked under a cross aimed for his skull.

Straight into the edge of Brontus's shield.

Face cage met banded iron with a startling *clack* of metal. The grill crumpled, squishing deep into Blacktooth's face, straightening the whole of his frame as if Seddon himself sought to yank him up by the collar.

Brontus followed up with a swing of his mace, completing a series of strikes practiced so often he could perform the combination while in his sleep. The spikes crunched into Blacktooth's midsection, buckling him. The Stable of Slavol's man crumpled awkwardly to a knee, his back exposed. His cry of pain merged with the crowd's horrified glee.

Brontus stepped in, taking what was offered, and slammed his shield's edge down across an ankle, breaking it. Blacktooth screamed again. The crowds rose to their feet, sensing a bloody end.

Brontus lifted his shield off the shattered ankle, leaving a mess of metal, meat, and purpling skin. The match was all but finished, and Brontus stepped around his crippled opponent to face him, rearing up his mace and intending to bring that evil chunk of black iron down with everything behind it.

In agony as he was, as vulnerable as he was, Blacktooth's blind instinct took control. He glanced up and recognized an opening in a fleeting instant of mind and reflex.

Thunder was of no use with Brontus's shield in place. Lightning, however…

Blacktooth sprang from the ground on his good leg, his ruined ankle flopping behind him, and stabbed Lightning with all the precision of a ballista. The sword lanced between mace and shield and slammed into Brontus's protected jaw so hard the very connection might have stretched bone and tendons a finger's width. The impact snapped the head back on its shoulders. Brontus staggered away, clearly senseless, and fell to a knee.

Blacktooth crumpled not a stride away.

Exquisite pain crackled through Blacktooth's foot and rang in his brain. His ankle unleashed a torrent of white-hot agony, refusing to exit his person by mere scream alone—so he channeled it once more into his sword arm.

Blacktooth lurched forward on his good leg, bashing Brontus across the helmet. The bigger man toppled in a plume of dust. Baring his one incisor and eyes watering with every jolt of movement, Blacktooth closed in upon his fallen opponent as the audience erupted into a frenzied backdrop of noise.

Sensing danger, Brontus drunkenly pushed himself to his knees as if in worship. His fingers grazed the shaft of his mace. A bare strip of leather from the weapon's pommel looped around his wrist in case of such a moment.

Broken ankle dragging behind him, Blacktooth clumsily launched himself at the stricken pit fighter and grappled him about the chest, bending Brontus back in a grunt of pain.

The spectators leapt to their feet.

Half mad with pain and lying across Brontus, Blacktooth tried to lift Lightning and discovered the blade trapped underneath his foe. He released the weapon and cocked Thunder, seeking to finish the fight.

Brontus caught the wrist in a vise. Blood from the pit fighter's temple flecked his eye and the skin surrounding it. Sand stuck to it all. Brontus bared his teeth as he exerted whatever power he had left.

Feeling that might, Blacktooth utilized his body weight and bore down on Thunder. A steel-eyed Brontus gasped. Spittle flew from his lips. Livid with pain, Blacktooth pushed.

And like the evening sun having had enough of the day, Thunder trembled and descended with all the grace of failing strength. The sword's edge crept to Brontus's throat with Blacktooth's insane grimace behind it.

"*Yield!*" Brontus barked in a spray of fluids and sand.

That one word unlocked the killer in Blacktooth. He eased off his sword, and Brontus relaxed underneath him. Blacktooth rolled off and around for a time, taking the pain. Both men sucked down much-needed air.

Blacktooth stopped, set his jaw, and glanced at Brontus.

"Well fought," he grunted, barely heard over the uproar of the crowds.

"Well fought," Brontus sighed in return, realizing the loss meant the end to his games, his first and last defeat.

"Next season." Blacktooth grimaced.

Brontus's brow shrugged understanding, but disappointment remained thick in the air. There were no excuses made, however, no vows of redemption, and certainly no threats. Brontus reached out and patted the other man's shoulder.

Blacktooth appreciated the gesture, but the painful wreck of his ankle screamed that his own ambitions had ended. There wasn't enough saywort in Sunja to set those bones right.

The crowd's enthusiasm had died down, prompting Brontus to stand.

"Brontus?" Blacktooth grimaced with a touch of hope.

"If you're willing… help me off the sands?"

The beaten man frowned at the fallen victor, and for an instant, Blacktooth thought the man would refuse. Brontus, however, cringed at the mashed ankle. He hauled the crippled man up without a trace of ill will and draped one of Blacktooth's arms around his shoulders before helping the older fighter limp off the sands.

"My thanks," Blacktooth whispered through clenched teeth.

"You're welcome, good Blacktooth."

8

Grisholt regarded the heat shimmers rising from the glowing sands and smiled. Beyond the stone arch of his private viewing chamber, the audience damn near shook the arena's foundation with their noise. The last fight had been an entertaining one, but Grisholt hadn't wagered upon it. In his mind, he'd chosen Brontus to defeat the aging Blacktooth. The victory by the Slavol gladiator surprised many from the collective groans and curses from the crowds. The sound pleased Grisholt, and he mentally patted himself on the back for keeping his coin right where it was—to be wagered on his own warriors. His blue eyes, normally fringed red with exhaustion, blazed this day. He had spared no expense with his perfumed water, taking yet another sniff of his shoulder and relishing the scent of lavender. His hand stroked his gray beard, coaxing it to greater thickness, while musing that the tides of fortune flowed with him rather than against.

That golden flow would deliver even greater riches this

day.

Behind him, Brakuss and a handful of warriors finished aiding Kossa with his armor. He would be the next fighter to drink of the Sons of Cholla potion after Barros's lopsided victory a few days ago. *Barros!* A chill enveloped Grisholt's aging bones as he remembered that spectacle of butchery. The devastation! His pit dog had mangled his opponent and left only bloody pieces. Any other time, fear would grip Grisholt for killing another house gladiator. That was before. This time, Grisholt actually looked forward to the blood match. The House of Razi would hunt for Barros down for the expensive slight of killing their man, and Seddon above, Grisholt hoped they would do something soon.

Barros's victory emboldened Grisholt to use the potion in the very next fight, despite the fear of arousing suspicion. Even though the Sons of Cholla's foul concoction had rendered Barros bedridden for two days without even the strength to walk to a latrine, Grisholt couldn't wait to use the potion—the *fire*—once again.

Victory, the stranger from the Sons of Cholla had called it. He did not lie.

Grisholt turned ever so slightly, struggling to contain his excitement, and sized up the gladiator about to sip from the iron flask. The potion had been revealed to his men. The stable knew about Barros, and Grisholt chided himself for ever thinking he could keep the potion's existence from the very ones who had to use it. The next evening, he'd gathered the lot of them in the common room of their barracks and gave them the speech—won the entire pack over. It wasn't difficult, really, convincing his lads to stay on his side. Thinking on the matter further, Grisholt realized his gladiators hated the repeated losses just as much as he did. They were tired of being mocked and scorned for being associated with the Stable of Grisholt.

They wanted victory in the Pit. They wanted to be feared. But more than anything, they wanted riches.

They *embraced* the potion. Grisholt appreciated their mercenary thinking. After all, they risked their lives every day in this profession until death, wounds, or age stopped them. Why not seize the gold and fame that had lured them to the games in the first place? They all fought for coin, family, or some other reason. And if they were discovered, they could plead ignorance, that their owner had ordered them to drink from the iron flask. At worst, they'd never fight in the games again.

For their loyalty, for their secrecy, Grisholt had promised them everything—nothing he didn't already have—but a noble sense of self overcame him as he uttered the words. If the potion continued working, he would share the riches won in the Pit. A few extra coins here and there. He knew he could afford it with the new wealth pouring into the stable. He stressed they should wager coin on themselves for even greater returns.

To his delight, they'd agreed. Not one deserted. And if one did, Grisholt would see to it the bastard would never leave the villa alive. Perhaps his dogs knew that.

He regarded the man about to drink from the iron flask.

A Sunjan by birth, Kossa's parents had come from far off Yanth or the Territories, somewhere from that southwestern region. Grisholt wasn't particularly interested in the details. Taskmaster Turst had given Kossa an exceptionally high grade, declaring the pit fighter would do quite well this season. To this point, the Sunjan-born had amassed three victories, all Free Trained, but Grisholt didn't care about that anymore.

Brakuss's one eye met the owner's, and they shared a knowing moment. The other fighters stepped away from Kossa's brooding form. Young, tall, thin of shoulder but thick of arms, protected by a leather cuirass and the usual armor, Kossa stood and glared. His shallow chest heaved, betraying excitement. Blue-eyed with short orange hair, the gladiator radiated a carefully cultivated confidence. He knew his worth.

"Are you ready?" Grisholt's eyes crinkled around the edges.

"Aye that, Master Grisholt."

"Show me your face."

Kossa snarled, twisting his ordinary features into something horrific. Even though Grisholt had witnessed this change many times before, it still fascinated and secretly shocked him. Kossa's neck corded, the veins and tendons popping out like the roots of some haunted, meat-eating tree. He bared yellowed teeth and hissed. His eyes narrowed into bloodless slits, every bit as shocking as a slash across one's guts.

The hairs on Grisholt's neck bristled. All gladiators had a secret face for the arena, a rarely-seen battle mask, but *Kossa's…*

Kossa's was special.

Grisholt approved. "Brakuss."

On cue, the one-eyed former gladiator produced the iron flask of the liquid fire that had transformed Barros into a monster. Brakuss undid the brass stopper and offered it to Kossa with both hands. Kossa took the flask and held it aloft.

"Careful," Grisholt warned him. "And only a taste. Not a mouthful."

Kossa sniffed at the container. He grimaced, repelled by the gut-wringing smell.

Grisholt suppressed the dark chuckle in his belly. Two nights ago, Brakuss, Turst, and Grisholt himself had gathered in his departed father's study. They'd surrounded the container in silence, marveling at its power. Armored by three bottles of wine, Grisholt had removed the potion's stopper and tempted Saimon to sniff. What he'd smelled had seemingly scorched the hairs of his precious nose, made his eyes water, and brought him to the brink of retching. Turst had sniffed as well. He'd managed to keep his supper down and compared the potion's aroma to rancid meat steeped in the bloodiest of scutters. That description alone almost made Grisholt sick. Brakuss had choked and grabbed his nose after the barest whiff.

Death, he'd called it. Death, Grisholt knew it to be.

"Barros drank *this*?" Kossa asked in undisguised horror. Grisholt nodded.

The gladiator became tight-lipped. He pinched his nose and tipped that awful juice into his mouth. His cheeks puffed out in reflex. His frame shivered. Brakuss snatched the container from the pit fighter as he struggled to send the mixture down. Kossa bent over, grabbed his knees, and swallowed with visible effort. He sucked down a great breath when he straightened, as if hoping air alone would remove the taste.

Grisholt doubted it would.

Kossa barked a series of coughs and wiped his lips. He gagged, appearing ready to vomit. Nothing came of it, however, so he hacked out another bout of coughing, his back bucking with spasms.

"Oh, sweet Seddon," he choked out between breaths, threatening to retch.

Brakuss flashed a concerned look at Grisholt, but the owner ignored it, focusing on Kossa's furious reaction to the potion.

"Do you feel sick?" the owner asked.

"Aye that."

Good, Grisholt thought, remembering Barros's identical experience. He glanced at the gladiators nearest the chamber door and sent them a silent message of *get ready*.

With a great gasping breath, Kossa held his stomach and straightened. His face reddened as if boiled raw. The cords of his neck stood out once again, but this time, they bulged and rippled with gruesome force. Brakuss flashed a second look of concern to Grisholt, and this time, the old man's outer calm faltered.

Kossa grunted, a long-winded sound as if he were about to lift a mountain. His bloodshot eyes flared, and a violent shudder ripped through his frame like a man impaled on a lengthy spear. He stomped his sandaled foot three times in succession, great smashing blows that caused Grisholt and everyone else to back away. The gladiator abruptly stopped, chest heaving, and regarded the sword brother holding his helmet. Kossa snatched it away. He slapped the open helm over his head with such force that Grisholt feared blood. An enraged Kossa grabbed for his small, rounded shield and fixed it to his left arm. He sputtered syllables that might have been a language but scorched the air as gibberish. He held out an impatient hand. A pit fighter immediately filled it with a long-necked warhammer. A single grooved spike protruded from the opposite side.

"Kossa," Grisholt managed to say, blinking in uncertainty and wondering if Barros had been a stroke of luck.

Bloodshot eyes beheld the old manager, freezing the words in his throat. Grisholt thought Kossa had looked frightening before. Now, however, the gladiator's unstable condition filled him with fear.

Kossa wasn't listening, anyway. Opening his mouth in a feral display of glee, the tall man spun around and barely cleared the doorframe on his way out. For an instant,

Grisholt thought the pit fighter would brain himself on the portal's upper crossbeam.

Then he was gone. His howls echoed in the white tunnel.

Brakuss's one eye appeared ready to pop free of his face. Grisholt exhaled and realized, with gratitude, that he hadn't pissed himself. He clenched a fist and shook it at the door.

"Make them fear," the owner whispered with newfound wrath.

*

The audience chatted, joked, ate, and drank in the stands, filling the time before the next clash of arms and wills. The odd yell spiked the rumble of conversations. The Orator stood on his podium positioned at the east end of the arena, dividing his time between surveying the masses and reading from a scroll. To his right and to the north stood the boxes reserved for the ruling owners and trainers, while to the left and the south was the raised platform, fashioned from rich hardwoods and drooping banners, reserved for the king and his guests. Qualtus held a scroll before his old eyes and inspected the names, remembering the house gladiators and noting additions. He scratched at his loose-fitting robes, fixing the material before it revealed too much of his skinny arms. Having done that, he went back to the day's schedule.

A savage pounding of metal on metal disturbed his thoughts.

Qualtus looked up and listened with a frown, pondering the source. He located it in short time: a relentless, rhythmic beating of iron coming from the eastern portcullis. Qualtus's puzzlement deepened, and he wasn't the only one. Each impact stole a little bit more of the crowd's attention. People stopped talking, stopped eating and drinking. Questions formed on their features. The seated section just above the eastern entrance became aware of the noise, and the people's yammering quieted in a spreading, wondering rush. In heartbeats, all conversation had stopped, and eyes and ears focused on the barred gateway.

Even the heads of the most skilled houses—Dark Curge, Nexus, and Gastillo—paused in their bickering and leaned forward, wondering what the hammering was all about.

Before its time, the portcullis cranked upward. A startling bellow issued from the depths. Some onlookers glimpsed a figure moving behind the crossed iron, throwing itself at the timbers and metal. Sand scuffed from the yawning opening. Another roar of impatience, a shocking bawl, was heard the length of the arena.

When the portcullis reached waist level, the head of a warhammer and a shield appeared underneath the rising edge, awkwardly lifting the gate.

Qualtus's puzzlement shifted into dismay. Dark Curge, Nexus, and Gastillo froze in place. The crowds shifted and muttered with unease.

And when the portcullis lifted high enough, Kossa

ducked out from under it and threw his arms wide as if newly birthed. He raged at the spectators sitting at the lowest level, causing them to draw back in terror. Kossa whirled in the rays of the sun, calling for Seddon or the Lords to strike him down, *daring* the divine entities to smite him. He cursed and stomped out a circle, marking the sands as his own.

Everyone seemed spellbound by the gladiator's frightening presence. The Orator adjusted his robes, gathered up his scroll, and cleared his throat. Kossa cleared his own pipes in a fearsome cry of discovery, rattling the elderly announcer and robbing him of his voice.

Heedless of arena decorum, Kossa charged the opposing portcullis, drawing the collective disbelief of all watching. He gripped the rising timbers and heaved, not moving the weight any faster but impressing onlookers nonetheless.

A sword lashed out, a thrust meant to ward the attacking Kossa away from the opening. Kossa jumped back, but only for an instant, before charging the gate again. This time, he ducked and disappeared within the tunnel.

A horrified Qualtus straightened and met the incredulous gaze of Dark Curge.

The sounds of a scuffle ensued, ending with a sword-and-shield-bearing gladiator being ejected as if forcefully shat. The top of his helmet *twanged* against the lower edge of the portcullis, and he staggered, arms floundering for balance, before landing on his back.

The fallen gladiator, called Stonum, belonged to the

House of Vandu. He clambered to his feet, teeth bared, as Kossa strode toward him. The Vandu pit fighter brought his weapons to guard just as Kossa reached him.

Stonum stabbed with his sword, aiming for a stomach. Kossa parried it with his shield, spun in a complete circle to the outside, and smashed the flat of his warhammer across Stonum's helmet, cracking it askew. The Vandu man collapsed in a heap, and Kossa brained him, flattening him on the arena floor. With a feral grunting, Kossa stood, stance wide, and lorded over the defenseless man before unleashing a horrifying barrage about his victim's head and shoulders.

Qualtus covered his mouth when Kossa paused long enough to turn the warhammer around so that he could employ the spike.

Some of the more bloodthirsty amongst the spectators yelled in delight at the spectacle, but the majority did not. Qualtus composed himself and waited, hiding his shock at the relentless killing. Every swing the hammer flung an arc of blood.

Eventually, the crunch of metal faded. Kossa straightened. He swayed on his feet as if drunk and backed off the unmoving lump that had once been a man. The crowds did not cheer, but a ripple of disturbed and stunned conversation swept through the Pit. Kossa regarded the dead man mashed into the ground and staggered to his side of the arena. The portcullis lifted as he approached.

Qualtus found his voice and announced the victor.

*

Kossa disappeared into the opening, and Grisholt released the widest of predatory smiles. A rush of excitement had overcome him upon Kossa's first strike, and after that, nothing else really mattered.

"Seddon above," old Turst whispered.

"Praise Seddon," Grisholt added with near-breathless delight. He quickly fixed Brakuss with a look. "You alerted our companions about Kossa, correct?"

The one-eyed guard frowned but nodded, having already answered the same question as he accompanied his employer to the private viewing chamber.

"Excellent." Grisholt felt even better, knowing that the Sons of Cholla would be happy with the day's victory. He did a quick mental estimate of just how much he'd won with Kossa's victory. The rich pot nearly robbed him of his breath. There wasn't anything better than gold coin spilling from stuffed coffers.

"He slaughtered that man," Turst said with awe.

The comment failed to ruin Grisholt's mood.

"And so will the others, Master Turst. So will the others. From this day forth, the denizens of the games will take notice of the Stable of Grisholt. They'll start talking. And they'll start watching for our appearances in the games. People will hail us, and our adversaries will tremble. Many years have passed since the Stable of Grisholt has been regarded as a threat."

Turst divided his attention between the body being

gathered up by arena attendants and his employer. "How many of these do you think you can win before you arouse the suspicions of the other houses?"

Grisholt studied Turst's sun-wrinkled face and sinewy frame. Sixty-seven years on, the taskmaster was solid of mind and body. He'd raised a valid concern. Grisholt had even wondered himself since Barros's victory in the arena. How many victories could his men amass before suspicions were raised? And what would he do if the other houses discovered his secret?

"Don't concern yourself with such matters, Master Turst. I'm already devising plans for that very possibility. We'll be selective with our matches, use the potion sparingly. If we do that, I believe our lads will still win without arousing suspicions. And if there are questions, we'll just attribute it all to your training methods. Who can dispute those?"

"That's two deaths on our stable," a pensive Turst pointed out. "Two blood matches."

The words still failed to dim Grisholt's cheery mood.

"And two examples laid out for all to see, Master Turst. Don't worry yourself about those deaths. The season's half done, so we'll be cautious with the time remaining and lay plans for next season. Instill some fear. The Stable of Grisholt will no longer be an easy mark. All will come to fear our name, and that's to our advantage. Far too long, we've been rabbits toyed with by wolves."

Turst looked at the sands, and Grisholt sensed his taskmaster's masked concern. Grisholt didn't worry. In time, Turst would relax. Grisholt had just won a considerable amount of riches, and with wealth came power. For years, his stable had been perceived as a joke.

It was time to become a force.

9

"What was that?" Nexus exclaimed with heat, his black eyes nearly bursting from his face. "What was *that*?"

"That," Gastillo rumbled from underneath his golden mask, "was a fighter from the Stable of Grisholt. Seems they're keen on spilling some blood these days. Wouldn't you say, Curge?"

"Mm," Dark Curge grunted, replaying the all-too-short match in his head.

Nexus thrust his almost nonexistent chin toward the sands. "That wasn't spilling blood, you gold-faced ass packer. That was butchery! That was an outright spreading of one's cheeks! As you said, one of Grisholt's hellpups killed a gladiator only days ago. Seddon above, I don't know what that man is thinking, but if—when—our paths cross, I'll tell him my mind. Saimon suckle his black heart if he thinks he can kill any of my investments."

Gastillo didn't comment, having been stung with the ass packer reference, so he sat and brooded in the shade afforded by the overhead tarp, his fingers tight around a goblet.

Dark Curge didn't blame Gastillo in the least for his silence. In his opinion, Nexus was an idiot of the worst possible kind, which meant the wine merchant not only held influence and power in certain quarters but possessed vast enough riches to back up his words. Curge had become accustomed to Nexus referring to his gladiators as investments, either sound or bad, and hoped the merchant would lose more than just a few by season's end. It amused him when Nexus ranted.

And the hostility toward Gastillo wasn't at all a result of the match they'd all witnessed. Dark Curge smirked. Nexus had been obviously forcing cheer and calm into his speech and actions ever since the day's opening fight. The effort reeked of ill-concealed nerves. Nexus had reason to be tense. Gastillo's man Prajus fought the next contest: a blood match, against one of Nexus's appointed punishers.

Dark Curge's smile widened, oozing smug wickedness. He could watch Nexus's and Gastillo's prized dogs bash one another all day.

"You seemed pleasantly happy, Curge." Nexus snorted, as if sensing those very thoughts. "Looking forward to the coming battle, are you? You must love it when you see our lads killing each other at no risk to yourself."

Curge reared back in his seat and lifted his goblet to his lips. "Nature of the games, good Nexus. I do enjoy it. Or would you rather I honey your ass and offer false well wishes? It's all sport, despite how bloody it becomes.

Don't tell me you didn't enjoy it when that Zhiberian defeated one of my lads."

Nexus's mouth became a slit. "I relished every moment, you one-armed punce."

"Take care, good Nexus." Curge bristled at the insult. One of these days, Nexus would catch him in a very violent mood. "You aren't among your merchants now. You're addressing a man who once took his share of lives and more within the Pit."

"I know your history, Dark Curge." Nexus sneered, condescension dripping from his words. "You might have killed a dog or two, but *I've* ruined lives on a scale you haven't even considered."

Curge didn't like the 'dog or two' remark. That one got his blood boiling. He'd take it from Gastillo or any other man who'd fought in the Pit but not from some merchant playing at the sport.

"I hear the Orator." Curge's mouth puckered into an angry bud.

"Time's come then," Nexus said and swung his attention to Gastillo. "Good Gastillo. And believe me when I say, my lad fully intends to open your man's throat and turn the air red."

Gastillo didn't appear to have heard.

*

Prajus lifted his sword to the crowd and received mixed applause. He paid no attention to the Orator's prattling on about his victories and his kills. Prajus knew his worth in the arena. All he had to do was impart that knowledge to everyone watching—including Gastillo.

The urge to slowly twirl took him, and Prajus did just that, embracing the theatre of it all and grinning with malice. He kept his broadsword high over his helmet and his shield at his waistline. His vest of meticulously conceived mail blazed in the sun like dragon scales, while the knee spikes of his greaves resembled upturned claws. When one possessed skill such as his, was it arrogance to know it? Prajus recalled Gastillo's warnings, and he smirked even now at the owner's words. Gastillo projected anger, but Prajus sensed fear lurking beneath, fear that didn't make any sense to him. He'd killed a warrior from the School of Nexus, but that didn't mean raw gurry. Nexus would have his chance at revenge, could take as many chances as he could stomach, but Prajus certainly wasn't about to lose to any of them.

Far from it.

Prajus decided that he didn't rightly care for Gastillo anymore. The weakness wafting off the owner offended him. He didn't understand why Gastillo would fear further retribution from those obviously lesser. The argument of not being able to afford a war didn't make sense. There would be no war, no risk. There would only be Prajus smashing each and every pit fighter into the dust, regardless of who they were or what house or school they belonged to. This season was *his*, and by Seddon's sunny ass, he'd take it and the lives of any who dared stop him. Gastillo might have provided training and comforts, but Prajus gave him riches and a measure of fame in return. The gladiator with the dragon's head upon his shield didn't like to be cautioned. He didn't like to be warned.

He didn't fight in these games. He was *unleashed*.

The Orator finished introducing the warrior at the other end of the Pit, a man called Parek.

Gastillo had already provided information about the warrior, gleaned from his spies. Parek had been a veteran of the games for a respectable seven years, a true warrior in his prime, mauler of flesh, and an agent of revenge to be respected and feared.

Prajus couldn't care less who the punce was. Whoever Parek had fought to earn his reputation didn't include him. As far as the Sunjan was concerned, Parek wasn't sent to avenge the School of Nexus. Parek had been sent to die.

The famed gladiator wore a vest of carefully fashioned leather sculpted to an impressive physique. His shoulders and elbows bore barbs of black iron. He carried a long-necked mace sprouting five spikes in his right hand while a short sword trembled with anticipation in the left. A faceless helmet, dull gray under the sun, had a happy smile punched broadly across its surface. Parek wasn't tall by any means, but he was broad across the chest and powerful looking, a bull trained for splitting heads.

That helm regarded Prajus in a sour moment of silence with an unspoken promise of pain. As the Orator heaped praise upon Parek's name, the School of Nexus fighter turned to his benefactor and lifted his mace.

Prajus did nothing of the sort to acknowledge Gastillo.

"Begin!" the Orator shouted to a burst of cheers.

Rolling his head, Prajus walked toward Parek, and the pair met in the center of the arena. Parek didn't say a word to him, and Prajus had to admit he liked that.

"No gurry out of you about life or death, eh?" Prajus said with an appreciative nod. "I like that."

Parek didn't answer. His baleful black eyes stared above that iron-freckled smile.

"Your he-bitch of an owner sent you to your death this day."

The words seemed unheard, but Parek's muscular chest and shoulders heaved ever so slightly.

Prajus brought his sword to guard and hefted his shield.

The movements unlocked something inside of Parek. The Nexus warrior mirrored his opponent's actions but did not attack. Both men circled each other to subdued cheering, warily, taking their time.

Despite what Prajus might have thought of his foe, a feeling of caution seeped throughout his person. Parek wasn't a man to be taken lightly. And Prajus wasn't a man to care.

He stepped into a powerful thrust aimed for a leather-bound gut. Parek parried the blow with his mace. The forceful deflection pushed Prajus's sword to the outside, and Parek stabbed for a head. Prajus ducked while swinging his shield up, connecting with the blade in a rattle of metal—only to see the mace fly at his face.

Prajus jumped back as spikes flashed before his eyes. He retreated three steps, surprised at the last attack and wary of any more unexpected combinations.

"You're more careful than that punce I put to earth," Prajus taunted.

But Parek didn't attack. Instead, he walked forward, stoically closing the distance and forcing Prajus to back away. Only for a few steps.

Prajus surged ahead, blade coming alive and chopping. Parek retreated. His stance widened and braced before meeting the onslaught head-on in a ferocious clanging. Neither man backed away, and for heartbeats, they eagerly traded blows, each man seeking to take the other's head off his shoulders. Prajus moved his shield up and down and side to side, anticipating half of Parek's strikes, dodging the rest. Three times, Parek stabbed for his face. Twice, Prajus's shield saved him from the mace. The blows crashed into Prajus's shield, bruising his arm and ribs, and he winced behind his face cage.

To the crowd's delight, Parek forced Prajus back toward the wall.

*

Watching the furious pace below, Gastillo leaned forward and lifted his golden face. He dabbed a cloth at his wrecked mouth. His posture suggested nervousness— understandable considering the mounting pressure being exerted upon Prajus.

Nothing was further from the truth.

Gastillo hoped with every fiber of his being for Prajus to be killed. He wanted Parek to break the man's skull with one blow. The death of that troublesome hellpup would brighten his spirits considerably and grant a short reprieve from this miserable existence. He'd even allow Nexus every opportunity to gloat, while he, feigning bitterness at having lost, would secretly work events to his advantage.

"That's it!" Nexus exclaimed, bony fingers gripping the low wall of the viewing box. "That's it! Press him! Press him, and take his head off! Press him, Parek!"

As if hearing his owner's voice, Parek doubled his efforts. His sword and mace flashed, battering his foe with an unrelenting rhythm of cross slashes, powerful stabs, and decapitating swings. Prajus stooped and swayed, bobbed and parried, seemingly without time to even draw breath, desperately working to keep the attacks at bay.

Nexus glanced at Gastillo with wicked glee. "Not this day, good Gastillo. Not this *day*."

*

Prajus ducked under a savage sweep of his adversary's mace, rose, and put his entire body behind a backhand cut that half-removed Parek's head from his shoulders in a spectacular mist.

*

Nexus's mouth dropped open in a thunderclap of shock. His entire frame froze. His eyes bulged, and the only sound escaping his lips was *guhh,* as if his very heart had just exploded.

Curge heard it all.

He missed Gastillo's paralysis entirely.

*

Blood erupted from the horrific gash of Parek's neck in a thick and pulsating arterial spray. He dropped his weapons and fell to his knees, the stoic mask splashed with red. For an instant, it seemed as if the man sought to rise. His hand lifted to mid-torso, but then the brain realized death had severed all control over the body.

Parek toppled, his neck a dying fountain.

With bloodied blade held steadily at the very end of his stroke, Prajus stood as if time had ceased. Ignoring the disturbing shiver of the dead man at his feet, the victorious gladiator retreated three paces and stopped, lapping up the raucous applause.

His victory had been every bit as unexpected as it was bloody. Shoulders heaving, Prajus raised his sword to the crowds. And turned his back on his owner.

*

"That he-*bitch.*" Nexus spat in undisguised loathing.

Gastillo's posture stiffened at the surprising finish.

Nexus whirled upon him, red-faced and livid. "You unfit *pisser!* You orchestrated the entire thing! Seddon's kog and bells, I had no idea I shared a seat with such a devious manipulator of flesh and bone. War, is it, Gastillo?

Is it war you desire? With me? You blackened cow kiss. I might be as fresh as a babe to these games, but I'm learning fast, and you'll find that what I lack in talent, I make up for in resources. *That* is a dead man basking in the adoration of the people, Gastillo, a *dead* man. Seddon above, I swear this."

Gastillo had no reply and only stared at the figure of Prajus departing the sands. Cold settled in around his pounding heart and slowly squeezed. Hatred oozed for the pit fighter disappearing through the far gate. *Prajus*, the owner seethed. Gastillo had warned the man of consequences if he disobeyed orders. He would have to be disciplined. Punished.

That thought curled in his mind as Nexus swore bloody revenge right beside him.

Punish Prajus, Gastillo thought darkly. Punish perhaps the greatest gladiator ever to train under his roof.

All the while, Dark Curge sat and smiled in contentment, playing with the goblet in his fingers.

*

Gastillo walked back to his home after the games, choosing not to be escorted by his trainers, guards, and gladiators, and ignoring looks from people and the children pointing fingers. He'd long since become immune to their attentions. He walked to clear his head, to cool the hot coils of anger building at his core. At times, he stopped and tossed a few coins to the unfortunate beggars holding out their hands without hearing their words of thanks.

Prajus. That insolent smiling bastard.

Instead of draining his fury, the walk intensified it. When he reached his property, he immediately went to the middle of the training grounds and commanded a guard to summon Prajus. Taskmaster Sowin, bent over like a broken reed in a windstorm, approached from the edge but halted when Gastillo held up a hand. The trainers Berlis and Pius, both valued staff, stopped their conversation and lingered nearby.

Prajus appeared a short time later, stripped to the loincloth and glistening with bathhouse waters.

"Master Gastillo." Prajus leered. "Something on your mind?"

Gastillo didn't immediately reply. He allowed the silence to swell like a ripe and angry boil.

"You disobeyed me, Prajus," he finally said, the words livid with heat. "You disobeyed the master of the house. I commanded you to not kill that man, and you did. What do you think happens now?"

"Nothing. Another dead dog is all. It'll make Nexus hesitate to send another after me."

"Wrong, you arrogant maggot. You're confined to your quarters this night. Tomorrow morning, Master Sowin will double your training, and you'll suffer through it under penalty of being cast out of this house entirely."

Prajus appeared unmoved. "That's my punishment?" His face cracked into a smile. "By the Lords, Master Gastillo, I have sympathy for you. You can't really beat me, can you? And you certainly can't dismiss me, for fear of the other houses recruiting me. So what's left? Nothing really. I'm your strongest man for these games, your best chance at riches and glory. Double my training. Triple it. I don't care. Confine me to these walls? After a good day upon the grounds, I'll need the rest anyway."

Brazen ass licker. But Gastillo held his tongue. If he'd spoken, the man would probably have laughed in his face.

Behind Prajus, the entrances to the common rooms and the bathhouse filled with the other gladiators training under Gastillo's roof. The owner recognized a few of the leering faces belonging to the little pack of admirers—and perhaps even friends—of Prajus.

"All of you," Gastillo barked, "because this disrespectful topper ignored my orders this day, you'll all be put through double paces tomorrow. He's part of your pack. You'll share in his punishment. No baths either. Sleep in your own filth tomorrow night. And no food. Only water."

That removed the light from a few faces, and Gastillo took some guilty pleasure from it. Still, the punishment, the threats all seemed light to him.

"Get out of my sight," he whispered at Prajus, very badly wanting to beat the man down. The temptation burned even more as the near-naked gladiator leered back, unmoved by the inclusion of the whole roster.

Worse still, the man stood before him, smiling that intolerable smile.

"*Go!*"

Prajus didn't, not right away. Three heartbeats later, he returned to the bathhouse, taking his time.

"Out of the baths," Sowin took up the cry, nodding at Gastillo. Thank Seddon for some support. Gastillo looked at his head of guard outfitted in leather and mail. "Jaco."

The tall man trotted to his employer's side.

"Have your men remove whoever's in the baths. And make certain the armory is locked up tonight. Post double the guards, and make certain no one leaves the grounds. If they do, you have my permission to beat them until they bleed. Understood? That includes Prajus. *Especially* Prajus."

Jaco nodded, a hand already on his shortsword.

"If one disobeys me, all will be punished," Gastillo announced to the night. "All will suffer. And at the end of the games, I'll cast out the repeat offenders and make certain no other house of worth will take you in on grounds of dissension. You'll be Free Trained or forced to fight in the lesser games. Go!"

The gladiators slunk back to their quarters. Gastillo hated doing it, feeling his house had suddenly come under siege. Lines had been drawn. His ranks had probably already fractured into segments, some loyal to him, others to Prajus.

Gastillo hoped he had the greater numbers.

10

The House of Ten gladiators focused on pummelling the wooden practice men, devising and slowly perfecting combinations under the watchful eyes of their trainers. Halm sat with Pig Knot and Muluk, all three watching and drinking from the most recent round of wine pitchers. Ananda had been quite willing to provide them with cups, but the three healing men—on their way to being well and truly pickled—declared that pitchers were much more suitable. They went through the first round slowly, enjoying the drink, and even Pig Knot's mood seemed to brighten. They eyed the pit fighters still in competition. Regret, envy, and even relief coursed through Halm. He wondered if Pig Knot and Muluk felt the same but dared not ask. Pig Knot seemed subdued with Halm's and Muluk's presence, and the periodic raising of a silver mug from the balcony, aimed directly at the three gladiators, lightened the mood considerably.

The wine helped. So they sat. And drank. Drank until

their senses swam.

"Care to see how a legless man pisses?" Pig Knot asked in harsh tone, despite the red hue to his face. Neither Halm nor Muluk had a chance to reply before the Sunjan screwed his pitcher into the sand and steadied it as best as he could. He pawed a hole out of the sand and rolled over onto his side.

"Not certain I care to see this." Halm cringed.

Muluk shook his head as well.

Pig Knot cursed for a moment before barking laughter. "See that?"

Neither man looked, but they heard the hissing stream.

When Pig Knot finished, he tucked himself away and sat up, slamming his back against the barrack's wall. He swept sand over the puddle he'd made, grunting all the while.

"Feel better?" Halm asked.

Pig Knot reached for his pitcher. "Aye that. Be even better after a few more of these."

"Wonder what the limit will be?" Muluk looked toward Clavellus's balcony and the two figures still there.

"We'll know soon enough." Every word spoken through Pig Knot's clamped jaw sounded ripe with anger.

At midday, Ananda brought them warm bread and dried meats on a platter, and they tore into the food with drunken enthusiasm. Machlann and Koba herded their three gladiators to the common room for something to eat as well, and Pig Knot took the opportunity to nod and wink at the scarred trainer. Koba scowled back.

While the men ate inside, the three drinking masters stayed outside in the sun. The wine truly soaked into their brains. After they devoured the food, the Zhiberian, Kree, and Sunjan continued to empty pitchers through the afternoon, conversing amongst themselves as drunken men do. And though Halm and Muluk cringed at Pig Knot relieving himself in the sands, they joined him after the fifth pitcher.

That drew murderous looks from Machlann.

Goll instructed clay bedpans to be brought to the three men, delivered by a former Sujin called Clades. Pig Knot attempted to get the man to join them, but Clades declined with a good-natured chuckle. A bedpan rested near each man's mat, and Halm wondered who would be first to try drinking from them.

Red-faced, insanely drunk, and mouth hanging open for unsuspecting sand flies, Halm sat and observed Junger going through his paces under Koba's watchful eye. Somehow, the three pit fighters had returned to the training grounds without him noticing. Sorcery! The Perician's striking was beyond compare in Halm's pickled mind. Never had he witnessed such skill. Even in the Zhiberian's smashed state, Junger seemed to perform magic with the drills. The warrior did not make mistakes, and the trainers didn't correct his form. There was no need.

While Halm drank and gawked, Shan's words floated in his mind and haunted him.

He's done, the healer had said.

Halm knew it to be true. Junger's frightening display of skill and his lean, untiring muscular body reminded the Zhiberian of his own aging bulk.

He's done. The words would not leave him. Perhaps he was done in more ways than one.

So this was how it felt when one could no longer do what he enjoyed, or so Halm thought in a fit of thinking so deep it made him dizzy. His senses dulled and bubbled and popped while Pig Knot and Muluk cackled in his ears like hellions. He'd known he couldn't fight in the games for much longer, but now that his season had finished, he wondered what to do next. As much as he enjoyed the company of Pig Knot and Muluk and felt the lure of a future with the House of Ten, it still shocked Halm that the end had finally descended upon him.

The end of his best run ever in the games…

He'd gotten through with his life, coin, limbs, and even more surprisingly, undefeated.

Undefeated and with a major role in a new house. The reality of it all shocked him. He should be dead three times over, yet there he sat, drinking good wine, eating bread and sliced meats, and feeling the need to once again empty the bull. *Wine!* He should tie a knot in his lad.

He's done. Shan voice repeated in his head.

"What's that… that dreamy look about?" Muluk's face bobbed atop his shoulders as if ready to fall off.

"Dreamy?" Pig Knot repeated. "Dreamy. Bedded down several dreams. Curvy, lovely dreams. Nightmares were the best."

A bleary-eyed Muluk dismissed that with a wave and focused on Halm. "Really, now, spit it out, and be done with it. Seddon above. Almost done with this pitcher. I should be squeezing the grapes myself. Now then. What's… what's on… your mind?"

"I'd like her on my mind," Pig Knot said.

"Not asking you."

"I'm done," Halm said, and that quieted his companions.

"You said that." Muluk studied the Zhiberian with all his might. "Earlier."

"My season's over."

Muluk nodded, attempting to understand. "It is."

"Done," Pig Knot added. "Unfit. I'm getting tired of this wine. Old Clavellus must have something better in his cellars. Something with more bite."

"Like you need more bite," Muluk muttered before shifting his attention back to Halm.

"I'm thinking…" The big Zhiberian bared the terrible teeth he still had in his head.

"Yes?"

"Of perhaps leaving for a few days."

That silenced both men, and for a noticeable stretch of time, all that could be heard was the straining of the gladiators and Machlann's barking.

"Leaving?" Muluk asked with a feeble smile. "You're joking."

Pig Knot leaned in, concern on his features.

"No," Halm went on. "I'm not. I'm leaving. Perhaps

tomorrow, once this is pissed out." He raised his pitcher.

"Why?" Muluk asked for himself and an equally attentive but swaying Pig Knot.

Even though brazen, ill-kept fangs filled his mouth, the warm smile spreading across Halm's face brightened his fearsome collection of scars and bruises. "Someone I want to see again."

Pig Knot barked a laugh. "The woman!"

Muluk joined him. "Karashipa."

"Moji is her name."

"I know that. I meant the village."

"Name's not *Moji*," Halm interrupted them both with a twinge of annoyance. "It's *Miji*."

"You can buy better in Sunja," Pig Knot declared. "Even save coin if you stay with the ones missing teeth."

Halm blinked dumbly. "I'm not going to…" he faltered, unable to finish. "I'm going to…"

His drinking companions waited with interest, their eyes swimming in their sockets.

"What?" Muluk asked gently, a surprise coming from such a black-haired brute of a man.

Halm didn't finish the thought.

Muluk hung on, waiting for words.

"She's got him," Pig Knot announced and clenched a fist in the air. "Fishhooked through the dewy pearls."

"He's not fishhooked through the…" An appalled Muluk squinted at the legless man. "The *what*? Where do you get these sayings?"

"I'm Sunjan," Pig Knot said, as if that explained

everything.

"Don't listen to him," Muluk said to Halm. "Listen to me now. Listen. I've known you for… well, not that long, but still… are you sure you aren't just very, very pickled right now?"

"He's not pickled enough." Pig Knot snorted.

Muluk turned and swatted Pig Knot across the shoulder. Though the Kree had only just escaped death himself a short time ago, his muscular frame retained enough of his considerable strength to flatten the Sunjan against the wall.

"Now then." Muluk took a great deep breath though his nose and resumed his line of thought. "Perhaps you should just think… or rethink whatever it is you're thinking about."

"Think *more*." Pig Knot righted himself.

"Aye, that. Yes, think more," Muluk repeated. "Thank you, you unfit bastard. Now then, good Halm, you only met this woman once."

"I did that," Halm agreed. "Think, I mean. I'll think longer on it. I'll give you that. Perhaps it is this speaking."

Halm held up his pitcher, secretly knowing he'd be leaving in the morning. From the dubious expression on Muluk's face, Halm suspected his friend also knew.

"What will you do if you do go to her?" the Kree asked.

Halm didn't rightly know and shrugged. "I'm not worried about it. I've lived all my life by doing first and thinking after. Probably not… not the best way to do things. If I travel to Karashipa in the morning, I'll think more about it along the way."

"And what if she wants nothing to do with you?" Pig Knot asked.

Halm shrugged again. "Then I'll return and enjoy your company every day for the rest of my days, good Pig Knot." At this he held out a fist.

But Pig Knot did not tap it.

*

The evening sun marked the end of the day's activities, and Goll descended from Clavellus's balcony to stalk the training grounds. He gave the word for the trainers to dismiss the gladiators. Torello, Brozz, and Junger walked to the bathhouse as the sweat glistened upon their persons.

"A word with you, Master Machlann," Goll said. "Master Koba."

Machlann screwed up one side of his face, skewing his great broom of a mustache. "Where's Clavellus?"

"Sleeping."

Much to the Kree's dismay, Clavellus had continued drinking well into the afternoon, and when Nala had called him, he'd looked to Goll with eyes so red rimmed, Goll thought they were prized rubies mined from the Valencian Spikes. Nala had appeared soon after and asked Goll to help her get Clavellus to bed. What surprised Goll even more was that the taskmaster allowed himself to be helped.

Machlann regarded the empty balcony with a knowing

chuckle. "What's the word then?"

"Blood matches."

"Ah." The older trainer exchanged a look with Koba. "Lead on then, Master Goll."

Goll did, walking toward his three companions still sitting on mats, their backs to the barracks wall. *A good thing*, Goll thought as his heart sank. Halm, Muluk, and Pig Knot all appeared clearly pickled after a prolonged drinking session. Pig Knot, in particular, appeared ready to fall over. Goll inwardly fumed at Clavellus for allowing spirits to flow to the three, but the taskmaster's stores had to have taken a heavy toll—enough to ensure sobriety for a little while at least.

Slowing to a halt, Goll nodded greetings to the three men.

Halm beamed at him. Muluk raised a hand. A dazed Pig Knot teetered and struggled to lift his pitcher. When he did, he checked on the amount remaining, tipping the wine onto his chest and staining the bandages there. He noted the spillage with a frown.

"We have to talk," Goll addressed them. Machlann and Koba stood to one side, neither particularly impressed with the three drunks.

"You lads look like the dew settled on cow kisses," Machlann remarked.

A wobbly Pig Knot took offence. "And you, you look like you… dropped out of a dead man's hole."

"Take care not to piss yourself, you rancid topper," Machlann countered.

"We don't have time for this," Goll interrupted the exchange. "As masters of this house, we have to decide how to avenge our fallen."

"Blood matches?" Halm asked with a visible effort to think clearly. "This is about… that?"

"Aye that."

"I'll fight them," the Zhiberian declared and slapped his chest hard enough to squeeze his eyes shut. "Hold on, hold on. I can't. Healer said so. I'm done. I'll be leaving in the morning."

Goll rolled his eyes. "Yes, well, before you do, I'm still asking for your opinion in this matter."

"I don't think he heard you." Muluk leaned into Halm.

"Don't think he did either."

"Or he doesn't *believe* you."

"Possible."

"You're a rat-pig bastard of a Zhiberian, after all."

Halm frowned at that.

Goll straightened and focused on the bulbous man with the bad teeth. "You're leaving?"

"I am."

"You can't leave."

"*I'm* a master," Halm pointed out, chin swaying. "I can do anything… pleases me now. Hm. And I'm pissed to leave."

Muluk chuckled at the slip.

The attention shifted to Goll.

"Do what you want," he eventually said. "But lend

your thoughts first. At least you won't be able to say I didn't include you in the decisions of the house."

"He won't be able to *remember* this," Pig Knot muttered.

"Let's hear it then." Halm ignored the comment.

"Yes, out with it," Muluk added.

"Need to empty the bull," Pig Knot remarked, dividing his drunken loathing between Goll and Koba.

"Two of our lads were killed," Goll began, trying not to dwell too much on Pig Knot. "And they were killed by Free Trained. Worse, they were Free Trained enticed by Dark Curge's bounty. With Halm falling out of competition due to the wounds inflicted upon his person—"

"His *considerable* person," Muluk interrupted with sly mirth, drawing a wary look from the Zhiberian.

Goll didn't smile at all. "Are you finished?"

Muluk nodded.

"We only have three fighters capable of pursuing the offenders," Goll carried on. "So I put to you, who should fight who? The Free Trained are called Cota and Bubruk, and despite being Free Trained, they handled themselves well enough to dispatch Kolo and Tumber."

"Who killed Kolo?" Muluk tried very hard to concentrate.

Goll gnawed upon his lower lip. "Cota."

"What about the Gladiatorial Chamber?" Muluk asked. "Might they take issue with this bounty business?"

"They won't care." Machlann growled. "As long as the fighting stays in the arena, all the more interest in the games."

"Let Torello have him, then," Halm declared. "The one that killed his friend Kolo. That's my thought on the matter. We've been watching them—him—most of the day. Right and proper serious, that one."

Muluk nodded. Pig Knot lost interest in dirty looks and resumed drinking. Neither of the men had been present at the games, but Goll still wanted them to at least think they were contributing. He glanced at his trainers.

"I agree," Machlann growled. Koba dipped his head in support, staring down at a detached Pig Knot.

"I agree as well," Goll said. "That's the easy choice. Torello will want to avenge Kolo's death. What about Bubruk?"

"Was he the naked one?" Halm asked.

"He was nearly naked," Goll replied. "Light armor. Used a short blade in his right hand and a spiked club in the other. Fast on his feet and eager to kill—at least for a pot of coin."

"Sounds like us," Halm said.

"How many of them pitchers did you have, Zhiberian?" Machlann asked without humor.

Halm gave it some thought. "Not near as many as your mother before taking your father on her back."

Machlann's face darkened, eyes narrowing into slits.

"Restrain yourself, Halm of Zhiberia," an angry Goll blurted. "And apologize at once."

Halm frowned, not pleased his joke had failed to amuse, and cradled his pitcher. He eventually nodded, surrendering to Goll's command.

"I apologize, Master Machlann," the Zhiberian huffed with as much sincerity he could muster. "That was uncalled for."

Machlann settled down, the heat in his scowl lessening.

"Apologies, good Goll," Halm muttered. "It was the wine."

"And the beer," Muluk added.

"And the wine," Pig Knot mumbled.

"And other… things," Halm said.

But Goll's anger did not lessen. "You listen to me. Free Trained you once were, but no longer. *Act* like it. What poor hellpup wouldn't trade general quarters for *this*? And here you are, sitting upon piss puddles in the sand and stewing and taunting your trainers! If you were in general quarters, what do you think would've happened? Hm? What? I'll tell you what—the Skarrs would drag you out with broken bones, kicking and screaming—or dead if you resisted. If you were taken in by any other House and insulted the trainer, you'd be beaten badly enough you'd not see that season or the next, and that would be only *after* you woke in an alley with the street gurry and maggot shite."

Goll let that sink in, glaring at each face in turn. Halm and Muluk appeared genuinely embarrassed, but Pig Knot had actually readied fists. The aggressive act bewildered Goll in the worst possible way.

"You've lost your legs, you brazen punce," Goll scolded in a low tone. "Not your brains."

That hit the mark, and Pig Knot eventually lowered his guard, downcast and taking time to adjust himself on his mat.

"Now then," Goll said, "if all poor humor is over and done, perhaps we can continue?"

No one said otherwise.

"Good. Now then, what about Cota?"

Halm shrugged. "Let the Perician have him."

Both Muluk and Pig Knot's expressions brightened with approval.

"Aye that," Machlann said, supporting the choice. "Make no mistake. The Sarlander would do the job, but the Perician would make an example of the man."

Goll wasn't convinced. "I think Brozz would be the better choice."

"Brozz?" Halm questioned with puzzlement. "You want to place fear into these bastards, you use Junger."

"I agree with Master Halm," Machlann stated while Koba stared over the older trainer's shoulder. "Use the Perician."

"I don't believe so. He disobeyed my command in his last showing. He didn't kill the man."

"But he defeated him," Machlann countered. "Soundly."

"He didn't kill the man," Goll repeated. "When I give a command to a gladiator—one of *my* gladiators—I expect him to do it. Why he didn't kill the man is still a matter I intend to straighten out."

"Then now's the time," Machlann said.

"Aye that," Halm said. "Dying Seddon, what better time? I mean no disrespect to the Sarlander, but the Perician is…"

As fluent as he was in the Sunjan tongue, Halm groped for the proper word. Goll waited.

"Superior," Koba said in a clear voice, filling the void and surprising everyone. "To them all."

The words failed to sway Goll, however, though he was very much aware of his being the only objection.

"You won't convince him." Pig Knot smirked. "Not the man who…who killed Baylus the Butcher. It's plain on his face."

Goll scowled a warning to be quiet. Unfortunately for him, the man he was attempting to silence was Pig Knot.

"I'll tell you something else," the Sunjan went on. "He doesn't want the Perician fighting because he's well aware of his skill."

Pig Knot's chest hitched with suppressed gas, and he softly tapped a fist to his right side.

"Very well." Goll still glowered at the legless man. "We'll do as you say. The Perician will fight Cota. I'll inform Borchus and have him make the arrangements. I want the blood matches to be fought soon. In three days, in fact."

Halm's eyebrows lifted in mild surprise. "That's early."

"We make examples of the offenders. I'd have the lads go tomorrow, but the training time will benefit."

"You don't care for him at all, do you?" Machlann put to the Kree.

"The Perician?" Goll asked. "No. No, I don't."

"Why?"

"I don't trust him."

"He joined us," Halm pointed out.

Goll paused, his face hardening. "I know. Exactly why I don't trust him."

That struck the gathered men.

"Why?" Machlann asked. "You think he'll cross over to another house? Like that other brazen ass licker?"

"I don't know, Master Machlann," Goll answered with all honesty. "All I know is… a man of his skill would have eventually attracted the notice and favor of *all* houses. Every one. Consider that. Yet, he decided to join us, as you've said, Master Halm. He could have waited and had his choice of any house, stable, or school in Sunja—in Kree or Pericia or beyond, for that matter. Yet, he didn't. No, I don't trust him. And with the desertion of Sapo, a suspicious nature is preferable."

Halm didn't agree.

"Be wary of the one called Junger," Goll told them. "I don't trust him. And neither should you."

11

In the western section of the great city of Sunja, off a side street and down the deep throat of another, a single lamp had been lit. Its flame shimmered and shifted beneath the wooden arm suspending the square bulb above the street. A slow, lazy burn meant to last the night, it barely illuminated the front of the storehouse behind it. Distant sounds of nightlife permeated the dark but did not come anywhere close to this recess. If people did find themselves within the lamp's glow, they were there for a reason and probably quick to leave for safer parts.

Above the fitted-stone street, in a restored warehouse attic, the Sons of Cholla held court. A wide Marrnite tapestry depicting a boar hunt lay upon the bare timber floor. It had been priceless at one time, but now stains darker than wine blotted the scene. Worn padded chairs that had suffered stab wounds lay scattered about the room. Three Sunjan Hrandwood sofas with flattened cushions were pressed against walls. Valuable urns from

Balgotha filled the corners and smoked with candles, their wicks glowing in the foggy crooks. Wisps of Mademian incense added to the evil magic of the candles, their cloudy ribbons hanging upon the air currents like dying snakes.

Figures lounged, drinking at leisure and breathing in the pungent haze laced with the barest hint of Osgarman crushed snow orchids, famous for their meditative effects. Cholla had long departed this world, but his sons filled the room with smoke, when they could, to keep his memory alive. Cholla had given life to and raised four sons, and his brood ruled the criminal web he left behind with a merciless hand—including the entire shadowy underworld of Sunja itself. The family of thieves and cutthroats had knifed its way to a bloody roost over a span of five generations, but it was Cholla's ascension that became legend—tales of tavern killings, late-night stabbings, back-alley butchery, bribery, debauchery, and sometimes, very public poisonings.

If King Juhn ruled the day, Cholla had seized the night—or so the Sons of Cholla, by blood or oath, liked to think.

Brejo sat on a sturdy, comfortable couch and waited. At forty-nine, he was the oldest of Cholla's sons and undisputed leader of the gang. Though he was not as tall as his brothers, Brejo's abilities lay in his brain rather than his knife arm, a fact his other brothers appreciated. He hooked a leg over one arm of the couch, leaned back, and tugged on red pants. He didn't wear a shirt, exposing a wiry mat of gray hair. Inked tattoos of chains and lightning flared up his arms. Brejo's grooved features were not entirely unpleasant to look upon but were decidedly cruel.

The incense has been his idea. It relaxed him, helped him think. In his business, thinking kept him alive and in control of the Sons' considerable resources.

A large man materialized through the white streamers on the air, surprising Brejo only enough to make him squint and scratch at the thick ash-colored hair atop his head.

Brother Jaro: Brejo's younger sibling at forty-seven. The passing of years made the aged muscle on Jaro's burly frame all the more menacing. A huge gray beard, pointed from years of stroking, concealed the cruel line of the enforcer's mouth. Bare chested and sullen looking, Jaro had killed his first victim—a merchant of fresh vegetables—by very personal strangulation, squeezing until the man's eyes and tongue had practically popped out of his head. Not even Brejo knew how many other necks his brother had wrung over the years.

He'd never ask. For Jaro *would* tell him. In great detail.

"Where's Strach?" Brejo asked in a voice that always cracked. He scratched idly at his nose.

Not knowing or caring, Jaro shook his head.

"That black-balled punce," Brejo muttered. "Whose crack is he tonguing *now*?"

Jaro stood, clasped one corded arm over his belly, and kept his thoughts to himself.

"Perhaps he's breaking a few new street beggars?" a

voice asked. Calagu lounged near a candlelit corner, making the most of the burning incense. His pasty-white face glowed as perfectly round as a moon frozen in a fog. A forest of hair sprouted from his head. The Iron Games existed and thrived solely under Calagu's nurturing hand. The youngest brother excelled at the blood sport beneath the city's streets. Brejo didn't know how many lives he'd taken either.

He dismissed Calagu's suggestion with a sour frown.

"Doesn't matter." Jaro shrugged, his mouth appearing to barely move beneath his bear hide of a beard. "Talked with him a fortnight ago. Business is the same."

"Always the same," Calagu echoed. "Except for the puzzling withdrawal of the Sujins."

Sujins. Brejo's stomach tightened. "What happened there? Has anyone discovered anything more?"

He looked for Linfur and found him leaning against a wall.

"They've withdrawn from the city, according to our eyes and ears," a cultured voice said. Linfur enjoyed the crushed snow-orchid bulbs far more than any of them. "No one knows anything, except that the Sujins have seemingly abandoned everything they once held."

"Hm," Brejo grunted, hating the most organized and most disturbing of all their rivals. For months, a new gang of unknown number had terrified the merchant sheep, one that confused the Sons to no end, as they believed they controlled all crime within the city. The Sujins would have been a mystery for longer still if it had not been for a pack of killers sent out hunting. The Sons' henchmen cornered a handful of the mysterious men, and only one survived to report the encounter. Soon after, the Sons unravelled bits and pieces of information about the secretive band invading their territory.

Sujins.

The killers who had invaded the Sons' territory were battle-hardened warriors from Sunja's own Klaws, a stunning discovery that rendered the Sons hesitant and uncharacteristically nervous. Breaking bones and murdering street thugs was one thing. Battling Sujins was entirely another.

The growing presence of these merciless Sujins had forced the Sons to abandon certain sections of the city or risk everything in a war of shadows. Brejo wasn't about to grapple with hardened hellpups and risk the Sons' existence, so he'd retreated, avoided selected areas, and observed from a distance—watched and waited for an opportunity to strike.

An opportunity that never arose.

"It is a time of war," Linfur pointed out in his rich voice. "Perhaps something arose that forced them to retreat? If so, better for us. We'll reclaim those holdings, squeeze a few more coins."

"Strach will find out what happened," Brejo asserted.

"Eventually," Calagu agreed.

"No doubt he's attending to business," Linfur said. "Busy, busy. Strach and his street rats clawing up something for the Sons' coffers. Never a notable amount.

Never notable. But steady. Consistent. *Persistent.* Like a sweet crust complementing a warm pastry freshly pulled from the oven. Filled with jam."

Not amused in the slightest, Brejo regarded the chosen voice for the Sons of Cholla. Linfur presented himself as a man destined for finer things—palaces, royal courts, grand halls, and women of noble blood. The man was a natural speaker and well educated, both formally and to the nefarious undercurrents of Sunja. Brejo never really knew Linfur's exact background, like all the rats drawn to the Sons' banner. Jaro had pulled the lad into their immoral embrace years ago when Linfur was still a teen. Jaro never recruited anyone unless he saw potential. Linfur *oozed* potential. Handsome. Gifted with a very physical frame and quick mind. A born talker. Over the years, he'd earned a reputation for being as vicious as he was well read.

And Linfur was exceptionally well read.

"You should have brought us a few of those pastries." Brejo's voice split from a lack of drink.

"I shall do so tomorrow," Linfur said with a dip of his slick head, flashing strong teeth.

"Then don't disappoint." Brejo grumbled and eyed the man's muscular arms and the impressive amount of ink fashioned into the likeness of serpents and chains from his wrists to his shoulders. In the day and in public, long sleeves would cover those skin badges.

"What about the games today?" Brejo abruptly asked.

"Very well," Linfur answered. "The Stable of Grisholt

isn't being shy about using the potion we've supplied. He's been an exceptionally… predictable sort, like a dog given permission to feast at the king's table. I daresay it won't be long before most or all of his men are partaking in that sweet, sweet wine."

Brejo fixed Linfur with eyes every bit as cold and serpentine as the ink drawn upon their flesh. "Your honeyed tongue truly sickens me at times."

"My sincere apologies, good Brejo."

Brejo didn't drop his menacing gaze until he saw the bob of Linfur's throat.

That brought a chuckle from Calagu. "Perhaps it's best you talk less, Linfur. Or curse more."

Linfur smiled briefly but not with comfort, as Brejo watched him.

"And?" Brejo finally demanded. "I said your tongue truly sickens me. I didn't say stop."

An uncomfortable Linfur cleared his pipes. "The coin we've won has already been added to the treasury, good Brejo. We know when Grisholt's men will fight again, so with your permission, I'll continue placing wagers."

"Of course, you buttery dog blossom." Calagu wiped his forehead, not bothering to conceal his amusement at Linfur's unease. Jaro watched the exchange without comment, his naked, muscular torso barely moving. Ink serpents and chains covered the Sons' chief enforcer as well, but a flying dragon, wings spread wide, spanned his chest.

"Grisholt." Brejo mulled, kicking his hooked leg.

"After so long, lads. After so long. Father would have been very pleased at these events."

"He would've," Calagu agreed. "How long do you think it'll take?"

Brejo shrugged. "Only a matter of time. The owners will start sniffing around with their agents and spies. Then…"

He shrugged again, answering Calagu's eager smile.

For years, the Sons had earned their coin from four questionable yet immensely profitable quarters. Calagu organized the Iron Games—the bloody yet always profitable alternative to the Gladiatorial Chamber's official games. *The Iron,* as Calagu referred to it, accommodated the minority who simply lived to place wagers upon grown men who hacked one another to bloody bits.

Strach organized and added to the herds of professional beggars infesting the streets and alleys of Sunja, a veritable army of lice besieging the city's kind-hearted populace for spare coins. Jaro and his men killed people for hire— quietly or publicly; it didn't matter. Brejo extorted coin from merchants.

In these hard times, however, the family business had suffered. The only notable coin filling the Sons' coffers came from Calagu's Iron Games, and even that wasn't as lucrative as previous years. Brejo's menacing of merchants failed to produce the gold of years gone by, and Jaro rarely had *any* requests to violently remove a person from life. Strach's beggars brought in the smallest amount of them all, but the years had transformed that stream into the most reliable, even more so than the Iron Games.

The Iron Games, Brejo thought. The Gladiatorial Chamber had successfully stopped the Sons from poisoning the fighting season with their influence. Thus, Cholla himself had devised a similar tournament with slightly different rules and an increasingly demanding crowd. It had been a success, but even Cholla knew Sunja's Pit would be worth so much more, a gemstone set into a crown. The Sons had approached selected owners with promises of victory if they worked together, yet none of them ever struck a bargain.

Honor still meant something in the games.

Cholla had confided to Brejo that times would change again, and when they did, the Sons would not have to contact the houses. Cholla said the right kind of owner would approach the Sons. That owner had been Grisholt.

Even years dead, Brejo knew his father smiled in whatever hell had taken him.

"All we have to do is wait," Brejo finished, "and keep abreast of Grisholt's fighters. There's no one else out there with the potion."

"What is the potion, exactly?" Linfur asked, regaining his confidence.

Brejo eyed the Sons' spokesman. "Victory, of course."

Calagu chuckled. Even Jaro smiled at the joke.

"Don't trouble yourself with the potion's contents, Linfur," Brejo calmly advised. "It does what we've promised, and that's enough. You know, I even considered using it against the Sujins, choosing just a few of our lads to take it before battle, but the weakness afterward prevented me from ever attempting it. Far too dangerous. That stomach-juiced concoction is much more effective in an arena setting than on the streets. Jaro, what about that other work Grisholt's man asked of us?"

Jaro's chest heaved with a deep breath, and the dragon's wings lifted. His black eyes barely reflected any light. "Men hunt the city even as I breathe."

"Ah yes," Linfur said. "I met with Grisholt's man, Brakuss, when he brought word of who is fighting and drinking the potion. He made it known Grisholt wants a man killed."

"No one *drinks* the potion, Linfur." Calagu scoffed and rolled his eyes. "They sip and endure it. I still think we should introduce it to the Iron Games."

Brejo frowned at the thought. They'd already talked about it. "The Iron isn't the place for that spectacle. It isn't grand enough, good Calagu. The Pit—the Pit *is*. Can you think of a better place to be corrupted?"

Calagu could not.

"Enough talk about that, Jaro. Thus far, Grisholt has done quite well, I believe. It's only in our best interests to honor our bargain with him. This man he wants killed… an agent, is it?"

Jaro nodded. "For the new House of Ten."

"The Free Trained one?"

"Aye that."

"A Free Trained house," Calagu said with disdain. "And the season half-finished. Gurry."

Brejo ignored his brother. "You have a description for this dead man?"

"We've already talked about this, too," Calagu pointed out.

"I was drunk at the time," Brejo snapped, growing impatient with his pale-faced brother. He settled back and studied Jaro. "This agent, you know what he looks like?"

"Short. Strong. Broad of shoulder. Dark hair but graying. Long sideburns on his face. No beard."

"The name again?"

Jaro gave it.

"And you haven't found him yet?" Calagu blurted with genuine surprise. It was rare for Jaro to have both a description and a name but no head to show.

Jaro flashed him a warning scowl, but Calagu dismissed him with a hand. The brothers had no fear of each other.

"It's a city, brother. Many places for an agent to hide. But I've been told he's been found. Even now, men follow him. I've given the word to kill him this very night." Jaro paused with dramatic flair. "The man's as good as dead."

"What was his name again?" Brejo almost pitied the poor bastard.

Through smoky veils, dragon wings fluttered.

12

"Borchus?"

His head bobbed up from his mug of beer to Sindra's face. The men and women around him were much taller, but he'd placed his elbows on the bar, and his thick arms gave most second thoughts about crowding him too much.

"Sindra." He gripped his drink. "A busy night here. It's good to see."

She glanced around the interior of what was once Hadree's alehouse. A good-sized crowd had crammed into the place, making it feel packed. When she looked, Borchus couldn't help being drawn to her pale throat. She'd tied her hair into a tail, which hung rather enticingly over her right shoulder, tickling at a low-cut dress.

"Surprised?" Borchus took a drink.

"I am," Sindra answered. "Yet part of me isn't at all. Do you know how damn stubborn you can be? Because I do."

Borchus swallowed, smiled weakly, and shrugged.

"Well, not this time." She leaned forward, placing her elbows on the counter, and fixed him with her huge brown eyes. "Look. It's simple. I'll explain it again in case you've forgotten. I don't want anything to do with you. I don't want to see you around here ever again. Whatever was then isn't now. Understand that? Do you? I've managed this place for years. It's my life, and I'm very much content. The roof over your head is mine. Everything you see under this roof is mine. Do you hear what I'm saying? Once you're done with that drink, I'll expect you to move on and never to come back. Not ever."

A scent of perfumed water hung about her, distracting Borchus enough to let his reply slip away. He kept his eyes fixed on hers, very much aware of the death trap set below her neckline. He knew Sindra and remembered her scolding any man whose eyes fell to her cleavage.

"I'm only here to drink."

Sindra gawked at him in suppressed shock, her mouth open. "Who do you think you're speaking to? Don't insult my intelligence with such gurry. Seddon above, a cow kiss has more sense than to believe you're only here to drink. If I had the patience or the time, I'd give you a history of how many times I've heard you say those very words."

She leaned in closer and whispered with irritated heat, "I *know* what you're here for. *You* know what you're here for. And I've already said my mind. Don't bother with anything else."

With that, she stood and glanced around the tight confines of the alehouse. Two other barmaids bustled around, holding platters of empty pitchers and mugs. A pair of men served drinks to an array of waiting customers. Sindra settled upon Borchus once more, regarding him with unconcealed dislike. She moved off to the other end of the bar, the full-length, bright-green dress she wore stealing his attention. It was tight but not nearly as tight or revealing as the ones she'd worn years ago. Perhaps the garment hung a little thicker around her middle, but it only accentuated her figure all the more.

Averting his eyes and taking a breath, Borchus sat and mulled and stared at the wall behind the bar, feigning interest in the kegs. The conversations buzzing around him seemed distant as he replayed Sindra's warning once again.

"Finished that drink yet?" An angry Sindra stepped back into his field of vision.

"No."

"Didn't I say to finish your drink and leave?"

Borchus thought about it. "You did not."

"I thought that might need repeating, seeing as the years are affecting your hearing—and your memory. Well, finish your drink and leave. You remember Gurga?"

Borchus had done his best to forget about Gurga. Luckily for him, the great ogre of a man positioned at the door had failed to see Borchus enter the alehouse. He'd timed it so he crossed the threshold on the heels of a group of men and women, thus evading detection.

"I remember Gurga."

"He's here every night."

"I'm glad he is."

"As am I. You finish that drink quickly, leave, and I won't introduce you to him a second time."

Borchus didn't recall being introduced to Gurga a *first* time, but he kept that to himself. He did remember the huge spiked club the enforcer carried, hanging from a belt that might've been fashioned from an entire cow. The image prompted the agent to hurry his beer. He inspected the remaining contents and made the effort to get more down.

Sindra's fingers rapped impatiently on the bar. "I mean it. When you finish that, leave this place, and do not come back."

Beer filled Borchus's cheeks and bulged them to the size of apples. He stopped, met her eyes for a heartbeat, then swallowed.

Sindra leaned in once again. "What's in that head of yours, anyway? Why do you always have to press a point?"

Borchus wondered that himself, answering Sindra's question with half a shrug. He finished his beer and placed the mug down. Sindra held out her hand, and he paused before settling the empty vessel into her palm. She snatched it away and regarded him with an unspoken *well?*

Sniffing and wiping his mouth, Borchus leaned back, lingering for a moment. Then he nodded at his old friend and gently pushed off from the bar like a ship leaving a dock. He slipped through the patrons and walked around tables, ignoring the laughter of people in much better spirits than himself.

Ahead, Gurga saw him and stood up.

Borchus sighed and corrected himself. The man *straightened*, his large graying skull only a head below the ceiling timbers. As Gurga partially blocked the door, it became plain how the enforcer would never clear the entrance without stooping.

"You," the oversize brute growled in a timbre that could rattle whole forests. "How'd you get in here?"

"I walked." Borchus gestured to the door. "Through that. Now I'm leaving."

Gurga's face hitched up into a questioning scowl. He looked past Borchus, in the direction of the bar.

"She doesn't like you," he informed the agent.

"I know."

"Don't come back."

"I'll try not to."

"If I see you again, I'll smack you 'til you're unfit in the head then toss you into the street. Understand that?"

Borchus sensed he was one smart reply from having that very threat become reality. Gurga didn't strike him as a talker, and so he was thankful for the advanced warning.

The agent kept his answer civil. "Only came in for a drink."

Gurga's harsh features screwed up into a bear's snarl. Borchus didn't wait for a reply or a second warning. He walked past the huge enforcer and into the warm night, leaving the merriment of the alehouse behind. The feeling of being watched came over him, but he didn't turn around. He selected a direction and walked away, not wanting to give Gurga a reason to strike.

As he strolled along beneath a festive line of glowing lanterns, Borchus concluded that Sindra would require much more effort this time. Hadree's alehouse could be a wealth of information concerning gladiators and, as such, could not be simply forgotten. And he couldn't allow Sindra to dissuade him from his goals, even though she'd done exactly that with ease tonight. Annoyance flared within Borchus. The woman kept him on his toes and could disarm or distract him with her wit, charm, and—dare he admit it?—curves.

Still, he had to bring her into the fold. He couldn't frequent the alehouse every night in hopes of overhearing bits of useful information. Having a person there was far more preferable.

He'd go back. In a couple of nights. When she wasn't expecting it.

Trouble was, Borchus *knew* she expected him to return, and when he eventually did, the question would be, what would happen? Would she finally listen to his proposal, or would she release Gurga to make his life considerably more painful?

As a rule, Borchus was adverse to pain.

It was worth the risk, however. Sindra was far too valuable to let slip away. Far too important.

I'm going to die there, the somber thought occurred to him. Sindra knew him better than he knew himself, even after all these years. Stubborn, she'd called him. Yes, he'd prove her right. It would make her happy. He recalled their brief conversation and how she'd kept it entirely vague. That made him smile.

The smells of the city wafted by as he arrived at a side street and turned. Men and women walked or staggered along. Some felt their spirits more than others, talking, giggling, laughing. The garish streamers crossed overhead. Some unattended merchant stalls had been covered with bare planks, while some larger stores had their shutters and doors closed. Sunja, Borchus thought: a city said to be over two thousand years old, which was reason enough for Marrn to say its own history reached back two thousand, five *hundred* years. He'd traveled that neighboring country on Sunja's northeastern border but didn't care for it. The people were far too competitive for his liking, far too convinced of their superiority.

Sindra. Age agreed with her. The thought pleasantly settled into Borchus's mind as he walked through thinning streams of people. He kept an eye on familiar houses and inns, looking for one in particular where an alleyway would take him through a maze of smaller streets and narrow lanes. The city hadn't changed much at all since his departure, and he'd only needed to walk a few paces before recognizing the area.

The inn came into view, a towering four-level frame built of sturdy oak and pine. Borchus crossed in front of an embracing couple and stole down the alley, sticking close to the middle to avoid tripping in any refuse along the sides. He got halfway through before he froze as if treading on a squeaky floorboard. An unseen force guided him to turn around and look back the way he'd come.

A man stood just inside the mouth of the alleyway, his form masked in shadow. The appearance of the figure startled him for a heartbeat. Borchus waited, hearing muffled strings and horns through the inn's walls. The heavy beat of a drum kept pace with his pulse. Borchus didn't like the way the stranger lingered there, but he forced himself to remain still, wondering what might be afoot. He preferred to avoid the main streets and keep to the back ways to identify any potential followers and lose them.

Or confront them.

The muffled music died away, but the drum pounded on relentlessly. The dark outline of a man lingered for a few steady beats, not moving and raising Borchus's concern. The thought of dead Strach rotting below the city came to him, but he'd been sure no one had seen that killing. He was certain of it.

The shadowy stranger lifted a hand to his unseen face as if scratching something. Borchus tensed. The figure took an awkward step, staggered really, before bumping into the inn's corner and disappearing out of sight.

Borchus let his breath out, relief replacing unease. He waited in case the figure might reappear. The horns and strings joined with the drum once more, rushing to a crescendo and finishing with a happy crash of applause. Voices babbled from the walls.

Replaced with a hurried rush of air.

Danger flashed through Borchus as he spun and

slapped away a dagger stabbing for his chest. A huge shadow crashed into him and slammed him to the wall. Garbage nudged and rattled at his feet. He held on to the knife arm as the shadowy presence wrestled for supremacy. Having missed his mark, the attacker jerked his blade back and cocked his arm to stab again.

Borchus kicked the man's knee, and the figure buckled with a grunt. The agent yanked his hidden belt knife free and barrelled into a torso, forcing the man back on his knees. Borchus punched three hard blows into a chest before jamming the short blade under a chin in a soupy gush of black. The attacker gargled horribly, attempting to draw breath past steel. Borchus withdrew his weapon, and the shadow sagged into a stack of crates.

Chest heaving from the short but intense combat, Borchus looked up to see another shadow walking down the alley—an extended arm ending in a curved dagger.

Borchus freed himself from the corpse. Blood from his buckle knife speckled the ground. He didn't run. Instead, he faced the approaching newcomer. Beyond the walls, the music started again. The drum pounded out a much faster beat this time, accompanied by an angry fiddle.

The approaching shadow blotted out the light of the distant street. *Big.* This new shade was much bigger than the dead one. Taking a deep breath, Borchus steadied himself.

The attacker lunged, slashing at Borchus's face. The dagger split air, whistling back and forth, before jabbing for the eyes. Borchus backed up with every cut, feeling the wind from those vicious slices. He ducked and stabbed, thrusting for a throat, but the larger attacker dodged easily before striking again. Borchus retreated a pace, expecting to hit a wall any moment. He slashed at his foe and heard a surprised hiss.

The man charged him.

A bolt of panic went through Borchus as the shadow bull-rushed into his chest and crushed him against the alley wall. Borchus threw out his left hand as if imploring the man to stop and caught a bulging bicep. Borchus gasped with the effort needed to keep that arm away. He braced his feet and *pushed*, panting, thighs knotting, and forced the larger man back. A faceless head buckled down, imposing his greater mass. Borchus bared his teeth, his forehead stopping against a muscular shoulder, and felt the surprising lick of a knife cutting, slicing, *sawing* away at his midsection.

Borchus let loose a short squeal of pain, felt the air biting at long cuts in his guts, and realized his own knife was pinned to his waist.

The cutting ceased for an instant as the killer refilled cavernous lungs. Black eyes narrowed as the man forced his weight upon his trapped quarry once again, long arm working the knife *deeper*, lighting up the agent's mind in a whip's crack of agony.

Borchus fell back, twisting the man and thumping him into the building, where he dropped to a knee. The hateful tip of the knife slipped out of Borchus's side. The relief was euphoric as the pain lessened by degrees. The killer's grip on Borchus' knife hand loosened, and Borchus ripped it free. He slashed a chest then the arm he still held.

A high-pitched huff of pain escaped the killer. He fended off Borchus's thrusts and slammed into him once again, trapping him against coarse timbers. The unknown attacker jammed a forearm across his chin, pressing Borchus's cheek to wood. Borchus grabbed the man's knife arm, slowing the thrust aimed for his neck. Flapping his own weapon arm free, he stabbed his foe's throat.

The shadow caught the arm at the bicep.

They stood there in that killing, ever-shrinking embrace as their strength burned away, knives poised only fingers away from jugulars. They grunted, the sound out of tune with the inn's music. Their arms trembled, pushing their blades ever closer to their marks.

The alley disappeared. The darkness deepened. Eyes narrowed. Teeth gleamed.

Blood and sweat dripped off Borchus as he pushed with all his remaining might. The tip of his blade crept forward, closer with every crashing heartbeat, closing with the shadow's exposed neck.

The man's eyes widened.

Though the stranger was larger, it became all too clear Borchus was stronger.

The shadow attempted a scream as his strength finally left him. Borchus's knife punched into his neck, right up to the bloody knuckles. A grunt escaped the man's lips, and he collapsed, suddenly boneless. Borchus kicked the carcass back and leaned heavily against the wall. He struggled for breath. He pressed a hand to his side and winced. Black motes filled his vision before he squeezed his eyes shut. Borchus gasped, sucked in air, and looked for other attackers.

Only then did he notice the music inside the inn had ceased.

Bandages. He needed something to slow the bleeding.

Grimacing, Borchus stooped. He released pressure on his wound to cut away a wad of dry cloth from the dead man's shirt. His breathing deepened. Blood seeped past his waist and down his leg. He focused on folding the cloth into a thick compress and applied it to the cut. The pressure almost brought him to his knees. He groaned, and hearing his own voice prompted him to check the alley once again.

Who were they? He regarded the unmoving lumps in the dark. The urge to examine them closer tempted him, but his bleeding side would have none of it. He needed a healer.

Placing a hand against the wall, Borchus moved at the best speed he could manage, exiting the alley from the far end.

Leaving a sprinkle of blood in his wake.

*

The third gang member sat upon the steps of a merchant's store. To passersby, he was a drunken reveller from the nearby inn, getting some fresh air before staggering back into a musical fray. He had an excellent view of the alley across the street, waiting for the deed to be done. Whenever Jaro took on a killing, he always sent packs of three: two to do the job and one standing back to watch and ensure the work was done.

Or to report back to Jaro if the attempt failed.

When Borchus staggered from the alley, the gang member expertly concealed his alarm. He watched the smaller man go, noting how the agent pressed a hand to his side. The agent was alive. That meant Jaro's killers were dead or dying.

Having worked the trade for a very long time, the gang member allowed Borchus to place some distance between him and the alley. A short time later, he stood, not as drunk as he'd seemed. He dusted off his behind and followed the agent toward whatever rat hole he might scurry into.

*

Halfway to dawn, Borchus nearly collapsed on the cellar door where he and Garl stayed through the nights. The stitches in his wound tugged uncomfortably. The healer he'd visited was the same long-bearded, rabbit-eating man he, Garl, and Halm had found days ago. Though well past closing time, the man still allowed Borchus into his workplace and treated him with the same stoicism as before. That kind of professionalism demanded right and proper compensation, and Borchus had paid the healer well.

With his side burning, Borchus paused before the cellar

door and regarded the alley. He'd been careful walking home, circling the area twice before deciding it was safe. Even then, he glanced over his shoulder far more often than he should. The only people in the streets lay out of harm's way, sleeping off the night's drinking. At one point, he saw the torches of the patrolling street watch but avoided them.

Home, his wretched home, had beckoned.

Facing the planks, Borchus winced as he bent over and scratched his fingernails on the wood three times. A dull clump sounded from below, prompting Borchus to scan the alleys' shadows again. Above the darkened peaks and spires, the night sky glittered.

The cellar door opened a crack.

"Garl."

"Borchus?"

"Let me in, quickly."

"What?"

"Let me *in*."

A scraping followed as Garl undid a pair of inner hooks. The one-legged man lifted the top of the lid high enough for Borchus to slip his fingers into the crack. He lifted, weak from blood loss and effort. He expecting his stitches to burst, but they held. As quietly as he could, Borchus descended to the cellar, making note to pay the cobbler for use of the space below his house. The sum was due at week's end.

To his credit, Garl held his tongue until Borchus was below ground and the door closed and hooked.

"Where have you been?" Garl blustered. "What's wrong? Has something happened? Why are you—"

Borchus waved a hand, indicating he wanted a moment to settle in. He walked into the deeper section of the cellar, rounded a corner, and eventually sat down on his cot with a sigh of relief. A second candle burned in a metal holder with a thick crown of melted wax at the base. An anxious Garl appeared on his crutches a beat later.

"Well?"

"A pair of dogs tried to kill me." Borchus gently laid himself down.

"What?" Garl's face bleached in the candlelight, and his breath quickened. "What?"

"I'd been visiting people when they came upon me in an alleyway. Tried to stick me with daggers. Two very eager bastards."

"Who were you visiting?"

"That's not important."

"It is if someone tried to kill you shortly after."

"No one who would want me dead."

"All right. All right, so who tried to kill you?"

Borchus stared at the ceiling. "I don't know. It was dark. I happened to be bleeding, so I wasn't so concerned with finding out who was holding the blades. I *was* concerned about finding a healer, which is why I'm taking my time walking around, and you're no doubt smelling something akin to onions. I swear that healer slapped me with an entire—"

"Were you followed?"

The alarm in his tone made Borchus hesitate. "What makes you think I was followed?"

"Borchus, we *killed* Strach only yesterday night. We killed him. I include myself because the Sons won't care. We killed Strach last night, and tonight someone tried to kill you. I think it's obvious. They *know*."

This time, Borchus's eyes narrowed. "The Sons? You think the Sons tried to have me killed?"

"If they did, then someone saw us kill Strach. They know what we look like. Oh, dying Seddon, dying *Seddon*."

"Be quiet, there's a family above us."

"A family that lives on a level *above* the level above us." But Garl glanced nervously in the direction of the cellar door.

"No one followed me," Borchus said.

"So you said, but obviously someone *had* been following you."

"The whole thing might have been a chance occurrence."

"A chance occurrence? Do you really believe that? In our work? After what we've done?"

Borchus mulled on that as Garl's infectious worry spread to him. "You have a point."

"Oh, dear Seddon above. Oh, dear Seddon." Garl rubbed his face. "Someone saw us last night. They found the body and started hunting for us."

"They could have, but one day seems quick to me."

"*I've got one leg!*" Garl blinked at his outburst and

attempted better control. "And you're not exactly forgettable. The Sons have eyes everywhere. *Everywhere.* They could find us easily enough."

"Listen to me. Listen. We're in a city of tens of thousands. It's wartime. There are several men around missing legs. You aren't the only one."

"What are you saying? They'll never find me? *Pah!*"

"All right." Borchus patted the air. "Calm yourself. We must think clearly."

Garl quieted and glanced back at the cellar door, his haunted eyes widening. He held up a hand. The sight raised Borchus's own alarm. He pulled himself to a sitting position, wincing at his wound's protests.

For long moments, the two men waited. Listened.

"It's nothing," Borchus said, but he whispered all the same.

"Thought I heard something."

"The cellar door is hooked."

"Are you *unfit?* If the Sons are out *there,* and they suspect we're in *here,* a cellar door isn't going to stop them."

"Then there you have it. They aren't out there. Calm yourself."

That point made Garl look back at the cellar entrance. His expression softened, and he started breathing again.

"It's the Sons. I know it," he whispered, terror rising to his face. "And they know about us. And if they know, we're dead men. The Sons won't stop until they find us. And being stabbed in an alleyway would be a blessed kiss from Seddon compared to what they *could* do."

Borchus clapped his hands over his forehead and forced his brain to work while Garl fidgeted. "Will you stop *moving*. Let me think. First, you don't know exactly if Strach really belonged to the Sons, correct? Only rumors, you said."

"I said that to relax you."

Borchus balked at that revelation.

"We should leave the city," Garl said in an urgent whisper, "at once. It's the only way to save our miserable hides. And our eyes. Oh, sweet... our *eyes*."

Garl set his jaw, trying with all his might to control the raw terror crackling through his person. Just watching him placed Borchus on edge.

"I'm not going anywhere."

Garl stared as if the man had sprouted a second head. "You'll die, then. They'll find you and gut you. You'll bob from the ceiling timbers by your own..."

The spy couldn't finish and clapped his hands to his cheeks.

"I've only just come back," Borchus said firmly. "I'm not letting the Sons of Cholla run me from the city. I have work here."

Garl shook his head. "Your work finished the instant they tried to kill you."

"Saimon's black hanging fruit! *You* brought this upon us! You never said Strach belonged to a gang!"

"Wait..." Garl's eyes widened. "Wait... wait. You didn't examine those men?"

"No."

"The ink! That's one way to be certain. Strach had the ink upon him. All of the Sons wear it. If those men you killed have markings, we run—run and do *not* look back. If they don't have the ink, it was a chance happening. They were a pair of cutthroats hunting for your coin."

"Are you saying I should go back there?"

Garl thought it over. "Possibly very dangerous."

"Ah-ha." Borchus nodded with sarcasm. "I'm glad you said it."

"I don't think you should go back. We should leave right now before the sun rises, just to be safe."

"Didn't you just say the Sons have eyes everywhere?"

"I did."

"Then if those punces *did* belong to the Sons, they'll probably have eyes on the gates, wouldn't you think?"

Garl actually whimpered, the sound as disturbing and pitiful as that of a trapped animal.

"Some time has passed. If they know about their lads failing to kill me, they might suspect we'll attempt to leave," Borchus reasoned. "They might have someone at the gates. If so, leaving the city isn't an option."

"Oh, sweet Seddon…" Garl slumped against the wall, almost losing his crutches. "We're dead men. There's no way out."

"There's always a way. We just haven't thought of it yet."

But in his mind, he cursed.

*

Dawn broke the horizon in a flare of light. Sunja's southern gates opened inward with resounding squeals and groans, revealing an inner corridor of stone. The people sleeping outside of the entrance came to their senses upon hearing that discordant sound and blinked at the thick moving timbers of the gate. Chains rattled deep within as an inner portcullis lifted at the end of the tunnel. Murder holes in the ceiling checkered the cobblestones with sunlight. A knot of battle-ready Skarrs marched through the tunnel with practiced formality and took up positions on either side of the square opening. Six soldiers separated from these forces and stood at attention around a wooden table where a single official stood ready to register the name and purpose of each individual seeking entry into the city.

The people struggled to their feet. They had arrived after the gates had been closed for the night and, rather than descend the long winding path to the flatlands below, chosen to make camp on the road itself or along its narrow shoulders. They hefted their belongings or climbed into the driver's seats of wagons or huddled around carts stuffed with food and other goods. Low grumbles, conversations, and morning yawns filled the silence while the day's traffic waited to be processed and admitted into the city, hoping to be inside well before the sun scorched the land.

Among the flow of flesh, wood, and metal stood a pair

of men, their clothing ordinary and dusty and smelling of dried sweat. Suntanned and weary looking, they stood in line with all the others, waiting for their turn to be questioned. When the city official finally greeted them and asked for their names, the two men identified themselves and their purpose for entering the great city. They were travelers from Anvar seeking their cousin, a merchant of leather goods, who had requested their presence so that they might discuss joining his business.

The official recorded all information in his ledger, including the merchant's name and whereabouts, while a pair of Skarrs searched the two visitors' persons. The soldiers forwent confiscating the shortswords the Anvar men carried, as it was common knowledge the journey from easterly Anvar to westerly Sunja was lengthy and fraught with bandits, Dezer horse barbarians, and Seddon only knew what else. A pair of blades would not trouble Sunja. As the travelers had nothing else in their possession, not even a change of clothing, the official waved them through, advising the two men to stop at the public baths.

The Anvar said they would and, without another word, they entered the city.

Their youthful expressions remained slack, expertly masking their true vicious nature.

And their bloody intentions.

13

Halm woke at dawn and rubbed his eyes.

Snores cut the morning stillness, and he rose with a grimace and a grunt. A wave of dizziness nearly toppled him, but he gripped the edges of the cot, held on, and rode out the feeling. Wine, beer, and some feral mixture that might have been firewater but probably was spiced horse piss that mule-kicked one's senses to the ground had been the stuff to finally knock them down. Whatever old Clavellus had in his cellar, he'd shared with the Zhiberian, Muluk, and Pig Knot, not caring in the least what Goll might say. And to the man's credit, Goll said not a word. By late afternoon, the three of them were right and properly senseless. Halm didn't even know how he'd found his bed.

The shuttered window above his head barred the light. He smacked his lips, felt the dryness of his mouth, and shuddered at the unholy poison nestling within his guts. He gulped down air and sat on the edge his bunk, staring at his sandals where he'd kicked them off the night before. The smell of body odor wrinkled his nose. He'd wash later, after the journey to Karashipa.

Karashipa.

Seddon and Lords above, was he really thinking about riding a horse out that way to see Miji once again? A shuffle to the nearest latrine seemed daunting. A powerful chill shook out all parched and sleepy thoughts. Halm didn't know if she'd even remember him, but the idea of traveling with a full purse and a clear destination was damn near overpowering and much more appealing than sitting and drinking himself into a pickled state with the others.

Not that he had anything against drinking himself pickled. Far from it.

In fact, he rather enjoyed becoming pickled as often as possible, even when such spectacular states of unfitness waited for him at the end—like this morning.

But the thought of Miji pulled, and he didn't think there was any harm in seeing what she was all about. He wore the title of master now and of an established house. That might even impress her, much more than his usual profession. His ample cloth sack containing his gear rested in a corner of his alcove, festering, badly needing to be aired. He wouldn't be taking it with him.

Feeling much better about the future, Halm gingerly slipped his hairy toes into his sandals and ran a hand around his belly and the cloth of his black breeches. Knees crackled when he rose. He stood and took a deep, settling breath. There was a water barrel in the common room, and he knew he'd have to be careful not to piss there by mistake. Or drink from the latrine.

Once he knew he wasn't about to fall apart, he reached for the fancy leather scabbard containing the Mademian broadsword. Eyes fixed upon the shuttered window and the tracery of light around the edges, Halm strapped on his belt and scabbard.

Heaving his bandaged mass through the doorway, he bounced off the doorframe and lumbered into daylight. The blanket of heat slapped him across the face, bringing forth a frown and a hiss. The sun was only a bright sliver over the eastern wall of the villa, but it was already imposing its will upon the land. Halm marveled at the breaking dawn and the surrounding emptiness. Not a cloud could be seen, and the sky was a blue deep enough to make one's heart ache. He stood there with a small sack containing his gold, a sealed jar of saywort, and a change of clothing—a second pair of old breeches—and checked on the numerous dressings keeping his person together.

"You're up early, Master Halm," a voice called.

Halm straightened and looked around, locating the white beard of the taskmaster. Clavellus sat atop his balcony, mug in hand, shirtless and damned near branded by the sun. He smiled pleasantly and lifted that familiar piece of metal in a greeting.

"Aye that," Halm answered, baring his teeth. "Looking to do a bit of traveling this morning."

A puzzled silence answered that as a frown darkened

Clavellus's snowy face.

"Traveling?"

"Traveling," Halm repeated, taking his time crossing the training sands. The stables were just past the taskmaster's preferred perch.

"Where, might I ask?"

"Karashipa."

"Karashipa? That's a half a day away—or more, in your condition."

"Aye that," Halm agreed, pain flaring throughout his frame with grim foreshadowing. "My condition has worsened."

"That's always the way of it." Clavellus lowered his voice when the Zhiberian stopped. The taskmaster leaned forward and rested his upper torso against the railing. "The hurts and aches and bruises rise to the surface after the fight when all's done. Flesh swells. Joints seize. Well. The healer's looked at you, right?"

Halm nodded. "Even have a container of that saywort to take with me."

"Saywort. Ever there was a gladiator's friend, it's that ripe concoction."

"It is that."

"Why Karashipa?"

Halm smiled, remembering the fury Clavellus had released upon them weeks ago, when the Free Trained fighters first visited his villa. How things had changed. "Shan's said my season's done. Truth be known, I feel that it's done with every swallow, breath, piss, and step. I... I can't bring myself to watch the training here, Master Clavellus. I feel I should be training with them. Doing something. And I've other things on my mind. Some time away from all this will do me well, I think. I'll return, however."

Clavellus listened, his brow knotted in concentration. Sounds of people rising reached them: thumps issuing from the pit fighters' barracks.

"You have coin?" the taskmaster finally asked.

"I do."

"You'll need it."

"Master Goll has given me everything I've earned." Halm lifted the cloth bag he carried.

"All that?"

"And a change of clothing."

Clavellus chuckled. "I know I haven't known you for a long time, Master Halm, but it seems to me you rarely wear clothing, except for those rags you're wearing now."

"Ah, I was going to leave a few pieces of gold in payment for a horse."

"I don't have many," Clavellus pointed out.

"Well, name your price. It doesn't have to be one of your better horses, just one that will carry me where I want to go and back again."

The taskmaster considered it. "If you're coming back, there's no need to purchase the animal. Just borrow it and return it when you're ready."

"I may not return, Master Clavellus."

That amused the man. "No, you may not. I took a

chance on you once. I'll do so again. And this time, with much more favor."

Feet crunched on sand-sprinkled brick, and Machlann came into sight, his tuft of gray hair bouncing like a lit flame. The trainer stopped in his tracks.

"Master Machlann," Halm greeted.

"So you're leaving, then?" Machlann asked in a near-civil tone.

"I am."

"He's borrowing a horse," Clavellus said.

"Be sure to bring it back," the trainer muttered with a hint of warning. "And safe journey."

"Apologies again for yesterday."

But the trainer scowled and waved a hand, dismissing it. "Heard better, Zhiberian. From better people."

"Well, then." Halm nodded at Machlann then Clavellus. With nothing more to say, he took his leave.

The stables smelled of fresh hay and well-tended animals, a level of cleanliness that impressed the Zhiberian. Halm explained his intent to a stable hand, who eventually brought him an older gelding standing a little over sixteen hands with a back just beginning to sag under a worn saddle. The horse regarded the Zhiberian's girth with a critical eye and snorted.

"Oh, we'll get along fine, saucy one." Halm smirked, taking the reins and handing the stable hand a single gold coin. "Does the animal have a name?"

"Lish."

"Lish. Like the dish?"

The stable hand didn't comment.

"Lish the Dish, then." Halm chuckled at his own humor and fiddled with a saddlebag, filling it with his few possessions. A moment's guilt ran its course, as the saddle and reins alone cost coin, but Clavellus had to have known that. Frowning, he positioned himself to take the saddle and pulled himself into it. Pain lanced through his gut, hands, and every other place cut and healing, while a nightlike swirl of stars gave his head a spin.

Lish took the weight but snorted again as Halm righted himself, its ears twitching as if the animal had just taken a blow to the head.

Or the back.

"Anything I should know about him?" Halm asked when his discomfort had passed.

"He's twenty-four now, so walk him when you can," the stable hand explained with a concerned look. "Otherwise, he'll take you where you want to go. Enjoys apples if you have them."

"What horse doesn't enjoy a bit of fruit?"

The stable hand had nothing to say to that.

"What hot-blooded punce doesn't like a bit of fruit for that matter, eh?"

The stable hand had nothing to say to that either.

Halm decided Lish wasn't the only saucy one around the stable. He flicked the reins, and the animal sauntered toward the training area.

The sight of companions gathered surprised him—even Pig Knot, sitting rather uncomfortably with his back against the living quarters' wall.

"I thought to be away without notice this morning," Halm remarked, eyeing the three men.

"These Zhiberians," Muluk said to Goll, "they don't really say goodbyes, do they?"

"This one doesn't," Goll said. "And he isn't saying goodbye. He'll return one day, once he's sown whatever it is passing through that fat slab of his."

"Harsh words." Halm glowered. "You won't bring me back that way."

"But we'll send you off that way," Goll countered and stepped up to Lish. "You didn't pay anything for this cow kiss, did you?"

"Clavellus wouldn't let me."

"Hm. You're truly going to leave us?"

"For a short time, at least."

Goll remained silent for a moment. "Remember, you have a place now. Here. If you want it."

Halm nodded.

"Safe journey, then." Goll stepped back.

The other Kree took his place. Dark haired and shaggy looking, a hungover Muluk squinted at the overweight pit fighter and marveled at the mess of him. "Half a day on that beast will rip you apart."

"Well, good for me Karashipa is only half a day away," Halm reminded him. "Maybe a young lady will have pity and put me back together."

Muluk wheezed a short laugh. "You have a way about you, Zhiberian."

"And you look very much like a Paw Savage, now that I see you from above."

They pressed fists, smiling fondly at each other, before Muluk backed away.

"Tell the lads… best of fortunes with the remainder of the games," Halm said. "Ho, Pig Knot. Until the next time we meet. Mind the women but never the pitchers."

But Pig Knot sat and simmered on his mat, appearing none too happy.

"You'll see me again afore too long," Halm went on. "Have no fear of that with my luck, anyway."

"Safe journey," Pig Knot muttered and lifted his fist as if to tap another. Halm did the same, a pang of unease going through his heart and mind at the downcast man. He kept his eyes on his friend's face and not his missing legs.

"I'll return," Halm said, surprising himself.

Having said his goodbyes, he tugged on Lish's reins and glanced up at Clavellus. The taskmaster nodded agreeably, as if knowing the pit fighter would return before too long. Halm wondered if he wouldn't be back in the villa by tomorrow. Or this day's evening.

Nothing more to say, he guided Lish toward the villa's gates, where a pair of Clavellus's sentries opened them.

Halm of Zhiberia passed through. He did not look back.

*

"That's it then," Goll said to no one in particular when the departing man winked out of sight.

"Too early in the morning for such goodbyes." Muluk groaned and held a hand to his gut.

"Agreed," Goll said. "He'll return before too long, perhaps after the games. There's too much for him here to simply give up. And that man is a fighter if ever I met one."

Goll cast his attention to his taskmaster. "Good to see you survived the night."

"It is good." Clavellus sounded amazed himself.

"I hope that's water you're drinking."

"Hope is a good thing." The taskmaster took a mouthful.

That set Goll's head to shaking in disapproval. He frowned at Muluk for his part in the daylong drinking session. Muluk wilted with guilt and averted his eyes.

Message delivered, Goll looked at Machlann's bearded features. "Today… we prepare for war."

The trainer liked the sound of that.

*

Later that morning, Torello placed his bowl of warm stew on the table shared by Junger and Brozz and plopped down beside them. "Halm's gone," he said, spooning breakfast into his mouth.

The other gladiators exchanged looks. Neither had expected Torello to join them.

"So he has." Junger moved his elbow to accommodate the man.

"Never expected," Torello mumbled as he chewed,

"him to leave. Not this. He's a housemaster, even. What else is out there?"

Junger glanced at Brozz, but the big Sarlander had nothing to say. They'd only known the Zhiberian for a short time, and while it would be strange not to see him about, they never really knew the man. The games would carry on without him.

As would they.

As if sensing that very sentiment, Torello shrugged and continued eating.

14

Muluk and Pig Knot sat on their mats, watching the remaining gladiators being put through their paces by the trainers. Goll wandered the fringes of the sands, scowling at things only he saw. Clavellus remained nearly stock-still on his perch above it all, the goblet in his hand flashing whenever he lifted it to his lips.

"Lords above," Muluk commented, "that man can drink."

The words stirred Pig Knot to life as, up to that point, he'd been sitting in the sun's grace like charred meat dropped from a skewer. Pig Knot's squinting eyes flicked to the taskmaster, lingered for a hateful moment, and returned to the training. Machlann had the men practicing the same four- and five-strike combinations as the day before.

"You see him?" Muluk asked.

"Clavellus?" Pig Knot slurred though his bandages. He sipped from his own half-full pitcher of beer, wanting to return to his pickled state. "Aye that."

"He finishes whatever he has there and leaves for a heartbeat, just a beat, and when he returns, he's drinking from it again. The speed is damn near magical."

Pig Knot grunted.

"Oh, his missus comes out to check on him every now and then, even to steal a taste of whatever is in that shiny cup, but…" Muluk trailed off with a disbelieving shake of his head. "Lords above, that lad can drink."

"It's his wine and beer to drink."

Muluk looked around. "I'm wondering where it all comes from."

"The man owns farmland. Grape orchards."

"But that's *wine*. I'm drinking beer now. *You're* drinking beer. Where's it all coming from? Does someone bring it here or make it in the villa? Or outside these walls?"

"It's puzzling," Pig Knot said with the barest lick of interest. "Ask him if you're so curious."

"I will. I will. When I'm in his presence again."

"Why not now?"

"Now? Pah. I don't have the will or energy to walk over there. Unfit that I'm even drinking after yesterday."

With Halm's departure fresh on his mind and having consumed just enough beer to not give a good damn, Pig Knot lowered his pitcher, straightened against the wall, and shouted. "*Clavellus*! Clavellus! Where is it you get your beer? Muluk is curious!"

The bandages holding Pig Knot's lower jaw in place

trembled. Spittle flew. Cheeks reddened. Muluk froze in mortified fright as the attention of the entire villa fixed upon them. Machlann's and Goll's combined gazes alone were strong enough to ignite a forest. Pig Knot realized he'd failed the address the taskmaster with the proper honorific, but he didn't care. Interrupting the all-important training gave him a tickle. After Halm's leaving, he *needed* one.

Clavellus took his time in answering.

"From Sunja. When I can afford it. Usually from some nearby villages. My man Clurik makes the wine. He dabbles in mead as well, if there's enough honey."

"Your man Clurik does good work," Pig Knot bellowed, the cords of his neck protruding.

Another pause. "Many thanks."

"His man Clurik no doubt heard the entire conversation," Muluk muttered.

"You wanted to know." Pig Knot's jaw throbbed from the effort. "So, now you know."

"I'll keep my thoughts private from here on."

The idea sounded like a fine one to Pig Knot.

Machlann stood with hands on hips, waiting for either Pig Knot or Clavellus to continue. When neither man did, he looked at Koba and then the taskmaster above. "Permission to continue, Master Clavellus?"

Nala appeared next to her husband and draped an arm over his shoulder. The taskmaster raised his mug. *By all means.*

"Master Pig… *Knot?*" Machlann yelled.

In answer, Pig Knot sent a thin stream of beer through clenched teeth into the sand and raised his own pitcher in salute.

Visibly unimpressed, Machlann returned to his gladiators.

"You're unfit," Muluk directed at Pig Knot.

The legless Sunjan already knew it.

Looking ready to kill, Goll strode toward the pair sitting in the shade. He stopped halfway upon seizing Muluk's attention. The Kree master of the house gestured for his fellow countryman to join him.

"Now you've done it," Muluk moaned. "You've brought Goll down on us."

"He wants you, not me."

"Oh, you'll have your turn. I'll insist upon it."

"My thanks."

"You're welcome. Sweet Seddon. Near-pickled again. Not looking to trade barbs with him today."

With that, Muluk rose with a groan and limped toward Goll, lumbering around the edge of the training sands. Goll led him to the smithy area.

Pig Knot watched them for a while, thoughtless but pulsating with weariness, a despair from which there was no crawling out.

Hurt. The world hurt. And he was alone in it.

He hefted his pitcher and drank deeply, throat working until he dropped the container by his thigh and gasped. The pitcher shone in the daylight, but its brightness failed to move Pig Knot. *Clay*, he thought, hardened, but drop it, and it would shatter.

Just like life.

Pig Knot regarded his absent legs once again, thinking of the women in his life—too many faces and all without names. He decided he'd watched his limit of gladiators training. Leaving the pitcher, he dug his hands into the sand, palms sore from shuffling himself along, and eased through a nearby doorway. His bottom slid across the stone and wood of the common area. Tables and benches went by as he strained and sweated, moving his weight along in an awkward stop and go, mindful of his bits. A pebble bit into his left hand, the sting distracting him enough to ram his right stump into the nearing doorframe. A jolt of sheer agony blazed up his spine, and he collapsed on the threshold, black stars exploding in his vision. He bent over, swept away by a tall wave of nausea.

In time, he regained his senses. A soothing slab of rock pressed against one cheek, and he rested there, waiting for the pain to subside. Pig Knot stayed there for what felt like a year and eventually inspected the bandage of his stump. The tight wrap *appeared* fine, but he knew, just *knew*, stitches had been broken somewhere underneath. The knowledge infuriated Pig Knot, and he used that anger to power himself to his alcove.

Inside, he yanked the curtain across and stopped before his dishevelled cot. A thick blanket covered the straw, unchanged so far this day. He recalled waking and being covered in sweat from the night's thrashing, but on the blanket rested a knife, one he'd used a day ago to slice apples. He was alone. No one watched. Just as well. It would be better this way. The short knife caught the scant light. The steel was dull, worn, but sharp. Sharp enough to do what needed to be done.

Machlann bawled commands in the background. The shouts sounded far away, as if emanating from a deep, dreamy tunnel. Pig Knot gripped the small knife, considering its purpose. The outside noise bled away into a fever-blunted hush. The blade's straight edge fascinated Pig Knot as never before. For him, it was no longer a weapon but an escape, an escape that would hurt for a short time, perhaps a very painful short time, before… well, whatever came next.

Pig Knot realized Halm had it right. The Zhiberian's season was over. To watch Brozz, Torello, and Junger preparing for the games would torment him, aggravate that sense of loss, of defeat, especially when he'd been experiencing the best season yet. Seeing them sweat and strain and work would frustrate him and leave him in a bad mood. Halm understood what he had to do. He'd left. That Halm *could* leave infuriated Pig Knot. Unlike his friend, Pig Knot had no choice but to stay. The rest of his days would be here, watching warriors prepare for their contests, battles that would no longer involve him. He would sit and watch people with all their limbs go about their lives.

Or so he'd thought.

The blade shone in his hand, the old metal scratched by the years, the edge sharp against his thumb. One cut. One quick, deep lick, and Pig Knot could leave, leave this place, this ruined existence. Perhaps he'd even be whole again in the next life. Hope flickered at the thought, an ember glowing in the faintest of breaths.

Pig Knot placed the edge of the knife to his throat, felt the indifferent metal upon his skin. The edge prickled the stubble of an unchecked beard.

His mouth became a line of concentration. The steel didn't waver.

So easy to do, the words blew into his mind. *So easy. One deep stroke.*

Do it.

Blood thumped in his temples. His vision narrowed and centered on shadows that spread across the walls, drawn to death. Pig Knot took the deepest breath of his life and set his jaw.

One cut.

But he couldn't flick the knife across the thick string in his throat. He *willed* his hand to obey, but it refused. The coldest sweat coated his flesh. His hand trembled. He gripped the knife with both hands, as if his right had betrayed him, and still couldn't open his cheese pipe, could not slash and soak the cot with his life.

Machlann bawled again, right in his ear this time, a hateful whisper, urging him to *do it*. Just *do it*. And Pig Knot *wanted* to do it. His hands shook from the stress. But like a bar of steel refusing to bend, he did not.

An idea struck him, and he braced the knife's pommel on the cot's wooden frame. He angled the tip straight up and held the knife firmly. Pig Knot leaned forward and positioned his bandaged chin directly over the point. He lowered himself until the prickly contact brought a grimace. The knife pushed, almost penetrating his skin. All he needed was one great shove to drive himself down upon the weapon.

But something stopped him again.

Snarling, Pig Knot shut one eye and dipped his face right over the knife.

One thrust, straight to the brain.

DO IT.

He huffed and whined. His grip weakened. The knife fell from his hands and landed on the floor. Pig Knot collapsed upon the cot, miserable. Death, he wanted… but he couldn't do it himself. Why couldn't he perish right there and then? He regarded the knife with loathing. Seddon above, it should be easy to take his own life after all of his practice killing right and proper bastards.

Pig Knot lay and stewed, badly wanting to die, yet unable to finish his life. Perhaps it wasn't meant for him to take. He didn't care for that thought at all. A second idea occurred to him, one that lifted hope in his beaten muscular frame. If he couldn't kill himself… perhaps another would.

With or without provocation.

Pig Knot mulled, exploring dark threads uncoiling in his mind. In time, he became aware of the training outside. Machlann bellowed a command and shouted for Koba, the big, scarred one-ear trainer.

Pig Knot's eyes narrowed.

*

"Junger!" Machlann shouted.

The man jerked awake from a personal daze.

"I suspect you've done all of this before. Am I correct, you cheek-spreading Perician?"

"I have," the Perician answered, unoffended by the insult.

"Then step over to me, my missus, and take up guard."

Junger didn't hesitate and moved as ordered, drawing all eyes onto the trainer and the nearly naked man who'd amazed them all in his opening match. He stopped in the middle of the sands and faced the trainer.

"Where exactly did you train?" Machlann asked.

"Pericia. Vathia. Some games in the Territories, not as well known. Minor compared to these."

"Where exactly did you learn the sword?"

"From a teacher in Balgotha."

"Pericia. Vathia. Balgotha. The Territories. You've done some traveling, my son."

Several of the onlookers noted that 'my son' was a significant improvement over 'my missus.'

"I have."

"I want you to defend against my attacks," Machlann said, "for as long as I'm able to swing at your head, not as long as you can. I have a suspicion I'll exhaust myself long before you. Understood?"

Junger hesitated, appearing somewhat uncomfortable. "Understood, Master Machlann."

Machlann turned a suspicious eye to Clavellus on his balcony. Goll sat nearby, intently watching the Perician.

"You impressed us with your level of skill yesterday, lad," Machlann said, mouth barely detectable underneath his thick beard and mustache.

A flicker of concern darkened the Perician's face.

"A damn fine display. Fine enough to make me wonder *how* good you are, you nimble bastard. Something I have to determine for myself."

Junger said nothing, his initial unease disappearing.

"Don't worry," Machlann said. "They're wooden swords."

Without warning, the trainer pressed ahead, sword stabbing, slashing, chopping, running through a masterful sequence of moves. Machlann flowed without pause, didn't overextend himself or place his person at a disadvantage. Despite the years upon his frame and the incident with Sapo, the grizzled trainer swung his wooden blade like a man of twenty, yet also wielding the weapon with years of learning behind it. Anyone else would have been immediately caught by its edge.

Not Junger.

As brilliant as Machlann was, Junger simply dazzled.

The swordsman, for this was no mere gladiator, parried, blocked, ducked, and dodged, and in the end, simply avoided the most dangerous of Machlann's cuts. He broke away from the older man and gave up space, not bothering to check where the practice men stood but inexplicably avoiding them all the same.

Machlann strode forward, cutting down the distance. His shoulders heaved, but he showed no sign of relenting as he went after the Perician again.

Junger met him in the middle of the sands. Machlann's feints failed to move the Perician. Razor-close slashes were deflected, and thrusts stabbed nothing but air.

Goll's features grew pensive as trainer battled student. Clavellus couldn't tear his eyes from the spectacle. At ground level, Koba and the remaining gladiators stood and stared in growing awe at the exchange.

The trainer whirled with a backhand cut, failing to connect with Junger's head. His left hand slammed into the Perician's chest, sending him flat on his back with a bark of escaping breath. Both legs kicked up in a wide V, and the startled look upon Junger's face informed the watchers Machlann had caught the pit fighter off-guard.

Machlann scrambled to cover the fallen man, placing his sword's tip fingers away from the grounded gladiator's chin. Junger relaxed and dropped his weapon.

Face flushed with sweat dripping from a soaked beard, Machlann struggled to catch his breath, but he didn't relax his stance. Deep gasps raked the air.

"Thank you, Master Machlann," Clavellus said loudly, scratching at his bare head. "Well done, Junger. Well done."

Machlann backed away and allowed Junger to stand, each man wary of the other.

"You want to inform them of the challenges, or will I?" Clavellus asked.

Goll grunted and stood. "We've decided who will fight our blood matches."

Torello's head perked up at the words.

"Torello, you'll fight Kolo's killer. No mercy is expected."

The announcement seemed to please the Sunjan. Goll hoped the man would avenge his friend's death for the house.

"Junger, you'll fight Tumber's killer."

"Bubruk," Junger said, giving the man a name.

"That's right. Bubruk. And I expect you to bury him. It hasn't escaped our attention that you didn't kill your last opponent as commanded. You kill this man. Make him dead for the slight against the House of Ten, and make no mistake doing it. A message must be sent to any other house, any other gladiator thinking our house is weak. Do you understand?"

"I do," Junger said without pause.

"Good," Goll added. "Continue on."

"Master Goll," Koba said after receiving a look from Machlann. Koba shouted at the three gladiators and got them to their places. Goll watched Brozz for a reaction, but the tall Sarlander showed no indication of being disappointed with the selection. That pleased Goll.

The gladiators paired off with their practice men, and Koba gave the command to strike.

"What do you think?" Clavellus asked over the clatter.

Goll returned to his seat. "The fight just now?"

"Aye that."

"Junger's a very good actor."

Clavellus nodded.

"I think he realized halfway through that dance that he had to lose, somehow, and convince us it was genuine, that Machlann had him."

Clavellus chewed on a thumbnail in thought. "I think you're right."

"There's no point in questioning him. The Perician would only deny it." Goll's thoughts churned. "I only wonder why…"

"Why the performance?" Clavellus asked.

"Why the performance."

"Well, in this case, I'm glad he did it."

This interested Goll.

"Remember what I said to you some time ago? About a trainer?"

"The trainer must always exhibit an image of strength," Goll immediately answered.

"And?"

"And it's the responsibility of a taskmaster to keep that image intact."

"Very good, Master Goll, very good. Well, this day, for whatever reason, *Junger* decided to keep Machlann's image intact."

"But why?"

"To save Machlann embarrassment? Perhaps it serves no purpose to Junger?"

A thoughtful Goll held his chin, wondering if that was truly the case. "You think Machlann knows?"

"I think if you ask, he'll *tell* you Junger spared him. Machlann is my last remaining true friend and companion. I know that man as well as this silver charm of mine. Between us, he'll tell you because it's his purpose in these games to prepare the men, to judge when they're ready. Machlann won't let pride cloud his judgement. As good as Machlann is, he knows he's getting older, as we all are."

"Unfit." Goll spat. "What's the reason behind it all?"

"Haven't a grain." Clavellus peered down into the training area. "But I do know one thing for certain. I'm becoming tired of these… mysteries."

As was Goll.

15

Just before noon, two of the four brothers from Cholla's accursed loins gathered for a late breakfast deep within their converted storehouse. They wandered into an eating area off a well-stocked kitchen, where the aroma of a roasting ham nearly twisted heads from shoulders. Windows with their shutters thrown wide allowed light inside, revealing a heavy wooden table, its surface pitted and scratched. Cups, plates, and old silver eating utensils covered the square slab. Cholla had instilled his sons with a strong sense of family as well as loyalty and mealtimes. Breakfast, in particular, was reserved for quiet conversations.

This morning, however, Brejo and Calagu sat and fidgeted while waiting to be fed, wondering where their other brothers were.

"You don't suppose someone's finally murdered them?" Brejo breached the silence.

"Damn fine beginning to the day, then."

Brejo tossed his head back and gave a soundless chuckle. "It would be. But really…"

"Possibly," Calagu ventured. "Strach at least. I've long suspected someone would kill him—been *wanting* someone to do it for years."

That drew a scowl from the older brother, but his expression lightened when Jaro appeared in the doorway. Jaro still wore no shirt, allowing his great beard to droop to his chest, where the black dragon remained poised and ready for flight. The Sons' chief enforcer regarded his siblings and shook his head.

"No Strach," Calagu said.

"No Strach," Brejo rasped. "We thought perhaps someone had murdered both of you."

Jaro's head scarcely moved on his shoulders, indicating the barest amusement.

"Still," Brejo said, "give him another day to appear. Then send out the dogs. Have Linfur take care of it."

"Linfur…" Calagu said, none too impressed. "You know he fancies himself one of us."

Brejo's eyes slid to his other brother, suggesting it was too early in the morning to talk about Linfur.

"Well, he's not," Calagu sputtered. "He's risen as far as he can in our ranks. That's all I have to say about that."

"I have news," the big enforcer said quietly.

Brejo rolled his eyes. "Business?"

Jaro nodded.

"Father would slap the skin off your cheeks for bringing up business at the table. Next time, remember him beforehand."

The mention of their father brought an embarrassed flush to Jaro's cheeks. The enforcer pulled a chair out from the table and sat down heavily, glancing toward the pantry and the crackling of grease droppings.

"Well?" Brejo asked. "You have our attention. Let's hear it."

"We'll be wondering all through breakfast," Calagu added.

Jaro considered his brothers. "Two of my men died last night."

Brejo's and Calagu's expressions remained unchanged, waiting.

"Killed by the one Grisholt wants dead."

"Borchus?" Brejo asked.

Jaro nodded.

"The third man told you this?"

Jaro nodded again.

"Did he find where this agent sleeps?"

"He did not."

This information interested Brejo in a very bad way.

"The agent managed to slip away."

"He what?" A disbelieving smile creased Calagu's face.

"He managed. To slip," Brejo said quietly. "Away."

"What was it Jaro said to us last night?" Calagu asked.

"The man's as good as dead," Brejo supplied.

"Yes, that was it. As good as dead. Imagine."

Jaro endured the ridicule, eyes darting back and forth.

"Well, you must have something," Brejo said after

allowing the uncomfortable moment to swell, "else you wouldn't be here."

"Yes, what is it? We're waiting," Calagu said.

Jaro took a deep, settling breath. "The agent didn't escape uncut. My man said he was holding his side."

"*Wounded?* And *still* managed to slip away," Brejo said with quiet amazement. He decided to wring every enjoyable drop out this moment. Jaro took immense pride in his force of killers, and with good reason. Jaro's cutthroats were ruthless executioners. It wasn't often Brejo or Calagu could enjoy a bit of amusement at their brother's expense.

Jaro sighed ever so gently.

"Sounds sloppy to me," Calagu said, "failing to track a wounded man in the streets."

"Perhaps even bleeding," Brejo pointed out and *tsked*.

"Bleeding *badly*," Calagu added.

"The man's an agent," Jaro stated as if that explained everything. Agents could be exceptionally evasive, especially if motivated—or if they suspected they were being stalked.

"Well," Brejo said in his rough voice, spreading his hands over the table, "what do you intend to do about it?"

"I've set men upon the gates. And at the koch bay. No one will get out of the city without me knowing. Sunjack and Bardal are hunting the streets. They'll find this rabbit."

Bardal. Sunjack. Brejo knew them as Jaro's more reliable killers. "Who died, then?"

Jaro frowned. "No one of reputation, a couple of lower lads attempting to move up the ranks. They failed. The others won't."

"And your man who allowed Borchus to escape?" Calagu asked.

"I've had words with him."

"Well." Brejo huffed and drummed his fingers. Activity in the nearby kitchen caught his attention, and his stomach rumbled. "This agent's wounded, you say? Daresay he'll stay out of sight for a while. Heal, rest, perhaps try to leave the city when he thinks no one's watching. You found him once. You'll do so again. In the meantime, I expect you'll have lads questioning the healers in that area. Perhaps they had a late-night visitor."

A brooding Jaro said nothing, his grim silence speaking volumes. Brejo looked toward the kitchen, deciding he'd had enough fun at his brother's expense. The ham smelled wonderful.

"Borchus," Calagu whispered thoughtfully.

"Hm?" Brejo asked, fingers spread wide over his mouth. "You know something?"

"Only that I'm hungry."

"As am I." Brejo glanced at the kitchen once again.

"I don't think he's coming." Calagu indicated Strach's empty seat.

"Have Linfur organize a search for him," Brejo said, which caused Jaro's brow to crease. "What?"

"I've got most of our pack hunting for that agent."

"Well, they can do both, can't they?"

"Suppose so."

"I know so. Release the snakes." Brejo exchanged looks with Calagu. "After breakfast, that is. No one works on an empty stomach. Sit, good Jaro. You look like you need a hot meal."

With that, the three of them focused on the kitchen.

"Bring us meat!" Brejo slapped the table.

*

In an alleyway, the cellar door trembled as the inner hooks were released with muffled *pops*. The slab of wood remained in place for long heartbeats before it lifted just a crack and stayed that way.

"See anything?" Garl whispered from below.

Borchus fumed at the spy's breach of silence.

"Well?" Garl asked.

"Will you shut up?"

Garl did.

Moving slowly, Borchus rested the cellar door upon his wide shoulders and peered up and down the alley's length. Passersby went about their business in the distant streets.

"Nothing."

"They could be waiting up there."

"Well, you have my shortsword."

"Aye that," Garl said in a deflated tone, prompting Borchus to face him. In the meager light, the one-legged man was barely visible.

"Now is *not* the time to argue the point," Borchus warned. "We've discussed this already."

Garl looked away.

"Stay here until I return. Keep the sword handy. If there are any more of them nearby, I'll draw them out."

"Don't leave me like—" Garl started, but Borchus's unwavering glare quieted him.

The agent didn't bother speaking his mind. Garl had a point. He'd abandoned him once before. Garl had no reason to believe Borchus wouldn't do so again, perhaps even suspected he might.

"I'll return," Borchus said. He eased out of the opening and placed the lid back down, glimpsing Garl's worried expression. Borchus straightened and dusted off his repaired brown vest and pants. His blood had stained his only white tunic, ruining it, so he wore a spare green one. The sound of the hooks fastening the cellar door made him cringe and glance around.

No one confronted him.

Feeling the stitches pull when he moved, Borchus walked to the end of the alley. He tried to stroll as he usually did, but the stab wound slowed him down with a sparkling *ah-ah*. His breath came in short bursts, and his knees weakened. Borchus pressed his hand against his side, placing pressure on a wad of cloth with a single dollop of saywort rubbed into the folds. The smell wasn't too bad, or so both he and Garl thought. Then again, the cellar reeked so badly of the ointment, it was possible they'd both grown accustomed to the smell.

Or had simply burned out that particular sense.

It wasn't safe for Garl, so they had decided he would

remain in the cellar until Borchus could return. That decision left the spy both relieved and nervous. If Borchus wasn't back by nightfall, Garl could assume the worst and would be on his own. The men had coin, but even Borchus knew their chances of leaving the city—escaping it—were low.

The Sons would find him.

At the end of the alley, Borchus leaned against a corner and watched the flow of people: women, men, children, merchants, and all manner of tradesmen, armed warriors, and hard ruffians. Borchus paid close attention to the rough-looking thugs, watching them pass and continue on, waiting for a head to casually look with the light of recognition.

Nothing of the sort happened.

Borchus stepped from one corner to the other, appearing unconcerned with the morning, but very much aware of everything. Satisfied that no one had detected him, he slipped into the stream of people and walked toward the koch bay. Ordinarily, he'd stay to the alleyways, but this morning, he would hide in the ebb and flow of flesh.

Naulis. Borchus needed to find the messenger who delivered correspondence from the city to Clavellus and Goll. Borchus and Garl believed the Sons had no knowledge of him, seeing as he wasn't involved with Strach's death.

Strach.

The memory of that night smouldered in Borchus's

guts. One act of revenge had placed him in a very dangerous predicament, from a foe even worse than old Tilo. The main reason for eliminating the street snake had been so that Garl could help recruit extra spies for Borchus, but that idea had all gone to gurry. Forcing the poisonous resentment from his head, he concentrated on the task at hand. He followed farm animals being walked to butchers, avoiding the fragrant plop and spray of cow kisses where he could. Wagons and koches rolled along, and he scooted between and alongside, slowing at the grumbling of his stitches. Once he caught the eye of an old codger sitting on the raised walkway in front of a store. Rheumy eyes tracked the agent, setting off Borchus's paranoia. He increased his speed, his wound cursing him with every step.

Naulis lived in a small, narrow hovel situated among hundreds of near-identical low-cost homes close to the koch bay. Though history wasn't Borchus's favorite subject, he knew Sunja had grown from a small village of farmers and herders at one end of the enormous elevated plateau, around the area where natural springs erupted, pooled, and eventually flowed from north to south, ending in a sizeable lake in the lower end. The palaces of King Juhn were the oldest constructions, while those buildings on the tableland below were the more recent. The Pit, however, had been constructed at a point in time that escaped Borchus, and housing and businesses sprang up around it. Over the ages, the wealthier Sunjans gravitated toward the northern end, closer to the security of the palace walls, as if the majesty of the royals might somehow elevate their own importance. The poor stayed in the south.

Borchus walked through the corridors of the lower-class district, not that it was a slum by any means. Overall, Sunja was a clean city with well-planned street and sewer systems. The southern quarters didn't quite sparkle like the north and even might have a bit of tarnish around the edges, but it was still Sunja. In Borchus's mind, it was the *real* Sunja. The merchants were a little louder, a little scruffier, their storefronts and stalls in need of the smallest repairs. Children ran through the streets, playing their games, disrupting traffic at times, and earning curses from parents and strangers alike.

Very much aware of his surroundings, Borchus circled areas and at times doubled back. He lingered in merchants' doorways and leaned against the corner posts of stalls. Any other day, he wouldn't be so wary, but today wasn't so ordinary. In the early afternoon, he walked down a lane lined with doors of small but well-kept homes. Borchus walked past the rows of residences until he located Naulis's front door, wormed in between a pair of similarly built houses.

A window lay open to the right of the door, so Borchus stopped in front of it, glancing around before moving on to the end of the lane. There, he waited at a narrow intersection, finding a small nook between a pair of houses.

Naulis appeared moments later.

"Something to run out to the villa?" he asked.

Borchus regarded the skinny man with his huge overbite and sunken chin. Naulis wasn't a particularly pleasant-looking individual, but he was loyal and dependable about delivering messages with haste.

"Yes, something to run out to the villa," Borchus replied, "after you go to the Pit and check with the Madea on behalf of the House of Ten."

"The Pit?"

"The Pit."

"Ah, I don't want to go to there," Naulis whined, massaging the back of his orange-haired head. "That place reeks of shite and piss and *more* shite and piss. What's there, anyway? And isn't that your job?"

"Yes, well, my job has changed since last night."

"What happened last night?"

Borchus eyed the messenger. "Nothing that concerns you."

"Suppose so."

"So you'll go to the Pit and—wait. Can you read?"

"A little," Naulis admitted. "Something I'd like to improve upon."

"Certainly. Good for you. Now then, hop to the arena, and check with the Madea. See if there are any matches scheduled for the House of Ten. Then ask if there's any news for the houses and report back to me. I'll be here. Regardless of whether there's any information or not, you'll be traveling to the villa to see if Goll has any messages for me."

A patient Naulis nodded.

"You have all that?"

Naulis nodded again.

"All right then. Off with you. And quickly return here. I'll be waiting."

"What? Right here?"

"Yes, right here. Now go."

Naulis frowned in good humor and held out a hand. Annoyed, Borchus filled the empty palm with a single gold coin.

"Just one?" Naulis protested.

"What do you mean?"

"Well, I'm doing your work as well this morning, aren't I?"

"You're only checking in with the Madea."

"Who dwells in that shite trough called Sunja's Pit. I despise the place! Did you not hear me talk about the shite and piss? Why not ask me to crawl through the city's sewers? They're cleaner. At least then I won't have that stink clinging to me or be shoved about by those swaggering savages calling themselves gladiators."

Borchus pointed a finger at the man's nose. "Don't be saucy with me, you brazen kog. Do *not* be saucy. I'm short on patience. Here."

He slapped a second coin into the messenger's hand. "Never say I wasn't fair."

"Not I." Naulis grinned, winked, and dipped his head before moving off.

Borchus stepped out of the alcove behind the departing

messenger. He watched until the back of Naulis's head disappeared in the trickle of people. Borchus lingered and walked a few steps before returning to the little crook between the houses. He leaned against the wall, favoring his wounded side, while furtively studying the passersby.

Without Garl panicking, Borchus could think clearly and wondered just how bad things had become. Could the Sons have discovered Strach? Might someone have witnessed them leaving the place of the killing? Or were the two would-be killers simply after his coin?

Regardless, Borchus reaffirmed what he and Garl already decided that morning: they'd exercise caution for the next few days.

*

Garl stood at the back of the cellar, in the cloying dark, strangling the hilt of the shortsword Borchus had left. The blade failed to instill any confidence. He doubted he could even swing the thing without toppling, but he held the weapon at his side, where it shivered. Garl's chest heaved. His heart thumped. His lower leg thrummed with unspent energy, and he wanted badly to run, to bolt—or swing— for the forest beyond the plains. Find a small village somewhere and become forgotten. The sound of the cobbler marching across the floorboards above drew Garl's anxious attention. What worried him the most were the sounds he couldn't identify. Several times, he thought he heard voices beyond the cellar door.

The Sons. The Sons *knew.* Of that, the former beggar

was certain. Those torturous hellpups knew Strach had been murdered, and they hunted Borchus and Garl. Memories tormented Garl of how Strach punished street filth like him, of how Strach laughed when he stabbed his victims—and the blood, oh, sweet Seddon, the *blood*. Garl wasn't unaccustomed to violence. He'd made a life of it in the arena, but that was sport. What Strach did was simply… *evil*. It wasn't a man who inflicted such pain and misery upon the weak and hungry. It was a monster wearing a man's skin.

Something crashed to the floor above Garl's head, and he whimpered. His head bunched into his shoulders, and he lifted the blade up as if it would ward off evil. Muted gibberish permeated the planks, even a short laugh. The laugh was the worst. Strach would bray laughter as he drew a knife across a person's bare belly. Garl shuddered at the horrors his memories conjured and wrung the sword's hilt even harder. He waited, expecting a second clatter any moment. Perhaps the Sons were above him, torturing the cobbler for information.

Garl wouldn't blame him if he talked. He wouldn't blame him in the least.

Garl held his breath, hearing scratching at the cellar door. Eyes near ready to pop from his skull, he waited for the door to fly open and bodies to tumble through, charging into the depths that stank of that Saimon-cursed salve Borchus smeared over himself. The Sons would find Garl at the back and swarm him. Maybe he'd strike one down if he swung in time, but in the end, the Sons would have him. And they'd punish him.

Garl waited and waited, his ears cocked and straining to hear, his tongue lapping at the cold sweat coating his upper lip. The drumming of his heart became footsteps. The churning of his stomach became evil whispers.

Nothing came through the door. Garl didn't relax. It was obvious. They wanted him to come *out*.

Gulping and hearing his throat click, Garl whimpered and clamped a hand over his mouth. More voices overhead, no doubt the treacherous cobbler explaining that *yes, they were down there. Just wait for them to come out.* In the dark, Garl rubbed his face as he mouthed another anguished oath.

They'd take him easily. And they'd torture him. They wouldn't have to torture him for long because, truth be known, Garl would give Borchus up right there and then in exchange for a quick death. He would scream out everything he knew about the agent because they were the *Sons of Cholla.*

His throat constricting, eyes watering, and sinuses drooling, Garl slid to the base of the floor, letting his crutches fall with the barest rattle. His hands shook—actually shook—with fright, raw and unchecked. He swore he felt his hair whitening.

Shadows flickered across the lines of light outlining the cellar door.

They'd found him. Garl knew it. There was no escape.

But then he realized he had Borchus's shortsword, an old length of well-used steel that might have trouble cutting butter, but it certainly had sliced Strach's miserable carcass. Garl wondered if the weapon retained enough of an edge to cut his own throat, or if its point would pierce the soft flesh under his chin.

The light fluttered again.

Seddon above. Garl decided the Sons would not corner or capture him. Not ever again.

He held his escape in his hands. He hefted the sword, took a deep steadying breath, and with a boyish sob, placed the weapon's point beneath his chin.

The light tracing the cellar door remained unbroken…

Muscles tensed, Garl waited for it to open.

*

Before mid-afternoon, Naulis walked down the crowded lane hedged in by low houses, sometimes disappearing among clusters of people. Borchus tracked the man. He quickly scanned the figures and faces behind the messenger, ensuring that he wasn't followed.

In short time, Naulis arrived at the alcove.

"Were you followed?" the agent asked.

"By who?"

"Nothing. Never mind. Any news?"

"The one called Brozz is scheduled to fight the day after tomorrow. The Madea said he was waiting for the house's decision on the blood matches."

No surprise there. "That's all?"

"All he would tell me," Naulis said. "Right and proper hole, that place that is. And the smell…"

Borchus held up a hand. "Forget that. Who's Brozz scheduled to fight?"

"A gladiator called Zilos from the House of Tilo."

The House of Tilo. The mention of the name chilled Borchus. *My old friends.*

"Anything wrong?" Naulis asked, sensing something amiss.

"Nothing. Right, then. You're on your way to the villa right now with that very information. Inform the house. Tell them I don't have any information on Zilos, but I'll attempt to find out who he is. Find out if they have any reports for me. Now hurry. I'll meet you here tomorrow at noon. Understood?"

"Understood."

"Good man." Borchus sent him on his way. He waited before venturing out into the streets, wondering about his next move. He hated to think what his choices might actually be. In the end, he decided that this day was the same as any other, except there was the very real possibility of men hunting him. And he'd be much more careful of alleys and side streets at night. A dull, painful throbbing reminded him of his near-fatal stabbing.

Taking his time, Borchus did his best to blend into the crowds.

16

The flickering brazier hypnotized Arrus for long moments. He sat on his cot—the only other thing in the cage—with his back to the far wall, facing the line of light. A small wooden bucket of water lay inside the bars to the left of a slot just big enough to slide the container through. The cot possessed one blanket and nothing else, but compared to his previous accommodations, this was a vast improvement.

Arrus scratched at his beard. Scratched at his crotch. He wished he could have left the gnats behind.

Outside his cell, voices babbled in that unknown Sunjan tongue. Attempting to understand the language exhausted him. He quickly isolated and remembered the few words he heard most often but didn't know what they meant. He'd try them sometime, perhaps on a jailor. Balazz had appeared earlier that morning, making his rounds with a few others Arrus didn't recognize. He remembered the big jailor from the other dungeon. He might have been a man once, but Arrus didn't like the gleam in Balazz's eyes. The jailor looked upon his prisoners like pieces of meat in need of cutting. Runson prowled about as well. Balazz once stood next to Runson, discussing matters in that maddening language of theirs, dressed in the same garb all jailors seemed to wear. Runson was a big man, but Balazz towered over him almost a full head taller and just as powerful. The jailor had no definition in his musculature as a ruddy layer of fat covered it all, but anyone could tell Balazz was an intimidating ogre of a lad. He'd chosen his profession well.

"Anyone there?" a voice yelled in Nordish.

It took Arrus a moment to realize he'd understood the language. He bucked off the cot, springing for the cell door.

"I'm here." His eyes searched. A hairy face not two cells away turned and brightened.

"Arrus, this where you landed?" the man called Heelslik asked, his shaggy head offering a rare smile.

"It is. Good to see you."

"And you."

"Where are the others?"

"I don't know," Heelslik admitted. "This place is big. Maybe another section or level. They only just moved me here."

Arrus nodded. The prisoner occupying that very cell had talked to Balazz last night. The message had been lost upon him, but the tone was one of madness. The fearsome jailor had stopped before the cell door and regarded the insane man like an annoying dog. Balazz had unlocked the cage and entered. Arrus remembered a short but violent scuffle before a squeal erupted—then nothing.

Balazz eventually emerged and strolled away as if in a garden. The cell door had remained open in his wake. A short time later, a pair of underlings had dragged the dead man past Arrus's cell, the head rattling upon the uneven floor. Arrus remembered the head twisted all the way around and how stone tiles peeled back lips.

A burst of angry Sunjan echoed along the corridor, and the Nordish men paused.

"That sounded important." Heelslik winked.

"Have you picked up any of the language yet?" Arrus asked.

"Not really. A few words perhaps. Un-fit. Ah… piss-her?" Heelslik thought about it. "Dog blos-som."

"That last one seemed interesting."

"I don't think it is."

A Sunjan appeared behind the bars of the cell located just next to Heelslik's. The prisoner shouted and offered a ruined smile. When the Nordish didn't answer, the Sunjan's tone changed, as did his temper. He ranted at the pair and ended with a stomach-turning gob of spit lobbed onto the floor.

Heelslik chuckled at the outburst. "I have a friendly neighbor, it seems."

Arrus smiled, appreciating his countryman's humor. "If we live long enough, perhaps we'll learn a few Sunjan words to share with the man."

"With that miserable curnos?"

Arrus chuckled. "It's very good to see you, Heelslik."

"Hm, well, we'll see how good it is after a week of my conversation. I bore myself very quickly."

"I don't believe you."

"You say that now. I'll remind you in a week."

"Will we be alive then?"

Heelslik quieted. "Good question. No idea. By the grace of Ivus, we might, if we fight and live. We're in the Sunjans' arena. We're not here to visit."

"You think they'll make us fight?"

"Make?" Heelslik chuckled. "Not me. I'll gladly limb these Sunjan bastards all day and every one after that. Whoever they put in front of me—as long as he's not Nordish. I'm not particular. I hope they have a few Sujins waiting for us. At least that will be a challenge."

Arrus didn't share the Jackal's view.

"Do you hear any hammering?" Heelslik asked.

"No."

"Sometimes, I do. Hear a hammering. Metal being pounded upon. Fashioned. There might be a smithy nearby."

"Or a length of iron just being straightened," Arrus offered.

"Yes. That could be."

"I think you're right," Arrus said. "We're here to either fight or be butchered. I'm sure this is the hole, however."

That quieted Heelslik. "The what?"

"The hole. That's what the Sunjans call this place."

"They call it a hole?"

"I think."

"Strange name for an arena."

Laughter erupted across the way, harsh and evil.

"Not very flattering," Heelslik continued, ignoring the outburst, "but I suppose it fits. And they *are* Sunjans, which is reason enough."

Another babble of angry syllables issued from the cell next to Heelslik's. The imprisoned Nord paused until the words stopped, but his once-friendly expression darkened into something unforgiving. Arrus didn't really know the man beyond sharing a few words around a campfire, but Heelslik had survived the Sunjan wilds for a long time. Kra had spoken briefly about him, calling him a good warrior to have at one's back.

That look, however, suggested that Heelslik had two sides to him, the friendly one and the one that would lop a man's face off his skull.

"He doesn't like our talking," Heelslik commented, still making hateful eyes toward the cell door. "That's unfortunate. For him."

"Unfortunate for many," another voice said in roughly accented Nordish, from two cells farther down.

The words caught both Arrus and Heelslik off-guard.

"You speak Nordish?" Heelslik peered in that direction.

"I speak Nordish." A pale face appeared at the bars of his cage door. "It's been a long time, however."

"You're a Norseman." Arrus recognized the accent as

belonging to Norjos—the small but populous country situated on Nordun's northeastern border, a semi-frozen timberland that barred the way to the fractured Ice Kingdoms. The two countries shared the same tongue, heritage, and interests, but the Norsemen possessed a rougher, thicker accent that some Nordish characterized as noble yet barbaric.

"Aye that," the man from Norjos said. "You're Heelslik, and you're Arrus. Well met. I'm called Rullik."

Greetings followed.

"You were the one that laughed a time ago." Arrus tried to separate shadows from Rullik's heavily bearded face. The Norseman's pale head was bald, marred only by a few scraggly wisps of hair.

Rullik chuckled softly. "It was, Nordish. It was. You're in the *Pit*—Sunja's *Pit*—though I've often heard it called a hole. Not in the Nordish tongue, you understand, but that's how it is with most languages. They have different-*sounding* words, but the meaning is the same as our own. And with the same… ah… power."

"You speak Sunjan?" Heelslik asked.

At that point, the vocal Sunjan next to Heelslik's cell rushed the bars and unleashed a hot stream of sounds.

Rullik barked back in that foreign tongue, and the Sunjan quieted almost immediately, surprising Arrus and Heelslik.

"What did you say to him?" Heelslik asked.

"That he'd best quiet down, else they—meaning you—would paw their way into your cell and eat your tongue straight from your head."

"Blessed Curlord," Arrus whispered while a huge smile split Heelslik's face. "I like you already, Norseman."

"It shut his mouth," Rullik observed. "But in truth, he's not the smartest. He'll start swearing again once he thinks things through. Sunjans. It's a wonder they lasted this long in your war."

"How long have you been here?" Arrus asked.

"Ah, long enough to learn the language."

"Then why are you here?"

Rullik looked at the ceiling and sighed, the sound mournful. "I'm a thief by trade. Not a soldier. And I robbed the wrong people."

"Sunjans?" Heelslik asked.

"Merchants," Rullik clarified. "Sunjan merchants. With exceptional Harudin mercenaries' protection. It's a long and terrible, terrible story. I'll tell you sometime."

"We have plenty of time now."

"Suppose that's true. And it might be the only time. You're half-right, Heelslik. We're in Sunja's Pit to fight to the death as long as we draw breath. I've heard the jailors speak of it. The Sunjans are in the thick of the blood-sport season, and it seems their pig bastard of a king wishes to clean out his dungeons."

"So that's it," Arrus said.

Rullik agreed with a barely audible grunt. Their conversation lagged, the silence filled with ghostly Sunjan voices, close and far, engaged in their own conversations.

"That's it," Rullik repeated, resigned to his fate.

"We suspected as much," Heelslik said.

Arrus felt his stomach drop, and his eyes studied the floor.

"Don't worry, Nordish," Rullik said. "After all, you'll die killing Sunjans, your sworn enemies of twenty years or more. You'll get to face them upon the sands in single combat, one last chance—perhaps even several—to send as many of those ass lickers to their death as you can." The Norseman's face brightened. "Personally, I can't think of a better ending to my life."

Rullik's words brought a smile to Heelslik's face.

And Arrus had to admit, his blood quickened at the idea.

17

There was a time when, upon entering the city of Sunja, anxiety gripped Grisholt's perfumed person, a dreadful, buckling pressure that tortured him ahead of the day's competition, knowing that his gladiators had been prepared by his trainers to the best of their ability but that their stock *still* paled in comparison to their opponents. His own financial woes weighed heavily on his wagers, forcing him to lose fights to simply keep his father's stable alive. Word had gotten out, as reported to him by his right hand and bodyguard, Brakuss. Even the other owners knew his real worth in the games and no doubt laughed at him.

Now, however, times were changing. Grisholt sensed the momentum shifting, gathering behind his stable. His men, their egos and spirits usually inflated with good—but false—bravado, sensed it as well.

The Stable of Grisholt had halted its losing ways. Their fortunes were turning for the better. No longer did unease plague Grisholt while passing through Sunja's gates. Excitement replaced his doubts. With the aid of the Sons of Cholla and their heavenly potion, victory had returned to the stable like a sun finally beating its way through an overcast sky.

Victory, the messenger from the Sons had called it—and rightly so.

Grisholt had thought to use the potion sparingly, but his mind had changed since yesterday's fight, especially after his agent Caro had requested Brakuss and a few more guards to help him transport the sizeable winnings from the Domis. The amount of coin won from Kossa's match had *astounded* Grisholt. He'd barely contained his excitement in front of his men. The immense sum had set his skin and soul tingling, his mind racing. Never before had wagering returned such a bounty.

And he realized the potential for so much *more*.

At first, he'd decided that discretion with the potion's use was best. It seemed the sensible path, the careful path. Stay low, secretive, and selective in choosing who swigged that foul concoction. After Kossa's win, temptation got the better of him. Greed sank its claws into his mind.

And, truth be known, with victories delivered to the stable by Kossa and Barros, just how *secretive* could he remain? He'd try. He told himself he'd try. But the urge to have his fighters wreak havoc remained. The yearning for more riches tested his willpower.

On this day, two of his lads were slated to fight. Barros was one. The House of Razi had lost little time in calling for a blood match. Perhaps the sting of losing to Grisholt's stable was too much to bear. Best to correct that loss before it drove old Razi mad. Unfortunately, fate would not be kind to the third-line house. Grisholt did not intend Barros to lose, not to Razi. The punce. The potential coin to be won guaranteed Barros would, once again, partake of the Sons' potion.

Grisholt stared out the koch's window. Faces and figures blurred against a background of houses and taller buildings, but he didn't take any further stock of Sunja's sights. He held an old but still usable goblet from his mother's collection and sipped Sunjan mead. Mead today, but firewater lingered at the back of his mind, as did perfumed water other than lavender. He suspected his lads didn't approve of that particular kind. He wore the best clothing left to him, fully intending to add to his wardrobe. A rosy vest of satin covered a black shirt. Beige breeches hid his legs, complemented by high leather boots of worn but distinguished-looking leather. Grisholt paused with his drink and inspected his boots. Perhaps he'd flick a coin in Marrok's direction and see if the cook could put a shine to the leather.

The koch stopped just outside of the city's bay, and Grisholt's head rose. He glimpsed Caro moving around the corner of the lead wagon, toward the koch's door. Grisholt pulled the shutters closed and waited for the knock.

"Enter," he said when Brakuss rapped on the wood.

Caro climbed aboard with a huff. The agent seemed

brighter in recent days, as did they all, but Grisholt still couldn't gaze upon the once-gladiator's hard features for too long—not with a belly full of mead.

"Master Grisholt," he greeted.

"Caro. Thank you for not keeping me waiting."

"When have I ever kept you waiting?"

"Never comes to mind at the moment, but I am halfway through a bottle of mead."

Caro glanced at the bottle. Grisholt could have offered his agent a drink, except he didn't have a second goblet. A pity.

"Well, then." Grisholt drained his last mouthful and placed the cup in a nearby slot. He pawed at a red cushion until his fingers hooked an edge. He pulled the cushion away, revealing the wooden underside and uncovering the koch's private latrine. Rolling back the sleeve of his shirt, he reached in and pulled forth a small cloth sack, much larger than the usual leather purse he kept there.

"That's quite the sight," Caro exclaimed softly.

Grisholt handed it over and replaced the cushioned lid.

"And a weight. How much is there?"

"Five hundred," Grisholt stated with a poised smile and shifted his bottom.

Caro paused in mid-heft and regarded the sack and his employer.

"Two of the lads will accompany you to the Domis," Grisholt informed the agent. "For added protection. Five hundred. A pleasantly *rounded* figure, wouldn't you agree? When I considered the match today, I said to myself, I said…'Borl, the odds are against us this time.' That set my mind in motion. With Razi looking for blood, he'll send his best after Barros. All the managers know this. The audience will know this. And even though the stable has been victorious recently, sentiment will attribute our good fortune to luck. Thus, what better opportunity to truly empty the pockets of whoever wagers against us, hm?"

Caro had no reply, so Grisholt continued. "Don't worry. When we win, I'll have the lads accompany you. I daresay—no, I *expect* the coin to be considerable, enough to raise some interest."

"Perhaps too much interest."

"For the future, yes," Grisholt admitted with a frown. "But not today. The arena still doesn't respect the Stable of Grisholt. I believe they will, eventually, but not this day. As such, the time is ripe to win a fortune. A *fortune*, Caro. It's been a very long time since I've held a fortune in my hands. And here." He handed over a leather purse. "Take this. Pay yourself first and then whatever you usually give your spies. Place your own wagers, if you wish."

The hefty weight in this hand caused Caro to place the sack to one side. He glanced at the coin, and a rough smile split his face.

Grisholt answered with a smirk, his fingers playing in the ashen wisps of his beard.

"A fortune, good Caro. A *fortune*." He looked at a shuttered window. "Many consider these games to be of spikes and edges, of blood and consequences. They're only partially correct. Truth be known, these games are all about coin. Coin is the lifeblood, more so than bone and flesh, more so than skill and spirit. Coin—*gold*—draws us here, much more than the spectacle of butchery. There is nothing foul or distasteful about any of that… I just want my portion."

Grisholt flicked a finger across his nose and met his agent's eyes. "Place the wagers upon our lads. Both of them. We'll collect at the end of the day. Don't worry about our… benefactors. Brakuss will alert them."

"Anything else?" Caro asked.

"I was about to ask you the very same."

"I've nothing to report."

As Grisholt expected. Caro did his job quite well, and the lads slated to face Grisholt's were known to them all. It would have been helpful if perhaps one of them had sustained an injury while training or even during a match. With the potion, however, Grisholt didn't think any extra information would be needed.

"Then I'll see you after the day's matches."

Taking his cue, Caro nodded and opened the koch door. Once it was closed behind him, the vehicle lurched into motion, and Grisholt cracked open a window, eying a few overhead lines of festive streamers. He shook the bottle at his side.

Enough for one more drink.

*

His name was Jonca, and he waited at the base of stairs leading up to the closed portcullis. The gatekeeper stood by idly, an older man with a beard so unruly, it reminded the pit fighter of shredded washrags or sacks with the bottoms frayed away. The thin iron mask of Jonca's helm hid his smile.

The House of Razi had charged Jonca with avenging Shoor's death. Jonca didn't know what had gotten into the likes of Grisholt's lads. Like any good pit fighter, he kept abreast of the history of all the houses in the blood sport. Despite collecting a deplorable record of wins and losses last year, Grisholt had still somehow managed to have his stable listed as a second-line house, a feat of magic many believed Grisholt had purchased with whatever gold he might have remaining in his coffers. The stable rarely killed anyone in the games, simply because they couldn't afford the wrath of the opposing houses or schools. Even the Free Trained might cause the stable trouble if one actually managed to kill a pit fighter under Grisholt's roof.

Yet, here Jonca was, seeking to avenge a friend's death, a friend slaughtered by a fighter from a stable of questionable history and reputation.

Jonca listened to the Orator overhead, introducing him. He inspected his chainmail vest and the various slabs of metal protecting his limbs. Jonca heard the crowds cheer his name, but he knew their fickle nature all too well. Thus far, he'd managed to stay undefeated this season, with five victories credited to his name. Old Razi knew—Seddon bless his fat belly—that Jonca would want the blood match against Barros, a man whose life was about to be as fleeting as an unfit stream of dog piss.

Old Razi knew.

Jonca lowered his head. He held his long-shafted mace across his pelvis. The weapon bristled with spikes filed to lethal points. He flexed fingers encased in metal gauntlets, the knuckles rippling with shiny pyramids. Jonca had crushed bones and taken five lives over the course of his career. Old Razi didn't have to tell him to take one more. He fully intended to rip it from Barros's chest.

At thirty-one, Jonca had stood against some of the best in the sport. He'd fought fellow Sunjans, Vathians, Pericians, and every other nation that had sent a son to the games. In the off-season, he felled trees until it was time to report for training. He had a pretty wife and two children. When he finally became too old to fight, he imagined he'd take to chopping down trees and selling them to mills. His wife, perhaps like all wives unfortunate enough to be married to pit fighters, pleaded with him at the beginning of each season not to fight, to find something else.

The Pit called him back, however. It always called him back.

This time, Sunja's Pit wanted him to exact revenge for an old friend, and Jonca would not fail. So he shut away his wife's cries. He didn't think of his children's worried faces.

The Orator finished his introduction.

Shrugging shoulders that topped the heads of most men, Jonca watched as the portcullis rattled open. Taking steps three at a time, he went forth to kill a man.

The crowd *oooooohed* when he stepped into the glare of

the sun, his towering size impressing all who laid eyes upon his bulk. He regarded them once, unmoved by their vocal enthusiasm, and settled against the portcullis.

A roar blasted the air, making Jonca squint in grim amusement. They'd all seen and heard this before.

A brief shower of sparks flickered as something struck the portcullis from the inside. A hand appeared underneath the lower timbers and heaved, actually lifting the heavy gate up a fraction. Such a feat of strength had amazed Razi the first time. Jonca had been beside the owner and witnessed it firsthand. Barros had displayed incredible power.

But Jonca was strong too, and he meant to inflict that strength upon his opponent.

Not waiting for the portcullis to fully rise, Barros ducked under the lower edge and straightened. A pot helm masked his features. A vest of studded leather stretched over his chest. He bellowed once again, stunning the audience with his ferocity. He brandished a long-shafted war hammer and not the sword-and-shield combination from before.

It didn't matter to Jonca. Unable to wait any longer, he hefted his mace and walked toward his opponent.

Livid with frightening energy, Barros sighted him and charged. Great chuffs of sand flew with every step. Each expulsion of breath was an enraged squawk.

Jonca angled his shoulders toward the attacker and cocked his heavy weapon to his shoulder, ready for that almighty first swing. He smiled at the inevitable contact.

The pot helmet lifted with another beastman shriek, and for a heartbeat, Jonca thought he glimpsed madness filling a set of wide black eyes.

He swung his mace. Barros swung his war hammer.

The two heavy weapons crossed in a deafening *clang*, the impact causing both combatants to tremble. The jarring contact rushed up Jonca's arms, and he experienced something he'd never felt before: a force greater than his own.

Jonca staggered to the side, hooking Barros's war hammer while he attempted to recover. Barros recovered faster, however, much faster than Jonca had anticipated.

The Grisholt pit fighter yanked his weapon free with a grunt, almost ripping Jonca's mace from his grip. Jonca fell back as Barros swung for his head. Jonca parried with his mace, but the war hammer's momentum drove the spiked ball back into his mask. The visor crumpled, crushing his nose in a spurt of red.

Jonca's legs buckled, leaving time for Barros to smash his foe's head to one side, the connection ringing over the hot sands. Jonca dropped to a knee.

Barros's war hammer swept over his shoulder and down like the arc of a wicked moon and squashed Jonca's helmet. Blood gushed from underneath the metal. Jonca teetered long enough for Barros to reset his swing and, with a scream of unchecked insanity, attempt to take the dying man's head clean off.

*

Grisholt cringed with evil delight as Barros's war hammer crunched into Jonca's face visor, backing the head up upon shoulders before slamming the entire torso to the ground. The impact didn't decapitate the gladiator, but Grisholt was both horrified and astonished all the same.

"He nearly took his head off," Brakuss muttered nearby.

"That man," Grisholt said as he massaged his throat, "was dead from the first blow. Just didn't realize it."

On the sands, Barros roared, demanding *more*—more opponents to kill. He stomped around the unmoving carcass filling the middle of the arena, waving his hammer as if fighting ghosts. He punctuated his rage by pounding the body even more, splaying the dead man across the arena floor like a bleeding warning to all. The audience drew back, fearful of attracting his attention.

In time, however, Barros tired. His shouting lessened. His curses became gasps. His arms dropped, and he looked around as if awakening from a dream. He quieted and, with barely a word, walked unsteadily to the rising portcullis.

"He's spent." Grisholt tugged on his beard. "Brakuss, send two lads to help him back."

Brakuss did as instructed.

Voices cheered the victorious gladiator, a few at first, then more. The sound distracted Grisholt. He stood at the arched window, drinking down the people's growing enthusiasm, an icy smile spreading across his face. The Pit damn near vibrated with applause, praising the brutal death. A warm tingle overcame Grisholt, and he knew his stable had just crossed a threshold. No longer would they be laughed at behind closed doors. In the stands and alehouses and taverns, his name would be spoken with a genuine awe. And perhaps even fear.

Grisholt wanted that. More than anything.

Then he remembered the five hundred gold pieces upon Barros's head. *Five hundred gold pieces.* Sweet Seddon above, the potential winnings stunned him as effectively as a blow from Barros's hammer. He was rich.

Rich.

The word crashed down upon his senses and lit up his brain. Better food, more servants, women, and drink. Firewater and perfumed water. Clothing. Everything and more. *More!* All the luxuries denied him because of dismal finances. No longer.

His gaze came to rest upon the iron flask. His thoughts whirled with extravagant possibilities. When his men returned with the exhausted Barros, Grisholt smiled broadly.

"Well done," he said, hiding his excitement. "Well done, indeed. Brakuss. Get Olibo ready for his match."

"He gets a taste?" That was what the one-eyed gladiator had come to call the Sons' potion.

"He does indeed get a taste." Grisholt turned to the waiting gladiator set to fight three matches later. "You're willing to partake, of course?"

Olibo nodded eagerly.

"Excellent," Grisholt said, nearly trembling. "You

know the effects and the aftereffects?"

"I do." Olibo, a stout Sunjan, nodded as he spoke. He reminded Grisholt of an energetic hound anxious to please.

"Excellent, excellent." And with that, Grisholt turned his attention back to a wasted Barros. "Get him some water. Watch over him. He's—"

Three short, hard blows struck the door to the private viewing chamber, rattling the wood and startling everyone. Grisholt didn't know what to make of the interruption, and he glanced from face to face. He eventually signaled the nearest gladiator to see who had come knocking.

In strode a red-faced, bulbous Razi, of the House of Razi.

Facing his unexpected visitor, Grisholt's brow lifted in a question. "Razi, this is unexpected."

"*Unexpected?*" Razi spat. "You've killed two men of mine! Saimon's dry crack, what are you trying to do? You know as well as I how expensive it is to train one of these louts! What are you *doing?*"

Two of Razi's men stood in the doorway, armed and with swords in scabbards. Brakuss and the five other pit fighters tensed, watching the armed visitors for any aggressive moves—not that Grisholt expected any. He studied Razi's ruddy features, his loose white robes that draped him from shoulders to ankles. The red vest hung open, allowing his boulder-shaped belly unrestricted room to bounce.

"I'm truly saddened by your—"

"You don't know what saddened *means*, you ass-packing topper," Razi snarled, dispelling the words. "Don't try to butter your words. I'll not stand for it. Know this: if it's a war you want, it's a war you'll have. A war, Grisholt. A right and proper *war!*"

The raging fat man's perfectly round eyes almost popped from their sockets. He jabbed a finger at Grisholt and his gladiators. "You think you can kill off my dogs without consequences? There are always consequences. *Always.* I'll make it my personal hobby to ensure you suffer from here to the end of the season."

Grisholt smiled calmly in the face of Razi's storm. "Come now, good Razi. It's blood sport. You wouldn't be here—"

"If you were Dark Curge?" Razi stuck out a chin and took two steps toward Grisholt, violating the edge of his personal space. "Is *that* what you're about to say? You're right. I wouldn't be here. If it had been one of Curge's butchers, I would've stayed well and clear of the man. But it's *not* Curge. It's *you*. And you're the most underhanded and shifty slip of gurry these games have ever known. You're the foul crust on the lip of a pisspot, the piss stain upon the front of a drunk's breeches. Just being in your presence turns my guts, but I wanted to see your face today. Next time, *you'll* feel the pinch of losing one of your dogs. Not me! And I'll not stop there. From here on, my fighters will look to decorate my mantle with the heads of yours—one by one—just so you feel the bleed."

Grisholt's mood darkened. "Leave, Razi. You've had

your say. When you send another of your bastards after one of mine, you'll see what I think of today's visit."

"I look forward to it! Oh, I intend to make my thoughts known to the Madea immediately."

That almost made Grisholt laugh, but he suppressed it and caught Brakuss's eye. "See this unfit honeypot to the door."

Razi's cheeks quivered at the jab, but he realized he stood within Grisholt's quarters, where the man possessed greater numbers.

"I'll have my revenge. I'll have my revenge!" the heavyset owner shouted. Brakuss herded him into the corridor.

Grisholt inhaled and showed his back to the departing Razi. The open arch of the window framed the arena attendants dragging Jonca's body out of sight. Heat shimmers warped the air, suggesting it was all a dream. Grisholt hoped not.

"Another day, Grisholt!"

The slamming door cut off the words.

Grisholt lost himself in the delightful thoughts of what awaited at the Domis. Razi's rant had failed to move him. He didn't mind having an open enemy within the Pit, especially one of Razi's quality. It might even draw more interest to the fights and make every loss sting all the more. Not that Grisholt intended to lose, not to that overflowing shite trough.

He caressed the iron flask and tapped the stopper with a single finger. "Razi, Razi," Grisholt muttered. "You'll regret your visit."

His thoughts returned to all the coin he'd just won and the potential gold Olibo would bring.

18

Torello punished the practice man, savaging the wooden frame with strike after battering strike. Dents appeared upon the outstretched arms and trunk. Fibers splintered and flew. Sweat fell from Torello's slick torso with each connection, and he paused at times to violently shake his black hair. When he did stop, he took a quick moment to refocus, scarred features set and stern, before resuming smashing the target.

"Flow," Machlann bawled over the barrage. "Flow, I say! *Eeeeee,* one murderous strike to the other. Take off that *arm,* take off that *head,* but Seddon squeeze my bells and make me sing, *flow* from one to the other. If you aren't flowing, change the strike that's hindering the combination, and start anew. Don't make me repeat myself, my missuses! Change it, and Saimon take you, *work* it. Until your arm drops off. Until your legs feel dead. Work! Only then will it benefit you. Only then will your body remember of its own accord, and when you're in the Pit, slashing for that leg or chopping for that arm, your own limbs will move as if possessed by hellions. *Hellions!*"

Machlann stopped alongside Torello and watched with furrowed brow, gauging the pit fighter's every motion. And surprisingly, instead of saying something entirely saucy to the trainer, Torello labored on, smashing the practice man and making the frame shiver.

"Shorten up your stance," Machlann instructed. "Mind the extension. Keep at it. Pretend it's that sorry shagger who took Kolo's life, the same unfit rat-pig-bastard you'll be paddling to death 'afore long. *Eeee*, whatever gives you push. *Eeee*."

The trainer walked to Brozz.

Sitting on his mat, Muluk shook his head at the exchange. He watched Torello increase his pace, slamming the target until…

Seddon above. That lad's sword's going to—

Torello unleashed a flurry of strikes into the practice frame, breaking his sword on the fourth blow. The shattered piece spun end over end and landed in the sand. The connection turned the trainers' heads.

"Shattered that slab, did you, my missus?" Machlann yelled.

Sweating, glowering, Torello kept his thoughts to himself.

"Well, go get *another* one, my furious he-bitch, unless you *like* standing there like one fishhooked through both bells. Break five more like that, and I'll personally make arrangements for a keg of your favorite."

Surly but keeping his tongue under control, Torello walked off to a nearby rack for a replacement.

Muluk giggled in unchecked disbelief before he covered his mouth. Machlann wasn't so bad when one was watching from a ways back. In fact, the man was belly-shaking comical at times. Muluk didn't say this aloud, however. Nor did he ever want any of the lads seeing him chuckle at the raw storm Machlann rained down upon them. Though Muluk no longer trained, he had no doubt if Machlann caught him with anything more than a smile on his face, he'd hear about it. Damnation, the trainer would probably unleash hellfire upon him. It was wiser—*safer*—not to draw the trainer's attention.

The Kree lowered his head in an effort to hide the rumbling laugh in his belly. He realized that Pig Knot had been gone for quite a long time. A *very* long time. It was nearing evening. That seemed odd to Muluk, so he struggled to his feet, embracing the aches and pains of his healing carcass. The open door of the living quarters beckoned, so he lumbered inside. Tables and benches filled the common area but nothing else.

"Pig Knot?" Muluk studied the chamber for clues. The door that led to the sleeping quarters lay open. Slanting beams of light pierced the shadows.

"Pig Knot?"

Muluk unconsciously clenched his hands, feeling the skin stretch uncomfortably over the knuckles of his missing fingers. He leaned on the tables for support as he limped toward the open door. Dread enveloped the base of his skull and chilled his back. His stomach twisted and coiled as if he'd swallowed a snake.

Where was the Sunjan?

He hurried to the doorframe and leaned against it. Stitches pulled taut and gave warning. The chunk of meat cut from his shoulder burned at the press of wood, prompting him to straighten. Inside the corridor, warm air felt as dense as water. The curtain to Pig Knot's alcove had been drawn across.

"Are you sleeping? Pig Knot?"

Behind Muluk, Machlann's voice carried on, giving out instructions and reciting bits of wisdom from the arena. Muluk concentrated upon the curtain. A dull ringing started in his head, where his left ear had been removed and a knot of scabs remained. His forehead beaded sweat.

"You'd best be sleeping, you unfit topper," Muluk growled, half in humor and half in growing unease.

The curtain didn't move.

Muluk hobbled to the curtain and yanked it back.

Pig Knot lay on his cot and regarded him with a look of annoyance. "How can one sleep with your long tongue bawling?"

Relief flooded Muluk, and it showed on his face. "Well, answer me next time. Save me from wandering the halls like a mother."

"With a mother as ugly as you, perhaps I don't want to be found."

"Well, then," Muluk said, unable to parry that last jab. "If you're sleeping, I'll leave you be."

But the knife in Pig Knot's hand caught his attention.

"What?" Pig Knot asked.

"Nothing."

"You've something to say?"

"No. Well…"

Pig Knot waited, resting the knife upon the fading bruises of his toned belly. "You look like you've something to say."

Muluk hesitated. "Ah, we're nearly out of beer."

That put a poisoned look on Pig Knot's face.

"The young one," Muluk explained, "Ananda. She told me just a while ago when she brought another pitcher."

"Damnation."

"I thought so."

Pig Knot deftly flipped the knife to an underhand grip and punched it through blanket and straw. He left it hilt up and folded his hands across his stomach. Shouts reached them from beyond the walls.

"Is all well, Pig Knot?" Muluk asked with genuine concern. "With you?"

"No. Not really."

"What is it, then? That troubles you?"

"You'll think it foolish."

"You won't know for certain until you tell me."

Pig Knot considered it for several heartbeats. "I… miss the Zhiberian."

Muluk gave a rueful smile.

"What's that for?" Pig Knot demanded in annoyance. "Seddon's rosy ass, man, you asked."

"No, no, I understand," he managed. "The Zhiberian's a presence, certainly a character. It hasn't troubled me yet, but I imagine I'll be missing him as well. Soon enough. But he'll be returning."

"Perhaps."

"I think it's a better chance than perhaps."

Pig Knot studied the ceiling. "Have you ever wondered, Muluk, what it's all for?"

The unusually solemn question put Muluk on guard.

"What do you mean?"

"This. All of this. And… this." Pig Knot indicated the ceiling, the walls, and finally the stumps of his legs. "Before, I lived from day to day, season to season, and woman to woman. Never thought any further than the end of the week, and even that didn't happen often. Always thought about where the next few coins were coming from. And who I might have to break or kill to get them. Honorably, of course."

"Of course."

"But here I am. Finally. Cut up like a bad ham and left to rot in the sun."

Muluk blinked. "You're hardly rotting."

"But without purpose. I have no purpose anymore. I'm no use to anyone, unless it's emptying beer kegs so that fresh ones can be brought in. I don't even know why I'm still here. Goll doesn't need me."

"You helped establish this house," Muluk pointed out.

"You're a part of it."

"By losing on his orders." Pig Knot scoffed. "History won't remember me. I'm worthless, tortured by daily routines I should doing, not watching. Daresay it's only a matter of time before Goll realizes I'm a drain on his resources, a bother best cast out."

"I don't agree. He doesn't think that. Or like that. Goll might be many things, but…" Muluk couldn't finish the thought, so he started a new one. "Your …boredom is twisting your thoughts."

"You'll be fine," Pig Knot carried on. "You'll be looking after that smithy."

In answer, Muluk held up his crippled hand.

"Well then, he'll find you someone to help."

"So…" Muluk concentrated on the thread of thought. "Goll will help me… but he won't help you?"

"No. He won't."

"I'm not entirely certain why you might think that, but you're wrong."

The silence swelled, aching to burst.

"I'm tired, Muluk," Pig Knot whispered. "It's been almost two weeks for me like this, and I'm very, very tired."

The words worried the Kree. "You'll get used to it, Pig Knot. You'll get used to it and learn to live again. In time, you'll find a purpose. It might not be bashing heads and breaking bones or soldiering or guarding or whatever else you might've done. But you'll find it. And only you will recognize it for its worth."

Pig Knot didn't comment.

"Goll will *not* cast you out."

"I don't want to speak of it again."

"If you ever do…"

But Pig Knot shook his head.

Muluk hesitated, sensing the moment passing. He nodded and glanced to the common room. "Clavellus's cooks are bringing in the evening meal. Get some hot food into you, something other than drink."

"They're serving now?"

"Not quite now, but they're getting ready."

"I'll be along when they are."

Not wanting to depart, Muluk lingered for a short while then conceded and drew the curtain across.

He walked away.

He hoped the man would think about their short conversation. He hoped Pig Knot would feel better in the days to come. And he felt he spoke the truth about the Sunjan finding his purpose.

Whatever that might be.

*

"Well?" Goll asked Machlann after the gladiators had been dismissed for the day. Clavellus, still without a shirt, had been lured off of his balcony and lingered beneath it, along with the pair of trainers.

"Well," Machlann said, "the Perician is ready. That one could fight any number of matches in a single day, no doubt in my mind. Torello has certainly shown improvement. He's right and proper motivated to fight

Cota. Whether he can kill the man is another question."

"You believe he can?"

"I believe so. Koba and I will devise a strategy for Cota tomorrow and put Torello to it. Nothing fancy, considering the shortness of time. After that…"

Goll didn't like to think it was out of his hands.

"That's all?" Clavellus asked, red-eyed and unwell looking. His condition amused Machlann.

"Not a word, you gray bastard," the taskmaster grumped. "Nothing you haven't seen before."

The approach of the former Sujin named Clades disrupted the conversation. The guard led a man who appeared well and truly spent.

"Ah," Clavellus said. "Borchus has sent word."

Clades stopped just short of the gathering and indicated the messenger should start talking.

To his credit, Naulis quickly composed himself. "Masters of the House, Borchus sends word."

"Let's hear it, then," Goll said.

"Ah," Naulis began under the wilting gazes of Machlann and Koba. "The one called Brozz is scheduled to fight the day after tomorrow. He fights a warrior called Zilos from the House of Tilo. Borchus doesn't have any information about the fighter, but he will try to discover something. The Madea has informed me there are no other matches."

"The day after tomorrow?" Goll repeated.

"Aye that."

"Then that's when we'll have our blood matches."

"One moment," Clavellus said. "You said the Madea informed you. Borchus didn't speak with the Madea?"

"Not this time, no," Naulis replied.

"Why not?"

The messenger shook his head. "I don't know."

A look of confusion crossed Clavellus's face.

"When are you going back?" Goll asked.

"As soon as my horse has recovered."

"And you've had something to eat," Clavellus threw in. "Go on over to the living quarters. Clurik is my cook. Tell him to feed you."

Naulis brightened at the prospect.

"When you return," Goll said, handing a pair of coins to the messenger, "inform Borchus that we'll be in the city the day after tomorrow with Brozz as well as Torello and Junger. Tell him to make arrangements for the blood matches. Torello will fight Cota, and Junger will fight Bubruk. See me once more before you leave."

A revived Naulis took the coins and departed for his meal.

"Clades, have someone look after his horse," Clavellus ordered and sent the soldier off.

The remaining four men absorbed the news.

His blue eyes shone, and Machlann's great moustache barely moved when he spoke. "Well. Our first fight with a proper house."

"Our first fight with a proper house," Clavellus repeated, eyeing Naulis as he trudged toward the living quarters.

"And not the last."

19

The horse's short, chuffing strides set Halm's hips and hurts to aching practically as soon as he left the villa. His belly and lower ribs complained. The cuts and healing bones protested with Lish's every movement. The swaying of the saddle caused Halm to clench his jaw, and even that hurt. It occurred to him he'd been wise to leave so early in the morning before the day's heat truly cooked the land, but he wondered if a wagon might have been more comfortable, and a touch more stable, than noble Lish.

"Lish, you dish." Halm held the reins slack in his good hand. His left, the one Skulljigger had feasted upon, was wrapped in the same strip of cloth bandage from two days ago. Shan had been occupied with Pig Knot, and Halm felt the wound would take care of itself.

"Ever fight in an arena, Lish?" Halm stared across a high-growing sward of grass, imagining Sunja to be somewhere to the north. Picturing the city alleviated some of the pain. Not much, but it helped.

The horse ignored him.

"Well, you're fortunate, you ancient beast, you. You never had anyone try to take your head off. Not that I'm complaining. It's the life I chose, the profession I'm bound to. It's also the reason I'm so battered this morning. My own blossom feels like it's been split by someone's crusty boot. If you saw me all healed, you'd have a different opinion of me."

Lish's head bobbed as he trekked toward the face of the sun. His ears twitched, dislodging a black fly.

Halm leaned forward in the saddle, groaning softly as he did, and patted what horseflesh he could reach. Lish snorted at the contact.

"I'm not so good with animals, Lish, you painful dish."

Enjoying the name put a smile on his face. He thought it fitting, especially since the Dish might be deliberately making the ride uncomfortable for him.

"But if you can, I swear by Seddon's rosy red ass, I'll feed you whatever you want once we get to Karashipa if you would… just smooth the ride. Just a little. If you haven't noticed, I've been right and proper fishhooked."

No response. Perhaps he needed wine on this trip. Halm chided himself for not bringing along a bottle or two of something. The saddlebags would have held them. Missed opportunities, he thought, and pictured Pig Knot without his legs. That poor bastard. As well as he knew Pig Knot, Halm didn't know what the Sunjan would do with himself in the years to come. Perhaps, upon his return to Clavellus's estate, he'd find the man in better spirits.

If you return, a voice whispered in his skull.

"If I return," Halm said, drawing comfort in the sound of his own voice on such an empty plain. Clumps of trees grew from the tall grass, appearing small in the distance, but Halm had traveled this way before. He knew those beasts towered over himself and Lish. Lovely countryside, however. And a lovely day for traveling.

"If," Halm repeated, wondering what was hidden over the next rise—and the days to come.

"Stop. *Stop*, you ripe Saimon-spawned bastard. Seddon above, stop before I kill you."

At midmorning Halm drew back the reins and halted Lish. They had traveled westerly until joining with a southerly road, and were currently stopped on a narrow dirt strip. Halm bent over in the saddle, cringing, his miserable bulk hammered with long nails of agony. He was certain if he placed a hand to tender parts, he'd color his palm with blood. Worse, he knew the trip had barely begun. Breathing as if on the cusp of giving birth, he hauled one leg over Lish's back and slipped off the horse, groaning as he fell. His sandals slapped the earth, flattening grass and sending shots of agony up his thighs and torso. Halm swore softly at the flood of discomfort and leaned over to grab his knees.

"You wretched, unfit hellion." Halm dabbed fingers here and there and wondered if he leaked blood. When he straightened, he wished for a bottle of drink again and discovered he'd released Lish's reins.

The horse remained by his side.

"Well… good Lish." Halm panted and stroked the animal's neck. A sheen of sweat came away on his palm. He frowned and rubbed it off on his breeches while Lish's breathing slowed. The tall grass to the side of the road tempted the horse, and he nibbled on select strands. Halm took it upon himself to take a blanket from a saddlebag and wipe off the horse's sides, making a face as he did so. Seddon above, he thought, the horse sweated more than he did. When he finished, Halm regarded the blanket, gave it a tentative sniff, shrugged, and draped it over his shoulder. He glanced back into the shine of the sun and shied away from its hateful brilliance. The day had hardly begun. The heat would damn near kill them both later. Halm shook his head and wondered if he should have taken a wagon instead.

Lish chewed away contentedly. Halm chuckled despite his misery. The stable hand's words came to him, and he patted the horse's neck.

"Eat what you will. And when you're ready, we'll walk. Give you another chance at torturing my fat hide."

In a short time, they resumed walking.

Pebbles and dirt brushed his toes as Halm led the horse along. The stable hand had said to walk the animal often, and Halm decided he preferred walking. It wasn't as painful. The heat bore down upon his back and shoulders, slow-cooking his skin until he could smell it. A fly buzzed in his ear, prompting a violent shake of his head. He scanned the open plains, looking for other travelers, and sighted none.

Empty.

It had been a while since he'd been on his own. Halm felt the need to fill the quiet. "I imagine you've traveled this way quite a bit?"

Lish's noble head nodded with every step.

Halm figured that for a yes. "Good. Good. We're off to see a woman. See if she still remembers me. Seems she's been finding a way into my thoughts, and I'm one to wonder why, especially when it's about women—or a woman, in this case."

Lish's ears flickered, and Halm looked to the north. Some figures and perhaps a tall wagon traveled the road, seemingly floating above the grass. It took him a moment to realize they were traveling toward Sunja. Still, seeing people gladdened his heart.

"Women. When I was in a city, I was never without one for long. Had them all shapes and sizes, Lish my lad. All shapes and sizes. And personalities." Halm didn't mention the gold he'd had to pay for the company or the drinks to make them stay.

"Beauties every one," Halm said as the horse scuffed up dirt. "There was one whose blond hair reached well past her waist. Lovely personality. Very popular at one alehouse. I remember a pair of sisters, one red haired, the other dark, small enough to sit on either knee and cuddle. Seddon's heaven, Lish. If I think hard about it, I can remember their touch, the smell of the perfumed water they wore. Right and proper ladies."

The sound of something plopping caused Halm to stop and turn in time to see Lish dropping a cow kiss—or rather a *horse* kiss—into the dirt. The animal eyed the Zhiberian, challenging him to comment.

Halm made a sour face and continued walking.

The southern stretch of road remained empty of travelers, not even a bird, though he heard some calls. Halm looked ahead, searching for the westerly turn that would lead them to Karashipa.

"Seems longer than the last time. The lads and I came out here not two or three weeks ago. You should've been there. What a time we had. Oh, my. All got resolved in the end. That's where I met her: small village to the west. You'll see. And don't expect me to walk you the entire way. I'm only doing this to rest you. When you look ready, I'll climb back on that bony back of yours, and you can torture me again."

Halm chuckled. Here he was, having lengthy conversations with a horse. The lads would call him unfit for doing such a thing.

"As if I expect you to say anything. Though if you could, I imagine you have some interesting stories. Wouldn't you? Of riders and places... maybe a mare or two?"

Lish let slip another chunky stream into the road.

A pensive Halm turned back to the empty road.

"You do that a lot..."

The day baked man and horse as they traveled farther west. Halm walked the animal more than he rode it. The animal's gait became too painful for him to bear. Lish also labored in the growing heat, and Halm didn't want his only companion to suffer needlessly.

Around noon, Halm crossed a small, solid bridge spanning a brook. On the other side, he spotted a comfortable-looking clump of trees with the stream running beneath its generous shade. The flute sound of the slow waters convinced him it was time to rest. He led Lish off the road and noted the scuffed earth and grass around the bases of the tree trunks. Other travelers had stopped under the wide spread of leaves. As Halm inspected the spot, the smell of nearby water made his throat ache.

"Right here then." He halted Lish. "Right here. Get out of the heat of the day. Seddon above, I feel terrible. Drank a little too much yesterday, good Lish. Drank a little too much. Don't hate me for it. I'm paying now."

Halm kept a steadying arm over the horse's saddle and took deep breaths. Under the shade, the brook's waters flowed, flashing speckled rocks at the bottom. Halm left Lish and walked to the stream, rubbing his lower back.

"You've done this to me," he muttered, casting a vengeful look in Lish's direction. "I was fine this morning. I'm unfit, now. Unfit. All because of you."

At the water's edge Halm dropped to one knee and then the other, bending over as if in worship. He clutched at wet rocks and lowered his face into the shallow depths. The water's touch revived him to a degree, and he stayed that way, alternating between dunking his face and drinking.

"Seddon above, that's good," he said when he came up for air. "Sweet Seddon. Ah, that's so good."

A scuffing of hooves and a snort made him look to his right. There stood Lish, drinking and appearing in much better shape.

Halm splashed water over his head, neck, and back. He crawled away from the edge and eased his back against the trunk of a tree. With both legs splayed out before him, he sat and breathed and watched Lish.

"Drink your fill, and don't go far. I'll rest here for a while. We'll make Karashipa by evening. You'll see. Just as the sun is lying down on the lake, we'll get there. Take your time. Seddon's burning hole, I'll never drink again."

Halm closed his eyes.

The sun rested on the horizon when he woke. Halm groaned upon seeing that great blazing ball sinking into the grass, knowing full well he had slept too long. Lish stood a few strides away, watching, ears flickering.

"Well, this is a time." Halm sat up against the tree. "You could have woken me."

Lish blinked and looked away.

Halm sighed. The horse sauntered to the nearest grass, nibbling on the more attractive strands. Eating wasn't a bad idea, but Halm hadn't thought he'd be falling asleep in the middle of the day, and as a result, he hadn't brought anything with him. The evening sky bled red, blending into a deepening purple. Nothing moved besides Lish, and the calmness of the scene rendered the big Zhiberian speechless. He sniffed and scratched, realized he wasn't so uncomfortable, and decided to stay the night right where he was. He had no food but doubted he'd starve, not with the stores upon his hips and ribs.

"I'm good for at least a week." He rose to his feet and pulled the saddle from the horse's back.

"There, in case you decide to lie down for the night. I don't understand how you beasts can stay standing for such a long time. Don't your legs get tired?"

Lish ignored him.

Halm was getting used to it. If he had any treats, he figured the animal wouldn't leave him alone.

"Eat," he said to the horse. "Drink and stay close by. Don't leave me during the night."

Lish made no promises.

Grunting, Halm walked into the tall grass and relieved himself of the water he'd drunk earlier. When he returned, he placed the saddle on ground not veined with roots. He lay down, slowly, cursing the pain in his sides and joints. He folded the blanket into a thin pillow, covered the saddle with it, and got as comfortable as he could with his head at the base of the tree.

The color slowly left the sky. The smell of the stream mixed with the moist heat. The night air buzzed with unseen life, and Halm hoped nothing would make a meal of him. In time, tiny bulbs of light appeared and drifted across the plains. He watched the tiny creatures, not knowing a name for them, but thinking them magical all the same. He watched until his eyelids grew heavy.

And despite his aches, a warm feeling of ease led him to sleep.

A splash of water woke Halm.

He thought he'd been dreaming. He lay on his back and realized he couldn't see the night sky through the leaves. A second splash broke the stillness, sounding close by, raising the hair on his head and neck. He scrambled to a sitting position, his senses crackling, eyes scanning the suddenly ominous dark.

Nothing.

He found the hilt of his sword and got up, wholly awake and searching. Stars glittered on the horizon, a sheer spectacle of celestial wonder surrounding the little knot of forest where he'd stop to rest. That vast cosmic space filled his vision, clouded in places by strands of milky silk. For heartbeats, Halm forgot everything and stared.

A snort from nearby and Lish's dark outline came into view, almost within arm's reach.

Halm waited and listened, hearing a low chatter of nightlife and nothing more. The second splash came from the north, or so he believed. Nothing else happened, so he decided not to pursue it. Lish remained quiet and untroubled, so Halm believed the danger—if they were in danger—had passed. Perhaps a single animal had wandered by. Maybe a bear?

Or a troll?

The thought fouled his calm, but he discounted the idea a moment later. Trolls were rarely seen across the land, driven into forgotten places by the insane fools who hunted the beasts. There were other dangerous creatures of the night, but if some horror or other did prowl the night, Halm doubted Lish would be so calm.

Still, Halm stayed awake long after the disturbance roused him from his sleep.

In time, he sat down, watching the glittering dark framed between a line of grass and one of leaves.

In the morning, Halm awoke with a snort and attempted to look everywhere at once.

Lish studied him with little interest before returning to munching on a breakfast of grass. Scowling at the animal, Halm rubbed his jowls and stood. He stretched his back and limbs, growling at the pulling and popping. The sun hung above the eastern horizon, and there was very little else to be seen.

Keeping his sword handy, Halm emptied the bull in the same area as the day before, looking around as his stream fell upon grass. When he finished, he tucked himself away and gripped the sword hilt, wondering what had disturbed him during the night. He marched in the direction of the noise, the grass reaching his mid-thigh, and slowed to a stop.

"It was near here," he muttered, turning in a circle. He realized he'd traveled a good distance from Lish, who continued eating. Well over thirty paces.

"Hm." Halm grunted and made to turn back when he noticed a depression in the grass, as if something had rested there.

Sword in hand, he approached the small hollow and discovered a skeleton lying on its back, its jaws split in a howl. Bones protruded from a mesh of rusted chain links and torn leather. A discarded spear and shortsword rested at its feet, the metal fouled by time and elements. Halm didn't go any closer, nor did he bother following what appeared to be a trail. Instead, he backed away, retracing his steps back to the clump of trees where Lish waited.

When he reached the horse, Halm wasted no time saddling the animal.

Wisps of smoke rose from stone chimneys as evening fires grew hot enough for cooking. Riding Lish once again, Halm rounded a bend of forest and spotted the first house. His spirits lifted considerably as other little village houses came into view.

"Thank Seddon," he muttered. Everything hurt, despite Halm spending an equal amount of time walking, riding, and resting during the trip. Not even the sights and clear air of the countryside could distract him from his growing discomfort, but seeing the little community put a weary smile on his bruised features.

He leaned forward and patted Lish's neck. "Almost there."

Lish ignored him.

By noon, Halm had passed by a scattering of barns and single houses on the land known as Plagur's Reach, but he did not approach them, focused on getting to Karashipa by the end of the day. Now, the rough houses came into full view, dark shapes detaching themselves from the deepening shadows of the timberland. A few voices broke the sleepy quiet, while at the very end of the road, the sun reflected in the mirror of the lake.

Halm spotted the place where he and the lads had slept when they first came to the village by koch. Lish slowed, and Halm let him, not wanting to exhaust the animal. Some men and women sat outside their small homes, watching the Zhiberian ride in. Some even raised their hands in greeting, remembering him and how he'd killed Thaimondus. Halm lifted his free hand in return and rode on toward the lake.

Lish snorted, and his ears fluttered, indicating he was growing tired of carrying the Zhiberian's weight.

"Almost there," Halm repeated, nodding at a few villagers along the road who stopped their conversations and turned to watch him. He recognized the fellow who'd had the word *punce* carved in his forehead by Torcul, son of Thaimondus. Halm couldn't remember the lad's name, but he nodded at the man and got a smile for his trouble.

More villagers peered out of windows. A few children playing by their front doors turned and stared. Halm didn't stop.

The alehouse waited down by the water's edge, the surface so calm he almost forgot about his aches. A smoky ribbon issued from the chimney. The walls of Thaimondus's residence came into view, the gates open wide. Halm wondered what the village had done with the space or intended to do with the land. He supposed he'd find out soon enough.

Lish continued along the path to the alehouse door, and Halm eyed the small but well-built alehouse. The building certainly wasn't as fine as anything in Sunja or any other city he'd visited, but its thick log walls appealed to him—rough, but comfortable.

A short laugh perked Halm's ears as he dismounted, and he saw windows covered in thin netting. Lamplight glowed from within. He saw that no one had bothered to replace the door, which remained ill fitting in its frame and looked as if some drunken lout had put boots to its wood.

"You stay here now," Halm said to Lish. "Don't wander. I might need you for a quick escape."

Lish looked at the lake and made no promises.

Rubbing the horse's sweaty neck for good fortune, Halm drew himself up, saw that none of his bandages were stained with blood, and walked to the front door. He opened it and didn't really see the rough stone fireplace. Nor did he notice the coarse canvas painting of rolling hills and a sun. He paid little mind to the three men sitting around one of four tables.

The woman behind the bar, now…

She captured his attention entirely.

Lit lamps and a low-burning fire cast the room in a red hue and darkened her complexion, but it was Miji, her black hair tied back from her narrow face. She wore the same green dress with a white apron tied around her waist. She looked up from cleaning a mug, and Halm's heart warmed to the recognition on her features, which he thought quite lovely.

But then she saw his condition, and her mouth dropped open in horrified alarm.

As the door closed behind him, Halm smiled back, making a conscious effort to keep his bad teeth hidden.

"Hello, fair Miji."

20

"What of our stores?" Sindra took her friend and cook Telda behind the bar, ignoring the shouts and laughter filling the alehouse.

"Well," Telda began, her head tilting, "we can probably make it through the night. There's a roast of ham, a roast of beef—but that's going quite fast—and one rabbit and one pheasant."

"No chicken?"

"All gone," Telda said. "Took the head off the last one earlier this evening. One chop and…" She fluttered both hands before her chest, showing how the headless animal's legs moved upon decapitation.

"You're bad," Sindra said.

Telda giggled, delighted with her friend's reaction. "You'd say different if the little feathered bastards ran across the floor. And they would, too, if I didn't turn them over."

Sindra had no reply to that image. "Well, make a list,

and tomorrow we'll head to market. We'll take Gurga along. We'll need him to carry everything."

"Need a few kegs of Sunjan Gold as well."

"Make note of it. When I said 'we'll' I did mean both of us."

"And Gurga."

"And Gurga."

"Your friend's back." Telda looked past Sindra, causing her to turn.

Sindra's heart skipped.

Borchus. The man tipped his head in her direction.

"Didn't you—" Telda started.

"I did." Sindra cut her off and immediately felt bad for doing so. "Sorry."

"I'll get Gurga."

Sindra caught her friend. "No, I'll talk to him again."

"Best make it clear this time."

"I will."

"Clearer than last time."

"Aye that."

"Because he *clearly* didn't understand last time."

Sindra fixed Telda with a silencing look.

"I'll check on the vegetables," she muttered and moved to the kitchen door. "Put honey on that ham. Maybe do a little chopping."

Sindra turned back to Borchus, her surprise slowly replaced by disbelief. The man refused to listen. Minding an alehouse and all her other duties and obligations were busy and stressful enough without having to deal with *him.* Anger welled up. She would make him understand that tonight. She crossed the space between them, frustration bubbling to dangerous levels.

Sindra stopped right in front of Borchus, slapping the counter with both hands. "What're you doing here?"

"Sindra."

"Answer me."

Borchus shrugged a shoulder. "Only here to drink."

"What did I tell you last time?"

"Sindra, I need to talk to you."

That set her head to shaking. "What's wrong with you? You're unfit. I don't *want* to talk. I've said that time and time again. I don't want to talk. Did you hear me that time?"

A downcast Borchus shifted on his seat and avoided meeting her fierce eyes, loosening another memory in her head.

"What's wrong?" she demanded.

"Nothing."

"What was *that*, then?"

"What?"

"*That.*" Sindra mocked him with his own expression. "What was that?"

"Perhaps the little man's kog is twisted." A nearby patron smiled through a heavy black beard.

That drew dark looks from Sindra and Borchus.

"Mind your business," Sindra snapped and stared knives at the man. The bearded fellow shrugged and turned away. She kept her eyes on him a moment more before speaking to Borchus. "Well?"

"Nothing."

But as Seddon above was her witness, when Borchus said it was *nothing*, he really meant it was *something*. A bout of indecision swamped her mind. She knew full well she was asking for trouble if she pursued the matter any further, knew he *hoped* she would anyway. She didn't owe him anything and probably had plenty of reasons to hate him.

Borchus waited for her decision.

Sindra's mouth became a tight white line of annoyance. She hesitated, eyeing the patrons on the other side of the counter. With a hiss and a scornful shake of her head, she walked to the bar's end and opened a door. She bade him enter, furtively scanning the alehouse's interior. When Borchus took his time, she almost screamed at him and conveyed that thought with a glare.

"Follow me," she muttered over the crowd's rumble. She led him past her workers, through the door to the kitchen, and past a surprised Telda, who'd just split an enormous potato in two with a cleaver.

Sindra stopped at a second door and opened it, waving Borchus inside. She followed him in and lit a lamp on a small table. Having done that, she closed the door and didn't bother sitting at any of the room's three chairs.

"This place looks cleaner," Borchus noted.

"That's because I clean it. I cleaned it when Hadree was alive as well, at every opportunity in fact, except when you came around, and Hadree was mucking around in here."

"He did that quite a bit."

Sindra waved a hand. "What's wrong with you?"

Borchus pulled a chair out and sat down, cradling his left side with a hand. "I had an incident with a pair of cutthroats last night."

"What?"

"They tried to stab me dead," Borchus continued. "Right here."

"Who tried to stab you dead?"

"That's what I'm attempting to find out."

"And you came back to me?" Sindra backed against the door, offended. "I didn't have anything to do with that. I hate you, Borchus, but I don't want to *murder* you."

The words left her like a team of runaway horses pulling a driverless wagon, but she did not correct herself or apologize. Borchus stared as if he'd been slapped by a mallet.

"I see." He recovered and absorbed the outburst. "Well. That's good to know."

"Was there anything else?" Sindra asked coolly, wanting to end the conversation.

"Just…" Borchus trailed off. "No."

"So this is what you wanted to talk about? Someone tried to kill you? Is that really any surprise to you?"

Borchus took his time in answering. "No. I suppose not."

"This won't work, Borchus. Attempting to get sympathy might sway a wench with half a pitcher in her, but it's not going to sway me. Have you forgotten that?"

"No."

"Then…" She opened the door and indicated it was time to move along.

An impassive Borchus stood and walked past her, not meeting her eyes. Sindra doused the lamplight and left the door open, emerging a moment later. She followed him out to the bar, three paces behind him all the way to the front door of the alehouse, where the ferocious presence of Gurga waited. Not once did Borchus turn around to speak, and that gave Sindra hope.

She stopped beside her hulking enforcer. "How did he get past you tonight?"

Gurga shrugged. "Little man is little."

Sindra glared, shaming the brute into averting his eyes.

"I'll be careful next time," he said.

"You be careful from this point on."

"Aye that."

Sindra looked out into a night sparsely illuminated by lamplight and caught sight of Borchus, just a glimpse before he vanished into the shadows.

"You hear me?" she asked Gurga.

"I do."

Sindra turned on her heel and walked back to the bar. She paid scant heed to her patrons and felt better when she got behind the counter. Her serving staff looked to her for assurance that all was well, but she ignored them. Borchus lurked within her thoughts, as did the attempt on his life. He could spin a tale back when Hadree was alive, but she'd never once sensed he'd ever lied to her. She didn't believe he lied to her now, even though it had been years—*years*—since he'd left Sunja. People could change in such a long time. People could change several times.

Had Borchus changed?

She went to a keg and grabbed a mug, intent on filling it with mead and retreating to her private room. A good drink helped her think when needed and forget if necessary.

When she turned to leave, a man at the bar caught her attention. She stopped in her tracks.

"Sindra," the man said in a voice that reminded her of warm honey, his blue eyes dazzling to an almost supernatural brightness.

"Senturo." Sindra forced herself to sound unconcerned.

The handsome man placed his hands upon the counter and drew himself up to his full height. He studied the room. "Quite busy tonight, I see."

Sindra nodded.

"Who was that man you were talking with?"

"No one."

"Of course, he's *someone*," Senturo stressed with a shark's disquieting smile. "I want to know who."

"The woman said it's no one," said the same heavy-bearded man who had joked at Borchus's expense. "Leave her be."

Senturo regarded the speaker, lips curling in distaste, and ignored him completely.

"Mind your business," Sindra snapped at the patron for

the second time that night. He questioned her with a scowl as he turned away. Sindra knew the fellow was only trying to right his earlier slight at Borchus's expense, but his timing couldn't have been worse.

"So." Senturo's unnatural eyes did not blink. "Who is he?"

"Just a patron."

"You take all of your patrons behind the counter?"

"He herds cattle out beyond Plagur's Reach. Wanted to know if I wanted his business."

"Doesn't look like such to me, certainly doesn't smell like such."

"Well, he is."

"Ah. And?"

"And what?"

Senturo waited expectantly.

"Senturo," Sindra said sternly, peering at him from under her lashes. "I don't tell you *my* business. I don't *ever* tell you my business. And if Tilo has somehow changed our agreement, well, I'll be visiting him myself to clear any confusion. Understood?"

Senturo's expression didn't change. He shook his head, his smile widening. "You have fire, Sindra—*push*—though I detect a slight irritation in your tone. Was it something your cattle man said?"

"No, it's just you. What is it you want?"

"The usual." He sauntered past her to the door behind the counter, knowing she disliked it when he did so without invitation. "Shall we talk?"

Sindra did not move.

Senturo gazed down his hawkish nose at her and bared his teeth again. "You're unusually defiant this evening, Sindra."

"I'm getting tired of these conversations."

"Saucy," Senturo said with slick admiration. "Master Tilo sends his regards, by the way. Let's have our talk, and I'll be gone. I'll be thinking of you, however."

The barest chill stropped Sindra's spine. She didn't want this shite snake to have any thoughts of her, none whatsoever. But she knew Senturo's reputation, knew what he was capable of.

Restraining yet another insolent retort, Sindra led him through the door to her private room.

*

Later that night, Borchus scratched three times on the cellar door and waited, holding a cloth sack in one hand and his aching side with the other. He hoped that his efforts to elude any would-be pursuers were successful. It had been difficult. The disastrous encounter with Sindra muddled his thoughts. He glanced up and down the alley. If he had been followed, they would be on him at any moment. Thus far, nothing.

And no Garl.

His lips tightening into an annoyed button, Borchus scratched out the code on the cellar door once again, hoping the cobbler and his family were sound sleepers.

"Who is it?" a voice whispered from within.

"It's me." Borchus sighed and lowered himself. "Open now."

"How do I know it's you?"

"Garl, I have food and drink, and I'm growing impatient."

"I was sleeping."

"You want to hear the scratching?"

"Yes, please."

Growing annoyed, Borchus did just that, feeling the drag on his fingernails.

"You'll wake the cobbler," Garl warned, followed by the pop of one released hook. Then another.

"Open it, please," Borchus said.

Garl didn't answer.

His hands full, Borchus dropped the sack and pried the door back. He got inside, snatched up the sack, and dropped it on the nearest step. A moment later, he closed the door and locked it.

"You were sleeping," Borchus said unkindly, moving toward the back room, where a candle burned.

"I was." Garl eased himself onto his cot. "Bit hungry at that. Haven't had anything all day."

Frowning, Borchus opened the bag and emptied it, pulling out a roasted chicken, a round of cheese, and rolls of bread. Two bottles went onto the table as well, crowding the candle.

"A feast," Garl said.

"Are you all right?" Borchus asked, detecting wrongness from the man.

"I'm… well. A hard day. My nerves almost got the best of me."

The agent's eyes never left the spy. "Why is that?"

Garl frowned in answer.

"Well, then, you eat. That's wine and beer in those bottles."

"My thanks."

"Any trouble here?"

Garl shook his head while pulling a leg off a chicken. Borchus had eaten in a small tavern earlier that evening, so he stripped off his shirt and lay down on his cot, still wearing his boots. He said nothing for a while, resting as Garl ate.

"Visited the Street Watch today," Borchus finally said, his lowered voice booming in the close confines.

"And?"

"Learned that two men had been killed, gang members, both belonging to the Sons."

Garl's mouth hung open.

"I overheard them speaking about it. I didn't speak with anyone."

"You went to the Street Watch?"

"No one followed me there. Or here. They had all day and night to try and kill me, but no one did. I didn't take any unnecessary risks."

Garl resumed chewing, tasting nothing. "So it is the Sons."

"It is."

"We are well and truly fish hooked."

Borchus sighed in answer.

"What do we do?"

"We become invisible. Stay below ground. Stay away from the arena and our more frequented places in the city. I'll meet with Naulis tomorrow. I'll use him to go to the arena and such. I'll try to meet with Goll when he comes to the city."

"Will you tell him about the Sons?"

"I don't know. I suppose I should."

Garl took a swig from a bottle and stared off into the dark.

"We stay out of sight for a few days," the agent said. "Perhaps they'll lose our scent."

"They aren't going to lose our scent, Borchus. These are the Sons of Cholla. Their reputation is known far and wide."

"Well, I have a reputation of my own," Borchus whispered. "Though only a select few know of it. If you wish, I'll mention you to Goll and convince him to take you out of the city."

Garl brightened.

"If the Sons wish to attack a wagon full of gladiators in daylight, let them. It'll be the last mistake they'll make."

"They'll only send more. You don't know these people. They have an army at their command. If you cut down one, three more will take his place."

"Leave that business to me," Borchus said. "And finish eating. I can't sleep with you chewing like a damn horse."

Garl continued with his meal.

Borchus tuned out the noise as thoughts swirled within his head. Thoughts of Sindra.

21

"What do you think they're talking about?" Torello asked Junger as they lingered outside the common room. Goll, Clavellus, and the trainers had pulled Brozz aside on the rest day to discuss his upcoming opponent. Muluk was also in attendance. They wondered if Pig Knot was in there, since he was a housemaster as well, but they didn't hear the man's voice—or rather his cursing.

Junger shrugged and pulled at the shirt clinging to his shoulder. "Some last items, I suppose. I can't imagine anything new, not a day away from fighting. It's a little late for changes."

Torello eyed the closed door and then the walls of the villa, squinting in the morning sun. As there was no training, it seemed unusually quiet.

"I hope he wins," Torello said.

"He's prepared for it."

"But for a house gladiator?"

Junger pursed his lips. "Don't be misled by the title. A

house gladiator might have the training and the experience, but Brozz is more than capable of putting one down."

"I don't doubt that."

"You just focus on avenging Kolo."

Torello regarded the Perician. "You remembered his name. That surprises me."

"I remember all the names."

"He was a good man," Torello said quietly. "I knew him well. For years. He was the only one who endured my gurry. I'll avenge him. You can count on that. I'll put the bastard that killed him into the ground."

"I don't doubt it."

"You believe I can?"

Junger's dark eyes met the Sunjan's. "I do. You've changed, Torello. We've all noticed it. I'm sorry that Kolo perished in order to bring it forth, but you've changed. No longer are you the constant complainer I first took you for. Truth be known, I wonder who you'll be after the blood match."

"Who are you, Perician?"

A disinterested Junger shrugged and looked at the wall. "No one."

"I don't believe that."

Junger didn't comment.

The door opened, and Brozz stepped through, stooping to clear the upper frame.

"All done, Sarlander?" Junger asked.

"As much as one might expect."

"All ready for your greatest challenge?"

Brozz's great flowing moustache twitched with wry humor.

"That was almost a smile, good Brozz." Junger feigned caution. "I don't know the pair of you, anymore. Torello has changed. You're almost friendly. It's strange."

"And you're talking more," Brozz remarked. "There might come a day when I'll wish you never said anything at all."

"Might come sooner than you think," Junger said. "Well then, lads. Since the day is ours, I believe I'm going to eat, drink—water that is, as I doubt Master Clavellus or Master Goll will allow me anything else—and sleep."

"Not you," Brozz remarked, black eyes gleaming. "Master Goll wishes to speak with you next."

"Does he now?"

The tall Sarlander nodded.

"Well." Junger inspected his clothes. "Best not to keep him waiting."

With that, he left his two companions and entered the barracks.

The windows were open, but the heat still leeched moisture from Junger. A lingering smell of sweat hung on the air. Clavellus and Machlann sat at a table, while Koba stood with his back against a wall. The taskmaster was without his silver mug, a rare sight. Muluk sat off at another table, an island unto himself. Goll stood and didn't bother with greetings. Pig Knot was nowhere in sight.

"Keep that door open," Clavellus said. "Too damn uncomfortable in here now."

Junger did as instructed and faced the men.

"Junger." Goll locked eyes with the Perician. "I won't waste time. Over the last few days, I've been watching you. *We've* been watching you. And we've concluded that you're something of a mystery—mystery that seemingly does what it's told, but therein lies the ruse. In my time as a gladiator, I've never encountered one so… *carefree* in their training as you. You do what you're told and perform exceedingly well, yet it's obvious that you're restraining yourself."

Goll leaned forward and planted his palms on the table, studying the Perician. "Anything to say for yourself?"

Junger shook his head.

"I don't know what you are playing at," Goll resumed, "but we've noticed it. Discussed it. You're within the House of Ten now, and you'll do what you're told to do to the best of your abilities. You know the challenges facing this house, the collective hatred for a handful of former Free Trained warriors banding together—during a season, no less. Many, if not all, consider us a mockery of everything they attempt to achieve at the games, an insult to their months of hard preparation. They consider us maggot shite. In all fairness, I'd think the same way. But I'm not them. We're not them. *You're* not. We aren't fighting to prove we belong in these games. We belong. And we're fighting to win, to claim a championship for the very first time."

At this, Clavellus and Machlann exchanged reserved looks.

"To do that," Goll continued, "each of you has to compete at their very best. *Your* very best. You are not. You are playing as if in a grand game."

Goll straightened. "Stop. Playing. Show us everything. If you're the swordsmaster we suspect you are, show us. Impress us. Hypnotize us. Make it known that you represent this house. Make others fear you, *remember* you. What you do in the arena reflects upon every one of us. Do you understand?"

A relaxed Junger stood with his hands clasped behind his back. He looked into each face before returning to Goll's. "I do."

"Do you understand what you must do tomorrow?"

A pause. "Avenge Tumber's death."

"And?"

Junger offered nothing more.

"You kill that man tomorrow," Goll said with an edge to his voice. "Kill him and put fear inside the rest. To take one of ours invites bloody consequences. Let the Pit know we'll put the offender in the ground. Do you understand?"

"I do."

"Will you do it?"

"I will not."

Goll's eyes narrowed, and the room suddenly became much cooler. "What... did you say?"

"You want me to kill the man, but I won't do it."

"And why is that?"

"I have my reasons."

"Let's hear them."

"No."

Anger rippled through Goll's expression, and Junger could see he was but a word away from exploding. Clavellus leaned forward, not as offended as Goll but clearly exasperated with the answer. Machlann's back stiffened, and Koba's folded arms slowly dropped to his sides, as if he were suddenly very interested in the discussion.

"My reasons are my own," Junger said. "As are the reasons I fight within the House of Ten. I'll be clear. Despite what you might think, you do not own me. If you press me, I'll leave through that door and not look back. Not once. If you do not… I'll fight for you. And I'll win for you—for the house. If victory within the Pit is what you seek, I'll give it to you. If vengeance is required, I'll exact it. To a point."

The Perician locked gazes with Goll. "You want this man dead. I'll ensure that he doesn't fight again this season."

"That isn't good enough." Goll rose, baring teeth.

"That's all I'm willing to offer."

The ensuing silence swelled to a bursting point. Clavellus cleared his throat and regarded Junger.

"Never have I encountered a pit fighter dictating terms to his housemaster. That alone is enough to drive you from these walls."

"Then I'll leave," Junger said simply, causing Muluk to suppress a chuckle with a hand.

"I'll have you thrown from this house," Goll promised in a lethal tone.

Junger didn't flinch. "Master Goll, I wish to fight for this house. If you seek my promise for anything, I'll promise you that. Allow me to fight, and I'll impress you. Hypnotize you. And I'll make it known that I represent the House of Ten. Allow me to fight, and the others will fear me. And this house."

The setting of Goll's jaw betrayed his outrage. To his credit, he held it in.

"That will be all, Junger," Clavellus said. "We'll discuss this among ourselves and let you know in a short time. Let Torello know we'll summon him when we're ready."

Junger met the gaze of each man and gave a short bow. He turned and walked out the open door, leaving them staring at his back.

"Koba." Clavellus nodded at the door. The big trainer moved to close it.

"Brazen insolence," Goll seethed. "I'll drive him from these walls myself."

"You'll do no such thing," Clavellus said firmly.

"What?"

"You heard me."

Goll's eyes flashed fire. "Who are you to command me?"

"I'm the owner of this property, the taskmaster of these trainers. This house is as much mine as it is yours. Unless you wish to continue with the rest of your training somewhere between here and Sunja's gates? Gather up your two remaining pit fighters and carry on?"

Goll's face flushed red, threatening to ignite.

"Listen to me," Clavellus pushed on. "You have so *much* right now, Master Goll. You've achieved so very much in a short time. And whether you admit it or not, that man might very well be the prize in this entire venture. We cannot allow him to simply walk away."

His chest heaving, Goll didn't reply. His face remained set and stern. To his credit, he kept his composure and kept listening. Muluk thought he might see his fellow countryman fly into an unfit rage, but he did nothing of the kind. That display of willpower, of control, struck Muluk as commendable.

"If we allow him to leave," Clavellus continued, "then we have only two remaining gladiators. Two. The other houses have any number between thirty and forty-five. Most are experienced hellpups, who have devoted their very lives to the sport, carrying at least a year's training and having survived a previous tournament. I guarantee *half* of those are seasoned veterans, every bit as skilled and lethal as the Cavaliers, Lancers, and Sujins who guard our borders. And each one is starving for victory, conditioned for pain, prepared to kill, and possessing the mindset that *he* is the chosen one. That he cannot be defeated, that this season is theirs and theirs alone. *That* is our opposition, Master Goll. *That* is who we face upon the sands. All the while, the House of Ten readies its pair of hopefuls."

Clavellus took a breath and looked at his trainer. "Machlann, what are our chances to make it through a complete season, against such determined adversaries?"

"With two lads? I've a better chance of scratching gold out of my hole."

Clavellus's expression of *you see?* centered on Goll, and the taskmaster willed that last sentiment to sink into the Kree's skull. The argument reached the Kree master, however, as his head drooped between his shoulders.

The silence remained unbroken for a long time, until Muluk attempted to break it by clearing his throat. "Perhaps we should keep the lad," the burly man said, treading softly.

No one spoke, allowing Goll a reflective moment to decide.

Moments later, he did.

22

Heavy clouds gathered during the evening, and it rained overnight, showering a parched land. Dawn drove the storm away, and rays of sun split the ominous clouds, shattering them and leaving the air smelling clean. Under clearing skies and splashing through puddles, the House of Ten appeared in grim spirits as they climbed aboard their covered wagons.

Junger remained among them.

The fighters had eaten and rested well. The steady hiss of rain during the night had guaranteed a deep and uninterrupted sleep. Muluk had crowded into the lead wagon with Clavellus, replacing Koba, who'd decided to remain behind. The shaggy Kree looked forward to seeing the day's matches, and it showed on his eager face. For protection, Clades, Pratos, and Valka, the three former Sujins, would come along, outfitted for troublemaking or maintaining the peace. Clavellus tied back the canvas sheet separating wagon's interior and the driver. One could see the road ahead if one peered around the driver's torso. Machlann secured the flap in the rear, allowing a refreshing breeze to pass over everyone. The morning blazed with a glorious gold around the edges of the world, as if the very horizon was a gift to open.

After short time on the road east, Clavellus looked at the hairy housemaster.

"Not too bumpy for you?" he asked as the wagon bounced and splashed over the wet road.

"Not at all," Muluk replied. "Good thing I slept well last night, however. No sleep to be had on this trip."

The taskmaster exchanged looks with his trainer. Machlann regarded Muluk with something resembling wry amusement.

"The roads are rough this morning," Goll said. "Best tell the driver to make best speed."

"He knows, Master Goll," Clavellus said. "He knows we're not riding for pleasure—or our health."

"We should have traveled last night."

"It was raining last night."

"Master Goll appears nervous this morning," Machlann observed.

"He does," Clavellus said.

Goll drew a hand over his pensive features and fumed. "I am nervous. I know our men have a good chance for victory."

"I believe Junger has a better chance," Clavellus said.

"Aye, that," Muluk remarked.

"Nothing's done until it's done," Goll said, unmoved

by their confidence. "But I worry for Brozz. His fight with the house gladiator."

"Tilo is a known house," Clavellus explained quietly while examining his trembling hand, "a hard competitor with a long history at the games. His house hasn't done well recently, but he knows how to train gladiators. You should feel some unease with that match. Anyone would. But Brozz has displayed a skillset not usually seen in a Free Trained pit fighter. Don't forget that."

"But will it be enough?" Goll asked.

"Machlann?" Clavellus asked.

"It'll be enough," the dour trainer grumped.

Puddles marred the road to the capital city, and the wheels rattled through the deeper ones with splashes. The overnight rain had left the plains glistening and the air cooler than usual. In time, the crown that was Sunja rose up over the land and gleamed through the morning haze with formidable majesty.

Clavellus peeked around the driver.

"Bagrun, move yourself just a pinch so that I can see."

Bagrun complied.

"Wagon approaching," Clavellus observed.

Goll lifted himself to take a look. A solid bump forced him to check his balance and grab a support rib.

"Ah…" A smile spread across Clavellus's face. "I see it carries some very important supplies."

The wagon rattled closer, traveling west to east. A small hill of kegs trembled in the back. The driver, aware of the treacherous nature of the road and the approaching wagon, slowed his team of six horses.

Bagrun directed his own team to the road's edge as far as he could. The wheels left the dirt and rolled over tall grass, the ride suddenly violent. The wagons shivered past each other, minding the spacing as their sides were a mere half an arm apart.

They carefully slipped by each other, and Clavellus craned his neck to see out the rear. "The road widens—"

A great crash threw the men into one another as the front wheels dropped. The wagon stopped on an angle, and the passengers lurched to the front. Horses cried out. Bagrun yelled for calm. Machlann fell into Clavellus as if feeding on the taskmaster's shoulder. Goll stumbled, his hands going up and banging into the edge of the driver's seat.

"Ruts in the road!" Bagrun shouted.

The wagon rocked. Heartbeats later, the horses pulled the wagon free, and they rolled back onto solid dirt.

"That was a surprise," Clavellus said.

A cry went up behind them, drawing their attention to the following wagon. It had lumbered over the difficult section and came to a jarring halt.

"Stop, Bagrun, stop," Clavellus yelled, casting a look at the team of horses and the distressed driver. The man cracked the reins, but the horses couldn't pull the transport's weight free.

In the other wagon, the sudden stop squeezed the passengers together into the front.

"Seddon" was all Shan got out when he was thrown against Brozz. The wagon angled downward, and the sensation of sinking overcame them. As the situation settled in, the driver twisted and snapped the reins, coaxing the horse team to pull the wagon free of the miserable mire.

Brozz met Torello's irritated expression. Junger leaned out the back, attempting to spy the problem.

"Deep mud here," he reported. "I can't see what's ahead, but we're stuck."

"Out the back, will you?" the driver, called Almas, asked his passengers. "Lighten her a bit so the beasts can pull her free."

Clades smiled grimly. "This road always was a sore one after a good rain."

"More so this day." Torello made a face and rose. "As long as we don't miss our matches…"

"No fear of that." Clades gestured for Pratos and Valka to lead the way. "But your sandals will need a scrubbing."

Torello placed his hands on the wagon's rear gate and vaulted over it with both feet in the air. He landed with a jerk and a squawk, staggering against the wood. Torello hooked his arm over the gate as his lower half tugged on his upper. Hands grabbed for him, but Torello was already off-balance and sloughing into the mud. Junger and Clades climbed out and discovered unsure footing in an earthy stew of rocks and mud. With Brozz helping from above, they got their hands under Torello's arms and helped him hobble onto firmer ground.

"Broken," the Sunjan grunted. "It's *broken*."

They sat him down on damp grass and waited for Shan. Mud stained Torello's lower legs.

"I felt it break," he whispered in agony, lifting himself on elbows and gazing down at himself. "Felt it snap."

Shan appeared and dropped to his knees, hands out as if about to touch a hot pot. "Well, now, this doesn't look good at all."

"I felt it break," Torello said, taking in the pain.

"What happened?"

"He jumped from the back of the wagon," Brozz said. "Slipped in the mud."

The healer frowned and carefully prodded the ankle, already swelling around the joint with a rosy discoloration rising through the skin. While he tended to the joint, Almas the driver persuaded the horses to pull the wagon free of the mud.

"Foul luck," Shan whispered as he inspected the injury. "Foul, foul."

"Is it broken?" Muluk asked.

Shan shook his head. "Not broken… but might as well be. Unfortunately, I don't have anything to help him right now, not until we get to Sunja and my house."

He met Torello's watering eyes. "I'm sorry."

"What? Will I be able to fight?" he asked through clenched teeth.

"Fight? Blessed Seddon, no," the healer replied with a frown. "Can you lift him?"

Junger and Brozz hauled the stricken man to his feet.

Torello held on their shoulders.

"Help him back to the wagon, please," Shan said as Goll and Clavellus walked toward them with fearful faces.

"What's happened?" Goll demanded.

"The lad jumped from the wagon and sprained his ankle."

That hurried both men along in time to see Torello being helped along. His foot had swollen to near twice its size.

"Well." A frustrated Goll spat. "Wonderful. That's his season. Lords above, what were you thinking?" he asked at the pit fighter struggling into the wagon.

"Not the time," Junger answered for the man. "Don't worry about the blood match."

"Don't worry?" Goll demanded. "Who're you to tell *me* not to worry?"

Clades lent a hand at the rear of the wagon, relieving Junger. The Perician turned upon Goll and quietly studied him.

"Well?" the housemaster asked in a heated tone.

"I'll fight instead," Junger said.

"You'll fight it? Feeling confident, are you?"

Junger didn't reply, but the others stopped and watched the exchange, even Torello.

"You can't fight it." Goll waved a hand.

"I'll fight," Junger said calmly. "You wish to have people remember? I'll fight Torello's match. I'll avenge Tumber and Kolo both."

Goll searched the man's expression for insolence.

An impassive Junger stared back.

"It's been done before." Clavellus eyed Torello's misshapen foot. "Years ago. It's not unheard of."

"Fight it then," Goll said, not happy in the least. "Fight it. Fight and win."

Junger's blank expression suggested he'd do nothing less.

With a slap to the wagon's side, Goll stormed off. Clavellus spared the man a parting look. He moved closer to where Torello rested in the wagon, getting an eyeful of the pit fighter's ankle. Clavellus's bearded, weathered face puckered up with solemn distaste.

"Two months," he said sadly. "At least. But don't worry about it, lad. I'm sure Machlann will make time to pester you if you truly miss him."

The joke failed to produce a smile on the Sunjan's face. "I wanted to avenge Kolo."

Clavellus nodded. The taskmaster squinted at the sun and patted the wagon's gate as if it were a fat cheek. He faced Shan. "Take care of the lad. Slap on some of that saywort of yours."

"Different injury," the healer said. "He'll have to wait until we arrive at my house, though I'll do what I can along the way. I'm afraid this journey's just become exceptionally painful for our man Torello."

A disappointed Torello plunked his head on the wagon floor. Clades and Brozz stood over him.

"Do what you can," Clavellus said, gripping the lowered wagon gate. He peered in at the fallen gladiator.

"I know something about what you are feeling, Torello. You might even believe we're disappointed. And we are, but not in you. You would've certainly killed that topper, right and proper. I know you would've. Your trainers know, and even Master Goll knows. We knew you wouldn't disappoint. Seddon above has plans for us all, and in time, we'll learn what his plans are for you. So don't worry. You're among companions. And friends. I'm sure Kolo understands."

Red-faced and in obvious discomfort, Torello hissed but didn't reply.

Up ahead, an angry Goll berated Almas for not paying attention to the road.

The angry words spiked the air, and the taskmaster shook his head. Clavellus stepped back and slapped wood again.

"We go."

*

His balls and buttocks grazing wood and grit, Pig Knot shuffled out of the living quarters in that pelvic-thrusting movement he'd mastered. Daylight turned upon him, and he snarled at its heat. He positioned himself over his mat and settled in, bare back against the wall. His hands stung, so he paused to inspect the calloused palms, slapping them clean. Above the walls, thin clouds stretched out and snaked across blue sky. It was about mid-morning, so Pig Knot knew Goll and Clavellus and the others would reach the city soon. He didn't rise when the others did and clambered to their morning meal. He didn't bother with seeing them off, nor did anyone bid him goodbye. That drew a deep contemplative sigh from his wretched person.

He was forgotten. Felt forgotten.

And loathed it.

Worthless. The rancid knowledge churned his guts.

But this day, this day would be his. He'd planned to free himself of the villa. Of Goll. Not of Muluk, however, as he genuinely enjoyed the Kree's company. Muluk and the Zhiberian, he would miss. He'd known the Zhiberian the longest of them all, and thinking further on it, that wasn't so long at all. But Pig Knot believed Halm understood him perhaps the best. The Zhiberian would understand what he was about to do.

As unfit as it might seem.

So Pig Knot sat and fumed and watched the sun climb. The heat increased, and the sweat flowed. Moisture seeped under his arms and down his neck, making his tunic stick to his chest. At times, he dusted off his bandaged stumps, the depression nearly drowning him. Some of the guards on the wall walked by and greeted him, but he didn't answer. *Ignore them.* Pig Knot didn't care about greetings anymore. Didn't want to talk. All he wanted was a pitcher of something good to drink, something to drive the pain away, if only for a short while.

Koba, the big, scarred ogre of a man, passed in and out of sight during the morning. The man had stayed behind. Pig Knot didn't know the reason, nor did he care. His plan had just become easier. The trainer meandered through the main doorway of Clavellus's and Nala's household, but he didn't cross the sands to where Pig Knot sat. That would change. When Pig Knot wanted him, he'd get him.

When the lovely piece of fruit called Ananda appeared, Pig Knot's heart bounced. She started for Pig Knot on the other side of the training sands, but Koba called her back. She faced him, and they talked, too low for Pig Knot to hear, but he could see them. He saw their lips move, the smiles exchanged.

"You're so lovely," Pig Knot whispered to himself, mimicking the trainer's voice. "I've often thought about bedding you across a table, making you cry out loud enough to frighten any nearby children."

"You unfit brute. Of all the things to say to me..."

Pig Knot chuckled once and became still. Quieted. He continued watching Koba and Ananda talk. It occurred to him he'd only seen brief exchanges between them before, but then she had her household duties to fulfill, and Koba minded the savages. Pig Knot smirked with contempt.

Koba smiled almost shyly at Ananda, making Pig Knot wonder just how often the man had been around a woman. Pig Knot himself had been with several dozen, perhaps even more. Faces drifted through his mind. Some he could remember, some he couldn't. Some even pained him, recalling missed opportunities for something perhaps deeper than a brief physical encounter.

Ananda hooked a few strands of hair behind one ear and then the other. Pig Knot realized she, in turn, didn't mind the company of that unfit bastard. A short laugh chimed from her, summoning an even softer expression from the big trainer.

Sweet Seddon above. Pig Knot realized why Koba had chosen to stay behind.

The trainer possessed feelings for the woman. And the way she engaged him made Pig Knot wonder if she felt something in return. The very thought struck him as unfit. Could the two actually be nursing along a romance of sorts? In *this* place? Then again, if Koba's and his positions were switched, Pig Knot knew he'd be courting that honeypot and making it known to every other bastard within a day's travel.

His attention dwelled on the trainer's scar. No doubt the punce was self-conscious about that ugly parting of skin. Not too many women would take to him with that wound on the side of his face. Almost as bad as…

Pig Knot caught himself. His eyes fixed upon the ground below his knees—but only for a brief instant.

Ananda took notice of Pig Knot and, after a quick exchange with Koba, left him and approached the legless gladiator. She pleasantly graced him with her smile, and he answered with one of his own.

"Master Pig Knot."

"Pretty Ananda."

Her smile widened. "Honey tongued."

A cold realization as harsh and numbing as a winter gale swept over Pig Knot, chilling him, despite the heat of the sun. He recognized all of her giggles and word play with him were just to please, to make him feel better about himself, but her true interests lay with Koba. In a whole man.

"Is something wrong?"

Pig Knot sighed. "No."

"Would you like something to drink?"

He tried to be agreeable. "Yes. When you… you're able."

"I'll return shortly." She left.

The villa's gates opened, and four horses entered, pulling a wagon. One of Clavellus's guards approached and spoke with the driver.

"Ananda?" Pig Knot asked, taking notice of the wagon, *expecting* it.

I've already asked Clurik to have more delivered, so whatever we have left, let them have it. Clavellus called from some dark corner of his mind—words Pig Knot had caught and schemed around.

She turned around.

"Send Koba to see me."

Perhaps he'd said it too firmly. For brief flutter of time, Ananda frowned with puzzlement. She did as Pig Knot asked, however, and for that he loved her. Seddon bless her heart for keeping his spirits alive.

Ananda caught Koba's attention with a wave and called to him. The trainer lifted his head in Pig Knot's direction like some great ugly bear sniffing out a threat to his territory. He said a few words to Ananda and offered her a reassuring nod and a chuckle.

The pleasantry drained from his face when Koba walked toward Pig Knot. Pig Knot didn't blame him.

Halfway across the sands, Koba glanced toward the wagon carrying what appeared to be fresh produce as well as kegs of beer or other spirits. At the same time, Pig Knot reached around his back in one smooth movement, and pulled free the knife that had almost ended his life. He felt the rough hilt and pressed a thumb down on the blade's dulled back, slipping the weapon to the side of his thigh— hidden from the trainer's sight.

Koba's scowl deepened as he got closer.

Pig Knot's face twisted with dislike. The blade at his thigh felt cool. He knew that his newest plan was indeed the right one, the best one: to use Koba's wrath to remove him from this life. With their mutual distaste for each another, as well as a possible competition for Ananda's attentions, Pig Knot didn't think the trainer would object.

"What is it?" the trainer said in a voice attempting patience. He stopped two strides away and held his hips.

Pig Knot regarded him and didn't answer right away. He eventually—casually—lifted his knife and picked at a fingernail.

"There's something I wish to discuss."

23

The House of Ten's wagons entered Sunja's walls by late morning. They passed the koch bay and traveled directly to Shan's house, where his wife greeted him with a hug and kiss. She fixed Goll and Clavellus with a not-so-friendly look for keeping her husband away for so long. The pit fighters carried the injured Torello into the healer's house and deposited him on a table.

"I'll stay here with the lad," Shan said. "The ankle needs looking after."

Goll stood in the doorway, listening.

"The arena's infirmary will have to do until I can reach you later," Shan said to him.

"That'll be fine." Clavellus stepped in with Machlann on his flank. "Take care of that one. Do what you can."

"I will," Shan promised and moved away.

"We have other matters to talk about." Goll watched the streets.

"Really?" Clavellus asked and saw Borchus appear from

an alley.

The stiffness in his walk caught Goll's attention.

"Something bothers you, Borchus?"

"It's best explained inside, if you please."

Goll got out of the way, allowing the agent to enter. Inside, Clavellus led the way upstairs, and the others followed. Borchus took his time climbing the stairs, keeping a hand to his side. He sat down heavily on the nearest cot. The House of Ten surrounded him.

"So then," Goll said, "I imagine this has something to do with you sending Naulis to the Madea."

"Nothing of concern," Borchus said through clenched teeth. "I'm putting together a network. As soon as I'm able to afford it, I'll take on more spies to reduce my presence in the Pit. It's best to keep a low presence there."

"Else you get stabbed?" Clavellus asked with a critical eye.

The room quieted as all attention focused on Borchus.

"You were stabbed?" Goll asked with mild concern.

"Wounds happen all the time with agents and spies, Master Clavellus." Borchus winced. "A danger of the business. Sooner or later, house rivals may target each other's networks if they know who the people are. Just so happens the House of Ten isn't so popular at the moment. Have no fear. I'll continue my duties if you'll have me."

"We'll have you," Clavellus said immediately. "But you were truly stabbed? I spoke partly in jest."

"You're wise beyond your years, Master Clavellus."

"Who did this?" Goll demanded.

"I don't know."

"An attack upon you is one against the house."

"Leave all that to me. I'll find out who's responsible, and I'll deal with it. Unfortunately, I have other real information for this day's fights. And I won't be present at the Pit." Borchus let that sink in. "From this day onward, you'll see less of me. I'll be in the shadows. When you enter the city, I'll meet you when I deem it safe."

An exasperated Goll couldn't believe what he was hearing. "That's an inconvenience."

"You'll barely notice, Master Goll. Don't worry. I'll still perform my duties to the best of my abilities until I'm no longer needed. If, however, you do arrive in the city one day, and I fail to contact you, you can assume the worst."

"Shan will see to you below," Clavellus said.

The agent smiled thinly and regarded the view of the city through the open window. "I've already been tended to."

"Then he'll check you again," Goll said in annoyance, "before you leave."

Borchus shrugged, conceding.

"Well." Goll glanced around. "We're going. Are you available to place a wager?"

"No. I'm not," Borchus answered. "I intend to avoid the Pit and related areas. Best I stay out of sight for a short while."

"More surprises," Goll grumped. "Well, I'll have Muluk do it. I daresay no one will challenge him. Hold on while I get Clades to pay you—and a little extra so that you may recruit more spies."

"Very good of you."

"Enjoy that extra weight in the purse."

"Be a long time before I see more?" Borchus asked.

"Might very well be the case." Goll looked at the others. "Shall we be off?"

"Good fortune," Borchus wished to them as they filed down the stairs. Once they were out of sight, he pressed a hand against his stab wound and hissed.

It occurred to him then that the Zhiberian was absent.

24

"The House of Ten wants you for a blood match," the Madea said without taking his eyes off the documents covering his desk.

The news made Cota uneasy, straightened him. He knew it would happen, though he hadn't expected it so quickly.

"This day?"

"This day," the Madea said. "The sixth match, in fact. Be ready."

In depths of the general quarters, with a low din of activity in the background, Cota barely nodded. He walked away in a worried daze, leaving the arena official and his impassive wall of Skarrs. The House of Ten. He'd wondered if they would want blood for the killing of their lad.

Now he knew.

"The House of Ten," he muttered and went to the armory. There, under the watchful eyes of the quartermaster, he selected the weapons he could've purchased new with the gold Dark Curge's man had paid him. Blood gold.

The memory of how he'd killed the Ten's gladiator troubled him. Cota was a forester and a hunter in the off-season. He chopped trees for the mills, caught rabbits, foxes, and all other manner of wildlife for the market. His father knew how to handle a sword and had passed that knowledge to his son, who discovered he had a talent for it but not the stomach to join Sunja's military. A few matches were enough for Cota, and he had no desire to go too deep into the season. Coin alone bade him brave Sunja's Pit when his finances demanded it. Three or four matches and then done, return to his wife and two little daughters.

Now, however, the House of Ten wanted their revenge.

Shouldn't have killed the man, Cota scolded himself as he carefully chose his twin swords. The name of the man was already lost to memory, but he remembered the face. Cota sighed. Rarely did anyone seek to avenge a death from those ranks. Cota considered himself Free Trained and knew no one would look to avenge him if he died in the Pit.

Seddon above, the thought of being a hunted man bothered him. Cota took the swords without thanks from the quartermaster and returned to general quarters. There he stood, in a pocket of shadows, among the swaggering brutes and grim cutthroats awaiting their summons. He already wore his armor—a light shirt of leather and a grinning helmet fixed with tusks. Standing there, Cota thought about his family and wondered if the man he'd so recklessly killed for gold had a family. He cursed himself for ever being tempted by Dark Curge's coin, for ever participating in these games of blood.

With a chill, Cota realized he'd done wrong. He'd done it for his wife and children, but he'd still done wrong. *I should have never come back.* He'd won enough gold for his family.

The dark enveloped his small frame, and he considered leaving the games right then. Leave and not look back. His family would understand without question.

But the family of the man he'd killed, however…

No. With a wretched sigh, Cota decided he wouldn't leave. He'd meet whoever the House of Ten would send after him. And fight. Saimon take him, he'd fight and risk death. Even that notion of duty, of honor, sounded hollow to him, for if he perished, how would his family survive?

Fool.

Cota shrugged. He'd killed a man for gold and would risk losing his life and family. He'd face the avenger, or else it would plague him for the rest of his days.

He'd let the story bring itself to a conclusion upon the sands.

*

The House of Ten wants their blood match. The Madea whispered in Bubruk's head, mocking him, or so Bubruk believed. Every time he replayed the exchange in his mind, words once thought of as emotionless became increasingly twisted. Tormenting. The Sunjan didn't trust many at the games, and he certainly didn't take lightly to being challenged by a group of Free Trained maggots calling themselves a house. Dark Curge had lived up to his promise and had paid quite well for the Ten's warrior's death.

The trouble with coin, however, was the more one had, the more one wanted. And Bubruk wanted it all.

Killing a pisser belonging to the House of Ten didn't bother Bubruk in the least. He came into the games meaning to win as much coin as possible by any means necessary, earn enough gold to carry him well away from Sunja. A Sujin by trade, he'd fought the Nords knee deep in mud and blood. He kept that history secret. Men on the front knew which way the war tipped, and Bubruk had decided long ago he wasn't about to perish for Sunja if given a choice. For eleven years, he'd killed Nordish solders for King Juhn… only to be rewarded with the opportunity of killing more Nordish soldiers.

The war had exhausted him. If word of his desertion ever became known, he'd be limbed alive, screaming as a sword brother took his time chopping off arms and legs.

One couldn't get far without coin, however, and the games offered plenty of that, so Bubruk plied the only set of skills he had. He took care in concealing his past, taking a blade and shaving off any flesh etched with ink marking him as belonging to a Klaw. Scars from the war covered his body anyway, so a few more only added to the collection. He grew his hair far longer than a Sujin's. He didn't keep any friends and issued poisonous glares to those crowding too close in general quarters—or at least, when he stayed within general quarters. The last few nights, he'd rented a quiet room with the coin he'd earned, even paid a woman for her company and slept quite fine. So very fine.

Bubruk wasn't a man of deep thoughts, but he knew a house would seek revenge for what he'd done in the arena. He might even be a little concerned if it were a true house. But not the Ten.

From what he understood, there weren't even ten of them anymore. That put a scowl on his face.

Dark Curge had paid three times the usual amount of gold for killing one of those gurry bastards. That was in addition to the arena's sum of twenty gold pieces. To a man like Bubruk with a long history of killing for bounty, it was a tidy fortune for such a bit of blood work. It had been exactly what he needed. Curge's man had even spoken of a favor from his master's house, but Bubruk didn't receive one. Only the gold. The coin was all he wanted, anyway. A good run in the games would earn him a life, a luxurious one at that, somewhere far away from the Nordish conflict.

Now that the Ten sought him out for the seventh match of the day, Bubruk wondered if Curge's bounty remained in place.

Torchlight flickered as figures passed and shadows

flittered across his powerful form. The intimidating Sunjan stood with his weapons in hand, his face hidden by a caged helmet. A curved shortsword filled his right hand, while a club with a single spike filled the left. He scuffed his feet, the meager light flashing off brass greaves. Leather bracers protected his forearms. Nothing covered his chest, and the hellish heat of the confined quarters leeched his flesh of precious fluids. The warm, fetid air and trickling sweat annoyed him, made him angry. Vicious. Bubruk couldn't afford much armor, and he wasn't about to outfit himself because of the Ten. If he killed another, he'd ask about that bounty once again. If Curge paid the same sum again, Bubruk would be done. He'd buy a horse, armor, provisions and make for the gate—head for warmer climes and warmer women.

He'd do all that... after he butchered another one of the Free Trained pretenders.

The House of Ten wants their blood match. A scoff passed his lips. The very thought twisted his features in contempt. They could *have* their blood match.

Bubruk wanted Curge's gold. And he was perfectly willing to lop off a head to get it.

*

"So this is where the privileged watch the games?" Muluk asked in wonder as he limped inside the private chambers reserved for the House of Ten. "Even smells clean."

"Attendants clean the rooms at the end of the day," Clavellus said as he eased himself inside. "I wasn't sure they would these days, but I know they did so years ago."

"There's little time to waste," Goll remarked, paying scant heed to the condition of the warm chamber. "Master Machlann, see to the lads while Muluk and I see to the Madea."

Muluk's face clouded with doubt.

"Don't think you can make it?" Goll knew his countryman had been struggling through the streets. Muluk's wounds had healed quickly under Shan's skill, but the long cut to his right thigh left him with a limp not even the healer was certain about.

"Oh, I think I can." His hairy face bobbed eagerly. "Little bit more won't hurt. It'll spite the gash."

The bravado was lost on Goll. "This way, then."

With Muluk struggling to keep up, Goll followed the tunnels, grimacing at the growing stench. A foul blend of sweat, blood, and offal threatened to burn away his senses and made his eyes water. The smell was so offensive, his breathing in the very air brought him to the brink of sickness. He couldn't imagine what the place would be like at the end of the season. Nor could he believe he'd actually slept in such a hole.

"Dying Seddon," Muluk gasped.

"I know," Goll said.

The foul taint of the Pit's underbelly permeated their clothes and skin, but they eventually made it to the Madea's desk. The white-haired arena official with the near-perfect part down the middle of his scalp lorded over a gladiator, informing the man of his forthcoming battle.

Numerous Skarrs stood guard on either side of the desk, fearsome and unmoving. The huge matchboard displaying the day's fights hung over the Madea, so Goll took the opportunity to study the lettering. Familiar names had been written.

"I don't miss this place," Muluk whispered near his ear.

"Nor I," Goll agreed without stopping his reading.

"It's *ripe* down here."

"Hm."

"Looks even more crowded than before."

That prompted Goll to regard Muluk. Both Krees then peered into torchlit guts of the Pit.

"You're right," Goll said faintly. "There does seem to be more."

"How's that, you think?"

"No idea."

Having finished with his business, the Madea dismissed the man with a wave of his hand. The official paused and smoothed his white robes before taking notice of Goll. The older man inhaled sharply, unaffected by the dreadful air, and beckoned the pair forward as if calling dogs.

"Your business?"

Goll decided he didn't care for the Madea's authoritative tone. "I'm Goll of Kree, Master of the House of Ten. And this is Muluk of Kree, Second Master of the House of Ten."

"Masters," the Madea countered, his black eyes considering them. "It's not so often I greet masters of a house. Usually, they send a messenger."

"We're short of hands this day."

The Madea waited, uninterested.

"We have a change of fighters for one of our blood matches," Goll carried on.

"A change?"

"Yes. Our man Torello was scheduled to fight Cota this day. He cannot due to injury."

"Injury?" the Madea asked dubiously. "What manner?"

Goll didn't think the question was necessary, but he answered all the same. "Twisted his ankle."

The Madea stared down his nose at Goll and tightened his lips in distaste. "You say you're with the House of Ten?"

Goll paused. "We're the Masters of the House."

"The House of Ten."

"Yes, the House of Ten."

"So you wish to withdraw from the blood match?"

"No, we wish to substitute another gladiator."

"Ah," the Madea said with ill-concealed impatience. "Who?"

"Junger of Pericia."

The imperious arena official frowned and regarded his charts. He leaned back and arched his head to check the matchboard.

"Junger of Pericia…" he finally rumbled. "He already fights this day."

"Now he'll fight twice for the House of Ten. In both blood matches."

"In both?"

Goll frowned at the man. "Is that a problem?"

The Madea smirked as if entertaining children. "The change is noted. Will that be all?"

Goll met the other's stare and believed a much more respectful tone from the arena official should be in order.

"That's all," the Kree finally answered, his features becoming rigid with insult.

"Very well. Our business is done, then."

The official went back to his paperwork and charts, ignoring the pair before his desk. Goll tensed, unimpressed with the interaction and about to voice his feelings.

Muluk, however, hooked Goll's arm and pulled him away. "Let that one go," he said as they navigated bodies back toward the white tunnel.

"But you heard it as well?"

"Aye that," Muluk said. "Thick and raw. But then, I remember him treating the Free Trained no different."

"My point exactly. He still considers us Free Trained."

That made Muluk think.

Saying no more on the subject, they returned to their private chamber.

*

The arched window beckoned Clavellus the instant he stepped foot within the chamber assigned to the House of Ten. He went to the sill and planted his elbows upon its coarse brick, the curls of sand audibly shifting under his weight. For the first four fights, Clavellus remained rooted to that very spot, enjoying every moment that followed, the skill displayed, every clang of steel upon edged steel, and the blood that flew. He studied the Free Trained and often chatted with Machlann, who resided on the taskmaster's left, peering into the arena and watching with a subtle smile shining through his moustache and beard. They observed the gladiators and made mental notes for the future.

Goll watched the fights as well, committing the names of the victors to memory in case the same men might later be paired off against a House of Ten fighter. Clades and Muluk went off to place the wagers, while Brozz and Junger alternated between standing and sitting, mentally preparing themselves for the Pit.

And after the fourth fight, when Clavellus and Machlann quietly congratulated each other for predicting the victor, Goll spoke up. "You truly missed this, didn't you?"

The old taskmaster smiled the question away.

"The smaller games become boring after so many years." Machlann pointed out the window. "This, Master Goll, this is the premier event, the truest test of the fighting arts, the *grandest* of shows."

"Where even a lowborn hellpup can achieve wondrous heights. I often wonder why? Why do I enjoy it so? I shouldn't really. No civilized person should. It does nothing to advance us, as the thinking arts do. And yet…" Clavellus shook his head. "It's in our *blood*. Conflict. To fight. To survive. Either with the spoken word, clenched fist, or sharpened knife. For the noblest of reasons or purely for pleasure. And if we are moved to fight, we are equally moved to excel. Some may say this profession is the ruination of all. And I agree, even wish it wasn't so, but it's the way of things. The world will always need warriors. Always."

Clavellus's attention drifted to the arena attendants grooming the sands before the fifth match of the day. "You should get Brozz ready."

If he heard his name, the tall Sarlander didn't respond to it. Goll studied the gladiator. Brozz sat on a bench, hunched over and holding his helmet. His great moustache made him appear brooding, and the dangling necklace of screaming crow heads did nothing to brighten his image.

"Brozz," Goll said, prompting the Sarlander to look his way. "It's time."

He straightened and stood until the ceiling was mere fingers above his black hair. His leather armor creaked. He held his shortsword and small axe.

"Listen now," Goll cautioned. "Your opponent belongs to the House of Tilo. A house gladiator. Expect a much more experienced warrior, very well trained and not to be taken lightly. Don't be reckless. If the opportunity is there, kill the man, for he will have no hesitation about killing you."

At the mention of killing, Brozz's indifferent gaze flickered to Junger where he leaned against a wall. The Perician met the pit fighter's eyes for a brief instance before glancing away.

"Don't concern yourself with him," Goll commanded with a trace of disdain. "You listen to me. They're all still looking to collect Dark Curge's bounty placed on your heads. On our heads. Send them a message. To seek our deaths means their own. You understand?"

"Yes."

"Good," Goll declared softly, inspecting the Sarlander's weapons and armor. "Then fight hard. And win."

Brozz looked over Goll's head at the stoic faces of Machlann and Clavellus. The older men said nothing, but they heard Goll's words. Brozz couldn't read their expressions, but he sensed that they were as divided on killing as Junger.

An arena attendant knocked on the door. Exhaling, Brozz donned his helmet and answered.

Like the shadow of death itself, the Sarlander emerged from the doorway and stained the white tunnel with his presence. The arena official, a little man dressed in plain white garb, stood back and pointed. Brozz didn't need to be shown the way. He left the official with a relieved expression on his face, no doubt thanking Seddon for sparing him.

Despite his fearsome appearance, Brozz didn't especially like killing a man simply for the sake of killing. It was the sole reason why he'd left his homeland in the first place. To his knowledge, no one had ever deserted the Gorsha. The very idea of leaving was beaten from the heads of the men. One only left when one died and not before.

The Gorsha was the edged will of the Grand Vir, the most capable and deadliest of all within the Sarland's army. Brozz been given to the Gorsha as a child by his parents, to be trained from the very beginning. To be taken so young had been the highest honor for the parents he never knew. Brozz would be fashioned into a protector who guarded not only his ruler, but his land, people, and family.

When he was able to walk, the Gorsha began shaping him. They trained and conditioned him for innumerable hardships. In time, the Grand Vir's command was not only Brozz's duty but his life's meaning.

But somehow, the sense of right and wrong was never entirely erased from Brozz.

And over time, the Gorsha ceased being the glowing thunderbolt of might wielded by the Grand Vir. The Sarlander ruler used the Gorsha not only on the battlefield but also for more personal, more secretive, displays of power, each one more brutal and sinister than the last. The Grand Vir wielded his warriors like the sharpest knives, imposing his will upon even the very people the Gorsha had sworn to protect and defend.

Or so Brozz had believed.

The final act that had broken Brozz came when the Grand Vir commanded the Gorsha to execute an entire tribe of hill folk who had failed to provide sufficient tribute to the Sarland ruler. As punishment, children, men, and women numbering well over seven hundred had been put to the sword. Over wine, food and gold.

Like an unwilling player in a nightmare, Brozz had done his share during the mass executions. He remembered everything, every life he'd taken. Every face rotted his heart and left him hollow, ashamed. A part of him—the caring part—had perished with those doomed hill folk. The faces of the dying still haunted him, driving him. If Saimon indeed existed, Brozz knew he'd be swallowed in the hellion's fire and darkness for those evil wrongdoings.

Slaughtering innocents over goods the Grand Vir hoarded and ultimately wasted was wrong. Brozz had no reservations about killing as he'd been trained to do so since childhood, but a reason had to exist, a reason far better than taking away poor people's possessions simply because they were due.

That day broke whatever spell the Gorsha held over him.

At the end of the executions, while the Gorsha set fires to the village to erase the butchery from the land, Brozz had entered one small house and discovered a tunnel underneath loose floorboards. Without knowing where it went or how far, he decided to take it. He set fire to the walls and the doorway, ensuring he'd have time to escape if the Gorsha attempted to follow.

The question of where the tunnel went, if anywhere, didn't matter to him. He'd either die for his wrongdoings or get away. To his dismay and good fortune… he escaped.

The tunnel was actually a cellar laden with dried food

and clay jugs of water. He discovered another door at the back and, with his torch held before him, entered the real tunnel— one that took him all the way through a mountain.

Brozz remembered almost returning to the Gorsha, but only for a fleeting moment. The ghosts of those he'd killed stopped him. He struck west, looking back only to make sure he wasn't being pursued. If the Gorsha caught scent of his leaving, they would send hunters to find him. To his knowledge, they did not.

Three years later, he arrived in Sunja, just in time for the gladiatorial games.

Brozz didn't know if he would stay with the House of Ten beyond this season. He felt the games drew too much attention to him. But he needed coin, and his skills lay in taking lives. And escaping that feral nest called general quarters had been a gift in itself. Even escaping the city felt good.

Both Junger and Goll had reminded him of why he left Sarland. They made him think about what lay ahead and where he was going after the games. They also reminded him of who he was. If there was killing to be done, Brozz would choose who lived and who died.

As the Sarlander walked the white tunnel, he wondered if Goll would be angry.

He decided he didn't care.

25

When Brozz stepped through the raised portcullis, Zilos, from the House of Tilo, waited for him. With the butt of a short spear thrust into the sand, Zilos stood with his weapon and silently judged his opponent while the voices of thousands rolled across the expanse like an ocean's surf.

His legs drew Brozz's attention almost immediately, as they appeared thick and muscular and capable of carrying the man for days if needed. Zilos wasn't tall—far from it. He appeared just a few fingers taller than Borchus. Unlike other opponents, Zilos wore no armor at all, showing off a well-conditioned body, colored by the sun and lashed with an assortment of scars. A masked cowl dyed red covered his face except his eyes, eyes that blazed, warning the Sarlander's senses.

This was a house gladiator in all his deadly splendour.

Above them, the Orator completed introductions and shouted for them to begin. Zilos yanked his spear from the sand and whipped it around his body in an unsettling blur before pointing it at his foe's gut.

Brozz's hands tightened on his own weapons. He walked forward to meet this challenge. Tensing like a spider, Zilos crouched and waited. His skin gleamed with perspiration. He didn't speak, and in Brozz's mind, that was good. He really didn't care for the ones who talked.

The audience cheered and cooed in delight, anticipating the approaching violence.

Brozz circled to his left, wary of the spear's glistening blade no wider than a dagger. Zilos aimed its tapered tip at Brozz's abdomen, but his intense eyes locked onto Brozz's and held them. Zilos's coiled body informed the Sarlander that the man took him very seriously.

Zilos drew back as if wielding a battering ram instead of a spear and attacked, the weapon whirling about his small body in a masterful display of skill. Brozz parried the flashing blade twice and countered with his hand axe, but the smaller man darted well out of reach, kicking up sand as he went. The spear compensated for his short arms and lent the House of Tilo's warrior a reach equalling Brozz's.

Brozz waited, weapons held at guard, stooping only slightly, watching his foe's eyes.

Zilos wound himself up once again, spinning his spear from one side of his body to his other, and launched himself forward. That deadly weave enveloped Brozz, and for telling heartbeats, the pit fighters attacked and countered, adapting and anticipating each other's strikes. They circled left and right, marring the groomed sands.

Brozz knocked away the spear tip only to have the butt

slam upside his head, too fast to avoid. He staggered back. Zilos followed, slashing for an arm and drawing a bloody line across Brozz's left bicep. Zilos split the leather hide covering the Sarlander's chest. More blood flowed.

Brozz stabbed for a head and missed, but his hand axe chopped down—barred from parting Zilos's skull by the man's spear.

Brozz yanked, looking to pull the man off balance.

The crowds burst into cheers as Zilos leaped, kicking both feet into the Sarlander's hard stomach and driving him back. The sand scalded Brozz's skin as he went down, rolled over, and regained his feet in time to parry a thrust meant for his guts.

Brozz slashed with his hand axe and opened Zilos's cheek to the bone. The cut was enough to send the smaller man jumping back. His chest burned, but Brozz focused on Zilos, and the pair circled each other again, drawing closer, their weapons weaving and bobbing as if smelling blood. Fat beads of red trickled from their frames and dappled the sand.

Zilos lunged, stabbing for the taller gladiator's face. Brozz slapped the spearhead away, only to have Zilos spin the butt of the shaft. The length of wood crunched into the Sarlander's knee. Brozz crumpled to the arena floor. Zilos rushed in, spear poised to stab downward.

Brozz whacked the descending blade, sending it over his shoulder—but not far enough. The weapon pierced armor and grazed flesh, punching free of the leather and leaving a runnel of red.

With momentum carrying him forward, Zilos's eye widened as Brozz crunched his knees up. His feet caught and launched his attacker.

Zilos landed on his chest in an explosion of dust and grit. One hand still gripped his spear. Much slower to rise this time, he still recovered quicker than Brozz. The Sarlander stayed on his knees, stunned, and ripe for butchering.

The arena called for death. And Zilos shouted back.

Spear poised to skewer a heart and eyes narrowed into knife slits, Zilos kicked up a sheet of sand as he stabbed, seeking to end the fight with the Ten man. The spear lanced forward in a streak of light and got deflected into the arena floor. Zilos's body continued forward, and Brozz slammed the cage of his helmet into the unprotected face wrapped in red cloth. Zilos's nose squashed. Brozz pushed his head backward, his spine cracking like a whip.

Both men fell.

A ghostly chanting reached Brozz and summoned his wandering consciousness from the back of his skull. For a moment, he couldn't see clearly, so he gouged his fingers into his face cage, raking the helmet from his head. His eyes watered, blinded by grit.

Not a stride away, Zilos climbed to his feet. The pit fighter's face seemed to hang in bloody tatters, but then Brozz realized it was the cloth.

Zilos swayed without his spear, and his eyes fell upon Brozz's rising form. Without waiting, the warrior stepped up and smashed a heavy right fist across the Sarlander's chin, rocking it to one side. Zilos crashed a left fist into Brozz's face, mashing a nose with a distinctive *pop*. A third punch slammed into a cheek, breaking skin to the thunderous approval of the onlookers.

Brozz's watery vision cleared. He caught the fourth blow and heaved Zilos to the arena floor, slamming the smaller man onto his back like a sack of wet grain. And with the frightening nimbleness of a spider, Brozz pounced onto the stricken pit fighter. He punched the face beneath him twice and then a third time just because the fury was upon him. Breaking flesh, breaking bone.

Zilos stopped moving after the second blow.

Pushing himself back, a gasping Brozz reached for a weapon and grasped the spear that had bled him. He spun the weapon around and, with teeth traced in blood, pressed the tip to the soft spot under Zilos's chin. The man's bloodshot eyes cracked open and saw his predicament.

Brozz applied pressure, drawing a throaty grunt from the spearman. Blood beaded and flowed, tracing lines in flesh.

Zilos gripped the spear shaft. "Yield," the stricken pit fighter whispered, forcing his mouth to work. "I yield."

The word found Brozz's ears, slipping through the din of the audience. Zilos's hands dropped to his sides.

Three long heartbeats later, Brozz cast the spear away. He sat back, wondering if the storm crashing down would bring rain. As his senses returned, Brozz realized there was no storm. He sat and marveled how the crowds could make such a stunning volume of noise.

Once his senses finally righted themselves, he stood. The Orator's voice boomed overhead, declaring Brozz the victor. Zilos sat and plucked away the cloth from his battered head, unwrapping the strands as if they were leaves off a soggy cabbage.

"Well fought," Zilos muttered through smashed lips.

"Well fought," Brozz returned.

And to the surprise of all, the towering pit fighter bent and offered his hand. The gesture froze the defeated spearman. He considered it, and for a brief twinkling in time, Brozz thought he would take it.

But Zilos did not. He looked away instead.

The dismissal stung Brozz, and he withdrew his hand. Perhaps one victory over a house gladiator wasn't enough for such respect. *But at least you offered*, a voice informed him, and Brozz supposed he had indeed. That knowledge lessened the burn.

Perhaps next time would be different. Perhaps not.

Oddly enough, he believed the crowds would remember him anyway. And he believed he knew how they would judge him. That knowledge felt comforting.

Picking up his helmet, Brozz walked slowly to the rising portcullis.

*

When Brozz entered the door, both Machlann and Clavellus cheered.

"You didn't kill him," Goll said flatly, diffusing the

merriment.

"He did worse," a beaming Clavellus said and indicated the arena over his shoulder. "Zilos has to live with the knowledge that Brozz not only bested him, but Zilos embarrassed himself by not taking the hand of a house warrior, even one so lowly as us."

"They'll see it as an act of defiance," Goll said.

"A few. More will say it was a moment of spite. Mark my words, the arena will remember Brozz's honorable gesture."

But it was plain to see that Goll would as well.

Neither pleased nor disappointed but dripping blood with each step, Brozz sat down heavily on a bench. Machlann retrieved a wad of cloth bandages and moved to the Sarlander's weary side.

"I'll bind the lad up until we can get to the infirmary," the trainer declared. "Or our healer."

Goll turned to Junger, who lounged against a wall near the door.

"You're next," Goll said as if marking the pit fighter for disaster. "Return here once you're done. If you're able."

Showing no emotion in the least at the jab, an unarmored Junger straightened. He stepped close to Brozz and gently patted the big man's shoulder, receiving a tired look of gratitude from the fighter. Junger's dark eyes regarded Goll.

"You want us to be remembered?"

"Remembered," Goll answered, his jaw set. "Not slaughtered."

"Don't worry then." Junger pulled off his shirt and tossed it aside. Wearing nothing but his black breeches and a pair of high boots, he walked to the door.

Goll shook his head at the lack of protection.

"Don't worry," the swordsman repeated and paused on the threshold. "They'll remember."

He took care closing the door behind him.

In the ensuing silence, a puzzled Clavellus wiped away a single bead of sweat from his forehead. "He's walking out there a bit early, isn't he?"

26

Junger strolled along the white tunnel, glad to be free of the confines of the house's private room. The whitewashed brick ran left and right of him, and he stood a few strides away from the door to the Ten's chamber. An intersecting tunnel a short walk away led to the portcullis. It was much cooler in this part of the arena, and he appreciated the calmer atmosphere. Sword and scabbard in hand, Junger waited to be called.

Show them something to remember, Goll had said.

Don't worry. They'll remember.

That wasn't wise of Junger to say, but as with some thoughts, the words leapt far too quickly to his tongue. Junger chastised himself for saying such and promised to be more cautious in the future.

The white wall became a scrolling fog that freed his mind of worldly concerns. The mortar remained firm in between the brickwork, the floors surprisingly free of dust. Say what one might about the Sunjans, they treasured their arena. Junger couldn't understand, however, why the engineers built the tunnels so that they ended in the far-off hell of general quarters.

The wall hypnotized him. White memories drifted though his mind.

Memories.

Somewhere, a door opened and slammed. Voices spiked the quiet. The door to the Ten's chamber opened, and Junger turned around to see Machlann and Brozz emerge, no doubt heading to the infirmary. Junger nodded at the perplexed men. Then the arrival of an arena attendant caused the Perician to look away.

"It's time," the man said.

Show them something to remember.

Junger decided he would, after all.

He walked the tunnel, paying no mind to the Skarrs along its final length, and stopped at a gatekeeper with an impressive beard.

The old man sized up the warrior. "I remember you."

"You should," Junger replied, leaving the *by now* unsaid.

"You don't wear any armor."

"No."

"Why is that?"

"Too hot."

"Too hot?" The gatekeeper cackled. "You'll risk dying because of the heat?"

"I suppose."

"Seems unfit to me."

"Imagine there are many who think the same."

The gatekeeper inspected the undrawn sword gripped by the scabbard. His head moved this way and that, as if attempting to detect some sorcerous enchantment. Junger didn't comment on the glaring scrutiny. The Orator started introductions, breaking the gatekeeper's none-too-discreet inspection.

"Off you go then," the older man said. "Good fortune to you."

Junger made subtle side-eyes at him. "Many thanks."

The gatekeeper pulled the lever he worked. The portcullis at the top of the stairs cranked open, allowing the full might of the sun inside.

Junger went to the light. The day washed over him with its hateful heat. The expectant audience filling the arena to capacity cackled with recognition. The noise grew in volume until a virtual wave crashed over him, stunning in its strength. They remembered him, remembered his disregard for stifling armor and the sword that stayed within its scabbard, free of a belt. He looked over the collage of faces, settling his gaze on a few of the more attractive ladies in the masses.

The Orator announced the fight. Junger directed his attention to his first foe.

Cota stood on the other side of the arena, armored in a leather vest and with twin short swords ready. The killer's tusked helmet regarded Junger curiously, perhaps wondering why he chose not to wear armor.

The Orator bawled for the battle to commence, and

Junger casually walked toward his foe. Taking his own cue, Cota marched to meet him.

The gladiators slowed neared the center of the arena, and Cota made no move to raise his blades to defend himself. This struck Junger as odd.

"Greetings, Cota," the Perician said over the din of the crowds. "I've been sent to avenge a death at your hands."

"I know," Cota replied. "I expected no less. Not from a house. Even if it's Free Trained."

Junger smiled, knowing that response would poison Goll's sensibilities.

"Did it for the coin," Cota went on, his eyes barely visible above his visor. "And, truth be known, I regret killing the man."

"You think that will save you?"

Cota surprised him. "No. But if I'm to die this day, at least you'll know the truth of it."

"Well said."

They stood there for a moment, the cheers and curses of the gathered people failing to move things along.

"Ready, then?" Junger asked, dusky features scowling from the heat.

Cota rolled his shoulders and brought his blades to guard. "Aye that."

Junger nodded. He could respect this man.

The Perician blurred ahead at a speed that damn near rendered him invisible and clanged his leather-bound sword against the tusked helmet. The impact was so fast and so hard that Cota's knees gave way in spectacular fashion. Both swords dropped from nerveless fingers as the pit fighter crumpled backward, arms thrown wide. A knee awkwardly pointed toward the sky, the ankle twisted at a cringeworthy angle under the unconscious man's weight. Cota's chest heaved once as if he'd been stabbed in the back then settled.

A single hair could've settled on that stressed ankle, and it would've been enough to snap it.

The audience gasped, disbelieving the prompt dispatching of the Free Trained fighter. The Orator stood high in his podium, gawking at the fallen warrior. The owners and nobility attending the games in their own privileged viewing boxes stopped in shock.

Junger paid them no heed. He frowned at the twisted ankle, wondering if it might already be broken. He stepped in close to the senseless Cota and, with his weapon, hooked the crook of the man's leg. Junger lifted it, easing pressure off the joint until the foot sprang back to a more natural angle. He carefully laid the leg to rest on the arena floor and studied the fallen man once again.

Satisfied he'd made his point, Junger chose not return to the House of Ten. It would take too long. Junger decided the sun wasn't so hot after all. Instead, he took a walk around the arena.

*

"What… is he doing?" Muluk asked, returned from the Domis and crowding around the others in abject awe.

"He's… walking," Clavellus stated quietly, a hint of wonderment in his voice.

"Walking," Muluk repeated.

Attendants hurried out onto the sands and gathered up the crippled Cota. Junger let them be and strolled around the north end of the arena.

"Walking." Goll took a deep, settling breath as an uneasy mixture of wonder and envy filled him.

*

"Seddon above," Nexus breathed, his hand stopped midway to his face as if confused about what to hold.

Gastillo, the golden-faced owner sitting on the other side of Nexus, didn't say a word.

An equally stunned Curge sat and squirmed uncomfortably in his chair. For once, he was thankful he didn't possess a full goblet of wine. If he had, he would have surely spilled it.

Who *was* that half-naked pisser?

Dark Curge's agent and spies hadn't been able to discover anything about the gladiator called Junger. No one knew a damned thing except the glaringly obvious. The man fought for the newly formed house of Free Trained hellpups. And he was terrifying to see in action.

Those thoughts made Curge fidget. He lifted his goblet to his mouth, only to discover he'd somehow already drained it. Nexus and Gastillo were too captivated by Junger to notice.

Curge licked his lips and supposed Nexus spoke for them all.

Seddon above, indeed.

*

Faces. Some beaming with excitement, others ruined by anger. Underneath bright banners and streamers hanging in the hot air, Junger strolled along the walls of the Pit. He watched his boots mostly but glanced into the crowds at times, just to see if there was anything interesting—ladies in particular. After residing at Clavellus's villa, he'd forgotten how lovely the women of Sunja could be. They waved to him, and he smiled back, welcoming their attentions.

The bellowing of the Orator made him stop, however, just below the rich hardwood platform reserved for royalty.

"Men and women of the Pit…" The old man lifted his skinny arms to the sky as if to pause time itself. "It seems Junger of the House of Ten is no ordinary gladiator. He is a man of vengeance, of a hate hell-deep and chained by vengeful intentions. The House of Ten has sent their best man to fight twice in one day, to avenge yet another sword brother taken by the very Free Trained they once were and now strive to rise above."

Junger frowned at such dramatic liberties, wondering why the Orator inflated the introductions with such storytelling gurry. That last line about the Free Trained would rankle Goll to no end. Taking a deep breath of humid air, Junger proceeded to walk to the portcullis.

"You saw how he quickly defeated Cota. I draw your attention to the next opponent, a Free Trained slayer who doesn't care about houses, doesn't care about vengeance or coin. All he cares about is the man standing opposite him within Sunja's magnificent Pit." The Orator paused with evil delight. "A man he fully intends to kill."

Junger frowned again and regarded the old man high upon his podium.

"Junger!" The Orator exclaimed, his voice carrying over the rumblings of thousands. "From the house birthed in a Free Trained darkness faces Bubruk, a rabid dog hungry for fresh meat!"

The audience made their delight known. Their cheering threatened to bring down the very stands they sat upon. At the west end of the arena, the portcullis rose in jerks.

The cheering wilted when Junger's opponent stepped into daylight.

Battle scars decorated Bubruk's torso and limbs in a horrific verse. He stomped upon the sands as if attempting to awake whatever terrors might rest underneath. The pit fighter threw his arms wide and bellowed, shaking his curved sword and one-spike club at Seddon above, calling the god down and promising to make it hurt. A face cage lit by the sun hid Bubruk's face, but his powerful body glistened from exertion. He turned around as the portcullis descended and thrust his blade at the spectators cursing him. Then, losing interest in the audience, Bubruk slowly turned his attention to his opponent. He straightened to his full imposing height, bringing in his arms like some mythical predator retracting its wings.

"*Begin*!" the Orator yelled.

Bubruk hunched over and moved from side to side, his weapons slowly churning up the air like the cogs of a brutal, primitive machine.

Junger sniffed. He walked toward the hellpup who might've been whipped at childbirth and mangled every day since. Junger didn't know whether he felt the sun's heat or raw rage radiating off Bubruk's bulk.

Bubruk huffed, his shoulders heaved, and he broke into a jog. His battered frame aimed at Junger. The crowd's voice rose in pitch, signaling they were eager for the clash. Bubruk's arms chugged, his pace quickening, weapons flashing in the sun. The last few strides, the Free Trained pit fighter roared. The sound ripped through several hundred spines. Bubruk charged, striving to take his foe's head clean off his neck.

Except Junger, holding his sheathed sword by the hilt and mid-blade, ducked under the scything sweep of his attacker's weapon and crushed the Free Trained's abdomen, stopping Bubruk in his tracks.

The audience cringed, both visibly and audibly, at the force of the blow.

The pit fighter's forward momentum halted as if he'd struck a wall. He turned away from Junger, one awkward foot precariously rooted to the earth, before landing hard on his back.

There he stayed, weapons splayed out on either side of him. One hand flopped to his chest while a pitiful *hur... hur... hur* replaced the nerve-splitting howl he'd loosed only moments earlier. His mouth bit weakly at the air, attempting to pull it down into desperate lungs.

His posture relaxing, Junger approached the gasping man and hovered just out of reach. Bubruk's eyes fluttered in pain, but he hadn't officially yielded. Junger studied the wrecked form. He focused on one clutching right hand. This he stomped on, breaking the last two fingers.

The jolt of agony revived Bubruk, and he rolled onto his side, cradling his hand.

Junger stepped away and looked to the Orator, who struggled to find his voice.

"Your victor!" the old man finally bellowed.

The arena erupted with approval.

Junger basked in the unexpected adoration for a short time, feeling the sun's attention on his face. He backed away from the prone Bubruk, who struggled to sit. The stricken pit fighter finally got to his elbows and knees and stayed that way, his forehead kissing the sand.

Junger let him be. Tumber had been avenged.

At his end of the arena, the portcullis rose. Junger marched toward it while the crowds continued their applause.

The cool air inside the portcullis refreshed the victorious Perician, and he took his time descending the steps.

At the bottom, the heavily bearded gatekeeper regarded him with beady eyes and a ready smirk. "What are you about, anyway?"

Junger shrugged. "Didn't feel like coming in after the

first one, good gatekeeper. Hope I didn't offend."

Pleased at the genuine show of respect, the gatekeeper blinked before chuckling. "No offence taken. Just unexpected, is all. I don't remember a gladiator ever fighting twice in a day."

"Doubt it'll happen again," Junger said as he reached the bottom. Just ahead, a handful of Skarrs surrounded a pit fighter sitting with his back to a white wall. The helmet-covered head drooped to the man's chest. One of the Skarrs slapped him.

A pang of concern took Junger, and he halted, causing the gatekeeper with that great length of bear fur hanging off his chin to take notice.

"Just pickled, is all," the gatekeeper explained. "Not the first time one's tried to calm his nerves with drink—or strengthen them."

The Skarr handling the drunken pit fighter's chin hauled the helmet off. The soldier slapped him again and got a slurred string of syllables for a response.

"He can't fight," Junger said.

The gatekeeper shrugged in sad agreement. "Some get like that. Not all can handle being in front of thousands. Then there's the ones who realize *who* they're fighting— usually a house gladiator—and they go off and drink whatever they can before the fight. As I said, it calms them. Sometimes."

"What'll happen to him?" Junger asked.

"Skarrs will punish him, make it so he won't ever fight in the games again."

"Kill him?"

The gatekeeper frowned. "Well, perhaps, if the mood takes them. But… they will paddle him. Right and proper. Maybe even close to death. Can't let the Free Trained think they can decide not to fight at the last moment."

An uneasy Junger watched the Skarrs haul the near-senseless pit fighter to his feet, revealing a puddle of soupy filth. The drunk man groaned in protest, his lower chin covered in drool and blood. The lead Skarr pushed the warrior's head against the wall and ordered him to focus. The pit fighter's face was miserable, pleading. His eyes flickered in Junger's direction.

Show them something to remember.

The Perician approached the Skarrs.

*

A short time later, an out-of-breath attendant stopped at the length of another white tunnel, where a house gladiator waited for his introduction. The fighter, called Curn of the House of Vandu, turned his armored bulk toward the panting messenger and listened to what he had to say.

The pit fighter's eyes narrowed.

"Aye that," Curn said and sent the attendant running once again. Curn watched him scurry off, a steely leer growing behind his face cage. Day or night, in the Pit or outside of it, the gladiator didn't care who he fought, as long as he was paid for his efforts. He'd already killed one of those unfit Free Trained punces calling themselves warriors. He hated them, hated the Gladiatorial Chamber for ever allowing such gurry to poison the games. He hated the Chamber even more for allowing a pack of the walking maggots to form a house and formally enter the games. Curn didn't know what the exact process was for establishing a house, but the sudden formation of the Ten's house seemed as off as rancid meat.

News of the Ten had traveled quickly throughout the older houses and schools. There wasn't a soul in Sunja who didn't know about the house of Free Trained.

As well as Curge's bounty.

27

"Men and women of the Pit, I hope you're enjoying the day's entertainment?"

The raucous answer made Qualtus the Orator smile with predatory delight as his fists clenched and unclenched in the air, calling for quiet. When the arena settled down, he started again.

"This, the eighth fight of the day, has a killer from the House of Vandu making his fifth appearance of the games. This man doesn't fear. He doesn't panic or hear the wounded pleading for mercy. The House of Vandu found him savaging a pack of Nordish Grinders one day, managed to put a chain on him, and led him back to our fair city with the intent of unleashing him upon the games! He's already killed two men this season, and he's looking for more heads to split! Undefeated and unrelenting, he is a troll capable of ripping out limbs and throats alike! I give you Curn! Of the House of Vandu!"

From the shadows of the raised portcullis, Curn stepped

through and rolled his head left and right. Large and fearsome looking, the gladiator wore only spiked leather pads on his shoulders and his shins. A black band of toughened hide had been draped and tightened around his mid-section, leaving his thick chest bare. From his right hand swung a heavy broadsword. From his left dangled a war flail with a horsetail of chains that ended in chunks of jagged iron and spikes. Muscles bulged and flexed under a thin sheen of fat. A helmet fashioned in the guise of a grinning skull protected his head, the eyes dark and sinister.

That skull plate gazed expectantly across the arena sands at the other, still-closed portcullis.

"To meet this hellion upon the sands is a brave soul indeed, a Free Trained warrior who has battled to this point, defeating four of his own ilk to arrive at this juncture. He has proven himself to be made of ice with no fear of death and certainly no fear of Curn. He has clawed his way through a pack of dogs and emerged victorious, ready to lay waste to the gladiators willing to face him. He is… Worlo of Vathia!"

The gate of crossed iron bands cranked open as the crowds wailed their greetings. They made it known what they thought of Worlo's chances against the likes of Curn.

As quickly as the disrespectful sound grew, it abruptly died… then rose again, twice as strong as before, and with significant cheer.

The Orator peered into the Pit. His eyes near popped from their sockets at the half-naked bastard strolling back into the light.

*

"Well," Clavellus stated as Junger emerged from the brick mouth. "There's our missing lad. Returned to the sands and not quite done yet."

Machlann blinked. The unconcerned pit fighter was about to fight an unheard-of *third* match in one day and against a house gladiator.

Muluk simply stared over the trainer's shoulder, eyes wide, mouth slack.

Goll, however, could only gawk at the Perician gladiator. "What… is he doing?"

Clavellus didn't bother replying.

He didn't think the Kree would care for the answer.

*

Gastillo leaned ahead while Nexus spoke for them all. "What's he doing? What's that bloody bastard *doing*?"

Curge leaned on his left arm as he came to attention in his seat. "Seddon above, he's fighting again."

"Fighting again?" Nexus blurted and stared in horror at the owner. "How can he fight *again*? Is this even allowed?"

"If one fighter cannot fight for whatever reason and backs out with little notice," Gastillo said, "and the Madea is pressed for a replacement, it could happen. If the opponent allows it."

"That's what happened," Curge rumbled and scratched at his chin. "The Free Trained scheduled to fight could not. Surprising since they have the Skarrs nearby to discourage any change of heart. Something happened, and Junger was the closest to consider for a replacement. Or he volunteered."

"Three fights in one day?" Nexus marvelled in unchecked dread. "Has that ever happened before?"

Curge locked gazes with Gastillo. The gold-faced owner shook his head.

"Not to my knowledge," Curge admitted, the knot in his guts tightening with every beat of his heart.

*

The Orator called for the fight to begin.

The banners hanging from the arena heights stirred in the barest of afternoon breezes. The wind teased the sweaty masses, leaving them wishing for more. Amid the drone of anxious chatter, the skull-faced gladiator walked toward Junger. Cavernous eye sockets studied the Perician with cadaverous mirth.

"Free Trained," the skull said, its smile tainting the greeting.

"Curn," Junger returned, not bothering with anything else. Sour sweat wafted from the House of Vandu man.

"I've heard you've done well this day."

Junger nodded. He supposed he had.

"You enjoy punishing your own kind?"

"They weren't my own kind."

"I thought you Free Trained were all cut from the same hide."

"Not I." Junger's fingers tightened around his sheathed

sword. "And not the House of Ten."

"House of Ten," the skull scoffed darkly. "House of *shite*."

Junger's eyes narrowed. "I see you're the disrespectful kind."

"I'm the *killing* kind," the skull declared, those chilling twin wells of pitch still studying the Perician.

Junger didn't comment.

"Your run of good fortune ends here," Curn announced and cracked his flail of chains for punctuation.

Smiling thinly, Junger believed the conversation was indeed finished.

Curn charged without warning, chopping with his broadsword while winding up with the flail.

The broadsword missed. The flail missed.

Junger did not.

Stepping back to avoid the killer sweeps of Curn's weapons, the Junger darted forward and cracked his sheathed blade soundly across Curn's left elbow.

The flail flew from nerveless fingers.

Junger didn't stop there, and the House of Vandu gladiator discovered firsthand just how fast his opponent could be.

The Perician smashed Curn's head left and right. He slammed his sword into a spiked shoulder pad before thrusting the tip to the man's chest. He hit the left arm, the right, then speared the armored gut, buckling the man before uppercutting and nearly ripping Curn's skull helmet from his head.

Curn collapsed onto his back in an explosion of dust. There he stayed.

His skull faceplate lay skewed after the onslaught, uncovering part of a jaw. Curn's hands pawed weakly at the air, senseless as to what had just happened.

Junger knelt on the gladiator's chest and unsheathed a hand's worth of steel. He placed the edge to Curn's throat, scraping stubble.

The fallen gladiator had presence of mind to realize his predicament. Somewhat.

"*Yuh*," he croaked, wholly blinded by the shifted faceplate. "*Yuh*."

Yield.

The one word that granted life in the Pit.

Satisfied, Junger rose and backed away from the defeated man.

The audience exploded with approval.

*

From their private perch, not one of the three owners commented on Junger's speedy victory over the gladiator belonging to the House of Vandu. The boisterous cheering of the crowds soaked their skulls, as shocking and thought-clearing as ice water. Though Curn and his bloody reputation were known to a lesser degree to Curge and Gastillo, perhaps even Nexus, they did not consider Vandu's house to be a threat to their plans.

The hellion named Junger, however, was a genuinely *glaring* concern.

As soon as the day's games concluded, Curge would have his agent Bezange double his efforts and uncover any information on this gemstone of a swordsman under the House of Ten's roof.

"Master Curge?"

He turned at the sound of his name, as did Nexus and Gastillo. An arena attendant dressed in white-and-black robes held out a scroll.

"This is for you," the man said and handed him the document. The robed fellow moved to the other owners.

"What's this, then?" Nexus demanded, snatching his scroll from the messenger's hand.

Curge quickly opened his scroll and scanned its contents. His leathery brow furrowed with dangerous curiosity.

"Seddon above," he rumbled and stared into space. "Is this some kind of amusement by the Chamber?"

The attendant stood back after delivering Gastillo his copy. "I'm only the messenger, Master Curge."

But Curge had already dismissed the man. Never in his life had he ever read such news. Never. Yet there it was.

"The season's to be lengthened?" Nexus piped, attempting to fathom what that might mean for his school. "And what this other item? About forcing criminals to fight in the games? And… what's this?"

Nexus brought the scroll in closer to his face, not believing what he saw.

Curge said it for them all.

"Jackals," Curge cut him off, the cogs of his mind also

moving, wondering what it all meant for the future. "They're going to unleash a handful of Jackals."

*

In another part of the city, down a long alleyway where the applause for Junger did not reach, stood a pair of hard-looking men. They wore light clothing that hid ink picked and etched into the flesh, ink depicting serpents and chains and blades. A third man stood at the junction to the street, warding off any potential intrusions with hateful looks.

The other two gang members lingered around the sewer grate, taking great interest in the maroon stains splashed across the iron bars and surrounding stone. One fellow crouched and fanned away a few flies. The gang man froze, catching sight of something gleaming in the shadows. He went to the base of a wall and cleared away a few fragments of broken wood. In a short time, he finished and picked up the object that had caught his attention.

The second man watched, eyes narrowed with all the interest of a rat smelling fresh meat.

Without a word, the first gang man stood held out his open palm. Half a gold tooth lay upon it.

28

The afternoon sun cooked the ragged line of people and livestock waiting to enter Sunja's gates. A spicy blend of animal sweat, offal, and unwashed bodies clung to that long procession. Those travelers in need of relieving themselves did so along the sides of the winding road. Some individuals held up blankets for the privacy of children and womenfolk, while the men simply stood without embarrassment and let drift. A child sobbing sounded from farther back, awakening Pig Knot. He glanced up and took a moment to realize where he was, pushing away the blanket he'd bundled up beneath his head. Despite the blistering heat of the day, he'd still managed to fall asleep in the wagon's bed. He straightened and glanced over his shoulder, meeting the driver's eyes. Neither man said a word. Pig Knot twisted himself around to see how much closer the gates had become. Not far, he saw, and pulled at his sweat-sticky shirt, the only clothing he wore other than the loincloth. Having no legs freed him of breeches, which suited him fine.

A short time later, the driver stopped the wagon. Skarrs asked him questions and checked the wagon. The city guards took a quick inspection of Pig Knot, discovered him legless, and left him alone. That bothered Pig Knot. He knew the soldiers didn't consider him a threat. He *was* a threat. In his mind, he was probably the biggest threat entering the city this day.

After a brief inspection, the wagon rattled into the city. A fuming Pig Knot sat with his back against the driver's perch and glared at the passing Skarrs. Returning to the city, however, brightened Pig Knot's spirits… for a short time. The wagon rolled past houses and tall inns, storehouses and merchant stalls, tall wooden buildings of immaculate craftsmanship decorated with colorful streamers. A deluge of people crowded the wagon at times, some noticing the man with the missing legs. Pig Knot stared back. Sometimes, they met his eye and quickly looked elsewhere. Sometimes they just looked elsewhere.

"Here," Pig Knot said to the driver.

"Here?"

"Aye that. *Here.*"

The driver halted the team of horses in the crowded street and half-turned in his seat. "You want to get off in the middle—"

Pig Knot pushed himself toward the rear, startling the man. The driver tied off the reins and hopped down to the street. He rushed to the back and lowered the rear gate.

"No need to be like that," the driver said.

"Help me down," Pig Knot commanded.

The man hesitated. He didn't have the same muscle mass as the scarred trainer back at Clavellus's villa. Pig Knot didn't seem to care. He looped his arms around the smaller man and used him as a fleshy rope to lower himself to the ground. Once off the wagon, Pig Knot scooted along, his face contorted with an odd mix of freedom and pain. He wobbled over the road, through the masses, to an alley situated between a tall house and a three-story alehouse.

The driver watched him cut through the people, stopping some flat in their tracks. Shrugging, the driver returned to his perch and got his wagon moving again.

Pig Knot reached the alley mouth and shuffled inside. The short exertion left his heart and blood racing. Already, the grit bit into his palms, and he slap-wiped them clean. He had narrowly avoided a cow kiss on his left, and that was all he needed that day: for Sunja to welcome him with a handful of shite. Chuckling, Pig Knot leaned against the alehouse wall. He gazed out at the passersby. Some spared him a glance. Most did not.

That suited him just fine.

For if he was going to die, then Sunja was the place he'd do his dying. He truly believed he would perish upon the streets of his home. Koba wasn't entirely willing to get rid of him, which surprised Pig Knot. He'd figured the trainer would be quite happy to throw him onto the wagon. Koba did not; however, after a short conversation, Pig Knot convinced him to do his bidding. And for that, he was grateful to the ugly topper. In his mind, he wished him luck with Ananda. Oh, the woman tempted him, to be sure, but Pig Knot had already had his share of women. Koba certainly wasn't gifted at honeying words, and it was painful to watch the exchanges between him and Ananda. But the emotion was there. It took Pig Knot a while to see it, but it was there. And far be it from him to poison an infant romance.

But he did use it to get what he wanted.

Sunja. Back in his city. Back home. Pig Knot rested his head against stout timbers and peered up. The sun was nowhere to be seen, but the sky was the deepest blue, whitened with cottony cloud. He intended to live off the streets, as he had when he was a boy—at least until his few coins ran out.

Whereupon he assumed he'd eventually perish. Gladly. Eagerly.

Death. He often wondered what became of old gladiators when they could no longer pull steel for whatever reason.

Pig Knot relaxed, smiled faintly, and looked out from the alley's shade, partially hidden from the herds. For the first time in what seemed a very long while, he felt free.

The people walked by him without notice.

*

A pair of sun-browned men walked past the legless man in the alley. One glanced in his direction but rapidly looked away. There were better things to see in the city. The

Skarrs had asked the two travelers their purpose for entering Sunja. The newcomers informed the soldiers of their plan to make contact with the cobblers and leather workers, and with a little good fortune, maybe even negotiate supplying the merchants with materials.

That was good enough for the Skarrs. The two travelers had appeared honest enough and carried nothing more than spare clothing and boot daggers. Protection while on the road from Marrn, they'd said.

Entry was granted.

Once the two men had gotten past the Skarrs, their expressions changed from weary honesty to guarded determination. Their thoughts turned to a violent future.

And shortly after they entered the city, they disappeared into the masses.

About the Author

Keith C. Blackmore is the author of the Mountain Man, 131 Days, and Breeds series, among other horror, heroic fantasy, and crime novels. He lives on the island of Newfoundland in Canada. Visit his website at www.keithcblackmore.com.

DISCOVER
STORIES UNBOUND

PodiumAudio.com